Star Points

Connections Old and New

Star Points
Connections Old and New

Daniel O'Brien

Copyright 2011 Daniel O'Brien

ISBN 978-1-257-65812-1

Dedication

To all the Japanese people who showed kindness to me. Especially the older ones who I mistakenly thought would not like Americans because of living through World War II. They taught me much about the resiliency of spirit, and this book is a testament to their ability to survive a war and smile about life once more.

Table of Contents

Prologue: Explorations and Connections Old and New xi
1. Hurry Up! 1
2. Yuri Arrives at the Church 4
3. Yuri's Parents' Experiences 8
4. The Reception 10
5. Beginning Married Life 12
6. Summer Breeze 17
7. Work Life and Honeymoon 26
8. Back in Japan 31
9. Back in Egypt 38
10. Another Summer in Tokyo 40
11. A Second Trip to the Old Administrative Building 43
12. The Seals 47
13. Wedding Gifts and Remembrances 51
14. The Journey to Horyuji 60
15. Alexandria Revisited 64
16. Oomisoka 66
17. New Year's Day 71
18. Tokyo Again 80
19. The Plan 82
20. The Grand Assembly Meeting 86
21. Meeting the Members of the *Secret Society of the Stars* 97
22. Revelations of the Secret Society 108

23.	The Seals in the Grand Hall	119
24.	At Home	129
25.	A Call to Yuri's Mother	130
26.	The Next Day	132
27.	Becoming Students of Meditation	135
28.	The Next Morning	138
29.	In Tokyo Once More	142
30.	Again at Horyuji	143
31.	The Following Day	154
32.	Once Again in Tokyo	157
33.	A Picnic in the Park	160
34.	At Long Last the Couple Visits the Grand Hall Again	163
35.	The Next Weekend in Osaka	174
36.	Getting Back to Horyuji after a Brief Time Away	177
37.	Tea the Next Day	188
38.	Back to Tokyo	190
39.	Later That July	192
40.	The Next Day	196
41.	Further Exploration Needed	199
42.	A Fruitful Trip to Ise	203
43.	The Search for Proof	206
44.	What They Found	213
45.	Again With the Secret Society	219
46.	The Search for the Origin	224
47.	Archaeological Dig	229
48.	When in Rome	233
49.	What Yuri Remembered	242
50.	To Oxford	245

51.	Secret Society Meeting in Egypt	255
52.	The Last Treks of Confirmation	269
53.	Attending to the seals…	274
54.	*Tanabata* Festival	279
55.	Epilogue: The beginning	283

Pronunciation guide 285

Glossary 287

Prologue

Explorations and Connections Old and New

A very, very, long time ago ….

Nobody knows, nor seems to remember how long ago, but some untold thousands of years ago it so happened that on the top of a mountain, like anywhere, sparkling stars were out at night. And on this mountain, too, there was a person who looked at those sparkling stars in utter amazement. If it was evening, then surely this one would be looking at the stars, and more often than not he made it up on top of that mountain. It was as though he wanted to be as close as possible to the stars that had captivated him and gained his attention so completely.

For him, of all of the things in nature, stars especially made him think of the sacredness of life. It was also true that he had absolutely no idea why this was so. Even so, the stars in nature really moved him, moved him to come down from that mountain and take action. The story that follows is the result of his actions, being so moved by the beauty of nature so many thousands of years ago. Still, as we shall see, since very, very, long ago what this man accomplished when he came down from the mountain has remained …lost.

Hurry Up!

"Hurry Up!" she exclaimed, nearly tripping herself as she scurried around the room in an attempt to get ready.

Today was the day, she thought. The young woman continued whirling around the house in a flurry going from one room to another and eventually checking all the rooms over again to see that everything was just right. They were having guests from abroad, and she wanted everything in its place.

Because she kept thinking "Today is the day. It's my wedding day!" she could not think of anything else. Actually, it was as though the many things that she was thinking of, piled up a mile high in her mind, and then raced through her mind all at once making it so that she could not really concentrate on any one of them.

It was a first for this woman of whom everyone said, "She can do anything." All she could do was whirl around the house saying to everyone, "Hurry up! Hurry up!" an expression she learned while abroad. Her mother chuckled to herself and tried to get Yuri to sit for a moment. Her mother, Hisako, a traditional, and brilliant woman, wanted Yuri to sit down and have her hair done up right. It was after all, the wedding day of her one and only daughter.

"Sit down, Yuri," she said in vain as her daughter all but knocked her over going to the closet to look for something in her modest and well lit bedroom. "Only for a moment..." she continued, but this, too, was in vain as Yuri was already straightening her undergarments and smoothing her dress and looking as though she felt that she was ready to go.

She looked so beautiful, her mother thought. And then, demonstrating her quick wit she realized that all mothers must in some way think of their daughters as beautiful on their wedding day. Then as she was putting the futon they had slept on away she smiled a mother's smile while looking at her child from the side of the room.

They had slept next to each other on their futons relishing their last day together under the same roof. In fact, Hisako, who always puts the futons away upon getting up, prolonged putting them away this day not really wanting the feeling of being together to end.

Yuri was beautiful; however, it was true there was something else that Hisako noticed. Hisako noticed how beautiful one who is happy can be, something that goes further than only skin deep. Indeed, she noticed that beauty and happiness, at least in that moment, were somehow one and the same …. And then she came back to the business of the day, how to get her daughter to the church on time. And of course there was the matter of whether or not Yuri would finally allow her for once to help her pin up her hair.

Yuri was stubborn about allowing her hair free reign. Perhaps this, too, was part of her beauty. Wild hair had come to look natural on her. Hisako was sure that this was because of the confident way in which Yuri acted. This was fine, Mother thought on most days, but not on the day that she was getting ready to be in her own wedding.

Yuri's mother, Hisako, a short, stout woman, could be forceful, but knew that now was not the time for such action. Again, smiling the smile that comes from many such experiences, and chuckling to herself, she threw up her arms and resigned herself to the fact that for the time being her daughter was hopelessly out of control. She saw so many young people get married during her seventy years that she was not overly concerned. She knew that eventually one of two things would happen. Yuri would either come to her senses, or slow down when she became exhausted. Hisako, not being one to dally around, busied herself for the present moment by preparing things such as the guest books to take to the reception for all to sign.

Yuri, herself was quite aware that her hair was messed up or at least not pinned down. This allowed it to fly around and be wild, and even on this special day this did not bother her. Yuri was not against things traditional, such as the expectation of impeccable hair at a wedding, but neither was she one to stand on ceremony looking to feel self-important. Unlike almost everyone else at that moment, she felt that other things were so much more important than her hair. Much was on her mind now; greeting people she hadn't seen in years, whether the guests would be comfortable many coming from abroad, whether the food would be right for all, whether there were enough rooms reserved at the hotel etc….

Though she was someone of whom since she was a little girl everyone understood to be gifted in many ways, caring about her hair just wasn't one of them. About this she was indeed, as her mother thought, clearly stubborn. Yuri wanted things to be free and wild and her hair was just that today making it hard to pin up or even attach a veil to. She was thinking that she would leave it till just before entering the aisle of the church. And then she grew nostalgic.

While whirling around the house, she noticed the curtains of all things. They had been put up when she was going from sixth grade into the seventh grade, the first year of middle school. In her village the building for grades seven through nine was a school quite separate from elementary and high school. And in her middle school, grades were counted from the beginning all over again, first, second and third grade.

Looking at the curtains, she remembered now that she was just beginning to get lessons in English at the time those curtains were put up. And there they hung still, with the greens and yellows she had become used to, though hadn't really thought about ever since they were put up. She loved the pretty bamboo pattern as indeed, she loved bamboo forests. Sometimes she would sit in a bamboo forest, and lose track of time, and then suddenly become aware of herself again and go home.

Indeed, she could sit among the upright shoots for hours enjoying the earthly colors. Her friends never understood this. They preferred to watch TV and play video games while Yuri spent hours just being in nature, feeling the sand with her toes, running wildly into the water. Her friends thought she was unusually excited by simple things. Yuri only felt that simple things were real, and she was not even sure why she thought so. Yuri felt lucky that she never got into video games. Life seemed so much more real if you could feel it, touch it, smell it. She loved climbing trees and the feeling of rough bark and smooth bark on her hands. And the greens, wow the greens in nature are so wonderful, she thought. She remembered now that one time when she was quite young, she had scraped her knee and went home laughing even though it hurt, because it felt so "normal" to her to have a scraped knee that hurt.

So much had happened since the beginning of English lessons and middle school. She had traveled and lived in so many places around the world. She was thankful for having a family that, although with some reservations, allowed her to follow her dreams and do things like climb trees even if it did mean getting dirty, something often thought unbecoming of a girl in her island village. She was especially thankful for her ability to learn languages, picking up nuances easily. The curtains brought up some of the many great memories from this home that she would move out of today....

Yuri Arrives at the Church

The church doors were opened right on cue and light flooded into the foyer, crossing the statue of the Virgin Mary and lighting the aisle to the nave filling from back to front the distance of the crowded church. Those assembled there filled both sides with people there to see Yuri and the groom, Bernd get married. The atmosphere bubbled with anticipation of the bridal procession.

Bernd had taught Yuri that his name was pronounced, "Berent" and that was enough to get her interest the day they met. For whatever reason, as though it was predestined, they became friends immediately. Even so, neither of them fully believed that all events were foretold by God ahead of time. They had hopes of making a future together doing great things. Yuri now recalled that their first argument ended in Bernd getting the book, the two lovers of books were after, in the book store on their first day together. He had been quicker and reached the book before she did. They still laugh about this. The book was <u>Hamlet</u>, and living in England at the time, both wanted to read something of Shakespeare.

Bernd, who had been waiting with great anticipation since ten-thirty A.M., strained his neck to see if at last his longtime friend and soon to be wife had arrived.

Bernd was handsome with a boyish face that sat underneath a set of wire-rimmed glasses flat across the top and round otherwise. Like his glasses, Bernd had an intense side to him, that showed in his stiff, straight approach to study and attention to detail. However, he was also well-rounded in many ways such that that he could be very adept socially. He also had much passion for his many interests such as history and the use of artifacts. Surely this passion would make him a good husband as well as partner, Yuri thought.

Indeed, when he wasn't studying science, football or what Americans tend to call soccer, was his passion. In 2006, he did not miss one world cup soccer game of his favorite team, Germany, the team from the country of his birth. Unfortunately, though Germany hosted the event, the German team did not do as well as Bernd might have liked. However it *was* good fortune, he thought, that while hosting the event, the German team placed in the top four. Bernd could not attend the third place game, but was happy to watch it from his home taking his mind off getting married if only for the ninety minutes of the match.

So much was his love for the game that he would even get upset that the scientific precision with which he viewed the game did not help. His friends would tease him as he would sometimes claim that a forty-five degree kick would have gotten the ball down the field farther, and at other times that a thirty-five degree kick would have been better for getting a corner kick between defenders.

Jokingly his friends would ask, "Wasn't it really thirty-six degrees?" and he would laugh good-heartedly and reply, "You can only ask so much of the lads." Most of the English he now spoke well, he learned from British television shows.

He would have liked to have seen how Germany would have done against France or Italy in the final game, but had to watch as both teams played each other for the highest honors in football. Now they were getting married in the autumn to avoid the summer heat. This also allowed them to avoid the conflict that would arise out of having the wedding while the World Cup was being played that summer.

At any rate, he gave a sigh of relief to see Yuri standing there looking stunning with the light behind her, her shadow stretching into the aisle that was wrapped in lilies. Lilies were laid end to end down the sides of the aisle, a subtle reminder that her Japanese name, Yuri means lily in English. They were pure white and beautiful, she thought.

Also present was Yuri's cousin who had traveled to this remote island of Japan from the USA. Her cousin could not believe that, being from a small village, Yuri would be getting married not at a shrine, but in a church.

Getting married in a church was of course no different from the many other Japanese people who as of recent choose to get married in either a church, or some other setting made to look like a Christian marriage might. This had come to be called a *chapel wedding*. Indeed, chapel-like structures had been popping up in cities at hotels and wedding halls, perhaps first in port cities like Nagasaki or more recently Kobe. These were places where various foreign influences have been traditionally strong. And now they are spread across the country. This had become so much in vogue that foreign-looking people are often hired to perform the service, giving that added appeal of being something special, interesting, and exotic. Some people find it interesting and ironic that this practice is not limited to people who are qualified ministers.

While Yuri was not afraid to state her own wishes, she was considerate enough to ask her parents whether they would accept a *chapel wedding* or not. They were not convinced that it was a good idea at first, but agreed when Yuri said she wanted to have the service in a real Catholic church and not at a tailor-made wedding chapel. Indeed the church of her choice was on the island of her birth. It was established by Portuguese missionaries who had fled the mainland because of persecution several centuries before during the isolation of Japan in the Tokugawa period. This closed period is called *sakoku* in Japanese. The missionaries were somehow able to establish a small parish on the island before being unceremoniously kicked off of the island and out of Japan. Recently, a small Filipino population maintains the modest, yet ornate church that began in secrecy and had been closed down for many years until the new constitution was written after World War II.

That the local people refer it affectionately as *the small foreign shrin*e, may also be one reason why her parents agreed to have the service there and not the local shrine. More likely however, it was the fact that both Yuri and Bernd agreed to have their *kegare* or "impurities" removed at the local shrine earlier that day by the local Shinto priest. This was done separately for both bride and groom and was why Yuri was getting ready while Bernd waited at the church. Bernd had gone first. They joked that this was because he had more impurities to get rid of; however, in her heart of hearts Yuri knew that his sincerity made him most noble in many ways.

Part of the ceremony to get rid of impurities was dedicated to purification as well. And though they did not consider themselves superstitious, they held true to the tradition of not seeing the bride before the wedding ceremony on the day of the wedding. That is why separate Shinto purification ceremonies were held. It also explained Bernd's joy at seeing her now.

With Yuri's cousin sitting on the bride's side and Bernd's football friends on the groom's side and both sides filled with friends and family members, the bridal march was set to begin. It was early afternoon.

Yuri was truly nervous now, listening while her heartbeat rapidly to the sounds of the organ that filled the church as "Amazing Grace" squealed out of the pipes. It was a song she had heard while abroad and seen in movies in which weddings played a part, and so she chose it for their ceremony.

She had acted so confidently in so many areas of her life since she was a child that this nervousness, being uncommon for her, made her feel uncomfortable. This, however, soon passed as she also noticed that it made her feel rather alive, too. While she was coming to terms with her feelings, she did wonder what people would think of her if she tripped while walking down the aisle because of the mixture of excitement and nervousness that she now felt.

As she watched the last maid of honor reach the front of the church, she took a deep breath and after a moment asked her feet to move. The anxiety she felt made it so that she was no longer able to hear the organ play. It was as though, however briefly, she was in a sort of trance. And then, with effort she came back to herself and with great awareness of what was going on around her she walked effortlessly down the aisle toward her beaming father and smiling groom.

She was not sure exactly why, whether it was the flow of the events that transpired or just the pleasure of marrying someone she was sure would be a good partner, but Yuri felt as though the wedding service was over in a just a few moments. Now she and Bernd as husband and wife were in the back seat of a car. And though they were in Japan, it displayed a large sign that read "Just Married" in English, a common language for many in attendance, as well as in Japanese and German. In the car they were cruising to part three of their special day ….

Yuri's Parents' Experiences

Yuri's family line had been continuously living on the island for many centuries, and though they were not poor, neither were they rich. Yuri's mother noted, light-heartedly, that this was especially because of sending their only daughter to study abroad in Egypt *and* England. Of this her parents had no regrets except for missing some of their daughter growing up when she was in foreign lands. She had been away during a formative part of her life. A few years in high school and even in her third year of junior high she had traveled abroad with relatives to Hawaii. Though with as much Japanese as is spoken there, one wonders how much it was a foreign experience. All in all, they felt more than compensated for missing her while she was away now that they could see how successful she was in many ways. They were two truly proud parents Shuhei, her father and Hisako, her mother.

Seeing the changes in the world during their lifetime, they raised Yuri to be independent and caring. Indeed, they made sure to tell her of the trials they underwent during World War II. Still, they wondered what kind of strength would be necessary from here on out in this rapidly-changing, increasingly global, population. The problem, to them, seemed to be that while being confidently independent was necessary, it was also painfully obvious that the ability to cooperate and work together was necessary, too. And they felt that this was perhaps true now more than ever. In fact confidence and cooperation seemed to them to be skills that go hand in hand, but were horribly lacking in the present age. Why just the other day they had met a conscientious young American man who had originally thought that older Japanese would hate Americans. For their part they were pleased to meet a young person who was sincere, honest and caring. They had seen such misery during and after World War II, that they no longer had any patience for nastiness. They truly wished that no others would be subjected to such a horrible experience. Their compassion gauges were on high alert always. Those who were impatient, they hoped could see that they were purposefully considerate of others in an attempt to teach what they had learned from their troubles. In short, they felt that others mattered.

When their daughter included her parents in making the marriage arrangements they felt relieved. In this they felt that they had done something right. This was because their daughter was able to decide for herself, yet also willing to confer with them in something that was to them a very important matter. What they saw around them, the selfishness and emphasis on economic gain so pervading everything it seemed in so many places in the world, made them wonder as to where society was heading. They wondered, too, whether humans would, in the end, be able to truly work together. They also knew that there was no use standing around worrying about these things. That is why they took the action of sending their daughter abroad, and writing to her often. They had not the slightest idea, but the letters Yuri received from them while abroad were some of her most cherished possessions. This was probably true in part because Yuri's first trip abroad was when she was only 13 years old. Fortunately, it was a good experience for her. Now, unlike the superstition, she considers 13 her lucky number.

Their chief concern was that this self-centered economic gain paradigm was true not only in Japan, but also around the world. And the reports of their daughter's experiences and stories in the news seemed to confirm their fears. Their concern was very strong despite what they saw around them as an age of the world coming increasingly together, interdependent, and connected.

It was in this fact they maintained that there was some glimmer of hope. They also felt, coming from a society influenced heavily by Confucian ideals that people were basically good.

The Reception

There was quite an array of food provided at the wedding reception. It was a combination of Japanese style, *hundred dollars a plate dinner* and many varieties of food served with deserts from around the world. The sweet feast was from places where Yuri or Bernd had traveled.

There was baklava from Greece, strudel from Germany, *omanju*, sweet bean cakes covered in glutinous rice from Japan, and many others such as piroshkies from Russia, *kolaches* from Czechoslovakia and many more.

While no desserts from Egypt were present, a copy of a wedding ceremony invitation from Egypt was prominently displayed on a table to the side of the entrance to the main reception room. Its Egyptian characters, both new and ancient were in blue and gold. This represented Yuri's love for Egypt and hieroglyphics, but was set out especially in memory of her Egyptian friend, whose wedding she had attended when she was in Egypt. The main colors at the wedding were blue and gold. In fact, this was the wedding program from that very wedding. Sadly, her friend could not afford the trip to Japan, and would have taken great offense at suggestions to pay for the trip on her behalf and so was not in attendance. This was not such a bad thing, however, since Yuri's friend was at home having welcomed a new baby boy born just several months before.

The desserts were placed around the five-tiered wedding cake that Yuri, not even knowing why herself, demanded be five tiers. In Japan a four-tiered cake, representing an even number that some say could be evenly split up upon divorce, would just not have done. Further, the number four and the word for death have the same sound in the Japanese language making the number four undesirable. And a three-tiered cake would not have served the many guests they had invited nor sat well with Yuri who recognized the simplicity of three, but was not always simple herself.

The one Japanese custom they simplified was the *o-hikide mono*, or take home gift traditionally given to the guests by the family of the bride. In place of a physical *item* a gift card was given that could be used by their guests anywhere in Japan, or world wide. They could be used wherever JCB credit cards were accepted, which was indeed many places. Bernd thought giving a gift item, which would have been a nice thought, would be a nuisance since so many guests had traveled to Japan from abroad. The gift card was a great compromise solution. It would not be a dramatic increase to anyone's luggage.

After most of the guests had finished eating, the bride and groom hand in hand lit the marriage candle that to them signified unity. This was a practice that was perhaps more popular in Japan than in the United States and other countries where the custom may have originated. Next, they cut the wedding cake, again hand in hand, in a most fashionable ceremony fitting for such a promising couple. Someone was lighting candles at the center table so when the bride and groom returned their faces were surrounded by lit candles. Not only the candles, but the couple, too, glowed. They were happy to be married now having waited two years since their engagement. Bernd remembered now how he had proposed. He asked his Japanese friend how to say "Will you marry me?" in Japanese and then took Yuri out to view the moon on a full moon and asked her to marry him in her native language. She told him that this had made her feel special and was romantic.

Yuri chose not to change dresses several times throughout the day as is customary in Japan. She was satisfied with the white laced wedding dress Bernd had bought for her in Europe. Everyone seemed to enjoy the reception, and gave her many nice comments on the dress purchased at an upscale shop in Paris. She normally would not like Bernd to spend much money on her, but made an exception for the dress. She was very pleased with it right down to the last sewn on pearl surrounded by lace. She was glad that it was a high neck dress, too. While she liked to allow her hair to run wild, in this case she was modest. Her athletic figure would have looked nice in any dress, Bernd thought.

The day was long and enjoyable. Some of the Japanese people noted that it was *ii o-tsukare* or a good tiredness, a tiredness that comes from doing something worthwhile.

Beginning Married Life

Bernd and Yuri moved to the Kanto region of eastern Japan, having found jobs in Tokyo. From there they could easily visit Yuri's relatives during the *O-bon* holiday or ancestral holiday in summer. They could also visit Bernd's relatives for the Christmas and New Year holidays. The trains were top notch and regular and international travel was easy. Though this summer-winter visit schedule was the preliminary plan, they had not worked out all of the details yet. It was complicated, since Yuri really liked visiting the island of her birth for the New Year, especially on New Year's Eve.

First, they set up their apartment. Not expecting to stay in Tokyo forever, they were in no hurry to buy an expensive house. They were able to find a cozy place with the help of a relative that had been living in Tokyo for what seemed like forever to such a young woman like Yuri. Her older relative knowing much about the area was of much help. She showed them where to shop for items to fill their place and how to find the local green grocer to buy fresh vegetables.

Yuri was sure that the kind of place they lived in didn't matter much since she felt so good about being married. She felt that she would make good use of anyplace and that building a life with Bernd would make it all the more enjoyable. Bernd for his part was very pleased feeling that he was married to the woman of his dreams.

Though they wanted to be in a place that was more remote than in a busy part of the city, they realized how difficult that commute would be. As a result they settled on a small apartment in the Shinjuku area because of its ease of access to train routes that took them directly to work.

At any rate the three room *apaato* or apartment would suit them just fine. In fact it was called a three LDK, which meant that the apartment had three rooms in addition to a Living room, Dining room and a Kitchen area.

One room was for their combined office space, one for their bedroom leaving one to spare. They were lucky since many families with children lived in places with fewer rooms. It was sparingly decorated, though tastefully done. The walls were painted over with earth colors, hues of green and one room done in yellow which was slightly darker than mustard yellow. Bernd insisted on the color, though could not say as to why he wanted a room that color. The sliding doors, that moved side to side, called *fusuma*, separated the bedroom from the living room. They were decorated with shoots and bamboo trees flowing across them. The *tokonoma*, or alcove in which decorative scrolls made to be wall hangings are displayed was just off to the left as one entered the living room. And the living room was near the *genkan* or entryway to the apartment where people took off their shoes upon entering the home. There was on a lower stone floor area at the entryway below the level of the wooden floor that goes into the home. Some entryways are only slightly lower than the main floor going into the home.

In the apartment there was no carpet, but the three rooms in addition to the living room space were decked out in *tatami* or woven reed mats common in Japan. Taking off one's shoes was important especially to avoid getting dirt in the tatami mats. Indeed, no type of footwear is worn on tatami mats.

Bernd got a job as an assistant to a physics professor at Sophia University, Ichigaya Campus in Tokyo. This job provided him with access to up to date research in the sciences and had another benefit as well. For example, his love of history was encouraged by various friends he had met who work in the history department at the university. His wide range of interests gained him friends in many of the departments at the university.

He was excited about working at Sophia because he knew from acquaintances that the Asian Studies seminar held there brought together quality scholars from around Japan and the world once a year. Given his passion for Eastern philosophies and religions, he hoped that he would be able to participate in the seminars. Interest in these fields was a close second to his interest in physics. Constrictions on his time only allowed them to become a minor degree taking a secondary role to his studies of the various sciences which truly thrilled him. Still, history was a favorite of his.

More than anything else he loved learning about and figuring out how things work. Discoveries along this line made him tingle with joy. He loved his job. Mathematically describing how things work was an especially rewarding challenge he thought. His recent passion was taking on something unusual and new. He had begun to study the science of how the brain works. He was truly amazed at how flexible and malleable the brain really is.

As for his own research he was proud of his idea to combine philosophy, sports and physics. He carried out research about the ancient Greeks, the early Olympians, and how far those people threw Javelins starting with the first Olympics in 776 BC. He admired the Greek penchant for a sound mind in a sound body. He learned how the ancient Greeks philosophized about the merits of getting together and taking a break from war during Olympic competitions. He also enjoyed the study of other Greek philosophers thinking much of Socrates, who Bernd considered as rather ahead of his time. Bernd thought this was because Socrates considered women and slaves as being equal to, or at least no less than, men. This was notably unlike many philosophers and politicians as well as people of distinction who came after him in history.

Unfortunately, regarding the Olympics, the discussions regarding putting war on hold in the pursuit of fair, athletic competition were not broad enough and did not include either the right people or enough people to be long lasting…. Bernd's logical mind took over his enthusiasm as he mused on this fact. He thought that this was evident because of the fact that wars have continued to be fought up to the present day.

Bernd was sad that all disputes could not be as easily decided as a football game. He really could not understand why after thousands of years of interaction, humans had not come up with a way to all play by the same rules. This astounded him as he thought that humans seemed to have the same basic needs and those needs could be met better by cooperating than by fighting. He believed that fighting produced at best only temporary gains. There must be a scientific way to figure this out, he imagined ….

Indeed, he had read the science reports that claimed humans could all be fed if there was the coordinated distribution of food that is currently produced. He thought that what must be lacking was the ability to coordinate *and* cooperate regarding this matter. He felt this intensely, almost as intensely as he felt about Germany playing in the third place game in the World Cup. To him it was a distribution problem, not a production problem. We really could do better as a species at getting along, he thought.

He was equally puzzled when he heard that our genetic differences are really rather minor. He read that human genes and DNA compared among peoples of the expanse of the ancient routes of the Silk Road differed only slightly. Indeed, to him it was puzzling that humans could have such similarities and still not get along. After all, wasn't mapping the human genome or DNA already happening? He could only hope that this would not lead to even more thoughts of our differences, when the same mapping would also point to the overwhelming evidence that humans are more similar than different. Indeed, more similar by far! Human genetic make-up is more than 90% similar, according to some studies. After reading that article in a science journal, Bernd noted it and intended to follow up on this work ....

When he thought about the World Cup, he was heartened. He realized that it was an example, if only one, of humans being able to coordinate and work together for a common goal over time. Certainly there must be other examples if only he could find them. If ever the possibility arose to help others come together he was sure that he would do everything in his power to make it happen. As for himself, wasn't his marriage to someone from a culture different than his own an example of the wonderful possibilities available in the modern world?

He had been thinking of these things for some time one evening. While mulling these things over, and in part because of the exhaustion he felt from the load of tests and correcting that had taken place during the week, he fell asleep. Yuri noted how the moon shone on his face in the *shinshitsu* or bed room. Lying beside him, if she closed her one eye, the moon disappeared behind the silhouette of his face.

Eventually, Yuri and Bernd felt settled into the apartment and began to enjoy their lives together. The challenges, the successes, and even the learning that comes from the failure to get along were all amazing. Each proved to be an opportunity for growth.

Though Yuri and Bernd felt that they fought over silly things, they felt that their problems weren't really that unique. They came to the conclusion that two people, even of the same cultural background would most certainly experience difficulties in marriage. It seemed unavoidable that newlyweds would argue over such everyday things as whether or not they agreed where to put the toothpaste, from which end to squeeze the tube etc.... They also realized that two people from different cultures such as themselves might not even easily see from where their troubles originate, but nonetheless, have to work through them just the same. It was no surprise to either of them that life together would be a challenge. Both thought that it was naïve to think otherwise.

By the time they had been married almost a year, they had worked through many points of contention and were happy that they had devised various ways to work out the challenges posed by married life. In order to keep the peace in their home, Bernd and Yuri devised various plans to continue relating even when they disagreed. For example, they established a special place to be separate from each other if necessary, and agreed to always be willing to come back and talk things through at some point. This got them through many tough times as they continued to learn more and more about each other especially during that first year. They also discovered that as they took the effort to learn more about each other, they did not have the same fights over and over again. While they did grow through some of their points of conflict, they noticed that some took longer to get past than others.

Over all, they felt that they were making a very good life together and considered themselves to be very fortunate to have each other and so many good things, not least of which were families who cared about them. And neither of them took lightly having decent jobs in occupations they adored.

Summer Breeze

One night they had an argument over what each considered the suitable use of the *zabuton* or seating cushions in their living room. As a result Yuri had gone out on the *engawa* or porch-way that extended along half of the house on the outside. The *engawa* played a variety of roles in their life. It acted as a place to sit and have tea, enjoy the evening breeze on a warm summer night, and had yet one more important function.

On this warm night it was an area for Yuri to cool off while considering why she got so mad whenever Bernd moved things, such as the stereo radio, into the living room. She got angry since for her it was clear those things belonged in the dining room. *And he seemed as though he would never understand the correct use of zabutons. Who ever heard of piling them up to lean against to watch TV!* she thought. So she was out on the engawa catching her breath. She was thankful for the pleasant summer breeze.

It had been only a few minutes since she sat down on the *engawa* on this bright, moon-lit night, but already she was beginning to calm down. She couldn't stay angry in such an awe inspiring setting. She really enjoyed how the moon shone over the houses. Their place being located on a hill gave an excellent view of the city, or at least their small part of it. She could see a nearby grave yard or *hakachi* in which the grave markers, *ohaka* put up by families were lined up in rows and had been that way for many years if not centuries. The cremated remains of one's family members and especially the throat bones of deceased family members could be kept within a compartment in a grave stone. It was the custom that fresh flowers were maintained by a family member in front of the grave stone.

The way the moonlight bounced off of the roofs before her made her wonder what they might have looked like during the Edo period, many years before. She could almost see a bamboo forest off in the distance. Still, she knew that Tokyo had been rebuilt many times as the old was pushed aside by the new.

It was also apparent that much had had to be rebuilt after the *kuushuu* or firebombing air raids that destroyed much of Tokyo during World War II. The moon not only made her think of these many things, but also gave her space to calm down, and rather quickly, too. The free and carefree side of her fought with the side that wanted to see things used properly. It seemed silly to fight over the use of seating cushions, but this came from how she was raised in Japan and the idea that things were meant to be used a certain way and that that way was, well, proper. She had to trust that the customs had been devised, at least originally, according to what works best.

For a while she was lost in the thought of people having to stay inside on hot summer nights hiding any light they used so that their house would not be seen by World War II bombers. Then, Bernd slid open the *shoji*, or paper door and offered her a reconciliation *o-cha* or hot green tea. She gladly accepted, taking his hand and leading him to sit down beside her. She especially liked making up never able to stay angry with him for long. She admired him, and he her which really helped when wanting to make up. Simply put, they both shared a passion for their interests and for each other.

One passion they shared was learning about this wonderful world in which they lived. Bernd had turned his keen mind to the composition of their universe many times. He loved discovering super novas, and volcanoes, how birds fly and so many more things in and of nature. She for her part enjoyed immensely learning about different peoples of the world. She did this mostly in her learning of various languages and the culture points that came along with that study. She was pleased that she was able to combine a love for languages with making money. Her job was working at an internationally recognized dictionary making company.

As the two sat there enjoying the evening breeze and drinking the *o-cha* they started to play a game called *shiritori*. In the game one person states a noun in Japanese and the last part of the noun, the *shiri* or tail end is then used by the next player in forming the beginning of the next noun and so on taking turns. This made good use of the syllabic form of the Japanese language in which a consonant is followed by vowels each in turn, and was a great way to pass a summer evening. For example, the word for moon is *tsuki* and so the last part "ki" would be used by the next person to form the next word such as <u>*ki*</u>*mono* which means Japanese wrap around clothing.

They played for about twenty minutes when Yuri suddenly stood up on the engawa and exclaimed, "Just a minute, look at that!" As quickly as he could Bernd stood up and looking to the right between two nearby houses gray in the moonlight he saw an old building in the distance that looked like an abandoned apartment building. At least this is what he thought Yuri was pointing to, but could not immediately make out what it was, nor was he sure that it was the thing she was pointing at.

At first he was not even sure why she had pointed it out and then it suddenly became clear. He saw a light that flashed. It was not a bright light, it flashed intermittently, and the fact that it was randomly going on and off, would normally have hindered people from noticing it at all. However, since Yuri had noticed it and pointed it out, Bernd was now sure of it. There could be no mistaking that there was something flashing in that building in the distance off to the right along a characteristically narrow road in Tokyo this night.

And tonight in that building in the moonlight along that narrow road, it looked as though someone was turning a light on and off seemingly on purpose. It was as though someone was trying to draw attention to the building or so he thought. Though for all his trying, and through logical reasoning, he could not imagine why someone would want to do that. As far as he could see, all things otherwise seemed normal, safe and all right.

Yuri had that look she gets when she is really thinking hard. She holds the edge of her mouth up on the right side and holds her lips together solidly.

Bernd was about to ask her what she thought it was, when she was down from the *engawa* and into the *niwa* or garden. She was gone before he could utter a word. Bernd looked for his sandals and finding them stumbled into them and quickly went after her. She was walking down the alley her wooden sandals, called *geta*, making the click-clacking sounds that Japanese say sounds like *karan koron, karan koron*. It was like something out of the *edo* period in which samurai flourished, but with an intensity and purpose that would surprise even samurai so Bernd thought. Then he, too, quickened his pace hoping to catch up.

Bernd thought they should be more quiet, but Yuri was walking so quickly that it was all he could do just to catch up to her, and that happened when they were only a few paces away from the building they had seen from their own *engawa* moments before.

"Now what?" he said between breaths as he looked over the building before him.

"We'll have to go around to the other side," she said quietly, noticing how odd it might look if someone noticed them observing a building that may not have had tenants for the past twenty years. And so they began, now ever more careful to be quiet, to go to the other side continually thinking about who or what they might find inside the building. They could not help but wonder who was turning the light on and off, nor could they figure out why …at least not from where they were.

They made it around to the other side, being sure to walk in the shadows when possible. They were convinced by now that it would be best not to be seen trying to get a look into the building. They also gradually came to the understanding, without having to say anything to each other, that they would have to go inside.

They arrived at what seemed to be the front of the building directly in front of an imposing, wooden door. They would have held hands when going in the front door, but Bernd kept watch while Yuri tried the front door …with no luck. It seemed as though it had been rusted shut for years. If that was not the case, then it most certainly was locked tight. Aside from that it was the same as any other door to any entrance to any building.

They did not ring the bell, wishing more and more to not be seen and not even sure why they were feeling that way. After all, they had done nothing wrong, at least *not yet*. They then returned to what seemed the side of the building. On the side of the building, where a street light did not reach, they found a window by a fire escape. The window, too, was locked, and because of the darkness and the curtains that hung in the window, they could not be sure what was on the other side. They had to look into the room through a small opening where the curtains that met side to side hung slightly parted.

Through that small opening, they looked through the window and into the room which was pitch-dark. Well, almost. There was a crack of light coming in from another room though not constantly. Immediately they guessed that the light they now saw, that was being turned on and off intermittently was the same light they had seen while at home. It had a most irregular pattern and so they still could not imagine why it was being turned on and off in this way. This did, however, make them all the more curious and now even a little worried that there may be someone in there that needed help or some other kind of pressing issue. Again they felt that they did not want to be seen by anyone outside the building. And there was a new feeling, too, that neither did they wish to be seen from anyone *inside*. A shiver ran down each of their spines, making them feel scared, and for Yuri, very alive, too. Bernd was cautious. Though they had much that they wanted to say to each other, neither dared speak.

Anyway, when the light was off the room was black as pitch, and when on, but for the moment they could see that there was nothing directly on the other side of the window. They could also see some of the outline of the room. The room looked like an apartment, and it looked as though it had been empty for years or at least that was the impression it gave with the table being empty and the furnishings being meager. Bernd looked around nervously hoping no one had seen them by this building. When the light flashed all they could do was to keep pointing out things that they saw to the other.

Up close the building looked as though it was ancient. It truly had been around for years, maybe even centuries it seemed, though this fact struck Bernd as odd since Tokyo had been so thoroughly bombed during World War II, and was a relative newcomer to the world as an industrial giant. Japanese buildings were made of wood, before stone or brick, but this building gave you the feeling that it was built many years earlier and built very well though he could not say why he thought so. It was a feeling.

There was no use arguing about it; both Yuri and Bernd knew that they had to get into the building and the sooner the better. They felt drawn to find out whom or what was turning the light on and off like that. So next they devised a plan using as little words as possible. Bernd, knowing the flexible capacity of glass, figured that they could get in the window if there was no alarm attached to it. Being seemingly such an old building it was unlikely that it would have an alarm, yet since it had been made into an apartment building, it may have had an alarm system installed in it at that time.

Sure enough they spotted a wire going across the window sill. Since this was in between flashes of light they could not make out what kind of wire it was and so for a moment pondered its purpose and took no action. And then Yuri made perhaps the most important discovery of the evening. She saw that the wire ran over and seemed to end at a socket in the wall. It was clearly a telephone wire as the socket connected to the outside of the building and the telephone wire ran underground only yards away.

Both gave a sigh of relief as Bernd began to move the window in a way that allowed Yuri to use the pin on her hair clip to push the small arm of the lock from the upper to lower position unlocking the window. They were thankful that the building was not more than an abandoned apartment and that the locks were simple and easy to get past. Though they were able to open the window, both were frightened when it made a scratchy noise while being opened. Yuri almost screamed and noticed Bernd grimacing. Wondering what to do, she grabbed his hand in hopes of making a connection so that they both could stay focused.

Once inside they stood still for a moment taking in the environment around them and waiting for their eyes to adjust to the darkness and intermittent lighting. Of course, there was much to consider. Did anyone see them entering? Did their entrance into the building go unnoticed by anyone who might be inside the building? In an instant so much went through their minds that they instinctively stood still attempting to calm their heightened state of unease. So, too, they had to consider whether or not someone would hear them moving about, or who it is that might be either in danger or, this was a new consideration…lurking around inside for some other purpose.

Almost right away they were a little relieved as they could hear the wind blowing through the room, whatever kind of room it was, on the other side of the door in front of them. Yuri thought that they wouldn't be easily noticed because of the noise the wind made or at least this was her hope.

They walked the few steps from their point of entry to the door that led into the next room, and listened carefully for anything audible. Bernd even placed his ear onto the door to see if he could get a sense of the happenings on the other side. For the time being there was …nothing.

They were also relieved to find that the door was locked, though the lock was on this side. They took a deep breath and gathering all the courage they possessed, unlocked and opened the door slowly. Then, after looking around and believing that no one was near the door, they went through the doorway and entered the next room.

They expected to find someone in need of help sending some kind of SOS, or a secret coded message being sent, but the room into which they entered was as far as they could tell, empty. It was empty with regard to people anyway.

It was only just barely lit, making things almost impossible to distinguish, by the pale moon. This they only understood a moment or two later. There was no light "on" in the room. The shining moonlight came in the window and *wow*! It lit up the room if only for a second.

"What was that?" Bernd exclaimed though careful to keep his voice as low as possible. Yuri kept a hold of his hand, but was lost in thought. She thought to herself what would light up the room for brief moment and then turn out the lights again. After the flash of light their eyes were no longer adjusted to the darkness, and so they could not see anything for a brief moment. That may have been the best thing that could have happened because it allowed Yuri to use all of her senses. She felt something …. Yes, what she felt was definitely a breeze coming across the room hitting her on her sleeveless left arm. Now she heard the breeze, too, as they had while in the other room. She noticed that there was some other noise as well. The scratching of whatever it was that was hanging overhead in front of them near the wall. It was scratching along the wall she now realized as the wind blew whatever it was back and forth. And there it was again, a flash of light bright as …the moon! And then in an instant she realized what it was. It was the moon being reflected off of a mirror or something. It was hanging fairly high up on a wall in what must be a very large entryway though not to an apartment building, but a very fancy building. They were standing a ways back from the entryway in a large room. Of course the entryway they were now looking at was over that very sturdy door they had encountered only moments before. Bernd longed to talk to Yuri, but dared not.

Careful to avoid looking directly at the flash Yuri and Bernd's eyes became slowly accustomed to the dark. Making use of the brief flashes of light, they were able to see what was seemingly an old administrative building of sorts built, according to what Bernd felt was during the Meiji Restoration. The Meiji period (1868-1912) was a time in which Japan copied a lot of things from abroad including architectural styles of the West. This must have been one of only a handful of buildings in the area that had survived the fire-bombing air raids in Tokyo during World War II.

At any rate Yuri felt a little let down that the culprit was only a mirror catching the evening breeze coming in a window. They both thought that the window had probably been broken for years. They turned to go out the way they had come in, still cautiously not wanting to be seen coming out of the abandoned building and not knowing why they felt this way.

Bernd had been looking down to watch his step when bam, the light flashed across the room once again. He noticed a seal of some sort on the floor encircled by some saying.
    "Yuri, did you see that!" he said in his amazement, then quieted down in case someone else could hear them.
    "No, what did you see?" she asked in a whisper, her mind still on the window, the moon, and the mirror.
    "There's some kind of marking on the floor," he explained.
    They stood as still as statues waiting for the next flash of light their eyes trained on the spot where they hoped would be the wording of the seal on the floor. Yuri imagined where Bernd had been looking based on his brief and careful directions. Their patience paid off. The words read, "The world will come together by being together under the stars." They realized that this was some of the language from the Meiji Period, when the world was coming ever closer together as the result of automation and improved technology. It was a time in which the development of steam power on ships brought people farther and faster around the world. It was also not missed by them that the Japanese considered themselves like a rising star in the world around the turn of the century. Bernd remembered reading of the Japanese victory in the Russo-Japanese war in 1904-05. Indeed, the victory seemed like a miracle at the time, especially for those who could remember the "backwardness" of Japan not so many years earlier when Admiral Perry of the U.S. naval fleet *opened* Japan in 1853. He had been able to do so with the threat of force contained in only one naval ship. Yuri had heard as well that English became a major topic of study as were other languages during the Meiji Period. The Japanese truly were on the rise to global exchange even then.
    Not wanting to risk being found in or even near that building, they decided to leave after memorizing the words on the seal. They called it a seal not knowing what else to call a round decorated disk that reminded them of a government seal and looked almost like a trademark. As they walked back home, careful to make as little noise as possible until they were a comfortable distance away from the building, they talked about the wording. Bernd told Yuri what he thought the words meant, his theory of the seal being created during the Meiji Period in Japan. Yuri listened but was lost in her thoughts now, too.
    Yuri shuddered remembering what her grandparents told her of the indoctrination of the Japanese under the militaristic Emperor

System that developed during the Meiji Restoration and continued ruling Japan up to and throughout World War II. Her grandfather had lost three brothers to the war, each having received a red paper called *akagami* which was a compulsory draft notice. During the war as prospects for the Japanese military became increasingly worse, in Japan a draft was imposed. Each brother was taken in turn and each was increasingly younger.

Her grandfather had only survived because he had been the youngest, and he had been undergoing Zen training at the local temple on their small island. Because of these things he didn't receive an "*akagami*" draft card. This was one of the few means of succor people found during the war. Having their dead buried by Buddhist priests was the custom, so temples remained important as places to come together throughout the war. They were also lucky in that the four hundred year old bell at a local temple on the island was not melted down to make bullets or munitions for the war effort as others had been. It was one of the many that avoided that fate though all were seemingly at risk at one time or another. The temple bell was on the way to the war-time factory to be melted down only to be sent back to the original place where it now hung. It was returned because of the end of fighting in mid-August 1945.

Though, they did not find anything of substance in the building, they both stayed up late into the night talking about their adventure. For some reason it reminded Yuri of her trips to the pyramids in Cairo, Egypt. She had gone there on a study trip to specialize in reading hieroglyphics. This allowed her to use first-hand the Egyptian language she had been learning in university while giving her the opportunity to see hieroglyphics up close, her longtime dream. She was fascinated by all languages and especially interested in those written with symbols. She was not sure if this was because her native Japanese was one such language including thousands of symbols or because she enjoyed putting together puzzles, solving riddles and the like.

At long last, after recounting the events of the night many times in the privacy of their home with a combination of peaked interest and nervous exhaustion, both of them fell asleep. Yuri was a little down since the trip to the building did not lead to anything, though this was a vague feeling. However, one thing was for sure, she was really glad that she and Bernd had had a fight that night, putting her in her cooling off place out on the *engawa*.

Work Life and Honeymoon

Yuri worked as a language specialist for a multinational corporation that produced dictionaries and had offices all over the world. What she liked best about the company was that it had branches in countries she held dear to her own heart, namely Egypt, India, Tibet and England among others. True, she had never been to Tibet but her studies in Buddhism while at Cambridge that told her that many devout Buddhists live in Tibet made her curious enough to want to go to Tibet. She even read further about meditation and Tibet. This was because Vajrayana Buddhism, the Buddhism of Tibet was something new to her. It was also because it was different from Zen or even Mahayana Buddhism both of which are practiced widely in Japan. This was of course, one of the hundred or so things she wanted to do or study in her life…someday. She laughed at herself wanting to study Vajrayana Buddhism because she realized that even though she was from Japan, she had still not taken the time to properly study Zen Buddhism or any of the Mahayana traditions that had come to Japan via the Silk Road, China and Korea.

    She translated documents from abroad and was an interpreter in the languages she knew when people arrived from overseas. She of course was instrumental in many of the dictionary projects being something of a specialist in various languages. Since the company dealt in dictionaries and language study supplies, many salespeople came to Japan some simply dropping in the office *while in Asia*. Japan had become a wonderful place to visit having recovered, it seemed, fully since World War II. This was especially the case for the Egyptians who decided that traveling all the way to Asia meant a mandatory stop at all three countries in which they were doing business: Korea, China and Japan.

    Yuri hoped that someday she could pay a return visit personally and explore the pyramids of Egypt once again. She really enjoyed trying to read the hieroglyphics since the study of them was among her favorite subjects. She just hoped that she wouldn't be too busy to drop by if ever she had the opportunity to go to Egypt on business. Her passion for understanding hieroglyphics made her the second best reader in her class during university and a favorite contact for Egyptian visitors nowadays. If only there was enough time to explore everywhere she wanted to go in the world! It thrilled her that the world had so much to offer.

She especially enjoyed the treasures left behind by the ancients. Like so many others she was impressed by the scale of the Sphinx, fashioned after the Pharaoh Khafre. When she visited Egypt she heard of Alexander coming to Egypt from Macedonia, fulfilling his destiny, so he said. Then he went on to conquer "the world" as known to the Greeks. She also appreciated Alexander's travels to Egypt because it was her personal belief that if he hadn't, the Rosetta stone would never have been found and the key to hieroglyphics might have been lost forever. Of course no one at the time in Alexandria, a city founded in the name of the conqueror, could imagine just how serious the "lost" library at Alexandria would one day become. The ancient learning lost was as much a tragedy she thought as the hieroglyphics were fascinating.

Yuri also wanted to explore other parts of the world which included the contributions of those in the country we now call Iraq. She was fascinated by their achievements in taking and utilizing for further study the manuscripts from the library at Alexandria. Saving these from being lost, these people eventually kept learning alive in both the sciences and mathematics. And this was accomplished at a time when Europe was in a dark time, the middle ages lasting roughly from the sixth until the fourteenth century CE. CE stood for Common Era and is a compromise way of noting the date since this way of referring to dates has become so commonly used around the world. And of course, while it is useful for many, one can imagine that using A.D. meaning Anno Domini or year of our lord could be just as easily something to be offensive to non-Christians.

Perhaps this is why she chose to go to Iraq for her belated honeymoon with Bernd. They had been married for over a year, and now that he was established in his position at the university and she was well thought of at her company they decided to ask for time off to travel. This fit well for Bernd as he would be paid his salary throughout summer even without giving lessons, this being the standard for those working at universities in Japan.

Yuri was pleased to find out that she would receive a summer bonus. This was a practice that remained from the period of major economic expansion in Japan, a period that began in the late nineteen-sixties and ended in the late nineteen-eighties. She was impressed that her company could afford to pay bonuses being in such a competitive business.

They would leave in the autumn, which was not long after the anniversary of their engagement which had been in the *o-bon* season, the Japanese season of welcoming back the spirits of one's ancestors. The o-bon season was special for them as they had gotten engaged while traveling during the o-bon season. The plan to travel in autumn would of course kill two birds with one stone or *isseki ni chou*. They would be traveling around the time of their actual anniversary and avoid the crowds as droves of Japanese traveled back to their family home place, one's home town or *furusato* during the o-bon season.

First, their travels would take them to what had been Mesopotamia in Iraq often called the "cradle of civilization," since that is where it is said the earliest civilization developed. They could hardly contain their excitement. Then, they would move on to a brief stop in Greece to see the Parthenon, an ancient temple. Next they would embark on a cruise through the Mediterranean Sea to Alexandria, Egypt before returning to Japan.

After flights with connections that seemed to be all over the world and all times of the day, they arrived safely in Northern Iraq, ready to cruise down the Tigris and up the Euphrates rivers of the ancient Fertile Crescent.

While Yuri could not read the cuneiform of ancient Sumer, she enjoyed immensely the translations provided in stops along the way. She was already figuring out several of the language patterns in the first museum they visited. The modern heirs to the ancient Sumerians really promoted connections with other countries in the region translating descriptions, through the help of their universities, into Arabic, English, Persian and other languages. Yuri noted, too, that the connections made between countries by the Ancients via their economic ties and other means of communicating was fascinating. She realized even more deeply on this trip that she chose to study languages because she liked the bridge that was built between two cultures when one knows even a little of another language.

After visiting the Parthenon in Greece, they continued the honeymoon on a cruise of the Mediterranean Sea. Bernd and Yuri thoroughly enjoyed the cruise, taking every opportunity to eat the exotic foods available, and even taking time to lie in the sun. The sea lived up to its reputation. It was sunny and beautiful most of the days and one could see islands and bits of land jutting out almost everywhere. The deep blue green colors were wonderful, giving great pleasure to the honeymooners and others on board.

Bernd teased Yuri asking her if she could see the lost city of Atlantis rumored to have sunk many centuries before. Yuri stated emphatically that she did not believe the story, but nonetheless seemed to keep an eye out at all times to see if anything giving a clue of the lost civilization was to show itself.

After their Grecian leg of the cruise, next it was off to Egypt for the final part of their trip, the part Yuri had been anticipating most. They arrived in Alexandria.

In Alexandria, the couple explored the catacombs, said to have existed since the time of Alexander the Great in the fourth century BCE or Before Common Era. The underground vaults were magnificent to behold provided you were careful not to get lost in their maze-like walkways.

The pair had been looking very forward to visiting Cairo and the pyramids in Giza in just a few days, when Bernd fell ill. He had never been to Egypt or the Mediterranean before, and grew very ill from some unseen bug that he got from food or drink somewhere along the way. Yuri, of course, was saddened that they would need to return home earlier than what was planned, but knew better than to blame Bernd. After all, she had been sick while abroad with Bernd several times including a trip to Southeast Asia.

They simply did not have the amount of time off from work necessary to wait out the illness and continue their planned route, so they chose to return to Japan at the next possible opportunity. For a few days, however, they weren't going anywhere as Bernd was in hospital being tested to find out what was wrong.

When in the hospital, Yuri noticed a motto on the floor. She was not sure what it said, and could only read some of the hieroglyphics, but guessed by the pictures involved what the elaborate symbol meant. It had the hieroglyphic that represented the sun and a rough map of what seemed to be the areas conquered by Alexander by 324 BC. Yuri took a note and asked the nurse to confirm if the hieroglyphics that Yuri had written down meant, "All the world is united by the sun." The nurse agreed that that was a possible reading of the hieroglyphics involved and then hurried off. Yuri figured that this statement was a reference to Alexander, who considered himself the Sun God.

Alexander, being superstitious, based his belief on a revelation by a local oracle who he had visited. When consulted, the oracle declared Alexander the "Sun God." Indeed, this is what Alexander had hoped to find out and a main reason he pushed his armies to Egypt.

With more looking Yuri found out that this hospital is said to have been built here because it marks the location of Alexander's visit to Egypt. Of the symbol, no one seemed to know who made it or how long it had been on that spot. However, she was told indirectly that rumors claimed that it had been there since long ago. At least that is what Yuri thought she heard them saying to each other in the hotel front lobby. And then everyone went back to work.

At any rate it was a very nice, modern hospital, and for that Yuri and Bernd were extremely grateful. Unbeknownst to Yuri and Bernd, soon after Yuri's enquiry, the first nurse had gone "missing."

She had realized that Yuri was the only one in her thirty years of working at the hospital to ask about the symbol on the floor. Of course she had promptly contacted the *Society* headquarters regarding Yuri …and her husband who was reportedly "sick."

Three hours later, the nurse still hadn't heard back regarding the inquiry she herself had put in to the Society. The nurse just couldn't believe it. Certainly this would be given strong consideration by the Society members. This Asian woman would be *dealt with* if necessary, the nurse was sure.

Back in Japan

Yuri and Bernd were able to return to Japan safely. Rest was mostly what Bernd needed to make him feel well again. They were fortunate to be two healthy people that heal well. Since Bernd recovered rapidly and they still had a few days off from work, they decided to use the traveler's checks to travel within Japan.

Yuri had heard of a wonderful hot spring or *onsen* in Tohoku, in the northeastern region of Honshu, the largest Japanese island. The *onsen* was located in an area just across the strait from Hokkaido the northernmost of the four largest islands in the Japanese archipelago.

It is true that there are hot springs all over Japan, but this one claimed to be one of the longest continually used public hot springs in the country. It claimed to have been in existence as a bath house and a get away since the time of Tokugawa Ieyasu. He was the first ruler of the Tokugawa or "Edo" period which went from 1603 to 1867 CE. After the Tokugawa or Edo period was the Meiji Restoration or Meji Period a time in which the old *onsen* flourished.

The *onsen* was simply called Yamaro meaning mountain bath. Going to the onsen would give Yuri one of the greatest pleasures she could imagine, a soul cleansing, body-healing hot bath. For Yuri, going to a hot spring where the hot water came up out of the ground as it did in the volcanic islands of Japan was a spiritual experience. She absolutely loved it. This was among her passions, next to traveling almost anywhere and learning languages.

With only a few days left of vacation, it was the perfect place to go. It was about a half day ride away from Tokyo on the bullet train or *shinkansen*. It was a place that is easy to get to and there would be much to do around the hotel connected to the hot spring. Especially, Bernd was looking forward to drinking *jibiiru* or beer brewed locally. Japanese beers have many nice qualities that make them delicious, and when local brewers use good water they can be really quite distinctive and tasty so Bernd, the German, thought.

After a ride on the bullet train that began in the early morning, the couple arrived, shopped for a piece of art as a souvenir and walked around the pond at the hotel. Now they were relaxing in their room waiting for dinner. They had of course just gotten out of a hot bath.

Certainly the meal would be one the likes of which Japanese inns are famous for. It would be a wonderful selection of local delicacies including fish from the local stream or market, pickled local vegetables, sashimi, sushi, and a simple, local soup with all the rice you could eat etc …. This inn kept true to nature serving a different menu each season, and providing guests with the freshest version of local produce and fish suitable to the corresponding season. It was no surprise, Bernd thought, that Japanese people live to an old age. Scientifically he understood that not overeating was important to good health especially when matched with exercise. He also noted the wonderful variations in the "traditional" Japanese diet. He loved the variety of foods served at Japanese inns, and thought it was healthy, too, that they are served in season. He made a mental note as a reminder to himself that the Japanese word for inn is *ryokan*.

While waiting for dinner, Yuri was paging through an area guide book and came upon something in line with another one of her passions. She had found a local, and by the looks of it ancient, temple and thought it a great place to visit. *Teruji* which means sparkling or shining temple was the name of the nearby temple, but locals called it *Kagayaku ji* another reading of the characters. Knowing this nickname gave a clue as to whether or not someone was from around there or not. This was like how someone from Kyoto knew that sometimes Seventh Avenue was called *Nanajou*, though its regular name is *Shichijou*. Local tradition had it that true to its name people were said to come away from the temple with a smile on their face shining. Yuri wanted to visit the temple, and wondered if it would be okay to visit now, since there was still just more than an hour till dinner time. She wondered if the temple would still be open since it was later than four in the afternoon.

She decided that instant to try even if Bernd did not wish to come along. When she looked his way, she did not even need to ask him. Having only just gotten over being sick, and perhaps as a result of getting up early and the many events of the day, he was fast asleep. Yuri changed into a *Yukata*, the summer kimono provided by the Japanese inn for walking around the local area, and with a piqued sense of adventure left the inn. She loved visiting old temples!

It was a nice autumn day, and just as it said in the guide books, this area was blessed with *momiji* or Japanese maple trees. They were in the midst of changing colors. Indeed, there were so many, that in some places you could imagine that patches of the mountain were on fire making it a beautiful sight to behold. Within minutes of leaving the hotel, she arrived at the temple gate. Out of respect for tradition she was careful to step over and not onto the cross beam that ran across her path below where the doors of the temple gate hung as she entered the temple.

Thinking, *The temple is open,* she was relieved. Curiosity arose within her. She walked up to the main hall and taking a coin from her purse put it in the *saisen bako* or collection box. A very thick braided rope hung down available for visitors to ring the simple brass bell. She rang the bell in front of the grated window that looked in on the main altar. It was not a big booming bell like the one that hung in the bell tower off to the side, but one that made just enough noise for people to take a moment and prepare themselves and the scene for prayer.

As she looked more carefully through the wooden grating on the window, she saw the primary altar in the main building or *hondo*. Unlike other temples of this size there was only one main altar. And though there were side areas for respectful prayer, there were not many small altars placed here and there around the room with Buddhist statues and images.

Yuri was impressed with the obvious old age of the temple. She could not imagine just how old the temple was, but it seemed as though it had been there for many centuries. Certainly one clue as to the age of the temple was that everything was made of wood. This was not unusual, since most temples were wooden in Japan, but Yuri noticed the age of the wood, and the great size of some of the timbers in the structure and was impressed all over again. She itched to enter the main hall and walked to the doorway, that fortunately was opened just a crack. The scent of burning incense wafted out to her. Though the door was open, it did not mean that anyone could walk into the temple. You had to make sure there were no signs that read stay out. Fortunately the only sign in the doorway read, "No photographs."

Usually an altar contained Buddhist imagery such as statues of The Buddha Amitabha or *Amida Butsu* in Japanese. The historical Buddha, Shakyamui was also often prominently displayed. They might even contain an image of one of the bodhisattvas. Though try as she might, Yuri could not easily tell which treasures the altar held as the window was old and cloudy. The door being opened only a crack was inviting, yet no more help in seeing what the *hondo* had to offer. So this is what she did next.

She slid open the door, stepped into the main hall, and looked around. The incense she had smelled was burning in front of the altar. As is customary there was a cushion to kneel on if one wished to kneel in front of the altar and pray. There, too, was a bowl that can be rung, though this is used primarily by the priest of the temple Yuri knew. Yuri did not ring the bell, feeling that that would be far too forward since she was neither a priest nor a regular patron of the temple. In this case she chose to hesitate or pause something called *enryo* in Japan.

After looking to see that the altar contained the image of Amitabha also called *Amida* in Japanese, Yuri made a snap decision. She decided to sit a distance back from the altar and meditate. She decided to do the breathing meditation that she learned while at Oxford. It had been a while, but she had gotten pretty good at sitting in the full lotus position, both legs crossed while in the United Kingdom. She quickly became good at the breathing meditation, too. This surprised not only herself, but especially the many students who had been practicing and meditating for years and still considered the breathing meditation a challenge. Many envied her flexibility, but Yuri only thought that it was normal to be able to sit in the lotus position since she grew up in a place where she sat on the floor with her legs crossed to study. She also thought that doing yoga helped, too. She remembered pretending to be a Buddha when young, and she and her mother laughed when Yuri would strike a "Buddha" pose while sitting in the *butsudan* room, the room with the family Buddhist altar.

Now, it only took Yuri a few moments to relax into the posture. She was very athletic and thankful for the flexibility this gave her. After a short while she forgot what she was doing or even how long she had been there. Then she found herself being roused by a man who was seemingly very, very old. He asked her to get ready to leave as it was now 5:30 P.M. and the temple would be closing presently. It had officially closed at 5:00 P.M., but he did not have the heart to ask Yuri to move, seeing that she was so obviously relaxed into the meditation.

Startled she asked the time again. Since she had never *forgotten* herself while meditating before, she was really quite taken aback and concerned about her lack of concentration in the present moment. After repeating the time to her, the old man revealed that he was the abbot of the temple. He had grown up in that area, lived there all his life, and had taken over care of the temple after the death of his father, the previous abbot. Yuri noticed that even in his obviously very advanced age he had quite a twinkle in his eye.

What was most striking about him was that he seemed incredibly happy. Yuri thought he looked as though he were poor, but was at the same time, unmistakably happy, too. Yuri apologized for staying there after hours, and excused herself, planning to return to the *ryokan*. He stopped her abruptly and asked whether she had been meditating for long. She told him the truth that meditation was something she did in England, but it had been several years since she had meditated seriously. She also told him that she had not really practiced much when she started or even since then, a little embarrassed to admit that now.

He chuckled to himself and told her to come by the next morning at 6:00 AM. She was not altogether sure why she agreed to this unusual time to meet, though perhaps it was because she needed to get back for dinner, or for some other reason inside of her, but she did. As she hurried away it sunk in that she had just agreed to meet the old abbot at *6:00 AM the following morning*. She gasped, but there was nothing that could be done; as the Japanese say, *shikata ga nai*. She had agreed, and there was no taking it back. Besides, the temple was now officially closed.

Fortunately, Bernd was only just waking himself when she returned. They were able to get dinner since they were ready to eat well before 7:00 PM when the "dinner time" officially ended. After a brief discussion about the eventful and in some ways uneventful outing, Yuri and Bernd went for another bath. After the bath they returned to the room to toast each other with a local beer, and then got into their futons to sleep. It was a nice way to complete their honeymoon, she thought, as she fell off to sleep.

Not one to keep people waiting, Yuri was at the temple promptly at 6:00 AM the next morning. She thought the abbot was going to ask her to sit in meditation or clean the place as she had heard was customary in the Zen tradition, but he only offered to teach her the basics of *zazen*.

Having no experience in Japanese Zen at a Zen temple, she agreed wholeheartedly. After a short lesson on how to practice *zazen*, the Zen style of sitting, the abbot shifted the conversation to the history of the temple. But this was not before "encouraging" her rather pointedly to take up meditation practice when back at home in Tokyo.

He obviously wanted someone to tell about the temple. In fact his whole countenance brightened and his face seemed to light up all over again when he began talking of past events at the temple, of samurai who paused here before going off to battle, daimyo and even a shogun who had come by simply because the temple had been around for so long. He noted that the temple was one of the earliest temples in Japan, and that it had developed good relations with churches and temples around Japan. This came in handy both during World War II and when the allied occupation was in Japan after the war. As luck would have it, it was one of the few temples left mostly to its own initiative both during the war and in the post war period.

Yuri took her leave after their discussion thinking to herself, *What a great discovery*. She was also impressed by how kind this man was to give her a personal tour of the temple and describe its history to her. And perhaps most importantly she now had had a real lesson by a qualified teacher in Japanese Zen sitting. She smiled to herself as she met up with Bernd at the coffee shop near the hotel since she had missed breakfast at the inn. Bernd was kind enough not to rub it in, though he considered doing so.

"You'll be able to have roasted and salted fish in Tokyo, too," he said in an attempt to make her feel better about missing the wonderful breakfast at the inn. This didn't cheer her up, however. She loved roasted and salted fish. Especially she liked it when the fish was fresh from a local market nearby where it had been caught as was almost certainly the case with the breakfast at the inn.

Like all things, this brief vacation, too, came to an end. Even so, Yuri didn't really mind. She was too pragmatic, realizing that it would be pure fantasy to think that she could simply while life away in between relaxing hot baths. Indeed, her father often mentioned the saying, morning drinking, morning bathing and morning sleep; this lifestyle cannot continue. Anyway she so much enjoyed the fruitful engagement in life made possible by working with others that she looked forward to getting back to the dictionary company. She felt lucky, too, because she had a job, and it was one that she liked.

As for Bernd, he, too, was ready for work. In fact he was happy to go back to work for a very simple reason. He was filled with joy that he was feeling better and able to work. He'd have to go back to Egypt when he was feeling well, he thought. He wondered how long it would be till he got the chance. Like Yuri, he loved traveling.

They boarded the train just in time for the train conductor to tell them, "Thank you for riding our train today" which is customary on Japanese trains. As the announcements ended the engine shifted into gear, the train lurched forward, and soon was rocking them first briefly forward and backward and then side to side gently as it sped along the lush green mountains toward Tokyo. The windows rattled with a *clang* when they entered the mountain tunnels which could be quite startling, but other than that it was an enjoyable and uneventful train ride. They were lucky to live in a country where so many things worked so well, and Japanese trains were famous for working well. As for timing, Japanese trains were "dead on" as the British say, meaning perfectly on time. And Bernd was relieved that the swaying of the train did not make him feel ill ….

Back in Egypt

Back in Egypt below the floor of the hospital in Alexandria where Yuri noticed the symbols, there were some people holding a secret meeting. They were meeting in a temple that was separate from and predated the Alexander catacombs. It was not known to the public. This temple was not for tourists. It was brilliantly hidden and only theirs to use.

The members of the Society were incredibly frantic. Indeed, the room bubbled with nervous excitement, almost being loud enough to be heard through the floor or so some of them thought. This was only a little concerning since no one outside of the Society even knew that this room existed. Well almost no one above did.

The nurse, who had informed them of the big news, could not stay and participate in the hastily arranged meeting. She did, however, overhear as she left that the Society has been waiting one thousand years for someone to join them who could with grace unite the *star points*. The nurse had delivered a message to the Society about Yuri asking about the meaning of the symbols above this very temple room. However, if Yuri was of no use, that would be a totally different story.

The nurse hurried up the back stairs reflecting on what she had heard. She was not sure what the *star points* were nor how they could have know that Yuri could join any *star points* based on what she herself had told them, but then again, this was none of her concern. Either way, she had to get back to work. As this matter did not involve all of the Society she was ushered back to the elevator and thanked sincerely for her time. She trusted them, and they her something that had borne itself out over time. She would let the Society *deal* with Yuri. They always followed through to eliminate any threats to their mission.

It was always that way the Society noticed. When trust was given wisely it was always well received and reciprocated. And trustworthy people had been involved in the Society for a very, very, very long time. Like the nurse, others in the Society helped to protect its secrets and she could do so almost better today since she really did not know anything of significance regarding this ancient wish. This allowed her to be of use and to not put anything or anyone at risk. It was as though because she could not stay she became a buffer between the Society and the world so to speak. She would have other times to participate in meetings fully when she did not have to work. Indeed, if she had time to stay she would be fully briefed regarding the goings on .... Clearly something exciting was afoot!

Another Summer in Tokyo

They had been so busy with projects at the university and in the language dictionary world that the winter flew by and spring was a blur. Yuri was really pleased that they had decided to visit Bernd's parents for Christmas and would go to Yuri's parents' house for the coming New Year, a good compromise, she thought.

This summer was like all others Bernd had experienced in Japan. It was not only hot, but also humid what the Japanese call *mushiatusui*. This evening was hot, so Bernd sat on the porch waving the *uchiwa* or hand-held fan back and forth in front of his face with little noticeable effect. He liked living in Japan, and enjoyed the wonders of modern technology around him, but nearly melted in the heat and humidity every summer. This evening was particularly hot, and Bernd was the first out on the porch, but Yuri arrived just a few moments later looking as though she, too, would melt. As evening wore on the weather cooled down a touch providing an opportunity to give the air conditioner a rest. Yuri was glad as she did not like air conditioning.

Yuri was prepared for the heat and came out onto the deck carrying two glasses filled with green tea and ice. This was Yuri's own invention, and not something she would have wanted her mother to know about. Her mother would never approve of putting ice in green tea, but Yuri did not mind breaking tradition if it made sense to her. On the other hand she saw no reason to trouble her mother either, so she kept this tradition that she shared with Bernd between the two of them. There was no point in making an issue out of it just to make a point out of who was *right*, she thought.

Bernd, having finished his tea, got up to go in and take a bath when Yuri grabbed him by the arm just below where the sleeve of his *yukata* or summer kimono hung. "Say Bernd, don't you think that building is rather odd?" she asked slowly almost carefully.

"What building?" he replied not giving it much thought since he was sleepy.

"You know, the one that had the flashing light in it," she said trying to rouse his curiosity a little.

"Oh, you're still on about that are you?" he said in his typically British style way, the result of learning English language, pronunciation and style on the television in Europe.

"Of course, I am," she replied cheerfully and then turned serious. "It gave me a little bit of a scare. I mean, I felt uneasy when we were in there."

"What do you mean, made you feel uneasy?" he asked surprised. "You never mentioned feeling uneasy that night. And that was a year ago anyway," he noted, a little perturbed that she hadn't told him about this before.

"I was a little embarrassed. I mean, there was nothing obviously wrong, it was just a feeling that I got, that's all," she explained. She wished that she had not brought it up that way. But she knew that now that it was out in the open, the scientist would want to know everything before making his hypothesis and subsequent conclusion. He was so addicted to details that sometimes she wanted to shake him and say, "That's enough, don't worry about it." But she knew this time that that would be no good. Bernd would take this very seriously and want to get to the bottom of it, if there was a bottom to anything in what she was feeling.

He asked her at what point she felt uneasy, and she told him that it began when they went into the foyer of what seemed like an administrative building. It had been right before finding the wording on the floor. Bernd thought that it might have been related to getting flashed so directly in the eyes there on the spot. Even after some time passed, and though he asked her to think about what it may have been, she still could not say.

"So why do you bring it up now?" surprising her in his willingness to let it go at least for now. What she didn't know was that he was really asking the question hoping that she would let him go to bed.

"Well, I would like to go back again," she said.

"Not tonight, I hope," he exclaimed turning around from being already halfway back into the house through the shoji paper door he had just opened.

"No, no, no. I mean I would like to plan when we should go back and see that place again. It is such an unusual place right here in our neighborhood," she made her case being as convincing as she thought she could be.

"All right, then. How about this autumn when the moon is so bright that they say rabbits are pounding rice to make rice cakes on it?

September is after all, moon viewing month. Right now, I'm knackered" he said using a British term which meant that he was tired. He also realized that even if he wasn't teaching the summer term, he had a lot of preparing to do for the coming school term. "And anyway it is too hot for breaking into buildings in this summer heat," he claimed, surprised at how it came across. One would almost think that they did this often, breaking into buildings, which was far from the truth. Though, it was true that they both loved to explore almost anything.

As for today, he had had a long day at work explaining advanced theories in basic terms to people who were enthused about the science of physics, but were not yet at the level they were asking about. This made for rather lengthy, drawn out explanations. He had to admit, however, that as tired as he was, he loved his job. Talking about physics was something he could do all day. He was glad that he had friends in other departments in the university; this gave him a change, if not a break, on days like this when he was tired from his regular job. Today he was particularly tired, and so he preferred to be going off to bed to discussing the neighborhood building.

This was just what Yuri wanted to hear. "All right, then. Tomorrow night well find out when the moon will be full and plan to go on that day this coming September," she said firmly and with a smile catching his eye as he turned to continue going inside. Her mind raced with excitement, yet she still did not really know why. It was only a feeling that she had. And she would only have to wait a few months to find out why. September, the month when rabbits make *mochi* or rice cakes on the moon would be here soon. She felt as though she just couldn't wait.

Though Bernd was happy that she was happy, he went in for his bath both wondering and anxious about what the autumn would bring. As tired as he was, it took him a few minutes longer to fall asleep than normal.

A Second Trip to the Old Administrative Building

The few months between the heat of the summer months and the autumn moon viewing went quickly. Both of them were busy, Bernd with his new class on Buddhism in Japan then and now: physics and temple building, and Yuri with her role in editing a revised edition of **Hieroglyphics and You**, the only book of its kind in Japanese and English explaining Egyptian hieroglyphics.

Their busy schedules kept them so engrossed in work that time flew and soon the autumn was upon them. When Yuri considered just how fast the time seemed to go by, she thought, *kou in no gotoshi* or time flies like an arrow. Suddenly it was time to make another trip to the "administrative building." On the assigned evening when the moon being nearly full made things bright they met on the *engawa* or porch way and drank tea silently, both wondering how the evening would unfold. They chose to go a few days before the full moon so that if they needed to abort the plan for whatever reason they had a few more days in which it was possible to go to the abandoned apartment building with the benefit of moon light.

"Bernd," Yuri finally said breaking the silence with welcome conversation.

"Yes," he said in reply, glad to be in conversation rather than mulling over the same concerns he'd been over a hundred times already about what they might find in the abandoned building.

"When shall we go?" Yuri asked hoping they could start immediately of course.

"Why don't we get ready and go now?" he said, then immediately realized that they should plan it out a bit more before they go. He logically thought that a plan was important in case something were to go wrong ….

"Agreed," Yuri said, and like the first time, she was off of the *engawa* and click-clacking along in her *geta* making the sounds *karan koron-karan koron* while Bernd remained behind startled and looking for his sandals. Though it was autumn, it was not cool out yet, so they were off in sandals and comfortably so aside from his having to catch up with her again. It did not escape Bernd's attention that the moon in its nearly full state looked larger than usual tonight or so he felt.

"Wait for me," he wanted to cry, but she was already quite far along, and again it was all he could do to try and catch up which didn't happen until he was standing once again near the old building by her side. This time, however, they were both right away positioned out of the light on the side that had no street lights.

"Well, what is the plan?" she asked.

"That's just what I was going to ask you," he said a little sharply. Then he noticed that she was quite serious now, and so he began to figure in his mind, carefully considering what would be the best approach from here on out.

"Well, let's get inside the first room and make a plan in private," he said catching his breath.

"That's a good idea, though let's make sure the place is empty before we get too talkative," Yuri replied. Bernd agreed to this right away already bending the glass so that Yuri could move the latch with the hairpin she was removing from her hair.

After they got inside, they first listened and hearing nothing, carefully checked the door to the *grand hall* as they now called it, to make sure that it was locked from the side they were on. They didn't hear anyone or anything, and were reassured since the door was locked. Thus, they decided they could make a plan in that room, the one that looked like an old apartment. Slowly they backed away from the door to the grand hall. Looking around the apartment they saw or rather felt something by the window where they had come in. As far as they now could tell the object was possibly an old side table next to a bed. They really could not see much as there was not the flashing light as there had been on the first night they were there.

At any rate their eyes did adjust to the dimly lit room, lit they considered by distant street lamps. They looked around and saw that it had been a place for perhaps a caretaker or someone to live in years gone by, it seemed. They were remembering the first time they were in there. It had the same curtains on the window of a flower design and little to no light. It had a strangely lived in feel to it, but initially they found no evidence that anyone had lived in that room for years. They looked around at the telephone jack in the wall, the light hanging from the ceiling and the curtains though they could not make out the colors because of lack of light. They saw that the room must have been a cozy one at one time in the past, but could not tell how long ago.

Then, both of them froze in their tracks as a chill went up Yuri's spine and down Bernd's. They somehow realized at the same time that something was wrong. Yuri said, "Bernd, what is it?" and he looked at her and simply said "There's more light in here than last time," He was obviously very uneasy.

"Yeah, and I didn't think anyone lived in here the last time we were here," she said after recovering from the shock she felt upon realizing that the room may not have been as unused as it seemed up until now.

They both began to breathe again, and their minds were as alert as ever. In fact both of them were on high alert and feeling anxious. Bernd had noticed how the light was dim in this room, but constant as opposed to the flashing light they discovered the first time. After a final look around, though they wondered if anyone had actually used this room recently or not, they decided there was no one currently here, so they moved toward the door to the grand hall.

When they opened the door, it did not even make a sound, something they thought a bit odd, since the building was seemingly so old and unused. Immediately it was apparent that the autumn moon was what was responsible for the steady light they now enjoyed as the mid-September moonlight illuminated the grand hall. They noted how as it was autumn the moon was at an angle that allowed it to shine in through the windows. The difference in seasons and the timing of the rising of the moon was significant Bernd's scientific mind quickly began to consider. He was about to calculate the angle of the moon, and then coming back to the immediacy of the situation he looked around to see that there was no one looking at them!

While looking around the room and being favored by the dim moonlight, the couple could see in each alcove the busts of great explorers, Japanese and otherwise. Many of them were old and unlabeled, yet some were familiar names such as Amerigo Vespucci and Peter the Great. The latter were confirmed as their placards were luckily illuminated by the moonlight. Many robed figures were prominent seemingly Greek in origin or so Yuri thought, though the name cards were covered in shadows and as such unreadable.

"Bernd, what is this place?" Yuri asked half expecting an answer and half wondering if anyone on earth new what this place was about.

Bernd, thought for a moment, and then he told her that the robes the Greeks wore were not the same as these, at least not worn in the same way. He had seen robes like these worn …but could not remember where he had seen them. One thing he was certain about. He was sure from his studies of the Greeks and the Olympics that the robes in Greece were worn differently. He paused.

"Yes?" Yuri asked her voice rising in tone wondering why he paused just then.

"Wait," he suddenly blurted out. "I have seen these robes in …They are Tibetan." He had come across them while preparing his course on Buddhism in Japan. His course was planned so that he would start by following the spread of Mahayana Buddhism along the Silk Road to China, through Korea and eventually to Japan. And he would note the spread of Theravada Buddhism also called *Hinayana* or smaller vehicle to Southeast Asia. He decided that he would end with the spread and development of Buddhist ideals to Tibet as Tibetan Buddhism or *Vajrayana* is among the most popular of Buddhist traditions in the West. Of course he would balance this, too, with the long experience of the study and practice of Zen Buddhism in the west.

This didn't help, though. Neither of them had any idea why the room was arranged the way it was and if there was any meaning to any of it, or just an elaborate display of art from around the world. They were about to discuss this when Yuri noticed that the floor, too, was completely lit up. Not only was the seal that they had been standing on lit up, but they could see that there were seals seemingly from various places around the world written in as many languages in true Meiji style ….

The Seals

During the Meiji period, in stark contrast to the exclusionary practices under the Tokugawa leaders, Japan had established relations with nations around the world and purposefully so. Therefore, there was nothing unusual about foreign languages being written in public places, however, Yuri thought it was odd that there was one written in ...Egyptian hieroglyphics!

Immediately she set out to decipher any meaning she could from the symbols. It seemed as though they were easy to translate, "Under the stars united across the seas." It seemed that the meaning was clear, yet the last hieroglyphic could be used two ways, as an ending to the statement and as a symbol for something that was unfinished and needed completing. The only way to know its proper use was if it was spoken, and there have not been people who read and speak the ancient Egyptian language well such as the symbols she was looking at, for many, many years. What it meant seemed to be apparent, but was it really? Yuri puzzled. "Across the seas" made a lot of sense, too, she thought for the Meiji Period. It was a time when shipping connected everyone virtually everywhere across the oceans and continents.

While Yuri was contemplating the meaning of the hieroglyphics, Bernd was trying his hand at the Japanese writing on the floor. It explained that this building was built in order to draw connections between the Japanese and others in the world. It was a history museum of sorts it seemed, and Bernd could only read this part of the floor. He had no other choice, not being able to read Russian and not seeing any symbols in German anywhere. He thought the wording he was looking at read *"Ten no shita de, sekai ha touitsu shimasu."* He translated it to mean, "Under the sky the world comes together, or "Under the sky the world will come together." He was very pleased when he found that Yuri agreed with the meaning he took from these characters. She was very impressed. She did note, however, that the reading "heaven" was probably preferable to "sky" in this context. This, too, seemed like a statement and an unfinished thought at the same time. It made him wonder if it really was meant only to describe the building or if it had something to do with the seals. He did not know that the description was a saying from the Meiji Period expressing a wish by the administrators in this building to make connections around the world. They also did not know that it was the only wording that was prominent during the day time.

The seal in English was easy for both of them to read, yet was the most puzzling seal yet. "The world will come together by being together under the stars." There it was, the first seal that they had seen the very first time they entered the building and this large room.

"Wasn't the world connected and unified under the stars so to speak during this period of interconnectedness?" Yuri asked the historian Bernd. This jarred him to attention. They had been so quiet and said so little to each other up until now that her full statement riveted both of them to the present.

"Well, yes that's true. The Meiji period was a time of making connections around the world, but why does it say *under the stars*? That's a little odd don't you think?"

"Bernd in Japan, a lot like in China, everything exists with the help of heaven. Everything is treated with respect as something under heaven. I mean, everything exists under the sky and heaven, doesn't it? The stars, too, are part of heaven."

"I see your point," he replied.

Bernd got excited and took out a small pocket flashlight he had brought along and attempted to observe the details of the seal with it. Yuri looked over at him and noticed that his face lit by the light of the flashlight, went blank. He had been trying to read deeper into the meaning of the pictures and symbols on the seals and look for clues to further understanding of the seal by shining the light on it. However, when the light shone upon the symbol it *vanished*. This made him go blank, and that is what Yuri observed as she looked over at him now.

"What is it?" she got out, and then she, too, noticed that the symbol was no longer visible in the light. Where the light shone it looked like tiles from any other tiled floor in any large marble building anywhere in the world, Yuri thought. Just like tiles in St. Peter's Basilica in Rome.

"Why would the symbols be made to disappear? Bernd asked.

And Yuri immediately replied, "Why would they be made to be visible only at night?" For a few moments Yuri was lost in thought, her quick mind racing around the many possibilities that were now coming to her, and then she had an insight.

"Let's look at them all!" she exclaimed. "They may be gone tomorrow," she added.

"Anyway we can always come back when its night," Bernd said, not wanting to see them all tonight as it was getting late.

"Maybe, but we must do all we can. We are not even sure that someone doesn't live in the room we came in through." And with that Bernd came to the realization that they must do all they can tonight not knowing when the next opportunity would present itself.

They looked around as quickly as they could and counted six seals in total written in various languages including two that took them both by surprise. In a way it was somehow greater than any surprise they had yet encountered that night. The fifth and sixth seals, whether they were illuminated by the moonlight or by flashlight were without a doubt …blank. Obviously someone has found it important to include these last two seals, for some reason seeming to notice that the others by themselves were somehow incomplete. For what reason a fifth and sixth blank seal were added, neither Yuri nor Bernd could even begin to imagine.

They noticed one more thing. The writing on the seals was written in English, Russian, Egyptian, and a language neither of them recognized. That one of the languages was unknown to either of them was astounding. They couldn't even guess what language it was or where it was from. Again, that the fifth and sixth were completely blank, in fact everything they had come across that evening they now realized remained to them yet a mystery.

At that point, not having had time to completely read all the seals or take everything in, they heard a noise. They did not waste any time wondering where it could be coming from. Nor who might be making the noise behind the large wall at their backs that they had thought was an outer wall made of solid brick. They quickly and as quietly as possible went through the door into the side room and out the window replacing everything as carefully as they could and went directly down the street in the opposite direction of their home.

Bernd and Yuri were lucky that they were both married to sensible people. Though they were on an adventure like none they'd ever been on, each was relieved to be with a partner who they could trust to do the right thing. At least both of them simultaneously having chosen to walk in a direction away from their apartment seemed a good indication of this. It was a decision that they hadn't discussed, and had not been necessary to say out loud. For this, too, they were thankful. As they considered this and the night's events, they kept walking. With more than a little tingle running up their spines, their pace quickened.

About an hour and a half later, after returning home by a very round about way and having taken several taxi rides, they entered their bed room, laid out the futons and began a discussion that took them almost to the light of morning before finally they both all but passed out from nervous exhaustion. This was the first time that they ever took a taxi to their house and the only time they were ever completely silent for one and a half hours continuously while together. Neither thought it wise to break the silence till they were safe at home and inside their apartment. After breaking the silence both agreed that this was a good choice. It had after all, been a shocking night of discoveries. It was also a night of new mysteries.

After becoming silent from exhaustion, Yuri remembered hardly being able to wait to get out of the taxi and walk the remaining short distance into their home. She had known full well that it was of the utmost importance to look as though there was nothing special about their returning home and to not attract attention to herself. She had been incredibly glad to be in her apartment, feeling safe and unobserved, yet extremely excited about their findings. She was also incredibly disappointed because she realized that there would have to be a cooling off period before she and Bernd could return to the abandoned building again, if ever. And this was her last thought before she fell asleep that night.

Wedding Gifts and Remembrances

Two weeks later…
 The couple had been wondering when they could get back to the building that they no longer considered abandoned. They wanted desperately to get back into the grand hall and read the seals again and gather any other clues to their meanings. They also knew that going there would be more risky than ever. If whoever or whatever made the noise the last time they were there realized that someone had been there or had seen them, getting in the next time might not be so easy.

They couldn't be sure and had been over the scenario a hundred times. Could they go back at all, and if so, how long should they wait, a week, two weeks, maybe longer? They really had no idea. One thing was for sure, however, and both of them knew it. Neither of them even considered *never* going back.

For the time being, however, they decided that it would be best to not go back for a period of time as yet undetermined. They also decided to not talk about their experiences outside of the privacy of their own apartment nor with anyone else. Especially, they were to be strict about not sharing their thoughts about this matter with anyone else.

They were relieved when they realized that it was now almost New Year's time, and so they would be preoccupied with visiting Yuri's family on the small island which was such a nice refuge from their life in the city. In light of the recent events they decided not to leave Japan to see Bernd's family. They would have to go another time. Even though life in Tokyo was by all accounts in modern terms quite convenient, it was nonetheless a huge city and could not compete with the serenity and quiet that could be gained on the small island where Yuri had been born.

Life there was much slower than in Tokyo, and the contrast reminded Yuri of some things she had read about mental health, meditation, and about getting away from the hustle and bustle that was almost everywhere in the *modern* world. Indeed the modern world with its ultra fast video images and flashing signs, lights and commercials was considered by some to poison or hinder the chances of people actually attaining a state of calm. According to one teacher, modern life all but prevented people from finding the state of blissful clarity sought after and considered possible by those who meditate.

Yuri loved so much about the island that made it unique, and quietude was only one of these things. For example, the islanders still kept up a language of their own. They of course all knew standard Japanese from school, but the remnants of an older dialect, which was almost like another language was something she missed while in Tokyo. In fact, when she learned standard Japanese in school, it was what started her being interested in languages. She found the differences amazing and very interesting.

It was their first chance to return to the island for the New Year since getting married two years earlier. Usually they planned to go see Bernd's family during the winter holiday. This year, of course was different, and they decided that they would alternate which of the two families was visited at this time. This return to the island was also happening because they had so many gifts that had been stored at Yuri's parents' house from the wedding. Now that they were fully settled into their life in Tokyo it was time to go collect them. Yuri's mother showed an unusually playful side herself and much to Yuri's surprise jokingly suggested that if they didn't finally come and get them, she would have to throw them in the sea since there was such limited room in their small home. Of course this was just playful banter as she felt the strong Confucian duty to her child and so would have kept them as long as necessary to give the couple time to come collect them. The child in a Confucian value system had duties, too. For example, going and collecting the gifts was the couple's responsibility. To leave them indefinitely in Yuri's parent's care would have been a disrespectful intrusion. Respecting one's elders remains highly important in Japan.

Yuri remembered growing up in that small home with the local fire patrol going by and warning of fires by clacking together wooden blocks. She also remembered that a whistle would blow at five o'clock signifying an end to a busy work day for fisher persons, those who made *tatami* or rice reed, straw mats and so many more people laboring to make a living such as by farming.

She really felt that she had had a blessed childhood growing up with plenty to do on the island and a family that took good care of her. She was truly glad that she had been raised in Japan, and that her clan and her community valued taking care of each other so much. They truly worked together well. They cooperated well in things such as when it was time to dig sweet potatoes a time called *imo hori*.

Of course there was bickering from time to time. And also the odd nagging at each other to have things done the "traditional" way which was usually considered superior to innovation, but by and large they got along pretty well.

Confucian based life styles may have drawbacks for the status of women in society, but the Confucian based life style that she was raised in had merit in it such that it promoted cooperation and taking care of each other, especially the old. She really appreciated that even at her young age. There was a strong sense of mutual responsibility. Not only were children expected to obey their parents, a component of the ideal of filial piety, but also the parents were bound in some unwritten way to provide for the physical, moral and intellectual care of their children.

So it had been set that they would leave on December twenty-second, the day before the holiday celebrating the Emperor's birthday. This was while many others were still not on holiday and would hopefully result in there being less traffic and congestion along the way. This was because the trip itself would take much of the day, and because Yuri's company had time off. Its foreign offices were observing the Christmas holidays by letting their families have a chance to get together at this time. As for Bernd, he had been off since the middle of December, the normal time to begin breaks for those working at universities in Japan.

Now it was December twenty-sixth and after observing the Christmas holiday with Bernd at the same church in which they got married, they were both relaxing between exertions related to the annual New Year's cleaning ritual. Throughout Japan people clean their houses thoroughly in anticipation of the coming New Year. Homes are cleaned and washed, paper doors called *shoji* are repapered and things are made ready for greeting a new year with a fresh start.

This day was closet day, the day to clean out closets some of which had been hardly looked in for years and others that were used daily. Last year Yuri remembered looking through closets in Germany. She could not believe the large size of the closets there compared to the home she was raised in. She also noted how different it was that futons, the mattress bedding and covers were taken out in the evening and put away in closets daily in Japan. In Germany, beds were common and left out in the bedrooms. How nice it would be to have that much space, she thought.

When cleaning out one of the closets in Yuri's family home, Bernd came across a little diary written in Japanese. He asked Yuri whose it was, and she said that it was not a diary, but a fancy copy of their *koseki*, their family registry book. Family registries listed the members of the family from as far back as had been recorded, which in some cases was many years and sometimes centuries. Some books of, for example, nobility may list previous family members back thousands of years. Many if not most Japanese families may have some kind of copy of these, and all Japanese are registered in their *koseki* at the city or town hall.

Yuri was not sure why her grandmother had given it to her for a wedding present instead of giving it to her father, the normal route of the book that was really a kind of long-term family registry and history. Yuri's father was after all, the oldest son in the family and as such was considered the rightful recipient. However, Yuri's father as the oldest son also had the *butsudan* or Buddhist altar in his home. Yuri had been enthralled with the *butsudan* since a very young age and often looked through the family registry. Grandmother admitted that she was not sure herself, but that she just had a feeling that it should be given to Yuri. It was her *kan* or feeling.

Yuri now wondered if it was her interest in the book as a young girl that made grandma feel this way. She considered, too, how they would talk for hours at a time when she was young. It was as though Yuri wanted to know all about her family's history. Grandmother enjoyed talking about the family history with Yuri very much Yuri now realized.

On the other hand, Yuri was the oldest daughter and only child of the family and eventually would be the one to take care of the Buddhist alter. She would keep it in her home, as the oldest son would have done. As a result while Grandmother was passing over Yuri's father, the end result was the same. It eventually would have ended up with Yuri anyway. Nonetheless, this caused quite a stir as some of the family members insisted that the registry belonged with the *butsudan* that of course would remain with Yuri's father while he was alive. Maybe Grandmother thought she should just give it to Yuri outright instead of making her wait till her father gave it to her. No one really knew why this was happening, but one thing was clear, Grandmother obviously wasn't taking any chances in getting the registry to Yuri. That is why it became a wedding gift for Bernd and Yuri.

Eventually the relatives came to the conclusion that Grandmother was not giving it to the wrong person so much as just being a bit premature. No one, however, doubted Grandmother's judgment. It wasn't necessary as she had proven to be very wise many times making things work for the family especially during the harsh times around World War II. She really had kept the family together through both good and hard times.

Yuri thought that a compromise solution was to leave it in her father's care and with the *butsudan*. She trusted that her father would let her have it if ever she needed it. He for his part was proud of her daughter's ability to find a solution that would keep peace among family members. He also pledged to himself to keep his daughter's trust. He would give her the book any time she needed it. That was a promise. He recognized it as hers.

Yuri hadn't opened the book when they received it for a wedding present. She knew her family history well, and was not concerned too much with very distant or long ago relatives at that time. Indeed, Grandmother said she did not think knowing the names of each was nearly as important as having a general sense of respect for those that had come before. She really was a product of East Asian Confucian thought, Yuri considered as she smiled remembering how Grandmother's face lit up when she had told this to Yuri.

In Japan, following along the lines of Confucian thought, obeying one's parents and being respectful amounted to what was called the *Yamato nadeshiko*, or essentially obedient or at least traditional Japanese girl filled with *real* Japanese spirit. In many ways Yuri was a combination of views it seemed. Yuri did not fit the traditional image of the *nadeshiko* wanting often to make up her own mind regardless of what her family felt about some issues. And she was also in many ways essentially the ideal example of the Japanese spirit. This was evident in the way that she cared about others, and really truly strived to do well and develop her skills whenever possible. This was not unlike the sense of Confucian morality that upheld self-development as a model. When considering Yuri, Grandmother thought that Yuri was a little bit like her.

When she opened the book to show Bernd the family line back from …she noticed that there was a small tear in the back cover. She had been reading an English book earlier that day, and opened the family history from the back since that is how you open English books. Though in the case of English books, it would be the front. At first, she thought nothing of the tear considering the age of the book, but then a nagging thought kept telling her to *go back*. She loved the decorations on the book, things of nature such as bamboo, pine trees and the like.

She really wanted to show the family line to Bernd and did show him the names of the most recent ancestors until about two hundred years ago when she could not fight the feeling any longer. She opened the book from the left side as you look at it, which was the back of Japanese books, and observed carefully the tear in the back of the cover. It was not much bigger than about three inches long and it was vertical. She examined it with her fingers this time and found that the cloth cover could be moved away from the binding to allow someone, if so inclined to look inside. There was no lump or hint of anything inside the cloth and so she did not think that there was anything contained within the cloth cover. Of course she felt that it was worth a look!

Upon looking inside she found ...nothing! Disappointed she went back to the page she had been looking at with Bernd. He really was wondering what she was doing by this time so he asked. "What is it?"

"Oh, nothing," she replied. "I just thought the tear at the back was unusual that's all. But there was nothing there." Bernd took the book and with his scientific mind gave it some consideration and then finding nothing in his initial observation said, "Let's have some tea."

While having tea it was the perfect time for Yuri to relax and for Bernd to think about the tear in the back of the book which of course was now very much on his mind. With his astute mind he considered that the book was very old and that having a tear or marks or scratches would be nothing out of the ordinary. In fact, if there had been no marks or scratches it would have been really strange he thought ...and then it came to him. There was something odd about the tear. Why would the tear be vertical, he wondered? He might have been stretching his mind a little too much to make a hypothesis he realized, but still he thought this was strange. If a book was to be opened side to side, he thought as was the case with this book, then wouldn't it have a tear that would go side to side and not vertically? This may have been simply guess-work, but either way he thought it warranted further investigation.

Yuri's increasingly emphatic claims that she really thought that it was *nothing*, did not deter him. He went into the back room where the presents had been stored in a closet and brought the old book out into the room where they were relaxing and having some *o-cha* or green tea.

Yuri was now playing a little hurt that he would not listen to her, but was also as interested in exploring the tear in the cover as ever. Begrudgingly, she came over to the central table under the light and looked over Bernd's shoulder as he opened the book to the back once more. First he held it up to the light, and that proved to be of no help as light could not penetrate the back cover from behind. Then, he held the cloth side directly under the light without any luck there either. Then he went to set the book down and clumsily got his finger caught in the torn cloth as he was setting the book down. He looked down at his sloppy handling of the book and the light shone on the cloth cover at the same time. This time he did see something. There was writing on the *inside* of the cloth on the inside of the back cover of the book.

Yuri following quickly behind Bernd, both of them flew to their feet even as the book settled sideways onto the short table. Instinctively they grasped each other he grabbing her shoulders and she his arms. They had no way to know this, but somehow they thought that the writing was something significant. Then, right away they both knelt down alongside the table, Bernd taking into his hands the ancient book this time with extremely great care.

He opened it to the back and carefully, ever so lightly pulled the cloth away from the back cover, and then angled the book so that the light would shine into the resulting gap. He got ready to read the passage that was written vertically as was customary in Japan when he found that he could not make heads or tails of the writing. Feeling not just a little concerned he looked to Yuri hoping that she could in some way be of help. As he held the book under the light just so, Yuri positioned herself so that she could see the cloth without getting in between the light and the written words, and then she did it. She saw what it said and growing ever more excited started to understand what she was reading. Though she was able to decipher the words in the ancient script, she had to read very slowly. This was ancient Japanese, perhaps almost as old as when written characters came to Japan from China between the sixth and seventh centuries CE, or so she felt. The characters gave an elusive description of where "something wonderful" could be found, though there was no clue as to what this wonderful thing was nor *precisely* where it could be found.

The clue stated that "something wonderful" could be found at a <u>flowing</u> temple, and it would be <u>established</u> at the <u>center</u>. It seemed as though there were a million temples in Japan that fit that description. After all in Japanese, the term Buddhism means the Middle Way and the character for middle was the same character for center in Japanese. And regarding the idea of "flowing" there was no end to temples that had been built around or near water sources such as rivers, waterfalls, and the like as is the case, too, with shrines representative of the Japanese native religion, Shinto.

The couple also noticed that the note was signed, "Prince Shotoku." This was a problem since there was no way of telling whether this note was actually from Prince Shotoku or a forgery. To even the two budding historians the name seemed likely to be a fake. Scholars would realize whether or not this was his real signature, it seemed, so Yuri and Bernd were puzzled by the enigmatic signature. This of course left them, not being scholars of Prince Shotoku, wondering whether or not the note was authentic.

Yuri could see that the signature was written sloppily and was inclined to accept this as a hoax, considering reports that Prince Shotoku had a reputation for attention to detail…Then, suddenly she remembered her visit to the temple on their Japanese part of their honeymoon trip. She remembered showing up promptly at six in the morning the day after she visited the temple the first time. She remembered thinking that the abbot was a great teacher. He was not only filled with wisdom of which he readily shared, but was also out raking rocks and obviously had been doing so for awhile already before she arrived.

Yuri had sat in meditation with him and he gave her some brief lessons on meditating in *zazen*, the Zen style of sitting. She also recalled now clearly one thing in particular that he had said to her, "You have good instincts and a good foundation. Trust yourself." She did not know what he meant by a good foundation, but she now realized that the latter part of his statement meant that he was urging her to trust herself, her heart or *kokoro* and her own judgment. That is just what she wanted to do now, trust herself. She couldn't help wondering, though, in what way?

She thought over the statement written at the back of the book again and again not wanting to be too hasty to draw conclusions as to what it meant. To Yuri, the hint in the old book could only mean one thing. They were being directed to go to the oldest established temple in Japan, Horyuji in Nara Prefecture. She had to trust her instinct that whether it was the signature of the real Prince Shotoku or not. The *ryu* in Ho<u>ryu</u>ji having the same verbal meaning as flowing in the sense of a river made Horyuji as good a place to start looking for this "something wonderful" as any. In addition to her feeling about this, Horyuji was located in the central part of Nara Prefecture in one of the oldest Buddhist regions in Japan. Further, the temple was said to have been built under the direction of Prince Shotoku. The catch, it seemed, would be whether the signature was authentic or not. They hoped that it wasn't a ploy to throw off unwanted searchers from whatever would be the true path put forward by the clue.

The Journey to Horyuji

And so now they found themselves the following day riding the train to catch the ferry to go back to Honshu, the largest island in the Japanese archipelago, so that they could catch another train deep into the heart of Nara Prefecture. They were on the way to Horyuji, they were excited, and they were still unsure just what it was that they hoped to find there. What this "something wonderful" was they could not begin to guess. Clearly more investigation would be necessary. Clearly they were up to it, being more excited than any other time in their lives…ever!

Before boarding the train, both had to promise Yuri's family that they would be back by *Oomisoka*, or New Year's Eve. The first visit to a Shrine on New Year's Eve is traditionally considered important in Japan. Many people visit shrines just as the New Year is breaking, that is, at midnight on December thirty-first. Having promised to be back they were on the train, and Yuri was lost in thought. She was thankful that she had gone to Teruji. She wondered if Bernd would have gone along with her to Horyuji if she had not related the story of the abbot to him. She adored how his face scrunched up when he is a little incredulous about her notions, like the time when she said that she wanted to go back to the *abandoned* building in their neighborhood. She was also glad that this time, he trusted her enough to go along on a whim. He was excited to travel to the temple and decided that either way it would not be a loss since they could learn more about the history of the oldest remaining temple in Japan.

When they arrived in the area, they stopped for a cup of coffee, one of their shared passions, at a coffee shop near by the temple. Then, not wanting to waste any time, they went in to explore the temple and its grounds.

At Horyuji they found various descriptions of Buddhism coming to Japan in the sixth and seventh centuries AD by way of the Silk Road. They saw evidence of this in the hall of relics, a museum established to trace the movement of Buddhism along the Silk Road complete with artifacts. This reinforced what they had learned about how information and culture flowed to Japan from China through Korea. Bernd also knew how later the Japanese sought out cultural exchanges with both of its East Asian neighbors especially China as Japan became a world power. Indeed, Prince Shotoku was intimately involved in delegations sent to China before writing the first Japanese Constitution.

They were amazed at the similarities in artwork, between the three East Asian nations. Objects depicted in natural settings with subtle hints and strokes were common. In some cases detail was amazing, too. They noted that during the latter half of the first millennium, Japanese culture really took off so to speak with Japanese adaptations of Chinese painting techniques including the painting of mountains and indeed temples in the mountains, temples by water falls etc …again, in nature.

Yuri groaned as she imagined the many temples built around flowing bodies of water. Indeed one time she had been to the south of Wakayama Prefecture and had been to a temple along the highway that was built near a famous waterfall called *Nachi no Taki* or the Waterfall of Nachi. She remembered buying snacks shaped like little bells called *suzu* in Japanese.

Along with these great cultural exchanges between the East Asian nations, came perhaps the most influential adaptation for Japan, the incorporation almost wholesale of Confucian ethics with its moral traditions. The adoption of Confucian ethics had created great stability in East Asian societies, but was also something that had generally, though not completely relegated women to the status of almost second-class citizens.

What they did not find, however, were any clues to anything that was "something wonderful." Nothing stood out. In the back of her mind Yuri was secretly hoping that they would find something that gave them a clue about the seals from the grand hall. Bernd was still puzzling about the ancient book, but also intrigued with the construction of the temple. He liked the layout of the grounds and buildings and was absolutely fascinated by the mathematical precision of the pagoda or Buddhist tower noting that there were five tiers to the roof.

Then Bernd said, "You know, there would be room for a sixth tier on top of the pagoda. This could be directly related to the six seals on the floor of the grand hall," he continued thinking out loud.

After he had said this, Yuri promptly pointed out to him that "Pagodas around Japan often have five levels," meaning that it was unlikely that there would have been six. She continued thoughtfully, "Though if you think about it, one could imagine them having many tiers, too," she went on. This ended the conversation for now, Bernd being a little hurt by the quickness of her reply.

Later, they were both looking up at the pagoda the sun shining directly toward them from the other side as it was beginning to set in the west. Then, they realized something that they hadn't noticed before.

The brightness of the sun reminded them of all the references to the stars in the seals. Pagodas point upwards they considered. In fact many religious monuments point upwards. They realized that two examples were steeples on churches and stupas or sacred buildings that held items of religious significance in Buddhist countries such as India, Laos, Thailand, Myanmar etc …. They wondered if there was any significance and connection to the seals in this pointing upward. They also considered the importance of looking up since stars were everywhere, when you looked up! And didn't a pagoda make you do just that, look up.

"Oh, there's nothing wonderful in that," Yuri exclaimed exasperated at their inability to find any clue at all.

Bernd, too, was a little unsure what to think. Both were concerned, thinking that though many of their discoveries at the temple were interesting and even significant, they could not be the "something wonderful" that was hinted at in the ancestral book. At any rate it was too late to go home that night so they decided to stay at a hotel and go back to the island the next day. Of course, they called Yuri's parents to let them know their decision.

That night, as they went over everything from the day's events, they became quite concerned. They thought that they would have to go to temples all over Japan to find the "something wonderful," and that did seem like a rather daunting task. There must be many hundreds if not thousands of temples in Japan, and this was without even counting …Shinto shrines! The thought of adding shrines into the mix made their heads spin. And since so many temples had been established alongside waterfalls, there was no shortage of "flowing" temples.

And Yuri said out loud, "Oh Bernd, this could take a very long time. Remember that Buddhism which is called the "Middle Way" in Japanese uses the same character as is used for 'center.'" So if it wasn't Horyuji, as the day's exploration seemed to tell them, then the task now looked almost impossible to solve. They wondered, what was this "something wonderful" that was *established* at the *center*? Nonetheless both knew that the other would not give up easily.

The next day, while riding the local train to Yuri's parents' house, Bernd looked up at Yuri, and she knew that he had something to say so she remained quiet and looked at him waiting ….

Alexandria Revisited

"Yuri, do you remember being at the hospital in Egypt?" Bernd said.

"Oh, of course, the one in Alexandria," Yuri replied instantly remembering the sudden change in their honeymoon plans.

"Yeah, didn't you say that there was a symbol there in the floor of the hospital that looked really old?"

"It *was* really, really old." She said seriously.

"Well, what did it say again?" he asked trying to remember what she had said about the symbol. His memory of this was blurred since he had been so ill at that time.

"It said, 'All the world is united by the sun,'" she told him looking a bit puzzled.

"And isn't Japan considered the land of the rising sun?"

"Yeah, but what are you getting at? That symbol seems especially linked to Alexander who considered himself the sun god."

"Well, we've established that there are four known seals in the grand hall, right?"

"Yah. And two that are blank. So?"

"So, maybe the fifth or sixth symbol has something to do with the sun."

"In what way?"

"Well, what if it is a sunny place where the world is united under the stars."

"Do you mean like somewhere along the equator where it is sunny most of the time?"

"Yah, something like that," Bernd said hopefully and with a smile.

"And everything, too, is included under the sun as under the night time sky," Yuri considered out loud. "The Aztecs admired the sun," she mused. And then she shook her head, became serious, and said slowly, "That's a good idea; though, I want to think about this matter a little more."

"Yah, I am just guessing, huh?" Bernd considered.

"Maybe …" she said contemplatively. She also knew of course that he had a keen mind for figuring things out so she wasn't ruling out anything he said yet. She just wasn't sure what to think now. Her senses were telling her to keep everything in mind, to not rule anything out, but also that it did not seem likely that so many clear references to the stars would suddenly in the remaining seals, change to involve the sun. Feeling alive, she smiled.

Oomisoka

Oomisoka is the Japanese name for New Year's Eve, or the night before January first. Yuri especially liked the New Year holiday, because without a doubt she would be free from her ordinary obligations with work. This meant that she was free to visit the little shrine, a place with very fond childhood memories on her little island between Honshu and Shikoku, two of the four largest islands of Japan. Indeed, many Japanese if not most visit a shrine as part of the long-standing Shinto tradition of visiting a shrine or temple in the New Year called *hatsumode*. She especially liked her first visit to a shrine to be on New Year's Eve, *Oomisoka*.

She really liked to go to the shrine late at night as was her family's tradition on New Year's Eve. They would go at midnight, just as the New Year was breaking. To her it just wasn't the same to go on the morning of New Year's Day or sometime during the first three days of the New Year. She thought so even though she realized that most people took those days off from work allowing time to make a visit to a shrine or even a temple.

The evening brought the chill of winter to your face, reminding you of the reality and the harshness of life, but was also a refreshing wakeup call greeting you as you entered the shrine grounds. And for those who get cold easily, Yuri thought, there were always long under ware of various types to ward off the cold. Indeed, getting out and participating in life like this made her feel very, very alive. The use of long johns she took as a sign of Japanese sensibility. She couldn't understand why in modern times the practice of wearing long under ware to stay warm had tapered off so much even with the use of indoor heating. Some people did not wear extra clothing because of the current fashions. She wondered about modern fashion, but not only with regard to long under ware ….

For years people have said that drinking *sake* was a way to tighten one's bond with the gods. It was also a good way to warm you up on the inside at times when it was really chilly at the shrine. She had heard from university friends who live in Wakayama that at a local shrine they drink warmed *sake* with ginger in it. She wondered if her friends felt the same respect for the sacred that she felt during this time. At any rate here it was New Year's Eve and Yuri wondered how to best put into words the feelings that she now had as she prepared herself to enter the shrine, to pray and to drink the warm, New Year's *sake* and bind herself *closer* to the gods.

Actually, her thoughts came quickly and raced around inside her head. For example, she considered whether or not to buy a New Year's arrow, getting rid of the one from the previous year as is customary or to buy prayer charms called *omamori,* also whether to wear new kimono for the first time during the New Year holiday or not. She realized as she stood under the *torii* or gate to the shrine, that she had so much to think about from the year gone by and so much anticipation regarding the coming year that she hadn't felt this way with her head this full of thoughts since …her wedding day.

Nonetheless these matters would have to wait. She breathed as she had learned on several occasions in Oxford and more recently at Teruji. She did her best to allow the flood of mind states to flow through hoping they would not take her away from being present, in the moment. After a few moments of breathing with awareness she really began to enjoy being back at the shrine, greeting old friends, seeing old neighbors, and reveling in the familiar sights and smells.

After reminiscing with people who had entered the shrine before her, and gaining control of her mind through consciously acknowledging her breathing in and out, she entered further into the shrine. She paid her respects at the main building that housed the local deity. In this case it was a rock with a rope around it. The rock was a symbol of nature, and the rope symbolized continuity. The rope is called a *shimenawa* and it is meant to make a connection with the item in nature and by implication the *kami* or gods. She realized that this rope that symbolized continuity was similar to the teaching in Buddhism that uses the symbol of a thread of continuity connecting human thoughts together and indeed all beings with each other.

Yuri also took a small cup of rice wine or *sake* and drank it. The heated sake felt good, and Yuri wondered as her spirit felt free and easy if this result was because of her joy in the good fortune of going to a place she adores, the work of the sake, or perhaps both. At this, her childhood shrine, like those in Wakayama, she wondered what it would be like if they included ground up ginger in the hot sake drink. She absolutely loved ginger and felt that including it would make the drink even more infectious for her. She chuckled finishing the rest of the *sake* in one gulp.

At any rate she moved on and finished making the rounds at the various smaller adjunct shrines. They were placed around the grounds inside of the main gate each signifying something unique. Some of the smaller shrines within the larger shrine were places where one could pray for good fortune in business in the coming year, and for many on this island that meant the business of fishing. Others were shrines dedicated to the good wishes for education, good health of the local people or various sundry purposes.

By chance she met an acquaintance, Junko Watanabe by the main gate, the *torii*, as she was leaving. They stood there looking at each other in disbelief. It had been years since they had seen each other. They were good friends in school, and since Yuri's last name was Yokota she often sat right in front of Junko from grade school through high school as Junko's last name Watanabe comes right after Yokota in order in the Japanese alphabet system. In fact they wrote New Year's greeting cards to each other to keep in contact through the years since they were in high school even though they had not met since the year Yuri went off to college.

New Year's cards are the customary way in Japan of keeping in touch with important people in one's life, not unlike writing Christmas cards for Christians or holiday greeting cards in the United States and other places.

As Yuri was about to leave, and since Junko was only just arriving, instead of catching up that night, especially since the breeze coming off of the sea was chilly, they made plans to meet the next day. This suited Yuri just fine, since for her, New Year's Eve was meant to be spent reverently visiting a shrine, but in the New Year she could visit a temple as well. Visiting temples in the first few days of the New Year was something Yuri liked to do, too, for *hatsumode*, or the first visit to a shrine, or a temple in the New Year. Still, she was glad that she could visit her home town shrine on New Year's Eve. Yuri noted as she turned to make her way home from the shrine that the ocean was flowing alongside the shrine. She was at first on edge about how many places would be alongside flowing water such as this, and then relaxing into the feeling, smiled. She was at her hometown shrine, reconnected to a childhood friend or *osanai*, and warmed by *sake*.

They planned to meet at Bentenji, or Benten Temple, the local temple dedicated to the goddess of music, literature and the arts. She was called *Sarasvati* in other traditions. Many on the island abhorred war, especially after the massive carnage of the Second World War that took many of the young men of the island. Fortunately this temple had served the island's people well for a very long time. It now stood in most islanders' minds as the temple to help *avoid* war, as so many of them prayed specifically for peace when visiting there. If one were engaged in the arts, one would not engage in war, they believed. Many, too, remembering the great suffering and sacrifices made during the war, took the opportunity to honor those who died in the war. Along with the memory of the dropping of the atomic bombs on Hiroshima and Nagasaki and the accompanying devastation, praying at Bentenji affirmed their resolve to be peaceful at any cost. Yuri wanted to meet Junko at Bentenji so that she could do just that, put in a prayer for peace, something she naturally felt inclined to do. She learned about many wars all over the world in school and regrettably more recently in the daily news, too. She was also thankful for the reminder of the importance of music, literature and the arts that she is attracted to in so many languages and traditions.

And so the time to meet Junko was set at just after brunch the next day. Brunch began promptly at 11:30 AM at Yuri's house on New Year's Day. Which meant, by Yuri's calculation, that she would meet Junko around one o'clock. When Yuri returned to her parents' house she told her mother of her plans, and reminisced with her mother about the fun time she and Junko had together as students. And as it was late Yuri went to bed thinking "what a small world" and soon fell asleep. Bernd had already gone to sleep, tired from the days of cleaning around the house in preparation for New Year's. He did not go to the shrine with Yuri, which she thought was fine as it gave her a chance to be alone and think things over by herself for the first time in a long time. They had a kind of respect for each other's traditions and needs that served them well and made their marriage work.

Before rolling over to sleep she looked at Bernd. She noticed that the moonlight coming in through the open *shoji* or sliding doors made of paper formed a beam that crossed his face that was without his square topped and round bottomed glasses. He had gone to bed tired, even after a bath, but was now in possession of a very relaxed face. She thought this relaxed look made him very handsome. She snuggled into the warmth of the futon and blanket covering her and smiled in appreciation of the many beautiful things in life from warm futons to faces illuminated by the moon.

Earlier that evening ending just before midnight, Bernd had watched his favorite Japanese TV program, *Kohaku*. It was a competition between the Red and White teams: the red team, all women actresses, singers and performers and the white team, singing and performing men from around Japan. Tonight the red team had won, and this suited Bernd fine as he knew so many of the women performers. He did, however, think that the men put on a good show. His competitive side, the side that watches football with such intensity, hoped the men's team would win the next year. Though what he really liked about the competition was that whichever team won it was clear that it was all in fun and everyone was a good sport about the whole thing.

New Year's Day

Yuri woke the next day unusually early for New Year's Day, but this didn't bother her as she did not need to get up right away. She soaked up the feeling of being able to lounge in her futon feeling luxurious though not lazy on this day alone when lounging. New Year's for her was in the time-honored tradition around Japan, a time for renewal. A renewal of New Year's vows, a renewal of spirit and a fresh start to another year of goals, activity and living life. This of course made her wonder what the year would bring.

Then something came to her. She realized that it had been a long time since she had meditated, so she took this opportunity to meditate while the house was quiet, indeed serene on this winter morning. It was the ideal time she thought.

Yuri nearly fell asleep while meditating. She was brought around by her mother calling out telling her to come down to help prepare a meal of *o-sechi* or specially prepared Japanese food served during the New Year holiday. Helping prepare the meal meant setting it out. It was still true that this job fell to the women of the family. Generally men did not help with food preparation in Japan, especially in traditional island villages. Nonetheless she was happy to do her part in assisting her mother with the preparation. She disliked the idea of her mother doing it all herself and was pleased that her mother did not act the martyr and try to do it all by herself. Working together made it for both of them a much more enjoyable task.

The food for New Year's dining had been prepared over the past few days, and was meant to last for a few days. The sight of the food brought back good memories for Yuri. *Kuro mame* or Black beans, *zenzai* a bean dish made from red beans, and *ozoni* a soy bean based soup made from *miso* or fermented soy beans were among her favorites. She felt that *ozoni* was especially good when her mother made it. Various kinds of fish dishes and more recently various fruits were prepared, though the fruit was meant as a supplement to have later, and not with the New Year's meal. Yuri especially liked the thick *miso* soup or *ozoni* which included some vegetables and her favorite, *mochi* the rice cakes made from special, pounded rice. Perhaps, she thought it would be more accurate to describe *mochi* as caked rice, rather than rice cakes the wording that is usually employed. They are served many ways. During New Year's they are often served in hot *ozoni* not unlike dumplings that are served in other places around the world. Yuri really liked the way the *mochi* melted into the soup. It truly was good food. She would bite into the stretching delicacy before it completely snapped in two as she held it between the chopsticks in front of her. Inevitably it would go plop into the soup seemingly wanting to return to the warmth it held.

Though she did enjoy *mochi* in *ozoni*, she really enjoyed another common way of eating *mochi*. For her family this meant roasting the *mochi* till it softened and puffed up and then dipping it in hot water and smothering it in sweetened and slightly salted *kinako* or powdered soy beans. She could even eat *mochi* plain when it was roasted over an open flame on a mesh grill. Since eating *mochi* plain was not common, it showed how much she really liked it.

After brunch she set out for the temple to meet Junko. This time Bernd was with her. It was their chance to make their first visit to a temple or shrine in the New Year, *hatsumode*, together. As they walked down the narrow alley that separated their house from the one next to it, Yuri thought that she would have *mochi* later for a snack, smothered in honey. When she told Bernd this, he laughed saying, "Didn't you just finish eating?"

It took only a few minutes to get to the temple since it was in the neighborhood. The whole island was only a few kilometers in circumference, so almost anywhere seemed like *in the neighborhood*. However, for Yuri this was a more accurate description of some places, which Yuri had frequented as a child, than others. Yuri knew the island well. The temple was one of the easiest places for her to visit. She had gone there often when little, enjoying the chanting of the resident monk, and sometimes several monks when there were others around. As a child she did not understand that chanting made one feel more concentrated and like the sake from the visit to the shrine on New Year's Eve, closer to the gods. As she understood this idea now, being more concentrated and closer to the gods, it was part of what Buddhists called the universe or the universal power, being a religion without a god. All she knew as a child was that it made her feel good to be around the chanting, enjoying the vibration and the sound. She tried it herself, too, but never loud enough for anyone to know that she was doing it. She laughed and ran home giggling more often than not. And now, here she was with her husband, Bernd, at the temple of her childhood. They had visited before, but it still felt strange to be here with him *this time* for some reason. She had been so many places since growing up here. It made her head spin, sort of.

When they arrived at Bentenji, they noticed that Junko was waiting near the main hall of the temple or *hondo*; she was always on time. For Yuri it was a joy to see her again so soon and to be reacquainted. As for Bernd, he had heard so much about Junko, and her quick wit that he was glad to finally meet her. Junko waved when she saw them and made sure to shake hands with Bernd, signifying some understanding of other cultures.

Junko had been abroad several times, but had never lived overseas like Yuri had. Junko was not only interested in things foreign, but also things of Japanese origin. In this way her interests were balanced. She was part of the youth of Japan that expressed a renewed interest in traditional Japanese culture; something she thought would be a waste to lose sight of. In part, young people were trying to reconnect with their roots, and this was a response to feeling disconnected. They felt disconnected from their cultural past in spite of living in the ultra-connected wired age of text messaging, Face book, and email all on hand held devices …. At least that is what Junko thought; the interconnected present confused lessons from the past. Nonetheless she did enjoy what she could do with a smart phone, which was more than was possible only a few years ago with cell phones.

She had just finished text messaging three friends and sending them photos of the beautiful *kimono* she had seen people wearing this fine day. New Year's visits to shrines and temples provided just the opportunity that so many had been waiting for, a chance to wear their best kimono. The pictures she took showed many kimono or traditional Japanese wrap around garments fixed in place with beautifully woven belts called *obi*. New Year's Day was one of the times in which kimono were saved from the fate of being left in the closet as they normally were year-round being taken out only for special occasions.

Junko was wearing a particularly ornate kimono of blue hues and leafy bamboo and small flowers, those delicate harbingers of spring. It reminded Bernd of what he had read about in a magazine, something called *harumatsu hito*. *Harumatsu hito* means someone who awaits and looks towards the coming spring especially after the New Year has been rung in.

"Hey, it has been a long time" or *"o-hisashiburi"* Yuri said, as she approached Junko, aware of the fact that she herself was not wearing a kimono. Junko put her at ease immediately saying how wonderful it was that she wore that color combination. Of these nuances, Bernd felt, that he would never understand the Japanese penchant for smoothing things out in social settings as best as possible it seemed. Bernd acknowledge that he would not be able to do this himself, but nonetheless noticed how good women can be about making things all right for each other. Bernd gave up trying to understand the elaborate greetings the two women performed since he was more concerned with the way the gate was put together and the pair of vicious looking guardian deities called Ni-o. The deities on either side of the gate were poised to greet all who entered the temple with a menacing look, as they had been doing for centuries it seemed. Junko suggested that first the group pray at the main building and then chat and decide what they would do next. All agreed to this plan.

While it was a simple process involving a small monetary donation placed in a box and a brief prayer, because of the crowds, out in great numbers even for a small island such as this, the time it took to carry out this normally short task was considerably longer than it would otherwise have been. At least that is what Bernd thought. As it was early afternoon still when they had finished their visit to the temple they went to get a coffee, at one of several coffee shops in the area.

"It was nice to be able to pray for peace today," Yuri stated emphatically.

"Yeah, I enjoy visiting this temple. It reminds me of the horrible loss of my grandfather in World War II, and makes me feel like really doing something with my life," Junko chimed in. Bernd kept silent observing his relief that they did not ask of his losses. His family has recovered nicely so to speak, but had suffered severely having gone against the Nazi regime on his father's side and gone along with the regime on his mother's side. This rift was poignantly felt for many years. Only recently perhaps was the family able to say that they were "over it."

"I have wondered why we continue to have war seemingly without pause as we have throughout all of history," Bernd added, wanting to steer the conversation away from his own family."When I studied the Greeks it was refreshing to hear that they at least paused during the Olympics leaving off fighting for athletic competition if only for a short while. I wish everything could be solved by athletic competition," he said hopefully. "But that is a bit too simple and naive, I suppose," he added in a more realistic manner. Still he mentioned how much he enjoyed watching the Olympics in Beijing in the summer of 2008. It did not escape his attention that China, known infamously for its record on human rights was a rapidly growing economic power. He hoped it could become a responsible, respectable and respected member of the world community as a result of hosting the Olympics. It is so important for us to all get along he thought. This was painfully obvious to him.

"Yuri, what have you and Bernd been up to since you got married and how on earth did you two meet?" Junko asked changing the subject in a way that was welcomed by all.

"Well, first of all we met while I was studying at Oxford. Bernd was there for special coursework in Architectural Physics. He's really quite good at describing how and why buildings are put together the way they are," said Yuri, starting an explanation of their time in the United Kingdom.

"Well architecture is fascinating, you know," Bernd began, taking the opportunity to talk about something that he was truly passionate about. He noted how varied architecture is around the world. "Humans have made such fascinating structures. How they have solved many problems of building and architecture is amazing," he stated enthusiastically. He began to go into more detail with, "The arch was just one of the many ways humans have solved making weight bearing structures …" when Junko stepped in. He was about to discuss how religious structures particularly fascinate him when she began.

"Well, I think I will leave that kind of study up to you, Bernd," Junko said, teasing him. "As for me, I just love going to see what people have built in so many places. I just love traveling and exploring this wonderful world," she exclaimed striking a harmonious tone for all of them. They all, indeed, loved to travel. So Yuri began next.

"Me, too," Yuri added considering how to explain more about how they met. "We met one day when I was checking out a book on the pyramids that had descriptions of hieroglyphics in it," Yuri said. "Bernd, of course, had been reaching for the same book wanting to see how the pyramids were put together," she said, and they all chuckled.

"Who won?' Junko asked.

"Why I did, of course," the competitive sportsman replied with a grin. "I just had to get that book. You must admit, having secret passageways connecting the tombs of pharaohs to the outside is pretty cool especially when they built the pyramids without any *modern* equipment," Bernd explained, though with an air of See-what-I-mean in his voice. He had emphasized the word "modern" demonstrating a bit of contempt with the idea that modern should be automatically considered better than ancient solutions to architectural or any problems for that matter.

"Yes, that's certainly true, isn't it?" Junko replied since she, too, thought of the pyramids as fascinating having wanted to travel to Egypt for many years now. It seemed that they all would be friends soon, Yuri thought, pleased that things were going as well as they were.

After several hours Junko excused herself since like Bernd and Yuri she was anxious to return home and spend time with her family. Unlike Yuri and Bernd, however, Junko lived with her parents. Many of Yuri's friends had moved away from the island, though those who stayed behind often followed tradition and lived with their parents until getting married or for longer if necessary. This would allow them to take care of parents as they grew old.

Junko was happy to hear about their married life and interested to hear about the "adventure" that they told her they had had, even if they would not go into detail about it. Yuri and Bernd realized that they had opened the proverbial Pandora's Box by bringing up their adventure and became at first concerned and then were saved by Bernd thinking to cover by talking, a little, about their honeymoon being an adventure. Yuri let the topic drop after a brief discussion, and Junko did not push for more information figuring that the couple wanted to keep their honeymoon particulars to themselves. Before they parted, however, Bernd took the opportunity to ask Junko what characters made up her name. He had guessed correctly that "*ko*" was the character for child, a common ending for female names in Japan. It was a little more surprising for him to hear of the character for "*Jun*" being the same as *meguru* or something that goes around such as the seasons which are cyclical in nature. He was amazed that a friend of Yuri would have a name that fit in so well with Buddhist philosophy which they continually seemed to be running into. The cyclical nature of life is a key component of Buddhism he noted to the other two. To himself he thought it was a bit preordained, and then his logical mind withdrew that impression.

For their part, the couple was relieved to have told someone that they had had an adventure, but was not at all sure that they wanted anyone to know what they had seen. That is why they were so relieved to tell Junko the stories about their honeymoon instead. Again, it was a mystery as to why they felt that way since nothing significant had really happened to make them feel this way. They just did.

While considering the trip to the *administrative building* yet again, Yuri noticed that she still felt a bit of wonder about the ancient, ancestral book and went through it again that night after everyone but Bernd had gone to bed. That night once again they stayed up late wondering what the coming year would bring. Would they be able to go back to the grand hall? Would they figure out what all this talk about stars was about? Would they be able to find out what the fifth and sixth seals were all about? All of these questions were of great interest to them, but for now having stayed up late the night before as well, both of them would have to get some sleep. The questions would have to wait.

As she was dozing off to sleep Yuri had an experience, which reminded her of something that had happened when she was little. She felt as though voices in her head were trying to tell her something. She could not remember the details, but felt as though something important was being said to help her understand something important …and then she fell soundly to sleep.

The next morning when she thought about this, she did not remember the statements or the details, but was left with the feeling that it was about spaces being made between two kinds of material. This was so little to go on that she figured that she would have to leave it for the time being, and began preparing herself mentally for the day.

Suddenly she fully awoke, brushed her hair out of her face and …bolted to her feet. She immediately went over and picked up the ancestral book, and went to the back page. She thought to herself, *There must have been something in this book that was taken out. And it must have been taken out through this torn section. What is it that was taken?* she wondered. She had to talk to Bernd about this.

They spent that day relaxing and visiting with Yuri's family while resting up for the long train ride to Tokyo. Bernd took the opportunity to learn how to play *goh*, a strategic board game that is popular in Japan. Bernd thought that it was harder than chess, but was fascinated with the logical strategy needed to play as one player captured territory on the board in an attempt to prevent the opponent from capturing or even maintaining territory at the same time. It was an incredible challenge, Bernd thought, and one worth the effort as he stretched his mind.

On the last day of their stay on the island, Yuri went back to Bentenji and at the temple's gift shop bought some incense to take back to Tokyo. She also bought some for the people at work. She knew that she couldn't go back empty handed. She needed *omiyage*, or locally produced souvenirs of which it is customary to bring back for one's kin, bosses and coworkers. Though her company was a foreign company enough employees were Japanese and the company had been doing business in Japan for so long that this was considered customary where she worked, too. She also thought that she would buy a temple remembrance card or *shuuin* for about 300 yen or three dollars. It was a piece of paper about the size of a post card that had the name of the temple written on it along with a distinctive stamp from the temple and the date of the visit. It was a great way to record one's temple visits.

The monk who was writing the calligraphy wasn't in a hurry like during the New Year rush, and so he took even greater care to write with his brush, the way that they had been writing for centuries. He wrote the name of the temple, the year, month, and day in Japanese characters. At New Year's time it was all they could do just to hand out previously prepared copies made with stamps scrawling out the date clearly, though as quickly as possible, the lines of visitors seemingly never ending. He finished with the obviously ancient, distinctive stamp of the temple.

Yuri took the page home and showed it to Bernd. He admired the beautiful handwriting and thought it would be nice to keep it safe in the ancestral book until they could get it home and paste it in their temple card collection book or *shuu in chou*. Both wished that they had brought it along.

Yuri agreed and went to place it in the book. Suddenly she stopped for two reasons. One, she realized that they would not be taking the book home having planned to leave it with the family Buddhist altar. Also, she realized that the card was the same size as the tear in the paper at the back of the ancestral book. In fact, she slowed down almost to a stop and began to compare the calligraphy of the temple stamp on today's card with the calligraphy on the inside cloth of the back cover. She noticed immediately the same distinctive style on *both*! Oh my god, she thought, now they would have to figure out if Bentenji and Horyuji were related! That would help them to determine if the place of the "something wonderful" was indeed Horyuji. She realized that the tear was not an accident, but a deliberate tear made in order to get something out of the book without otherwise taking the whole cloth cover off. She wondered if it was a temple card from "somewhere special," which is what she said to Bernd.

Since it was time to leave for Tokyo, they decided to talk more about it on the train, though it would be hard to keep other people from knowing what they were talking about. The most important points in their discussion would have to wait until after they got to Tokyo in the secrecy of their own home.

Tokyo Again

This year was different from the previous year they noted. For one thing, they were now used to being married. Also, their daily routine had changed drastically. Every night after work they came directly home instead of eating out as they had occasionally done early on after getting married. And now before, during and after dinner they talked about all of the events and happenings from the previous year. These talks continued often keeping them up until late into the night. Yuri especially liked going over the events they experienced in the grand hall. Bernd was wondering just how old Bentenji was and what the architecture was like before it was built as a Buddhist temple in the seventh century CE.

On one evening at the beginning of February they were talking about the so-called "something wonderful" wondering what qualities the ancients considered wonderful. They were also a little at a loss since they did not really know how old the writing in the registry was.

"Do you think when they say "something wonderful" they mean something magical?" Yuri asked.

"That could be what they meant," Bernd considered. "Then again it could be some specific object such as a room that did not exist until that time and was specially built for a particular purpose," Bernd went on wondering out loud. Then Bernd asked Yuri what the traditional Japanese concept of magic was. Yuri admitted that while she was not sure how to describe the Japanese concept of magic, the idea of psychic powers developed through performing Buddhist mantras or spiritual exercises was the closest she could come to understanding magic from the Japanese perspective. Some people were endowed with these magical powers and considered special, while others weren't it seemed.

"We have to go to Horyuji again," Yuri suggested cautiously, but with sincerity.

"We've been over that many times," Bernd replied still resisting the idea of going there when there were so many other temples to consider around Japan. But he knew in his heart that she was right. It was more a matter of when they could go rather than if they should or not. "You're right. I guess. We will have to go," he conceded. Though they had nothing specific to suggest this, they both had a gut feeling about Horyuji kind of like they had a gut feeling about keeping the visit to the grand hall a secret when they were catching up with Junko.

They discussed when and how to go about visiting the temple again and thought that the earliest they could go would be in spring. Then, when she felt that they had decided as much as they could about Horyuji, Yuri spoke up about another topic hoping to breach it while the discussion was going well.

"What about the grand hall?" she said, her whole face lighting up when she spoke. It had been a long time since they had gone there, and she really was interested in getting back there again. She told Bernd how her whole body felt energized whenever she thought about going there again.

Bernd hesitated and then at last said, "I think it has been long enough since we have been there. We'll just have to take a chance at some point," he finished decisively. Even so, his tone conveyed the sense of caution that he also felt. Like Yuri, Bernd felt an incredible pull to explore again the grand hall, their nickname for the large room in which the seals are housed, but did not want to be hap-hazard about it. After some more discussion he stated, finally and with determination, "If we run into trouble, it might as well be now rather than later."

Still, it was risky so they needed to develop a plan, to not get caught, if that was at all possible. They both understood this important point neither having to say it out loud.

The Plan

"Okay, okay," cried Bernd giving in the next evening. He didn't like it, but agreed that it was the best they could come up with not knowing much about the building that housed the grand hall. Now that the plan was in place, only carrying it out was necessary, and that would not be simple they both knew.

They both realized that it was risky, but both of them also desired to try and understand anything that they could from the seals. They were determined to see the plan through to the end no matter what might happen. They were determined to find out the secrets of the grand hall, and it really did seem to hold some kind of important secret if not many. It was the beginning of February, and *setsubun*, the festival of welcoming into the home good fortune and ousting from the home any evil that was afoot. They carried out the tradition, throwing beans in their home as was the usual custom, but with much increased gravity this year. They really were praying for good fortune harder than on any third of February of any previous year.

According to the plan, Yuri would go into the "grand hall" first, and Bernd would wait observing everything from the side room while she tried to learn as much as she could about the seals. It was not a great idea since being "caught" would mean that the one caught was Yuri, who would be in the most vulnerable position. True she would try and get out the front door, hoping that the sealed front door really only seemed that way from the outside, and it could be unlocked to escape. There were many variables, and everything seemed full of risks, since they knew so little about the building. One thing they both agreed on, however, was that Yuri would have the best chance of reading the seals. She knew the most about languages and symbols and was very in tune to subtle hints in pictures, characters and the like. She was certainly the best, of the two, for taking the risk of entering the room and attempting to interpret the seals while the other watched prepared to warn of any problems that were observed.

Bernd, too, would play an important role by helping to alert the whole neighborhood if necessary to try and keep Yuri from being in great danger were something to happen. This related to something good about living in Japan. One could count on one's neighbors, especially if they were relatives, to join together to do almost anything. The ability to cooperate in things considered necessary by members of a group to which one belonged was often considered important to all members of the group. And this was highly valued throughout Japan. Bernd would be ready, and at the first sign of trouble he would burst out of the building and somehow get help from their neighbors. It was fortunate that they knew some people who lived somewhat near the building, a green grocer and an old retired couple that they had met at the grocer's stand.

At the last minute it struck Yuri as a good idea to have Bernd carry a backpack with a number of items to help them if need be. First on the list of items to include were wooden blocks. These blocks are clacked together to remind people to be careful not to leave any fires unattended, a longtime scourge of Japan with so many of its houses being built of wood. Indeed, if one house caught fire, the whole block was at risk, so the idea of cooperating on this front made absolute sense. If they made an awful racket reminding people to be careful of fire, then they certainly would alert people if something were to go wrong while Yuri was in the grand hall, the young couple hoped. Especially in this case since click-clacking the boards together at this time of night, unlike the normal routine, would be so out of place that people were bound to take notice. And furthermore, it was hoped that if no one else took notice, then at least those who were the ones regularly assigned to this task would take notice.

All of this was difficult to plan since they really did not wish to draw attention to themselves going into that old building and hoped that no extreme action would be necessary. In fact they wanted to look up the blue prints of the building, but dared not, realizing how obvious it was that such an action would draw attention to them and their interest in this apparently abandoned building. Though neighbors shared many good points in wanting to work together, they also took note of each other, and in this case that could turn out to be a negative, drawing unwanted attention to them. They felt that they had no one that they could trust to get the blue prints for them secretly. Anyway, they did not wish to put anyone in that much danger.

They realized that there was not much chance of them going into the building unnoticed, and they were a little frustrated that they had no idea who might notice them from the inside. Indeed, they had gone over many times just who or what made the noise that caused them to beat a hasty retreat the last time they were in there, and they remained puzzled. There were absolutely no clues even for a logical scientist like Bernd. If it had been someone outside rather than "inside" the building it would have made them feel a whole lot better.

This time when they went to the building, Yuri did not stomp off of the porch. Instead, they carefully made their way to the abandoned building seemingly out for a leisurely stroll, however unusual for a cold evening in February. On the other hand, they could have been going somewhere for dinner for all anyone knew. Anyway, Bernd often wore a backpack as he was going to the University. Usually, though, being filled with books made it heavier than it now was. The other items in addition to the fire warning blocks were a flashlight, his cell phone and even a blanket just in case they needed to stay somewhere and be still for a long time on a cold, February night hoping not to be discovered.

As it was getting dark outside the couple found themselves looking at that same window that seemed to belong to an apartment sometime in the past. Of course they now thought that someone was often using the room that lay before them. Yuri felt a shiver run down her spine, but reaffirmed her resolve to see what was inside and said nothing to Bernd. This was probably a good thing since he, too, had butterflies in his stomach, but also the will to enter the building come what may and didn't need anything to raise doubts right now.

They knew the routine and in fact, they had practiced it in their apartment in hopes of being quicker than ever this night. All seemed to go well. They walked up to the building and entered it through the window Yuri using her hair pin to move the latch and unlock the window.

They were both breathing fast, though the room, what little they could see of it in the scant light seemed unchanged from the last time they were there. The first time they were there the light had been intermittent, and the second time, a moonlit night made it dimly but constantly lit. Tonight was not like either of the previous occasions. Since the moon was waxing, it was lighting the room, but even more dimly than the time before. Neither had the stomach to wait for the full moon, and besides, there was no guarantee that any night they chose would be a cloudless night. Tonight being dimly lit was a blessing better than a cloudy night and provided somewhat cover for them as everything around was not lit up like it would be were it to be on a night with a full moon.

It was hard to tell whether the room was the same or different from the last time they were there. It seemed as though it was the same, but then something just seemed wrong. While they both thought so separately neither felt at liberty to discuss the matter. They silently exchanged perplexed looks. While considering what might be wrong Yuri bumped something on a table that they had been trying to go around. Bernd just had to know what could have been hanging off of the table, and so he turned on a small flashlight taken from his pocket and cautiously looked around. The light in the back pack was larger, and would be used if needed, but for now this smaller light would do. Yuri and Bernd's eyes met. They both could not believe what they saw. It looked as though someone had unpacked a suitcase and left it out in this room. They could not figure out whom or what left the suitcase because Bernd turned out the light as quickly as he had turned it on. There were noises coming from the other room. Of this he was certain ....

The Grand Assembly Meeting

Edging over to the door that led to the grand hall, both Yuri and Bernd held hands and stayed as close to each other as was physically possible while still being able to move. Their curiosity was piqued, and they were tremendously afraid all at once. It was a feeling Yuri had never felt before, and she wondered if she might ever experience it again. It was the most "alive" she had ever felt, she thought. Slowly she leaned her ear against the door to see if she could hear what was being said. They both knew that this was risky, since whoever left the suitcase could come through that door any second. At least Yuri wondered if Bernd thought so, too.

What they heard surprised them …voices. The voices were muffled, and so they could not understand what was being said. The voices were low and seemingly cautious so as not to be over heard, but they also seemed calm. There seemed to be some kind of meeting going on. Of this they were only guessing as they could not really hear what was being said which made them feel all the more uncomfortable. From the grave tone of the voices they figured that something important was taking place, but just what?

Yuri strained to see if she could hear more, and then they had the biggest shock of all. While she was leaning on the door …it opened. Luckily it only opened a crack. Even so, it was enough to let light from the grand hall flood in. They could see that the grand hall was filled by flickering candlelight.

Whoever had gone out of the room obviously hadn't closed the door all the way when he or she? had left. Or was it a group? They both froze expecting to be exposed immediately. Indeed, Bernd was already running through his mind how he would alert the neighbors and was picturing in his mind where the wood blocks were in the back pack on the lower left side just where he had left them next to his cell phone. To their astonishment, nothing happened. The meeting went on as usual, or at least that is how it seemed to them observing this group for the first time.

This had to be a really important meeting, they both thought. Neither was really sure what the other was thinking as both of them were still, frozen in their tracks, and afraid to say anything. Yuri motioned to Bernd to bend down so that she could better see what was going on. Seeing that she was in a position to see more, he crouched down, and she stood transfixed by what unfolded in front of her. After that, neither moved a muscle not wanting to make any sound.

Yuri observed about fifty people in the room, all wearing many different types of clothing. If Yuri wasn't mistaken, they looked as though they came from many different places around the globe. Even though she couldn't see much, Bernd immediately put his scientific mind to work trying to figure out the meaning of this great gathering in this unusual location at this unusual time of day. They noticed that there was someone speaking gravely and in a subdued manner to all assembled. It seemed to be a report of some sort as others were listening and not responding except for short acknowledgements showing that they were following along or so it seemed from the side room. The "meeting" or "report" went on for some time like this without any noticeable, significant change.

It was no use. They needed to hear what was being said. They backed away from the door, and cautiously, making as little sound as possible, they discussed what to do, being careful not to lose sight of the door for even a second and to keep their voices at an absolute minimum. They went so far as to use some sign language though both of them were a little rusty. It had been a long time since they took that class together in Oxford.

"Maybe if we can get over to the outside door, we would be close enough to hear what was going on," Bernd offered.

"That won't be close enough," Yuri responded thoughtfully. She felt that they would have to create some form of diversion, and then one of them could slip in while the group was distracted. Bernd immediately agreed, thinking that it was a good idea and also not wanting to talk for too long. Bernd felt that they had already risked a lot by talking at all. They set about at once planning the diversion using only gestures and signs.

After agreeing that one of them would try to slip in to eaves drop on the meeting, it was clear that they would have to decide on the best place to hide. The only place to hide that made any sense to both of them was behind the curtain just outside the door to this room *in* the grand hall. It was close by and would not take much effort or time to get to, and one could slide along behind the curtain and get near the assembly. A further advantage to this strategy was that the curtain hung to the floor and would cover Yuri, the one who would go in, completely.

Yuri was selected for this task as she would be the one most likely to be able to hide behind the curtain because of her smaller size, and also, they agreed, would be most likely to understand the language, if the one being spoken was not English. While he didn't like it, Bernd realized she was the logical choice for the task.

The plan was set in a few moments. Bernd would sneak back out and go around to the front door and knock the wood blocks together as though he was warning the neighborhood to be careful of fires. In some ways they soon realized beyond what they had been thinking that this might be the greater risk. This was because the members of this group might have someone posted to watch everything outside of what looked to be the main door to the building. Bernd might be seen and therefore never able to come in the building unnoticed again. He may even be followed and his life put in danger by the attempt to distract the group from seeing Yuri enter the room. They had neither the time, nor the mental luxury to come up with another plan, so this was it.

A few minutes later, Bernd was knocking the blocks together outside the "front" door. This created the stir the couple had hoped for, and Yuri slipped into the room unnoticed when the candles of the Secret Society had been blown out, in unison, amazingly without anyone coordinating it. It only took a few moments, but the members agreed, having seen Bernd go away from the building that there was no immediate danger of being found out. What they did not know was that Bernd circled back and went in the window again and was in the room next to where they were meeting once more. He had concealed his appearance and his identity by wrapping a towel around his head while outside. He looked as though he had been to the public bath just before making the rounds to bang the blocks together. He was proud of himself for this last-minute quick thinking and the good luck that Yuri had put the towel into his bag. Originally, he had not known that it was in there. Yuri, of course was in no position to know that that was what Bernd had done. For her the whole thing was nerve wracking since she could not see Bernd at all after he went out of the window. Hearing him bang the block was no help as it seemed that those assembled there had taken notice of his banging the blocks and might do something about it. The noise he made was finished already moments ago, and now she was relieved to see that apparently no one had gone after him. They must have thought that he was gone! She for her part thought that he might have gone home since it would be so risky to wander around the area. He might be engaged by members of this group or encounter a neighbor who he knew. *He must have gone home,* she thought.

Behind the curtain Yuri listened with anticipation to the "meeting" and found all that she heard riveting. She just could not believe what she was hearing. The meeting was conducted in English, but the leader of the meeting was speaking with a very heavy accent. Of course the meeting was in English she realized! It was the most likely way to have that many people from seemingly so many places all understand what was going on.

This is what Yuri heard:

"Tonight we have come here, observing our normal vow of secrecy even from trusted friends of our respective groups around the world. We are hopeful that finally the location of the remaining coordinate will be found. We are not yet positive, but all of the evidence points to the last star point coordinate being in Japan. Of course, of this we cannot be sure. Perhaps it would be better to say that the point does not seem to be anywhere else. A horrible way to figure things normally, but as you know this is in no way normal. Hopefully, this time someone can help us find the answer as to where this all began. It has taken us hundreds of years and a lot of exploration, ruling out other places, to get here. Now is the time. I feel it." He expressed calmness and careful wording, but was noticeably hopeful that what he was saying was accurate. Yuri wondered, *just what are they searching for?*

What Yuri did not know was how many times over the past hundreds of years those same words were spoken along similar lines regarding the star points, and had been so very blatantly *wrong*!

"We know that when conditions are right, the star points will be revealed. Each star point has been revealed that way, though no two were found in exactly the same way" he said, "mysteriously."

What are these 'star points,' Yuri wondered in her silence.

"No one knew why this was so," he went on. "Some thought it was because of cultural differences, and others still thought it to be because of the strange workings of the universe, but none really knew why things worked out that way each point being divulged differently."

"This brings me to the main point of our gathering tonight," he continued. "Not too long ago a lay member of the Society informed us that there was a woman who had great interest in our Society's seal inscribed on the floor of the hospital in Alexandria. Of course, it was not a hospital when the star point was engraved on that ancient floor. The interest of this woman, I mean an interest in the seal, as far as we know has never happened before. And in the past several hundreds of years we are pretty certain of this fact. Now we have come to see if we can find her and whether or not she can help us in our quest to discover what we think is the last star point.

The Society member in Alexandria said that this woman was from Japan, but could not get records about her as she was not a patient at the hospital herself. And no one knew why she was there as there were no Japanese people being seen in the hospital at that time. Nonetheless, it is our hope that this Japanese woman can, and some feel that she must be able to help us find the last point. With her help, if indeed she can be of any help, we can finally find that last coordinate. Then, it is believed, the origin to the story that began so many centuries ago can be found ...."

"Pardon me honorable chair, but that is very little to go on," inquired the delegate from Israel. She went on to point out that, "The first point was found after the tumultuous events of the crusades. It just jumped out of the wall so to speak, but that was big news, and very significant by all accounts. The Rabbi who found it, being able to read the ancient Hebrew symbols was truly a 'godsend.'" She pointed out that the information found revealed that the point was in Egypt. And that this had something to do with the campaigns of Alexander the Great. Then, she added dramatically, "Recently, there has been no such significant event or series of events." There was a stir around the room as old concerns propped themselves up again as though there was a historical wall to lean them against.

"Don't forget that all points have been found in different ways," the leader replied.

"How is it, that you think this woman can help us?" a delegate from Greece chimed in hoping to clear the air and get to what they could do rather than argue about what they could not control or take care of.

"One cannot be sure, but I have a feeling," the leader said as he began to feel the weight of being in charge of this important meeting. He had been chosen for his calm leadership within Egypt and was now for the first time in charge of a meeting of the world wide group. Calming himself by breathing consciously he began again. "The universe will either come together and help us work this out, or the mystery will have to wait some more perhaps. We must trust that things will work out."

"How can you be sure?" the delegate from India spoke up hesitantly remembering the many times that this sort of talk and meeting had led to nothing in the last several hundred years by various accounts.

"Again, I cannot be absolutely sure," he stated honestly. However, this woman spoke many languages, or, I mean, at least three," he was stating what the member of the society reported. "At any rate we have not welcomed anyone into the society for over twenty years, and we could use all the help we can get, now more than ever." Immediately there was a murmur in the room. Talk of inviting someone, especially someone they did not know into the Society was seemingly premature to almost everyone there. The Egyptian explained himself. "I feel that if we miss this opportunity the mystery will remain unsolved for many more years," he finished contemplating the seriousness of being wrong yet again.

"Especially since we are so close to discovering something, I can feel it," added the delegate from Central America enthusiastically. "And next we will discover the meaning behind the Nasca lines in the desert. It is all so exciting?" he added joyfully. He seemed more optimistic than most. He was a breath of fresh air, Yuri thought as she felt the curtain on her legs and right arm. It was made of a heavy, velvety kind of cloth. There were narrowly wound tassels at the bottom of the curtain that she now noticed were being reflected on the floor by the flickering candle light.

Many were worried about going too fast, though most of them recognized that taking action was the only way that things got done. Yuri agreed with taking action, though she was still on edge as to what kind of action they were talking about.

"Now calm down everyone, after the noise outside, we have to be sure that no one can hear us. Secrecy is very important. Are you all ready to join me in the sub-building if there is any trouble?"

Everyone present nodded affirmatively, and though Yuri could not see it, for some reason the agreement was clear to her, she could almost feel it. They wished that they had put the seals down there, but also realized that this was impractical.

While this last confirmation was taking place Yuri realized something both amazing and at the same time scary. While it seemed too strange to be true, it seemed as though it had to be true. They talked of a Japanese woman not long ago in Egypt, and at a hospital inquiring about some symbols. As preposterous as it seemed, she came slowly to the realization that they must have been talking about her! Bernd, too, in the other room while wondering what they were talking about, had a strange feeling he could not explain and a chill ran up and down his spine. Sometimes it was as though they could feel each other's feelings. It was wonderful and sometimes unnerving, too. *What was Yuri hearing* he wondered? He desperately wanted to know as he, too, was now feeing very much on edge and very, very alive.

Yuri wanted so much to hide, to run away from the building as far away as possible, but knew now that she needed to find out whether or not this group was good or evil. She also wondered why they needed to be secretive. She wondered what it was that they were so desperate to find, and how in the world she could be of any help to them. Her crime seemed to be her love of languages. The next line that came out of the leader's mouth gave her even more cause for concern.

"Brothers and sisters let us go downstairs to celebrate the recent findings. We hope to be on the verge of finding the last star point. Then, hopefully we can spread our knowledge around and let it take over the world," the leader stated with determination. Finding the last star point will put us in the most powerful position in many hundreds of years to understand the origin."

"This is the best thing to do for now," he continued. "Come on. After all, since we cannot find this woman tonight and have really only just assembled here to begin to plan looking for her, some rest and food is in order. Our pursuit of her will have to wait another day or two while we make careful plans. Anyway no harm done," he said. And then he chuckled. "After all, we have been waiting for several thousands of years already, haven't we?" Yuri for a moment wondered if he meant they were aliens, many hundreds of years old, but then shrugged that thought off, coming to the conclusion that he was speaking figuratively. She wondered if his chuckle was sinister enough to make her worry even more, and then other thoughts came to mind, too.

This was a lot for an evening of exploration. She was getting a little weary. She began to wonder how Bernd was and if he was at home by now. She then started to panic if only for a moment. The thought now came to her, *How was she to get home* …?

After the leader finished speaking, they went downstairs as a group. Their footsteps were amazingly quiet, virtually silent, a technique developed only over the past few centuries. Since the time of Michael Jackson, this technique has been called "moon-walking." In this technique first one finds out whether a person walks on the inside of their feet when placing them, the outside when placing them or straight heel to toe. Then, using this natural step one wears flexible, usually leather shoes and consciously steps from the natural position first and distributes their weight evenly throughout the step to silently and continuously move "through" the step. In many ways it is like the idea of slow continuous movement found in tai chi practice. This came as no surprise to those who had learned the stepping style. After all it was developed by a tai chi master who was in many ways like the ninja of stories old though from China and not Japan. This technique could be employed by those who were good at it at almost a regular walking pace.

"SS, SS" were the symbols made in the air by the assembly just before they had made their move to the lower level where if Yuri understood right they were about to have a feast. She had worked herself little by little to a place where the curtain parted and could see the group, though not all of them, wanting to disturb the curtain as little as possible. These symbols in the air were signs acknowledging the need for Secrecy in the Society and Safety while looking for the Stars points. The symbols were unintelligible to Yuri, but were easily enough made. One made the double "SS" by waving one's little finger and pointer finger in the shape of an "S" twice, both fingers in unison. This was referred to as "double, double Ss" by some. This "S" sign was made so that they could be read by others and not the one making the sign. This, too, was on purpose.

Yuri had her doubts as to whether or not the Society was a dangerous cult or organization. The way in which the leader addressed the group as "brothers and sisters", and that they were talking about stars made this unclear. Stars, seemingly from everything they had found out about them were nothing to be afraid of, though at the same time certainly much to be wondered at. She had to find out what the Secret Society was talking about, but that would have to wait. She could no longer ignore her concern for Bernd. She began planning to go home. She'd slip out while they were focused on making their descent.

As the assembly went below, she returned to the room to go out to find Bernd hoping to bring him back, even if that meant at some other time. Much to her surprise and putting her at ease, he was already there waiting for her. Saying nothing, they embraced warmly, but briefly, realizing the importance of getting out of there. At any rate now that they were together again it was as if they could both begin to breathe again.

Then they heard something that made them both freeze. A voice, louder than the others now rose throughout the grand hall. The reason for the voice being louder than the others who were going downstairs was that the owner of the voice stood only about three feet away on the other side of the door to the grand hall. He was overheard by the couple to say that he'd forgotten to take the suitcase down with him only arriving just before the meeting began. He stated that since they were all going down that he couldn't leave the suitcase unattended in the room. The couple's mutual panic made sense; they both realized that he was about to enter the room they were in to get the suitcase that had been left out on the table Yuri bumped earlier!

Yuri and Bernd almost ran into each other trying to move away from the door to the grand hall. Finally they squished themselves up to the wall on the side of the door that opens to the wall. When the Secret Society member came into the room, pushing the door open it shielded them from view. Neither of them dared to breathe. They were doubly lucky because the door shielded them, but also since it was a society standard to not use a light if at all possible. Fortunately, this man was so used to the room that he could have walked through with no light whatsoever and not bump into anything. He knew everything about the room, its smallest details. Therefore he required no light to close the suitcase, put it under his arm, look around, and leave to join the others at the gathering below. Being so familiar with the room, he turned and left it without bumping anything and hardly making a sound knowing which floor tiles to avoid, the ones that make noise and those that don't.

This familiarity is why when he left the room something that was totally unexpected by the couple happened. He came back, and with him he brought a group from the assembly only a moment later. The couple had breathed a sigh of relief and having moved the door away from themselves was making their way toward the window to leave when they heard ….

"Now who might this be?" They both froze in their tracks, and the tingling up and down the spine started all over again. Bernd could feel his heart racing and he began to sweat. With the man were the same people who had been waiting for him and with whom he had conversed before entering the room in the first place.

He was back with others because Bernd had not taken the time to shut completely the window he used to enter from the outside, and this had not escaped the man's attention. Upon reentering the building, wanting to see what was going on with Yuri, Bernd had immediately hurried into and across the room mostly, but not completely, closing the window. And though the window was only opened about a centimeter and there was no breeze this night, the man, trained to look for anything out of place had noticed that it was opened. Since he had been a member of the Society for so long, he had not let on that he had noticed anything. The couple had been completely fooled. Of course they couldn't even see him from behind the door, however, they had thought that he had left, and he wasn't coming back. He had not even paused, something that may have raised concern.

The others from the Secret Society congratulated him, and gave him some kind of secret sign, though Yuri could not make it out as it was so brief. The sign used was carried out by giving a three fingered tap with the left hand to one's own head, almost like a salute in the military. The longer version is to run three fingers across the top of one's head and then to point three separated fingers at the person who had accomplished something wisely and to draw the fingers together representing integration of thoughts, actions and words. It had been an abbreviated form of the sign which meant well done and signified maintaining safety in the search for the star points.

The members of the Society, now beginning to look menacing to Yuri and Bernd, took up places in front of and beside them and motioned silently that they were to walk with them into what the couple had been referring to as the grand hall. They had no choice but to come along. Being outnumbered and outsized, the young couple was in no position to resist.

Traversing the grand hall the couple was ushered down to the sub-level of the building flanked on either side by two society members who walked in controlled silence. Another went ahead, and the man with the brief case and another took up the rear. They did not know that this group of six had been ready to go after them even if the other man had not noticed anything out of place.

The Secret Society had been careful to note the time at which the local people have fire prevention parties out, and it had never been at this time before. All of these members had taken notice of this abnormal timing of the drill and were preparing to investigate as the man with the suitcase came out to get them. They really were an alert group. Yuri and Bernd had had no idea that any of this was going on, thinking it was bad luck and not polished skill that had sunk their plan. The Secret Society members included all kinds, and these six were like crack troops. Yuri and Bernd barely dared to breathe.

Meeting the Members of the *"Secret Society of the Stars"*

"How did you find us in this place?" they were asked by the leader. He went on to tell them that it has not been disturbed in the 60 years that they have held meetings there, and as such has been a quietly, useful place to keep their information safe for many years.

"We mean no harm," Bernd said. "It all happened by accident," he added quickly.

"We are sure that there is no harm done so far," he said, with an air of confidence that put them both ill at ease. The leader was not only speaking confidently, but also in a thick accent that once again piqued Yuri's curiosity as she wondered where he was from. That he used perfect English as well, made him all the more interesting, she thought, for someone who was from the countryside.

Her racing thoughts stopped. How did she know he was from the country? Why did she think so? She had to think quickly. Any clue could help them get out of this safely, she thought. She felt as though she had something in common with this man. Though for the life of her, and almost certainly because of the recent panic she had felt, she could not figure out what that was. She consciously began trying to slow down her thought stream, but with little success. Her thoughts raced around, filled with the events of the evening. This included noticing the people gathering closer and closer around her.

And then it hit her. It was the home stay that she had in Egypt that was coming back to her now. She and the family she stayed with traveled for miles to get into the city to see the pyramids because the family she lived with in Egypt had lived …in the country! And because the family lived in the country, they had quite a distinctive accent compared to Egyptians living in cities. It was not unlike the difference between the Kansai dialect and the Tokyo way of pronouncing and using "standard" Japanese in Japan. Everyone could understand each other, but the two ways of speaking were fundamentally different in intonation and even in the use of words. Indeed, there are many varying dialects in Japan, Yuri noted.

Yuri had felt lucky that she lived in the country when she was in Egypt. It made her feel as though she knew two different languages both rural and urban Egyptian so to speak. She learned "urban" or standard Egyptian when she studied at school and rural pronunciation from the home stay experience. The leader had obviously grown up out of the city. Just where, she was about to ask.

"Excuse me, where are you from?" She asked the leader taking him by surprise.

"Until we know more about you, I will be asking the questions," he replied firmly recovering almost immediately and consciously maintaining control of the flow of the conversation, though a little surprised at the question from her.

"Sorry to be so forward, but I know that accent. It is from a rural region in Egypt, I think." Yuri continued, hopeful that this would make a difference in their getting out of there in one piece. Then she froze again. *What if they were up to no good?* she wondered again. She may have just given herself away, she realized, and she immediately became concerned, her thoughts slightly muddled. She must be one of only very few people in Japan who can speak Egyptian at all and now she had shown that she understood some obscure things about the language as well. Perhaps well enough, they could now have wondered, to enquire about a seal on the floor of a hospital in Alexandria, Egypt.

Bernd was beside himself, wishing for Yuri to be as secretive as possible and still feeling a little ashamed that it was his fault, he now believed, that they were standing before the whole assembly. He still had no idea of the suspicions of the other six members, but considered that leaving the window slightly ajar was a bad move. He had wanted so much to confirm that Yuri was safe that he had been careless.

Bernd had been looking around while this discussion was taking place. He noticed that they were in a long room with large tables at which sat the big group rather comfortably. The tables were set with Indian curries and roasted chicken and other delicacies. It truly was a feast.

The meetings of the Secret Society always ended in a feast. It was a sure way to get everyone to attend, the members often joked. The jovial atmosphere that had been audible while descending the flight of stairs had turned eerily quiet since the couple had entered the room. As Bernd reflected on this he realized that this was not so strange since they were all looking from Yuri, to him and back again in obvious amazement, and getting ready to eat was joyful for everyone. *They* were the topic of the hour, a rather uncomfortable, unwanted honor.

As he looked around he noticed more and more of the building. It wasn't at all like the upstairs part of the building. If he was not mistaken, the below ground part of the building was built not unlike the gothic structures of medieval Europe complete with arches. How odd. If an opportunity arose he would ask just why the levels were so different. Then, suddenly, his thoughts were interrupted by a screeching noise. Well, rather, it was a squeal of delight, he soon realized, but for the life of him, he could not imagine why it rose and reverberated throughout this underground cavern.

What?! Why?! How?! The delegate from England, normally the most fluent and articulate in English was suddenly tongue tied. "Do we dare suggest it? Is it true to be? Could it be the fascinating fact it seems to me?" he said rhythmically not unlike Dickens, or maybe Shakespeare, though some thought his manner was in the likes of a crazed man as well.

"What are you on about?" the delegate from India piped up. Stop with the rhyming, and just say it!" he implored.

"Is it her, the one we are looking for in Japan?" he yelled, beaming at the same time and looking right into Yuri's eyes while waving his arms toward her.

The leader now looked at her, too, and a smile of hope, or was it mischief came across his face. Bernd felt that they were doomed. He did not know why, but a sick feeling in his gut told him to be careful.

Now Yuri was more on guard than ever. She was not at all certain that the members of this group were up to something good. She had more so hoped that they were before rather than knowing it to be true. She had to distract them in some way, she thought, till she was sure.

"While taking a course on Egyptian intonation, I saw in a television program that parts of Egypt were like the comparison between what is called Kansai and Kanto in Japan. The similarity is in the way the dialects are different based on the region in which they are spoken," she said in an attempt to clear herself of this inquisition. She noted for them that Japanese TV often played shows that explored interesting if not obscure parts of the world.

"But that still does not explain why you, living in Japan know that it is Egyptian that is my native language, does it?" retorted the group leader.

"So it is true, is it? Well, I have always wanted to go to Egypt, and so I have studied it and not only the languages, but the pyramids, too, are among my interests," she tried hopefully.

"Well, my dear girl, we are looking for a sign so to speak, and I am willing to bet on my best instincts now, that it is you who will help us find it."

"The whole world over the past several millennia has been waiting for you to bring us back to the origin," the member from Greece, a tall woman with long, straight, jet black hair said carefully and slowly while looking her in the eyes. This made Yuri, a Japanese woman unused to eye contact until only her recent, adult years, uneasy.

While it is true that Japanese are not apt to make eye contact, this was not what bothered Yuri most now. After all, she had learned to make eye contact while at Oxford. What bothered her now was being the center of attention and knowing nothing about the rather large group scrutinizing her every move.

"Wait, you move too quickly," said the delegate from India. "There is a lot to lose," he added. Nods of agreement were seen throughout the long room. And the leader once again moved to take control of the conversation. The delegate from Greece moved slowly back, but did not look away. This gave Yuri, and Bernd, too, a shiver which ran up and down the spine. They were certainly not gods to be stared at Yuri thought.

The leader continued. "Well, we are first and foremost wondering what it is that you are doing in this building?" he asked looking from Yuri to Bernd to Yuri again.

"Well, it was vacant we thought, so we came in to have a look around," Bernd replied.

"What was it that you hoped to find?" the delegate from India asked sharply with keen insight into Bernd's thoughts it seemed.

"Quiet and solitude," Yuri spoke up.

"Is that all?" the delegate from Greece resumed the line of questioning with interest.

"Well, what did we find?" Yuri asked, surprising the assembly with her directness for the second time this night, though it must have been getting close to the next day, Bernd thought.

So let's say that you are here innocently, and we are here innocently, well, I am wondering what you would say brought us together, young woman?" said the leader with a bit of curiosity in his voice.

"Fate," Yuri replied, without having given it much thought. She had always believed in fate. Not that fate was already preordained, but the kind of understanding of fate that led one to believe that things would always work out even if it did take some time.

"So what brought you to Egypt in the first place?" the English delegate asked.

"I did not say I had been to Egypt," Yuri stated quickly showing she understood the intent of the question and becoming pleased with her poise.

"How did you come to enquire about the seal in the hospital, then?" he continued.

"How did you know that?" cried Yuri, knowing right away that now it would be too late to deny anything more. He too had been ready for her reply.

"She's the one!" cried the Greek triumphantly.

"It would seem so," said the leader. Continuing with "Allow me to introduce myself. I am Avaad, and yes, I am from a rural region in Egypt. Pleased to meet you," he said in his impeccable, though heavily accented English.

Bernd was feeling less concerned now, but still wanted to be careful. He was also considering that it was amazing how well this building was preserved. He did not know that the fire bombings of Tokyo during the Second World War did not damage it, though this was only because of luck.

The Secret Society had built and rebuilt many structures over the years in places all over the world. Sometimes when they rebuilt, they used materials and styles from an earlier time period, as they had done here. For some of them, the older buildings gave them hope of finding out the mystery, preserving the atmosphere from earlier times. In this case they had incorporated medieval architectural styles such as gothic cathedral like walls complete with tracery around stained glass windows, vaulted arches and the like. It seemed rather eerie to him now that the stained glass windows were revealed only by moonlight the times that they had been here.

Yuri, who was a chess champion while at Oxford, felt strange being tricked so easily. Her only comfort was that at Oxford, she had never been brought down to a secret meeting before, nor been half scared to death multiple times in one night prior to playing chess. She only now realized just how cold she had become, and feeling somewhat ill nearly passed out. This was partly from the shock of witnessing the Secret Society meeting and the exhaustion which was the result of prolonged attention to and strain related to all the events she had been witness to this evening. Bernd was exhausted, too, but had not had to strain to hear, having given up trying to hear while in the back room. Further, they were tired from not being able to sleep the previous evening. Both were far too excited to sleep, though neither had anticipated that events would have unfolded as they did this evening.

"Get them some food," cried several delegates.

"Not so fast, cried the delegate from India. "Who are they, really? I want to know." Again murmurs of agreement rose from the delegation. Many were happy that the Indian was not easily fooled. It was true that there was much to lose, and so the use of such careful and logical sense employed by the delegate from India was welcomed by many if not most of those present.

"We, too, would like to know the meaning of this meeting," Bernd said, joining the conversation and surprising the delegation for the third time this evening. "It is not everyday that people meet in abandoned buildings," he added for clarity. He had regained some of his logical composure and realized that he had to be an active part of this gathering, or he would be subjected to whatever developments sprang from this gathering.

"We are meeting to find a very important set of information. This is a trek, a quest, something that has been going on for many, many years, but first, we must know who you are," the leader said with finality.

"Our names are Yuri and Bernd," Yuri said at last. I'm Japanese and he is German, Yuri added with resignation, believing that there was no use stating anything but the truth from here on out. She was not sure why she trusted, them, but did somehow and further, wanted to end this stalemate just as she wanted to avoid stalemates when she played chess; she'd rather win or lose. She'd lost many games that way, but really going for it, too, is what she believes got her to become a champion if only for a short while. And after all, she did believe in fate. *Why were they interested in her?* she wondered once again.

"We are here for a secret meeting," added the leader, in an attempt to put them at ease. He followed up rather commandingly with, "What brings you here?" asking the question himself for a second time that evening which had really become early morning of the next day. At his first statement it was noticeable that members of the Society looked to each other and back and forth seemingly concerned. After his second question all were listening intently.

"We first came here quite innocently," Bernd found himself explaining gradually growing more trusting now. "We followed a flashing light one evening, to find that it was a mirror that was swinging in the grand hall upstairs. Oddly, it was illuminating the entire room ... intermittently."

"Grand Hall? A nice name for the large room above," the Egyptian said, obviously amused.

"That was my idea," spoke up Jerome, the delegate from Central and South America with pride referring to the mirror that reflected moon light when it was at angles other than what it was this night and in early morning.

"It was me, who noticed it first," Yuri continued. "I am afraid I was in such haste to find out what it was that I left Bernd behind only just pointing it out to him and then scurrying off toward the flashing light."

"Fate," one delegate from Russia said aloud, though she was really echoing what all members present were feeling.

"I told you not to leave the window open even for the short trip to the supermarket for snacks," another delegate stated angrily to one standing beside him. "It was on our watch."

"Let it go Chou," said another, finishing with "It's history."

"Ahem," the leader cleared his throat quieting the room. "Yuri and Bernd, we are happy to make your acquaintances. You have come upon a gathering of high significance for our time, for a long time really. We are *the* Secret Society carrying out the duties imparted to us and our kin for many generations.

"What is it that you are being secretive about, and why such secrecy?" Bernd asked immediately still fascinated and amazed by the gothic construction surrounding them all. He could all but imagine that above the vaulted ceiling the construction would share the weight off to the sides with flying buttresses were this to be a gothic cathedral like those he had seen in Europe. They were upside down arches that allowed for weight bearing walls to be built and the inside of the large structure, such as a medieval cathedral, to be a tall, wide space indeed. Below where they now were the steep arches and pillared pathways looked like some kind of medieval crypt he'd seen time and time again in the old cities of Europe. He could hardly believe his eyes and was finding it a little disorienting to think that he was still in the heart of Tokyo, the largest city in Japan.

"It is our sacred task to find what we have come to call the star points," the leader gave in to his feeling that these two might be of help in finding the last point, which was thought to be in Japan. And he thought that if the last point was not in Japan, perhaps they could help to prove that, too. It was now his turn to take a risk and let them in on the business of the Secret Society. There was a collective gasp that was palpable among the assembled members of the Secret Society from around the world. Normally someone would have had to meet with the society on many occasions to have been given such confidence.

"This is an outrage," yelled Pankaj, the Indian delegate.

"My good friend, we shall be careful about the information we do give out," the leader countered. "I do not take my charge lightly, but feel a need to charge ahead," he added rhythmically. No one else knew that he was carefully watching the couple's reactions and sizing them up as he continued the encounter.

He took a breath and then went on, returning his gaze to Bernd and Yuri. He hoped he would come to trust them even more. He trusted the keen interest in their eyes which was absent of skeptical doubt. They were here to learn and be interested which seemed so much better to him than those who were on a quest to be in the world and gain experiences, but lack the clear thinking that would allow them to really experience things as they are. He was no ordinary Egyptian farmer. He noticed his own breathing now.

So many people nowadays, he thought, seemed to think having an interest in exploring the world and a little knowledge of say, Southeast Asia meant that they actually know about the place. What it really takes is *experience*, he thought. To truly be informed of almost anything, one needed the ability to see and hear what was going on, he thought. He felt that these two could do that. He could see that they were listening in earnest to everything that he said and with great attention.

"A gathering of this size has not happened in recent history. The last time such a large group of the Secret Society from so many places had met was when the fourth star point had been found in an icon in Novgorod, Russia almost three hundred years ago," the Egyptian now stated with gravity to show how important the present time was. That icon was a good place to hide the coordinates. It still remains untouched in a church museum created by Peter the Great."

The room was absolutely still. Many delegates were now so scared that Yuri and Bernd may be spies that they shifted positions where they were, and some even felt queasy. The Leader continued. "Many had no idea that Peter was secretly involved in the Secret Society. Involvement in the Society played a large part in why his capital, St. Petersburg, was established in 1703 to help create for Russia a *window to the West* which at the time meant a window toward European nations. And it meant for us easier access back and forth between members of the Secret Society in both Russia and in Europe as well as elsewhere by sea. And now there were delegates from around the world, members of the Society, having been carefully selected for their trustworthiness, something that had not faltered, but was hard to ensure nonetheless.

The small palace in Novgorod proved to be a good place to conceal a star point since it was not a highly traveled place as were the Hermitage and other palaces in St. Petersburg. And while Peter the Great was a member of the Secret Society, even he did not know exactly the place where the star point was hidden. It was a particularly hard star point to find for us because it moved, only within a small area to be sure, around a small village outside of Novgorod. It moved from relative to relative. Later it was incorporated into an icon and then later still, stabilized in one place after the Orthodox Church, the lead religious institution in Russia decided various rules about icons. The rise of Communism caused a scare for us, however, since being in the countryside, the Icon was left alone and at one-point even used as historical art within the building in which it was housed. This saved it from being tossed on several fires meant to destroy religious items. The Society had to be creative indeed not to let that happen.

The point itself, the northernmost point on the Volga River, had not actually moved far, but the knowledge of that point became confused after the one who knew where it was died without passing knowledge on of the exact coordinates of the point. This made the point seem well hidden to the Society, hence the long time in finding it. That it had not moved far made it easier to confirm than other points that had been lost to anyone's knowledge in both place and time and in need of being rediscovered all over again such as the fifth star point." The delegation shifted once again at this unprecedented unveiling of secrets. The leader may have been losing the confidence of all in the room. He pressed on.

"The coordinates for the fourth star point were clear given to us by Peter the Great, North on the Volga River, and on the east bank. The exact location only was what was lacking."

"You mean like the strange events that have been happening to us recently ..." Yuri commented, speaking mostly to herself, but yet audible to those in the immediate vicinity.

"What strange events are you talking about?" asked the Society member from Central and South America, Jerome.

"Oh it's nothing I'm sure," Yuri said while exhaling, and certainly not sure where to begin. "You see I ran into an abbot at a temple, who really seemed to understand meditation. And while practicing I kind of dozed off, or rather, well, I don't know how to explain it," she finished clumsily.

"This is good" the member from Greece said coming forward and looking at Yuri with great interest. "We have an ancient, though mostly lost on the present generation, tradition of meditation in Greece," she added.

"You don't mean, *initiation*, do you?" Bernd looked at her in anticipation, shaded with a bit of disbelief about the rumors of meditation in Greece since before the time of Christ. There were rumors that a type of *initiation* took people into altered states of consciousness and mystical experiences, though modern generations have not been able to confirm this. In fact, modern meditation in Greece as in other parts of the world seemed to have come from other places such as Zen Buddhism or the Tibetan Buddhist tradition. When Bernd began to ask questions along this line he was abruptly stopped by the same delegate.

"No, no, no, it is nothing like that. Each person has his or her own experience, and there is nothing in the way of magic or anything like that. Mostly, we prepare a room that is not so much secret as it is quiet! For those who were uninitiated it looked like it was strange and unusual. This is what happens when people judge something without trying it or knowing much about it," the Greek finished a little exasperated about hearing once again of the initiation and the biases based on rumors more than fact. While she was familiar with *initiation*, she truly believed that one's personal experience in meditation was what was important and not only having experience of *altered states of consciousness*. The Greek continued thinking out loud, "And it has been that way for many, many centuries."

Bernd, for his part noted that this was not so different from what he had heard of the Tibetan Buddhist tradition, though with its emphasis on the Guru-disciple relationship it had its differences as well. Of course, he had only read about both Greece and Tibet, and recognized that he had a lot to learn about both places. He would have liked to have discussed *initiation* further, but the Greek delegate, at least for now, wasn't interested. He hoped that this would change.

"That is for another time," the leader brought them back to the business at hand, but not before the delegate from India had caught Yuri's eye making her wonder what he was up to. Since the leader continued, the Indian delegate hadn't time to explain himself ….

"We had better get something to eat everyone. I think it is going to be a very long night," the leader continued, showing compassion for those who had been patiently taking this all in. All had already been here for a large part of the day, making preparations and taking the necessary precautions …though no one had eaten anything yet. This calmed many nerves as people would have a chance to discuss just how far to go with explaining things to Yuri and Bernd. The Egyptian, however, was prepared to *tell all* so to speak. He trusted the young couple; the universe told him that he should.

The Indian delegate noticed Yuri's sincere look and wonderment at his actions and was relieved. He, too, relaxed somewhat now, growing to trust the young couple, if only in a reserved and cautious way. All he wanted to know was whether or not they were trustworthy, and her meditative experience led him to believe that *she* at least was. He hoped Yuri didn't think he meant anything bad by the look he had given her. It was unfortunate that he couldn't explain, but that would have to come later.

Revelations of the Secret Society

"Now the time has come for us to hold a conversation about what is to transpire next. I mean let's discuss how we shall go further from here," the leader began as everyone was finishing up their desert. Once again a collective gasp, that was more of a deafening silence, was so obvious it could almost be felt. The discussions had led members to commit to giving Yuri and Bernd an assignment to prove their trustworthiness, but not to have full disclosure this night, which left a little bit of a gray area to be filled in by the leader. Even with the agreement, the meeting became somewhat tense. Clearly the Society members wondered, and some were worried about how far the leader would go.

At this gathering there was a selection of the finest drinks from around the world: Chinese tea, coffee from around the world-including the German varieties that Bernd loved so well, various teas and other drinks. It was decided that it was not necessary for all present to remain. That wouldn't be necessary until the general assembly meeting which would be held when they would collectively decide what the next action to take would be. They could set that meeting time and date only after the couple had been observed to have left the building.

After drinks were poured and the people who remained had settled around one large table, they were ready to begin planning the next action. At the table was one delegate from each place where a star point had already been discovered. Also, any senior delegates remained while all others had gone to rest. Engaging with the two newcomers was begun again in earnest.

During dinner Yuri and Bernd were quizzed heavily as to their connection to this building, and while they were aware that this was purposeful, they had been good sports and so were more than ever welcomed, even if only on a temporary basis, into the group. During dinner it had been decided that this opportunity should not be let to pass. The young couple would be given enough information to allow them to help the Society.

This was unprecedented, but so was meeting Yuri, the one they were looking for in this way. That she came to them was considered by many a reason for going ahead with giving the young couple their full confidence. At the worst it would only mean abandoning the building for good, which would be a shame since it had already served them so well for sixty years.

"It is really a simple story," the delegate from Tibet began seriously. He took the place of a very tired, yet observant, leader who was now acting as the delegate from Egypt. This was another time-honored tradition of the Society; they helped each other out when necessary. There was no long discussion, simply the recognition by the Tibetan that the Egyptian needed a break from leading the group. He went on, "It is a simple tale we are led to believe by the clues we have found. However, it is a tale of which the details have been lost for so many years. Therefore, we are still unsure exactly how this seemingly simple tale was started nor how it will end," he said. "It is more of a project, an effort," he started to say when he suddenly paused noticing the look of amazement that had come across the faces of both Yuri and Bernd. He had meant to explain of what they had found in clues that gave the Society hope and suggested a plan to return to the origin by ancient travelers when he noticed their awestruck faces. He had intended to explain how they didn't know much yet, and this was part of what he meant by the story being simple.

This pause gave them a chance to take in what had been said. They had heard stories of the supernatural and the sacred, but most of the time it was about something elsewhere like India. Now, Yuri and Bernd were listening to a group of which its entire existence was based on the search for something truly special, perhaps almost magical, and of a tradition that was very old. Most of all it struck them as amazing that the group was meeting in a building in their neighborhood. Yuri sat almost stunned in disbelief at the prospect of a fifth star point being in Japan …whatever it meant to be a star point.

The delegate from Tibet went on."Some people were sent out from some unknown place we believe. They were sent out in many directions, some think five, such as that of a common star. Several members held their breath as he said this tough Bernd and Yuri could not have known this. The Society has recently come to believe or at least hope that this belief has us on the right track. We do not know how or why nor when the use of the ancient five-pointed symbol, we call a star, began, but we have chosen to use it to describe our findings so far. What we do know is that the five-pointed star is as good a symbol as any to use to describe the places ancient explorers *established* when they went out on their journey establishing *points* around the world.

We do not really know for sure how many points there are. And it has taken a long time to find the ones we have found, however this belief, based on the scarce evidence is all that we have to go on. It was not easy. As you can imagine, without confirmed information from the original establishment of the points a lot has been understood through intuition, imagination, and I must admit some significant guessing," he finished this initial explanation and sat down at the head table on the wooden chair provided for the meeting leader used in a rotating basis by whoever is taking a turn at leading the assembly. It just so happened that for the time being the large wooden chair with engraved constellations that have been recognized since the classical period in Greece around the 700s BCE complete with the lore of the Olympian gods was occupied now by the delegate from Tibet.

"You see," the Tibetan went on. "Originally the Society had thought there were six-points as in the Star of David. It makes for slow going trying to find the last points when likely one of them doesn't exist! We then discovered or at least came to believe, having found points in the locations in which we have found them, that there are only five-points in all to be discovered. We based our inferences on what we believe to be the trajectory of each path and the distance of each path from the others, and well, you can imagine.

We found several points and considered what if anything connected them. "From where did these points originate?" became the burning question for our group. If we could figure that out, we'd have some sort of understanding as to what the quest was about, it was hoped, sometimes madly. That is what we are looking for, something that makes a connection between these points. After the first four were found we began to think that they formed the shape of a star with either five or six-points. The six-pointed star, however, left us, by our calculations, somewhere in the Indian Ocean, which is why we now think that there are only five star points.

There are many ways to think about it, but most of us agree that there were most likely five journeying groups on this quest in the ancient world."

"That's what makes it a bit suspect," the English delegate stated now loud enough so that all present could hear him. He was of the hold out group who believed that there were many more groups out journeying to the far ends of the earth so very many years ago.

Allowing himself time to relax and regroup his energies, the Tibetan began once more. Later, Bernd would remember this and note that the Tibetan had been breathing deeply.

"We looked in China for centuries. Even with their grand tradition of astronomy, we came up entirely blank on that one. Still some haven't given up on China, yet, right Chou?" Chou returned the query with a smile. He continued.

"Perhaps most perplexing is that the point of origin remains a mystery. The "Star Points," of course are what we call the five directions that those people went off in search of, or more accurately, the five destinations that they eventually reached. You may be wondering why there are six seals on the floor above us, then.

"Yes, I am," Yuri got out, but in answer to her utterance, the delegate finished his explanation.

"Well, we retained a seal to signify the point of origin once it is found.

He continued, "Now where was I when I went into that elaborate explanation of our journey up until now? Yes, back to the five star points themselves. Each of the five journeys was carried out in a different way depending on the direction, the circumstances of travel, terrain, geographic resources being different, etc …, but all with the same goal in mind. The goal it seemed was to make contact that is to make a connection with people from the five directions at the farthest extents of the earth. What we don't know for sure is *why*," he finished.

He stopped to let these ideas sink in and was interrupted by the delegate from India.

"Or at least this is what we *think* we know," he said always the realist.

"There have been many guesses as to what this quest may be about," the Tibetan continued explaining, "but they are all conjecture for now until the points are all found. Someone may have had the foresight to recognize that humans would be continually fighting each other, something that certainly was likely to have been happening at that early time already." The Tibetan stated this in an unaffected manner, not taking the Indian's comment personally. "Perhaps the realization meant that something had to be done to change this tendency toward war. It may also have been felt that there would be a need for unifying the peoples of the earth into one team so that they would not eliminate each other and perhaps the globe with them."

Again he paused, and noticed this time the great interest in the eyes of both Yuri and Bernd. He went on.

"What is important is that though this quest began in earnest many years ago, it has not been completed yet. We think that this is because the knowledge of what was to be done, why and especially *how* to realize the goal of uniting the world, if that was the goal, was lost along the way.

It has taken long to understand the quest because its scope is much wider than, for example, the United Nations. Though like the United Nations it is believed to be an attempt at making a volunteer, non-governmental organization. It was an attempt to make a really cooperative and actively engaged collaborative organization without borders or governmental influence in the future. At least that is what we imagine from the clues that we have uncovered.

One can imagine how difficult this will be to accomplish. As you can see, it is painfully obvious that we in the Secret Society, too, are among those coming from somewhere, each having his or her respective flag to live under. Belonging to a place on this earth is a major challenge that gets in the way of cooperation in many ways. So you see all is not yet clear it would seem, and besides, only four of the five-points have been found. The sixth seal, which must not have escaped your notice ...."

"It did not," Yuri quickly added cutting off the Tibetan ready for him this second time of mentioning the sixth seal. "I would like to ...."

Remaining calm and unperturbed the Tibetan went on, "Those who set out on this great journey, with much less information about the world than we now have, established clans that fulfilled this duty as faithfully as any society has ever carried out a secret plan." With this, Yuri understood that she should wait her turn and also astutely figured that the sixth seal would be addressed at the appropriate time. Still she hoped that that time would come soon.

"Why did the plan have to be secret?" Bernd now was the one who spoke up.

"Because, dear, sir, if it were not secret, then someone would have taken it over, we believe, and used the *team* so to speak for their own purposes. That someone could have created trouble out of the Secret Society, was dreamed up of course, in a world in which wars had gone on since the dawn of people kind at least people in what has come to be called *civilization*. The worry of abuse of the Society and its organs had to have been of great concern for them to go to such lengths to keep their doings secret."

"And the same problem remains, continual war, today, many centuries later," the English delegate added.

"Of course," Yuri chimed in the way Japanese people often join a conversation in an attempt to show understanding of the topic, that they were listening, and to add agreement to what is being said. She followed up with, "That makes a lot of sense, but leaves us hanging, doesn't it?"

"Well, yes," the Tibetan delegate resumed speaking, being in agreement with the two eager newcomers and the Englishman. "What that plan was, the details, and how to help it be realized is not easy to say. You see, the details of how to create unity, to make this *team* have remained a mystery to the Secret Society.

The Society, of course, was formed much later than when the original messengers were sent, and their secrecy has resulted in an almost complete loss of their original plans. The place of their goal, and the return trip, even what was to be said upon making contact with groups of people in the directions traveled, all of it must have had to have been sworn to be kept in the utmost secrecy. Almost nothing of the original quests remains. The places traveled to, and returned to, were to be revealed only when the last star point was put into place, that is, established in the place in which it was put. This meant that when the last groups of people were contacted at the farthest corners of the planet in, we believe, five directions, then the return trip could be made, and all five search parties so to speak would meet at the origin making the quest complete and their collective goal clear to all. In some ways it would really be a beginning.

"And if today you found the place where it all began, you'd be hoping to find the original instructions, the plan so to speak." Bernd's impeccable, logical mind had concluded what he stated now out loud to the group assembled there.

"You have that right, my new friend," the Tibetan quickly replied. The Egyptian, in a barely perceivable movement nodded his agreement.

"But wouldn't that be as likely to be information that was lost as were the points along the way, the "star points," Yuri inquired a bit doubtfully.

"Well, be that as it may, we have no other alternative," the Tibetan continued deliberately. "Do not forget, we haven't even found all of the star points yet. Events will have to take their course. We feel that it is worth the try. Does anyone disagree?" the Tibetan asked those assembled there.

There was not a word in the room. Indeed, Yuri and Bernd agreed with him, too. They couldn't help but think that it was worth the try even though they realized that they had the least amount of knowledge of anyone in the room.

The Tibetan went on to explain further the significance of finding the point of origin.

"Here is why we think this information has been lost. As it is, the world is indeed much larger than they could have known. They did not return in years or decades as was originally thought possible. As you have heard already, the fifth point is so well hidden from our sight that it is still not found as we sit here breathing and taking up space!"

All present took on a sincere and serious look at these words. And the feeling in the air that it might finally be possible to find the star point and indeed bring the world closer together was almost something you could touch. "Oh god, help us find it!" the Tibetan said out loud, seeking help, it would seem, from the very universe itself.

"It is now very, very late, my friends," the Egyptian said reentering the conversation and adding a sensible point to the now early morning discussion. "A break here seems appropriate, does it not?"

There was a murmur among the small group gathered there at which time Bernd had a chance to chat with a member of the society next to him who brought up the question.

"So what do you think was the beginning of the spread of trade in the ancient world?"

Bernd immediately had an insight into this point, and smiled. Anyone could have guessed that human interaction over large distances has always been based on economic gain. The delegate briefly told Bernd how among the members of the ancient traveling explorers, those coming from the point of the origin, went undetected because they looked as did any other travelers of the time to be merchants or perhaps mystics, but were in truth, neither.

After a brief interlude of murmuring, Yuri spoke up with sincerity. "I think that I would like to finish as much business as possible tonight as I have no idea when I can meet with any of you again."

"Well said, young lady," the Tibetan began again. Though he also noted how they would finish up soon as the Egyptian was right, it was already very late. "All that the Secret Society has had to go on were several check points along the road where all too few clues were left behind. You see, there were very few mistakes along any of the paths taken in the five directions. This of course, means that while we think we know where the travelers ended up, we are not sure from where they began only guessing at the clues found thus far. Their mission clearly had one component; leave no trail. As you can imagine this has left us with not much to go on.

Again, we believe, or at least hope, that the final star point will give some clue that will link all of the star points in a way as to suggest the origin. It is hoped that all of the star points together will somehow upon investigation reveal the meaning as to why these journeys were embarked upon in the first place. And, taken together this knowledge will help us to understand where to go from here!

You see, that is why we are discussing this tonight even though it is so late. "Where do we go from *here*?" is the ultimate, pressing question for us," he ended gravely.

"And where is here anyway?" one delegate spoke out contemplatively, which was not so much an interruption as an utterance they all felt, yet none were willing to say more about this feeling or idea.

"We feel that those of us in this room, many of us descendants of the original clans, or descendants of those who have become members of the early Secret Society, must do something to bring closure to this quest," the acting leader continued. This of course has been our mission for centuries, the Secret Society being very old. Understanding brought about upon finding each star point helps to make up a more accurate picture of the ancient world. We inch along, but get clearer about the search with each new piece of information.

Whether or not there is a sixth star point, as some have guessed is unclear. For now, the origin is the destiny of the sixth and last seal, that is blank for that reason. It was hinted at when point number four was found, but the clue again was it would seem, purposefully vague. It mentioned six ways of tying the star points all together. This information was found on the back of the Icon in Novgorod. This could mean, by night, by day, it could mean anything, not necessarily a sixth spot on the globe!

Finding the origin, would be the key, then, to finding what is either similar or uniquely important about all five star points as destinations and what to do from here on out we hope," he added contemplatively.

"To give you an idea of how difficult this has been, note that only since some of us are kin to the original clan members have we been able to find the clues that we have. It was then that we formed the Secret Society. Before the Society, there had been no connection between our clans for many, many years. Each struggled on its own for what seemed an eternity. We are hoping, and some of us think, that the conditions may need to be just right, for some miraculous occurrence to happen, that when the fifth star point is revealed, the original point of return will be revealed.

Our frustration is perhaps most great when we recount that even with the discovery of all four currently located star points, no understanding for a return route back to the origin has been found. We thought that finding four-points would have revealed some kind of clue, but as of yet, nothing definitive has been revealed. We see many problems with our quest. We realize, for example, that the place called Mesopotamia, the cradle of civilization no longer exists by that name. And complicating things further, various conflicts continue to erupt in what is currently called the Middle East, specifically Iraq, where the original Mesopotamia was located. This has slowed the work of the Secret Society much over the last 1800 years which has unfortunately, been witness to almost unending conflict in the Middle East.

"And the rest of the world, too, I might add," the English delegate noted. He finished with "And this is in no small way attributed to the nation in which I was born." The Society members did not continue in this vein since all present were well aware of the many conflicts around the world past and present.

"What are the four star points that have already been discovered?" Yuri boldly asked, but with a wavering hint of caution in her voice.

"My dear girl, you do expect us to tell you *all* at our first meeting, don't you?" he said hoping to point out how unique their trust so far has been. "Much is to be deliberated yet as to how much we can reveal to you, but for tonight, a more than brief outline may be in order. You know, even now we are prepared to be gone tomorrow from Japan, if necessary."

Bernd's face went white considering the prospect of such a disappearance. "But why?" he asked innocently as he felt that would be a bit of an overreaction to the two of them coming here now.

"Surely you can appreciate our situation. There is too much to lose."

"Yes, though I think it would be a mistake," again Yuri proved to be more bold than tactful.

"Perhaps," the Tibetan let no emotion show on his face, and then continued the story within the previously agreed upon context.

"We believe, based on the lack of evidence of anyone returning to a point of origin from any of the four star points, that all groups had lost touch with the point of origin over time. Even after the final star point was established it had taken so long that no one has returned to the center from all five regions, and it is not likely anyone remains to do so. He paused here, and all looked to him, some leaning toward him, and some obviously moving in closer seemingly knowing what was coming next.

"Finding the final star point remains our last hope …And we think that you may be able to in some way help us in finding the fifth point." He finished speaking, and the gravity of what he said was felt throughout the room. And this seriousness was not missed by either of the young couple. Bernd shifted in his chair while he quickly worked out why it was that these two, and in particular, Yuri, who the Tibetan pointed to, would be of any help in this matter. Yuri shrank for a moment and then sat up straight in her chair.

"Do the seals upstairs on the floor, have something to do with this?" Yuri asked hopefully. She hadn't forgotten the allusion to the seals earlier.

"Precisely they do. You see anyone who can find that final point and unite them all at the center will have completed the search. Especially important is the sixth seal. Completing the seals, it is hoped, will reveal something great that the ancients knew that we do not. We will then complete seals five and six on the floor so that future generations will not lose this knowledge."

"May I go see them again?" Yuri asked half thinking that the answer would be "no" especially since it was so late as to be considered early in the morning already.

"If there is any way you can help us understand this mystery, by all means do so, young woman." the Egyptian delegate chimed in still fully aware though looking pale from having traveled so far from his native land. "Though after looking at the seals, we must call it a night," he clarified his thoughts to them. He was thinking of others in need of rest, though he obviously did, too.

There were less gasps this time as many had gotten over worrying about Yuri and Bernd by this time. The Indian delegate did decide for himself that he would keep close to this couple. He couldn't believe they were being let in on almost everything they had discovered over the past five hundred years. He wouldn't allow them to copy anything he decided.

The Seals in the Grand Hall

Once upstairs members of this smaller assembly gathered around the symbols and hoped for as bright a moonlit night as any they could imagine. They were not disappointed. They could see beautifully. It was a clear and certainly a chilly February evening in Japan.

Yuri was amazed at the sight she was seeing. Yuri was feeling the happiness of having a long sought after goal accomplished. She had not forgotten any important details of the room. She remembered just how it looked, even the autumn moonlight on the night when she and Bernd hurried out shocked by the sounds they had heard. Bernd must have been thinking along the same lines because this is what he said. He was the first to speak.

"Was it members of the Secret Society of the Star Points who scared us out of here last autumn?" he asked, breaking the silence.

"Be careful when you use the full name of the society. You don't want to give us all away now, do you?" the Indian delegate said quickly though surprising everyone in how he said this non-judgmentally. He pointed out that they were no longer down below and that lower voices would be advised. Bernd was taken aback that his utterance was the full name of the Society.

"Indeed it was," chimed in the member from Tibet. Though it was not a full meeting of the society," he explained. "You see, we had only just found out about your trip to Egypt and were here on a preliminary trip to see if it was true, that there may be a woman from Japan who could help us find the last star point." He went on, "We have meeting places almost in the open like this all over the world. It is quite convenient, however, when we want to communicate with the level of secrecy that we wish to have, it does take a while. We use coded communication, saying only bits and pieces at a time, when we contact people all over the world. That is why it took so long to get us all here for the meeting tonight.

"Your timing is impeccable, you two," the Englishman chuckled.

"You know it really does take a bit of coordination, to get us all here," the Tibetan said smiling. We don't have it so bad, though, years ago it was much more difficult. The internet going worldwide really helps in the early stages, contacting areas of the world with bulletins using coded terms. Of course we don't trust the internet for any *important* communication. If you thought a paper trail was bad just consider the digital trail left behind by even an honest hello. "*Om ma ni padme hum*," he said reciting the mantra in Tibetan for the deity of compassion, Chenreizig. He added quickly for their benefit, "or 'My god' as someone might say in English." He also told them that Chenreizig is called Avlokitesvara outside of Tibet. He had clearly said a lot about the Secret Society. The looks from others told him to wait and not speak more at this time.

Yuri could not contain her anticipation any longer. "What language is that one? I cannot read it or even imagine what language it is written in," Yuri blurted out inquisitively while pointing to the third symbol in the group.

"That is the ancient and lost language of the original Mayans, Yuri. It is the only existing sample of ancient Mayan anywhere in the world we think. And we have only been able to roughly translate this one. We have done so based on modern Mayan derivatives and usages and, well, our best guesses.

Modern Mayans cannot clearly read it we found, so we have to do the best we can. It sure was helpful to find the Mayan remains on a cave wall in what is now Mexico. Even so, translating this one was one of the most serious challenges we have faced. This aspect of the Mayan language has been lost for ….

"Centuries" Bernd added finishing the Tibetan's statement for him. Though he had never seen their language or symbols written, the Mayans had been one of his fascinations ever since hearing of their lost civilization in high school. The Mayan palace ruins and temple remains together were something he truly would like to explore. *He would have to go there someday* he thought.

"Therefore, you see," continued the Tibetan, "Since we cannot translate it with confidence, though the message was written down for posterity, we are not sure that we understand it fully. After the symbol was placed in the Mayan palaces, it was meant for the people from that part of the world, not only for the Mayans, mind you. All in that region were now included in the unifying plan. However, it had taken centuries to complete this part of the journey, not years or perhaps decades as it was originally thought. And then, that they had been contacted at all was not clear until after the Europeans, too, discovered the New World. This separation by the oceans of the world has caused the problem of not being able to read an ancient, lost part of the language.

The members of our group, regarding the clans who contacted the Mayans, found out that the modern people could not really explain what had happened in that part of the world in ancient times. You see, it really is true that no one knows why the Mayan civilization went into decline years ago. This is in spite of the fact that the heirs to the Mayan society have developed so many beautifully developed cultural and societal achievements.

"The world was considerably bigger than the ancients thought," said the original leader who was still acting as the Egyptian delegate. He was restating an earlier thought, again adding importance to the moment with his serious tone. "So while we do not know what happened to the original Mayans, where the original people who traveled to that part of the world came from or even whether or not they attempted to return to the origin, we think that this symbol reads …."

While getting ready to listen to the translation, Yuri leaned forward getting close to the symbol so she could take all of this in. To her it was a new look on a language that had totally disappeared, or so everyone in the scholarly world thought save the members of the Secret Society of the Star Points. The Egyptian paused to let her get a good look and then began again.

Pointing to the words across the seal as he read them, "It reads '*All points far and near are united under starry skies.*' That is why we have nicknamed the four places found so far, *star points*."

All of us are worried that I am revealing too much here, but am increasingly interested in seeing if you two actually *can* help us. After all, your interests are seemingly all in alignment with ours. So now I am going to take a leap of faith and tell you some further important information.

You could do me or rather, us, the courtesy of trying your best to see connections in what we believe to be true with any explorations from your lives. Here goes. A compiled translation of the four main ideas of the discovered star points is as follows: "joined together as found in terms such as unity, interacting, under starry skies."

"We think that taken together they all mean collectively, *Under starry skies we can all live together when interacting and communicating with each other.* "And," he said with emphasis "we can only hope that finding the fifth star point confirms this rather than causes further doubt.

You may be wondering why it would have taken centuries and not months or years, perhaps even decades to reach this far point from where our enthusiastic friend comes. Mexico, with regard to the Secret Society of the Star Points was in the southern and not northern part of what has come to be called the New World."

Yuri and Bernd had to listen closely, because either the Egyptian was getting so tired he could barely speak, or he lowered his voice to keep their meeting secret. "This point has been revealed to *us* relatively recently as a place in the western hemisphere that was lost because of a very important logistical problem. Between them and the "point of origin" lies one very big ocean. Of course we are referring to the Atlantic Ocean.

The Pharaohs really benefited from Egypt being a crossroads of knowledge for centuries. Perhaps the ancient Egyptians who built the pyramids had developed shipping technology that has been lost. It is possible, too, that the original clan heading west was so determined that they did so and were successful in considerably smaller boats than we modern people would consider safe.

We are amazed that the group, that eventually accomplished getting to the Mayan capital, left no clues, it seems, behind. That they had arrived there at all was only understood after finding the point in Mexico at the Mayan ruins. That point was one that was cleverly disguised as a map used for recognizing the solar eclipses, the times of seasonal change etc .... The map was really pointing to the sky and the stars. You see, knowledge of it even being a star point was not understood as a result of them coming back and making themselves known! It had to be deduced later independent of their quest. There is no evidence that they returned to the origin. They hid any trails very, very well.

All had been severed it would seem, from the origin. No one had returned to the origin as seems to have been the agreement for all five traveling directions. And if instructions had existed for return to the origin, we have not found them. We found no map anywhere back to the point of origin. Information regarding the place of origin had not been found at either the site in Mexico or at the ancient Mayan temple ruins. The information of where to return was lost, perhaps forever, from that region especially, with the disappearance of the ancient Mayans. It could also be that the information was destroyed on purpose. We'll never know." The Egyptian sat down as the hour was now getting very, very late.

He went on. "Building on the efforts of the early Portuguese maritime explorers, later explorers such as Vasco da Gama and Magellan connected the Mayan part of the world with what was called and considered to be the "known" world up until that time. Of course Christopher Columbus' famous voyages of 1492 and thereafter are the most famous in that hemisphere."

"How the sender or senders knew that there were points of civilization around the world, or would be points to be developed is in itself a fascinating mystery. It showed great faith in their endeavor whatever that purpose was, and perhaps some form of knowledge that we did not possess until relatively recently about the earth we live on. It was only a few centuries ago, really, that the eastern and western hemispheres were connected, at least in our modern sense. It was also intelligent to have a plan for the messengers to come back to the origin hence *uniting all near and far*."

"So there you have it. We are now left with the task of finding the last point and tying it all together. This will then, perhaps, help in some way to connect the people of the earth and help them to live together united as some sort of team," the Egyptian delegate finished. He was looking more tired of body than ever, though his eyes could only be described as clear and hearty. "And, unfortunately, while we believe this to be the case we won't know for sure what was meant by the original people who embarked on their journeys until we find the last star point providing that it leads us to the origin. Can you see why we are so excited to confirm its presence or not in Japan?" He stopped overcome by exhaustion that came from a lifetime of expectations and hopes and loss.

"It was lucky that the Japanese were found, we think," continued the Tibetan once more. Yuri and Bernd both were amazed at the seamless way in which the Tibetan took over speaking from the Egyptian. He told them that when it became included in the explorations of the Secret Society, whether there really was a star point in Japan or not, it was found to be easier than other places to keep the star point maps and information safe. That was because in Japan during the Tokugawa period, the country was isolated, a period called *sakoku*. And that was until relatively recently by the Society's standards. Japan had been isolated for over two hundred and fifty years ending with the change from the Tokugawa period to the Meiji period.

"Yes. The Tokugawa regime ruled from 1603 till 1867 by the western calendar anyway," Bernd added ever the historian. Again, a collective approval was felt among the group, and for the first time it was approval that clearly included the newcomers. Though no one knew why this change transpired it was almost palpable. It was an unspoken feeling among those present. Although, this group was much smaller than the other that had gone off for some much needed rest, something significant was felt by all.

After centuries of searching we found a second point, sort of, in India with of course the help of the unbroken lines of communication established by one of the four major Tibetan Buddhist traditions. The Mayan Point was the third point found. The second point was found because the Tibetan Lamas remembered collectively their roots in India that allowed them to help us trace the star point there, kind of.

"Can you explain *kind of*?" Yuri asked showing that she was paying attention.

"The Tibetan help came, of course, since this point was moved out of India to Tibet. We still have no idea as to why. It may have moved along with the movement of Buddhism from India to Tibet. It might have been as a safety measure while other influences came into India since Tibet remained relatively isolated until recent times. The seal you found on the floor was the English translation of what was originally in Hindi or was it an old language from the Indus region?"

"It was from Hindi," the Indian delegate confirmed. He continued with, "It seemed to make more sense since the other, earlier language had died out." We translated the Hindi into English. That English was the common language for commerce and between those who spoke different languages was thanks to the colonization of India by the British for many years ending in 1947."

The Egyptian continued, "And the Tibetan lamas only agreed to help us provided that we honor their wishes for strict secrecy. They wish not to be named so that which tradition they are part of is not revealed. Of this they were certain. They also make the claim that they are not who their names are anyway. Many of us could relate to this feeling of humility, but all of us do not have experience with their meditative traditions. We noticed that the second point, too, had a reference to stars in it. It was found to be from what is now northern India. The confusing part, of course was that it was found in Hindi in Tibet. This may have been a way of keeping it secret. What we gathered from finding this point was that the star point, it seems, was originally simply headed "southeast." In the same way was the one headed to Egypt headed in the corresponding southwestern direction such as that of the *leg of a star*.

When stars are drawn in many places around the world these days, they are depicted as having five-points. That is the symbol we are using for the time being to describe our search, and it has served us well for several centuries. We will use it until it no longer serves any purpose. For the longest time we did not realize that the point in Greece was really only an outpost marker along the way as was another in Tibet that depicted the outpost on the way toward Russia. Also, the Mexican one is on the way to the ancient Maya. "But we are now overloading you with too much information. Let's stick to explaining the seals," he finished talking of star points abruptly.

We have included all discovered points here drawn with this special sand in hopes that if the points are ever united with the origin, or the origin is ever found, we have them here together. Also, it is our goal to see to it that if all is lost as we believe it once was, the information could be found by someone hopefully by someone like you and Bernd as you did last autumn.

This way the information would not be lost for all time. He admitted now another secret saying, "We haven't told you everything about these seals. Not everyone can read them you see." There was a murmur among those present. This was going very far and trusting the young couple with very much.

"Of course not, Bernd jumped in, "they are written in many languages."

"While that is true, more importantly, they can only be read by those endowed with faith, or in the presence of someone who really and truly cares about all of us on the earth. Someone who cares about unity, love and well you get the picture." The delegate from Egypt finished, sitting down now as he was really tired from the length that the night had become. He finished with, "This, too, is a secret of the lineage from Tibet." Don't ask me how it works because I do not know. It was however, what had led him to trust them. He gathered because of Yuri's great interest in the symbols that she could read at least some of them. Obviously that was why she had come back tonight. Bernd clearly could see them even if he could not read them all.

"The seals made of sand are truly remarkable," Yuri mentioned.

"That was my idea," the member from Tibet added, finishing with, "Thousands of years of making sand *mandalas,* and you do figure out a thing or two, you know." He was beaming. Clearly he was overjoyed to be part of something that was larger than him and carried out *on behalf of all beings.* This was in line with his Buddhist bodhisattva vow. He had pledged to *awaken speedily for the sake of all beings*, and while he was not yet awakened, he could not think of a better way to spend his time while he worked toward that goal than participation in the life of the Secret Society. He, too, asked to not have to reveal Tibetan treasures such as how or why the moon seals and the sand that they contained "worked."

The Egyptian delegate continued, speaking noticeably slower than before, though deliberately just the same. His face now, too, showed tiredness. "We have some thoughts regarding the placement of the point in Japan. Those who had visited Japan from the origin had left the clues to the star points on the island of your birth, we are guessing, because it was relatively secluded from the mainland. It took us one hundred years of making contacts with Islands in Japan just to narrow it down to, we think, the island of your birth. One clue was that on the island of Yuri's birth exists one of the oldest continuous religious sites in Japan, Bentenji. Research shows us that as a religious site it predates the advent of Buddhism in Japan. And if we are wrong there are three more islands that are possibilities. We were held back in our search by the self-imposed isolation by the Tokugawa regime. You see, we don't much look like Japanese most of us," he said now smiling.

At this last comment Yuri, too, smiled realizing the joke by the Egyptian. She also realized just how hard it would have been as a foreigner to explore anywhere in Japan during that violent and secluded period between 1603 and 1867-68 CE.

The Egyptian went on, "Thus, it was hoped, we believe, that the island would be safe from any political upheavals that might take place on the mainland. This proved to be true even in times of great upheaval such as World War II. What we do not know is where those clues are and to where they lead. Once again we've drawn a blank, only guessing; the clues having ended before they really began."

"Maybe we can be of some help at this point, though we have found nothing conclusive yet," Bernd added hopefully. The scientific half of his mind was now working on the clues they had come across.

"Well, it seems that they put the clues on the island and that the universe put you there Yuri to find them," the Egyptian delegate added looking from one and then to the other of the couple.

"And with a right able partner I might add," commented the Indian delegate in British style, a remnant of the British occupation of India.

This last effort to explain further to the couple required some exertion by the Egyptian delegate who now began to show his age. Though his eyes remained clear, the lines on his face seemed more prominent now.

Yuri grew concerned, thinking that it was not simply tricks of the candlelight. Perhaps this is why he suggested they go down one level where talking would require less caution and indeed, less energy from having to be constantly vigilant and careful not to be too loud.

Once down on the lower level where they had eaten, the conversation began anew yet again, the Egyptian taking the lead.

"We contacted the Masons, that famous Secret Society, to enquire about our search. Even the Masons were emphatic that these messages had nothing to do with them. Since they maintained a secretive tone about their own practices, though we were quite interested, we still know nothing about them. They were very clear that they knew nothing about this matter that would be of any help to us. Indeed, in this matter they seemed to know nothing at all, and at this they themselves seemed rather surprised," he finished his statement and sat down.

Then suddenly, for a reason that was unclear to Bernd or to Yuri, the tone changed. There had been a secret sign from the Tibetan to the other members of the group that one of their party needed rest. Unbeknownst to Yuri or Bernd he had touched above both eyes with the index fingers of both hands, and out of compassion all communicated in their carefully contrived style of symbolism to end the meeting so that the Egyptian could get some rest. It had all been done in an instant. All had been paying great attention.

The Egyptian of course knew that this was for his benefit, but nonetheless complied with the wishes of the group. This was compassionate and gave them a chance to be caring of another. He was aware that this meant he was helping to provide compassion for himself. He realized, too, that ignoring the wishes of the group would be, in the same way as ignoring the needs of the group, something that would be lacking in compassion. Indeed, he thought that it would not be a demonstration of good leadership at all. After all, he had opened the meeting as the leader.

Therefore he quickly complied by stating, "It is getting later than is necessary to continue this conversation tonight. We have been searching for many centuries now. The search can wait a while longer. We shall meet with you both again, but for now Yuri and Bernd, you must go to your home. Though before you go, leave us some way to get in contact with you. To be sure it is better that we contact you and not you try to contact us. That would draw far too much attention and even be a little dangerous. On this we will not be flexible. You can be sure, however, that we *will* contact you. He had placed a sincere and heavy emphasis on the word "will" that reassured the couple even while making them feel ill at ease since they were so obviously being dismissed.

"You can't just send us away," Yuri cried out. "There's so much we need to tell you about our explorations in Japan. And so much to ask you about, too," she exclaimed.

"Yes, I am sure, but it will have to wait till next time." Though he admired her ability to see both sides, the need to share and to learn, he went on. "There is already much to consider. Even finding you, whose existence up until tonight we were only just beyond the feeling that we were guessing about is how do you say it in English, 'big news.' You see we believed that it was someone from that island, but certainly did not expect her or him to sneak into our assembly in Tokyo," he finished good naturedly. He added rather seriously, "and do not, by any means, try to enter this building again until we contact you. We will set the time and the place. You *must* follow this plan."

He now addressed those of the Secret Society remaining there still. "Good night and thank you, those of you who stayed up for this important discussion. We will meet tomorrow at eight in the morning in, to use Yuri and Bernd's term, the *grand hall*. We shall see if there is any way we can support these two young explorers." He then addressed the young couple saying, "Yuri and Bernd, 'good night!'"

"But," Yuri tried ...

"We will contact you. You *must* rest now," he said with emphasis. "There is much to do yet. You can start by following up on your explorations in Japan, including any trails you may have already begun, and by following the clues that you do know. That will be the most help now." And with that he turned away resolutely and walked into one of the many magnificently carved archways lining the underground vaulted ceiling that Bernd had been marveling at. They could see that he was making a curving descent, and then, he was gone.

At Home

"Needless to say I can't sleep tonight," Yuri told Bernd more than a little frustrated with how things ended that evening or rather, early morning.

"I am excited, and a little sad that we could not tell them what we have discovered already," Bernd noted, being in agreement that it was frustrating to be dismissed. But now that the scientist in him was fully in charge he continued with, "We need to sleep now. Let's talk more about this tomorrow. It won't change the outcome one bit if we mull it over tonight while we are tired." He noted his own exhaustion now overtaking him as he let his body relax from the poised listening mode that it had been in up until just then. It was after all only hours before sunrise.

Yuri did not complain, but she did not sleep at all that night either and was tired all the next day at work. She noted happily, however, that in between bouts of tiredness she was feeling as alive as ever. In fact she had never felt this amazed and excited even in any of the cases of having traveled to, by rough estimate, over fifty countries.

The only saving part in all of this was that the second day after meeting the Secret Society was Saturday, and for both of them, fortunately, this meant not having to go to their places of work. Yuri decided to call her mother.

A Call to Yuri's Mother

"*Bikkurishita,*" Yuri's mother exclaimed, expressing her surprise. Since starting her new job, Yuri never made arrangements to meet Mother and Father out of the blue. It was the understanding that they could only meet on holidays. After all, working at the Yamato Dictionary Company was a fairly new job for Yuri. It was more likely that they would meet on a holiday such as Golden Week. Golden Week is a series of national holidays that string together to make a period, sometimes more than a week that could be taken off from work. It occurs at the end of April and the beginning of May.

"Sorry to surprise you like this Mother, but Bernd and I really would like to visit you both. *Otoosan ha Genki?*" she went on, asking in Japanese how her father was doing.

"He is fine, and of course we'd love to see you," her mother replied. "We are always glad to have you both for a visit, you know. Father can always use a good partner to play *goh* with. When will you come?" Mother asked. Yuri thought about *goh*, the Japanese game of strategically placing "stones" and them being placed around the board in turn one at a time.

"Yah, Bernd is much better at *goh* than me," Yuri allowed. And this was fine with her. She enjoyed playing chess so much that it didn't matter that Bernd was better at *goh* than her. He was the natural logician, after all. Chess was certainly intriguing, she thought, but all in fun, too. Her light-hearted approach is most likely why she won so much. She had no reason to give up. She enjoyed the games whatever the outcome. She did not take it too seriously. This allowed the game to be enjoyable even when she lost.

"We'd like to visit tomorrow," she said in answer to her mother's question.

"Bikkurishita," Mother said again. "That's rather sudden, isn't it? But oh well, why don't you come tomorrow? We'll have dinner waiting for you."

Yuri breathed a sigh of relief. It was not that she was bothered with surprising her mother with a visit. Surely, her parents would enjoy a visit from them. She was relieved because her mother did not ask a lot of questions as to why they were coming to visit. In Japan, a society heavily influenced by Confucian ethics and philosophy, she would have felt obligated to answer her mother out of respect. Now she had a full day to consider how not to tell her parents of their endeavors with the Society, *respectfully*.

The Next Day

Having gotten up before the sun, they were back on the island of Yuri's birth just after noon. On the train Yuri had been deep in thought. Of course they could not discuss the most recent goings on while riding the train whether they used Japanese or English. As for German, while Yuri knew some, she did not understand the nuances well enough to be secretive in German. Yuri knew that even though most people only speak rudimentary English in Japan, most people speak some English in Japan. And some people speak and understand English very well! So Yuri was left mostly to her own thoughts while on the train and Bernd his. Upon reflection of the recent events, her travels around the world seemed to take on an even deeper sense of importance.

Fate, called *unmei* in Japanese is something often talked about in Japan, and now Yuri believed in it more than ever. Indeed, she remembered that it was on the island of her birth that she had learned about fate. She was amazed that the influence and experience of the small, remote island had taught her so much. She thought to herself, *oboradani* or "thank you" in the local dialect that, being an island dialect was really nothing like standard Japanese. She was thankful for the many lessons learned on the island. The Confucian ethics in place here, her parents and all of those who supported her while she was growing up really gave her the foundation and necessary lessons for her to be successful on her travels and in her studies abroad. This was true even though being abroad was nothing like this place, an island off of the coast of Honshuu the largest island in the archipelago.

She had been reading recently how thoroughly Shinto beliefs run throughout so much of Japanese culture and that the influence of Shinto on Buddhism as it arrived in the sixth and seventh centuries was vast. Certainly, too, the Zen approach to the arts, somewhat responsive to Shinto sensitivities and even Daoist influences had a profound influence in Japan. Japanese culture was uniquely Japanese and at the same time an amalgamation of influences, she noted to herself.

After arriving on the island, there was still time to consider her travels on the last train ride that would take them to a station nearby her family home. It really was only a short walk from the train station. This was something the Japanese had done very well, she thought. Trains had been made to provide travel nearly anywhere among the four largest Japanese islands if one had the time and the money to go about.

Considering the island now, against the backdrop of her travels, she realized that she did not think that this place was unique. She felt now that places all over the world have many different ways of carrying out these same important steps, the passing on of traditions to younger generations. She also felt that we could learn so much from each other. She took a moment and acknowledged the uniqueness of so many places around the world, hieroglyphics, mountains and deserts …. Her travels had made it clear to her that there was so much to learn and that this made life extremely interesting and at times exciting.

She was saddened when she considered how often these very differences had led to war over the past five hundred years let alone since the advent of people roaming, walking and exploring this amazing earth. Yuri had an irrepressible enthusiasm about life and learning. Her parents commented that her willingness and openness when learning about other places made her seem especially vibrant. Still, the island was unique in one way. It was a special base for her. She always felt rejuvenated when here. It was her home place, her *furusato*.

Realistically, too, she understood that a good amount of creativity and effort was important. Fate could not be left up to only fate. It would be better to consider that luck, she believed. Therefore she really went for it, giving it her all in so many things. She felt that this was why people thought she seemed capable of accomplishing almost anything. Certainly having tried and failed at many things many times had taught her, even at a young age, much. And naturally, along with the failures, there were many successes. She was grateful for the many talents she had been given by the *kami*, the life supporting Shinto gods of the universe.

Now it seemed that her karma was to put those very talents to use to help the Secret Society find the last star point, the last clue to finding the origin, and they believed that it was in Japan. Wow! It made her excited and somewhat dizzy just thinking about it. After all, Japan was her home country and the clues to the final star point were thought to be on the very island of her birth. Wasn't life amazing, she thought? Was the last star point on the island of her birth? Well, that is what the Secret Society seemed to think. At least they thought that the clues would be there. And even so it now seemed that her travels around the world were why she just might be able to figure out those clues. And her studies abroad most certainly would help with interpreting them. The interconnectedness of it all made her head spin and her heart fill with joyful hope all at the same time. This was while she found herself walking down a narrow street in her childhood neighborhood. And then they arrived at her familial home.

"*Kyuugamera*," Yuri said upon entering the house. This was the local greeting to let someone know she was at the door. Since this was an island dialect, it was different from the standard Japanese version, *gomen kudasai* that could be heard elsewhere throughout Japan.

They spent what was left of the day relaxing and eating dinner with Yuri's family. Bernd had a chance to share some beer with Yuri's father and was told that Kirin Lager is the best beer in Japan. He didn't argue. He realized that Yuri's father was set in his ways about some things and beer was one of them. Logic would have been pointless. Anyway, Bernd liked almost any kind of beer, so Kirin was as good as any. For himself, however, if it were to be Kirin, he preferred either Kirin Black beer, a dark beer or Kirin's *Ichiban Shibori*, another popular brew. Asahi Black is quite good, too, he thought.

The couple had agreed that the next thing they were to do was to visit Bentenji. Bernd was sure that it held some kind of significance for their journey, and while Yuri agreed, neither of them could put their finger on just what that might be. She thought to herself, we better help fate along by going there. We'll see for ourselves what treasures Bentenji might hold. They planned to go the very next day.

Becoming Students of Meditation

At Bentenji the meditation style had continued uninterrupted since long before the Tokugawa Period. And the style practiced there had come to Japan along the Silk Road. This particular style was heavily influenced by *Cha'an* while in China and then *Son*, in Korea. These were the forms that in Japan came to be called Zen. There were many types of meditation around the world as well as in Japan, and this was only one of them they knew. However, for some reason, it was very important to both of them now that they throw themselves into learning this particular style. They wondered if, since the style was so old, it might hold some kind of clue for their journey. At any rate, meditation had become famous in the modern world if for nothing else as a way to achieve improved health both of mind and body.

Though they had no way of knowing this ahead of time, they were in luck. Abbot Kimura was one of the most experienced masters of meditation in Japan. Abbot Kimura agreed to give them lessons in meditation. To begin with he was convinced that they would benefit only from the simplest of meditations.

Yuri, who practiced Yoga and also tried Tai Chi, wanted of course to go for it right away, proposing to sit long hours and see what would develop from that. Abbot Kimura only chuckled to himself, noting how haste would not help her or anyone to learn anything deeply from meditation. He truly was a wise teacher. Yuri and Bernd had no idea how lucky they really were. It is said in many traditions that finding a skilled teacher is important. The abbot did not put on airs, nor did he act as though he somehow was so good that he *deserved* his position, a mistake of many people who are at the top of their profession. He in fact was very humble. Indeed he was very reverent about holding a position in which many would in turn revere him.

One thing Abbot Kimura told them that was similar across all schools of Zen was that at some point one would reach a place where *nothing* would be experienced. This meant that the practitioner would be experiencing no-thing-ness or what Buddhists since the historical

Buddha have referred to in many different traditions as *shunyata* or "emptiness." Of course he used the Japanese term, "mu."

One of their first lessons was on the basics of Dharma and why one meditates. For example, there was a discussion of greed, hatred, and delusion which in Japanese is stated: *yokubari*, *ikari*, and *orokana* respectively. These are generally speaking, the three main tendencies for sentient or living beings. There were also several other teachings. One such teaching was the three-point lesson that (1) there is no ego identity, (2) all things change, and (3) that life is suffering. Indeed, the Four Noble Truths: that (1) life is suffering, (2) suffering is caused by desires, (3) there is an end to suffering called Nirvana, and that (4) there is a path to the end of suffering called the Eight Fold Path were also discussed.

For practice this weekend, these topics were all the abbot thought was wise to present so as to not overload these new students. He wisely realized that the major hindrance to calm existence in life today was overload not only in information, but in how it is presented in the glut of media and advertising. Additionally, the problem originated from technological advancement and all the glitz that goes along with, for example, computer graphics. The abbot kept it simple, teaching them to practice awareness, or being aware in all that they do. He also taught them the proper posture for sitting in meditation. And then, quite decisively and against the protestations of both Yuri and Bernd, sent them on their way.

"I can't believe he sent us packing," Yuri complained, a little frustrated that they could not stay and enjoy the temple atmosphere for a while longer.

"I have read and heard that teachers can be very unpredictable," Bernd responded with a little seriousness in his voice. Nonetheless I, too, would have liked to have stayed a bit longer even though I was knackered.

"There you go sounding British again," Yuri commented. Bernd for his part was amazed at how clearly she could tell the difference between British, American and Australian English terminology and pronunciation.

"Well, we'll have to go and practice at my parents' house," she said giving up on the temple for the time being.

"I don't think he wanted us to stay away," Bernd said reassuringly. "He wanted us to learn to practice and be self-sufficient and then to come back, don't you think?" he said finishing his thought. "He must have been able to tell that we were there in earnest to learn."

"I suppose so," Yuri replied once again hopeful. "Though certainly he did not want us to return right away; I could see that," she added.

"No, not to meditate, but I have an idea. How about this? Let's go to your parents' house now, and come back with a thank you gift for him tomorrow." He said this while they were walking the narrow roads, the size of what would be alleys in much of the United States, back to Yuri's parents' house. Bernd was amazed that everything was paved. It seemed as though Japan was one large slab of concrete and pavement, he sometimes thought.

"The abbot knows that we are going back to Tokyo, so let's plan our next visit to see him and ask *him* when we should return," Bernd said, proposing their next step. Yuri immediately agreed, knowing that his instinct was spot on in terms of proper respect in relation to someone older than them, and so it was set. They would go back tomorrow with a gift and a request for another meeting at the time of the abbot's choosing. Bernd did understand certain Japanese customs well, Yuri thought, and she smiled while reaching over to hold his hand.

Yuri did not waste any time, however. That very night she was up until early in the morning "practicing" meditation and rediscovering what that meant. Eventually, when she truly got sleepy, she laid down on her futon. As she began to contemplate her various meditation experiences she quickly fell asleep and was lost in her dreams. Later, she would learn that lying down was one of the four basic meditation postures along with sitting, standing and walking. She also would discover just how difficult it was to carry out meditation while lying down. That is, without falling asleep.

The Next Morning

The next morning, Yuri woke surprisingly early for how late she had been up. Bernd for his part was up and moving in earnest by 6:00 A.M. They went downstairs to have breakfast with the family, though only Mother was up already. Yuri's father had been to a neighborhood gathering until late the night before so he was still sleeping.

"Are you going anywhere today before you return to Tokyo?" Mother asked.

"Well, we are planning to visit Bentenji today and give Abbot Kimura a gift for letting us come and visit with him for such a long time yesterday," Bernd said.

"That sounds nice. Why don't you take some of the peaches we got from our relatives? They're next to the Buddhist altar in the *butsudan no ma*," Yuri's mother said matter-of-factly.

The *butsudan* is the Buddhist altar, traditionally kept at the house of the oldest son of the family. In the case that the oldest son is without children, no longer living or had never been born, it is kept at the house of the oldest daughter. Usually the oldest son inherits the family home, and so moving of the altar is often unnecessary. The room in which it is kept is called the *butsudan no ma* or Buddhist altar room. In traditional families, when a daughter takes over the family home her last name is changed from her husband's, taken at the wedding, back to her maiden name. This is in order to accommodate an easy transition to become the head of the family home name intact.

The couple's errand was no surprise since gift-giving was a common way to show respect, honor others, and maintain good relations between people in Japan. And sharing part of a gift from someone such as relatives even had its own term in Japan, *susouwake*. Even more politely it is called *o-susouwake*.

Referring to the offer of peaches Yuri said, "That's perfect. Thanks Mother!" Bernd had wanted to rejoin the conversation, but it was over almost as soon as it began. Now, all there was left to do was to eat. Mother had prepared everything, yogurt, jam, coffee, fruit and toast. For Father, too, she had gotten breakfast ready, though with slightly different fare. Father ate almost anything, but on this morning had said that he wanted to eat a "Japanese breakfast." For him this meant grilled fish, Japanese pickles, rice, dried seaweed and a poached egg. Some people liked raw eggs, but Yuri's father usually had his cooked some way or other.

After breakfast Yuri and Bernd relaxed until midmorning and then got ready and took the peaches to the temple. Abbot Kimura was waiting for them almost as if he knew they were coming. He opened the sliding door with a screech as the small metal wheels of the door rolled across the door frame. He watched then as they walked up to the temple building entrance. They entered the temple, and he said immediately "what brings you back so soon?" as his eyes searched theirs.

"We are going back to Tokyo and would like to give you these peaches as a token of our appreciation for your taking the time to teach us important meditation and Dharma lessons yesterday," Bernd got out quickly. He was hoping to head off any concern that they might be back nagging the abbot for further instruction. This was especially since it was so soon after his specific directions to not come back right away, presumably to meditate.

"Thank you, that is very kind," Abbot Kimura replied. I wonder when we should get together again?" he proposed, once again seemingly reading their minds. "I will be available during the Golden Week holiday," he offered considerately not wishing to put them in a position of telling an elder what to do or being seemingly too forward.

In Japan, the influence of Confucian ethics made it important to not be too demanding of elders. Hence, Abbot Kimura realized the potential concern on the minds of both Bernd and Yuri of coming across as too pushy. And, of course, he was absolutely right. This offer was kind, because it let them know, indirectly, that he was available during the coming holiday. Bernd was pretty sure that is what this meant, but hesitated just the same.

What Bernd did not realize was that hesitating was exactly what one did around elders in Japan and was perfectly in order in this context. It is true that not everything can be learned from a book. For example, how low to bow is clearly defined in books about Japan, but understanding what it means to bow too low to someone younger than oneself or not enough around someone older is something that can best be gained through direct experience. The nuances are what make it all difficult, but interesting, too, Bernd thought now as he contemplated coming back to see the abbot in the coming holiday time.

"That sounds just fine," Yuri chimed in after a suitable pause, averting her eyes to the ground and back to the abbot again, not wanting to miss this good opportunity. This told Bernd that he was right on, that the abbot intended for them to visit in the coming spring holiday. Golden Week was called Golden since it was about a week long period where because of a series of national holidays that came almost back to back, nearly everyone in Japan was on vacation at the same time that whole week. For resorts, inns and tourist destinations it truly was *Golden*. For tourists it was a golden opportunity to go places farther away than a one-day trip would allow. Upon considering this, Bernd the logician, thought, *we better be on our way. We do have to go to work tomorrow.*

Little did they know that the very abbot they were talking to, because of his long practice of the techniques he taught them just the day before was one of the few truly awakened beings in Japan. Indeed, his practice had been so rigorous that he may have been one of the most experienced practitioners of meditation in the world. Neither did they realize just how long it took most people to awaken, nor how hard it might be. Especially for Bernd this was not understood since so much of this world, wrapped in Eastern philosophy was in practice new to him. Yuri, though from the East, had ironically been introduced to meditation at Oxford. That introduction now somehow seemed like very many years ago.

She realized that she had a lot to learn regarding meditation and changed her attitude from that of frustration to one of trust toward the abbot. She admired his understanding of this early stage and the grace with which he allowed them to get some more experience on their own and come back for more teaching later. He was pretty amazing, she thought, since he recognized that only so much could be done at one time with their busy work schedules. He had also intelligently planted the idea for them to want to come back. So many students come one time and then do not return considering themselves *too busy* to meditate. This was something the abbot knew all too well. The abbot realized that in this busy world, the best use of time at least for him, and now he thought for Bernd and Yuri, too, was to meditate for total health and wellness. Yuri now thought that she was up to it. Bernd for his part hoped that he was.

They made their parting greetings and tentatively set the early part of the Golden Week holiday for their next meeting with the abbot. Then Bernd and Yuri took their leave and went back to Yuri's parents' home, did one last check of their packed things and embarked on the return trip to Tokyo.

Though the stay on the island had been brief, they both thought it very productive. Yuri's parents had been so glad that they would come from far away Tokyo that they did not question the suddenness or brevity of it. They chalked it up to filial piety, a Confucian value in which the young and old mutually depend on each other, and especially the young revere the old. They felt they had done a good job raising Yuri because she was willing to visit them at just any time. Yuri noticed this and thought, *We must get back as often as we can, not only when we are searching for clues.* She had never thought of it much that way before. After all, her parents wouldn't be around forever, she realized. Besides she loved her former home with its tiled roof and it being situated near the mountains basking in the warm sun at daybreak. The local area was dotted with farms anywhere that space permitted. The smell of a fresh catch of fish, too, was familiar to Yuri and brought back memories of running through the morning fish market hearing *irasshaimase*, a greeting that means something like "Hi there. Is there anything I can get you?"

What they also had no way of knowing was just how in depth Yuri's understanding of meditation was even though she seemed to be a beginner. She had a natural ability regarding meditation whether this was from a healthy construction of the brain, experience in another life, yoga practice or from what it did not matter. She was already clearly in tune with the vibrations of the universe, and that was something the abbot had noticed to a greater degree that even she had. He was hoping that she would allow him to point her in the direction of further understanding. He also thought that such a developed being …just might allow this.

In Tokyo Once More

Both of them were glad to get to their apartment. They unpacked, rested for a while and then had tea on the veranda, ever their ritual on evenings when the weather permitted. Tonight it was cool, and with a fine moon overhead. They took in the evening amazed at their surroundings, modern society under a starlit sky. There was a light breeze. They took this opportunity to enjoy the celestial light coming from both moon and stars. Then as they were soaking up the heavens it came to Yuri.

"Bernd" Yuri exclaimed, quickly grabbing Bernd by the arm. This had been almost loud enough to rouse the neighbors though it could not be helped. She had just realized something important and could hardly contain her excitement.

"Yes, what is it?" Bernd replied a little stunned by the abruptness of her action and utterance.

"We must go to Horyuji as soon as possible. I think I can help to find the connection there," she said now completely excited in a way that almost scared him. She was remembering the dream she had the night after meeting with the Abbot Kimura at Bentenji. Her excitement and the mention of Horyuji, however, made Bernd hopeful, too. He wanted to help find the star point, if that really was possible. As he thought about this he got excited all over again. They agreed to go to the temple the very next weekend.

The week at work was hard, since all they could think about was the star points, going to Horyuji, and looking for clues. In the evenings, they went over everything they already knew writing down ideas and tying everything they could together. They took care to not write down anything from their meeting with the Secret Society and even were careful to not talk about it directly, only hinting at what really was the topic of conversation. In fact, the things they wrote mostly did not make sense as they instinctively knew to not write any specifics about any of this. One thing more they had to consider was how they could get into Horyuji …at night?

Again at Horyuji

Upon deciding to return to Horyuji they considered that since so much seemed to revolve around the symbol of "stars" they would go to the temple in the evening and better yet at night. That had been Yuri's insight. This of course would not be easy as not just anyone can go to the temple in the evening and walk around let alone later into the night when the stars would be out shining in their full glory. Many if not most temples in Japan are closed to the public by four, and usually at the latest there was not public admittance after five in the evening.

When they arrived, it was still early in the afternoon. They walked around the temple grounds and reviewed the many murals and paintings that they had seen the last time they were there. They were trying to take it all in even more carefully than before. Especially, they paused before the mural where Prince Shotoku was completing the first Constitution of Japan.

"Really it was a code of conduct," Bernd told Yuri, and she smiled at his wide base of knowledge. She admired him all over again in that moment. Yuri was each day gaining insight into the importance of being in and really *experiencing* present moments, each of them. She seemed to see Bernd more clearly as time passed, she now noticed.

Also, Yuri was sure that there was something of significance here, at this temple, "something wonderful." That is what she felt now as she tried to remember the feeling behind the voice in her dream. She remembered her dream in which all that was said was "'something wonderful' waits at a temple's gates." She could not be certain, and surely there were other temples, such as Shitennouji that the young couple had visited not long before or after that dream. She knew, however, that Horyuji had been the temple visited closest to her having that dream. And she now thought that Horyuji must be of significance to their search. Certainly she wanted to find out either way!

Bernd, being ever interested in how things work and are assembled, wondered about the makeup of the temple. He had many questions come to mind. *How did it come to be that Prince Shotoku had the temple built in the first place?* was just one of them.

Fortunately, the abbot was available. After politely confirming that the abbot had time to talk and was happy to answer questions about the architecture and the history of Horyuji, Bernd began to ask questions. Upon doing so they discovered an incredible almost unbelievable fact. By some amazing stroke of good luck the abbot at Horyuji had heard of the abbot at Bentenji. Indeed, they had gone to the same school of training in Zen Buddhism. This was in addition to their regular traditions. The two abbots had never formally met, but the two temples, were nonetheless run by abbots who had attended the same Zen training school at the same workshop and were part of the same tradition or sect. Indeed, they had long been part of an organization of temples along with others in the region, though there had been no recent connection or exchange between their two temples specifically. Yuri and Bernd were amazed by this *coincidence*.

Yuri and Bernd having mentioned the island where Yuri was from, immediately made the abbot who now stood before them ask about one of the organizations sister temples, Bentenji, and about the abbot there.

At Horyuji, the abbot, a Mister Furuta was surprised to find out that both of these two young people had met the rather famous abbot at Bentenji, Abbot Kimura. After all Abbot Kimura was someone he had never formally met himself, having always seen him off in the distance at anniversaries and temple organizational meetings and such. And on top of this, they seemed to have had a good long talk with him, too. Abbot Furuta, already impressed by this, was even more amazed then, to find that they had taken meditation lessons from Abbot Kimura. They regretted mentioning this now. And it was this fact that piqued Abbot Furuta's curiosity, even while the young couple hoped to talk about anything else.

Fortunately, however, this proved a good omen. This interest of Abbot Furuta in their experiences at Bentenji was just what they needed. The abbot invited them in, and after the regular formalities, greetings and appropriate hesitation, called *enryo* in Japan they had an opportunity to ask about Prince Shotoku and the construction of the temple. The Prince was such a famous figure in Japanese history that it was not in anyway unusual to ask about him. Yuri remembered reading in textbooks about the Prince completing the first Constitution of Japan, and so that is why she brought up his name in connection with the Constitution first.

Thus, they were quick to take advantage of their good fortune. They also asked about Buddhism coming to Japan and everything they could think of that might shed some light on or give some clue about the final star point that Yuri just felt was so near to being discovered. They framed all of their questions with regard to either the Prince, or meditation, and questions regarding the meditations that came along the Silk Road to Japan. This was successful they thought since the abbot seemed to think nothing of their questions other than two young people having more interest in mediation than any others he'd met who were so very young. At Horyuji, like Bentenji, they did not know that this abbot, too, was experienced in the advanced stages of meditation. And that he was, as a result of meeting with them, now preparing to make his own journey to Bentenji at the first chance he got. His interest was piqued as he wondered how the abbot there had gotten two young people to take meditation so seriously. He, too, would like to interest young people in taking up a sincere meditation practice.

So many people really of any age, he thought could benefit from practicing meditation and moment to moment awareness. And so many, especially the young had no interest in anything that wasn't *entertainment*. He thought to himself, "*If they only knew ....*" At any rate, it was clear that these two young people were serious about meditation. He decided that he could trust them for some reason or other, though this was only a feeling or a sense that he had rather than any logically drawn conclusion.

And this sense of trust was exactly why all of a sudden the abbot leaned nearer to them with the air of a great story teller motioning them to come near in confidence and said, "You know we have some keepsakes from the Prince's family," arousing their interest immediately.

"You mean Prince Shotoku's family?" Bernd exclaimed.

"Yes, the very same Prince Shotoku," he replied with sincerity, also making it clear with a short back and forth wave of his hand that they should not make a big deal of this and involve others who might be near.

"Wow, that really is something," Yuri began in a whisper, going on to ask, "Can you tell us about them?" Though she did not want to be too forward, she was now tingling all over with the anticipation of hearing about something that old. She thought to herself that in another life, if there was such a thing, she would almost certainly be an archaeologist. She wondered briefly now, what she had been in her previous life or *zensei*. But there was no time for day dreaming, the present grew ever more exciting as the abbot continued.

"I'll do better than that," the abbot said, giving them a mischievous smile. "Follow me," he said, and getting up quickly walked over to a side door in the room. Neither had to be asked twice; they were right behind him. It was now getting dark adding to the mysteriousness of the venture. They had planned to arrive late in the day and stay the next if nothing came of their first day's attempt at getting into the temple in the evening. Their plan seemed to be working now as the stars would be out soon.

They went down a long set of stairs that, to their surprise one could imagine was built not so long ago. Abbot Furuta began to explain about the place they were headed, once they were out of earshot of anyone else at the temple. He told them that this deep storage facility had been built during World War II.

"Horyuji" he began to explain, "is among the oldest temples in Japan."

"I thought it was the oldest continuous temple in existence in Japan?" Bernd stated inquisitively.

The abbot acknowledged that "As far as we know that is true," sounding very realistic and down to earth. He then continued the story without more explanation of the age of the temple, "And being so old Horyuji had many artifacts to care for. The resident monks at the time of World War II realized that they couldn't take risks with the treasures accumulated over the centuries. Therefore, they dug this deep cavern and carefully carried down into it all the treasures of Horyuji, including anything of value donated over the years. They began digging on December 9, 1941, the date in Japan of the day after the bombing of Pearl Harbor in Hawaii." Their foresight was a product of meditation you might say ...."

"Wow, this is a pretty tight passageway," Bernd noted commenting that large items could not have been carried down this way.

"This was just one of many pathways that had existed to access the underground vault," Abbot Furuta continued. "After the larger artifacts were replaced to their original locations after the end of the war, the need for large passages was gone, and so now there only remained access to this one, narrow passage. Any remaining artifacts down here are all rather small," he confirmed. "Other small items, too, were back up on display to be sure, but certain items were too important to risk having someone take them," he said, with a hushed seriousness.

"Do you mean that the allied occupation of Japan had no idea that this place even existed," Bernd asked with interest.

"It had been a well-kept secret," Abbot Furuta replied, though he had himself been only a young, novice monk at the time. "The allies trusted a bunch of monks, you see," he said grinning.

He told them that he had not gone down there very often. In fact he hardly remembered the many things stored down there. And he only recalled this one because the circumstances surrounding it coming to the temple were so unusual and as such became legend. The story was often told among those who were custodians of the temple, especially the abbot and his fellow abbots when they got together on retreats or for purposes of further study. This story telling had gone on for many, many generations sharing stories of temple goings on. Sometimes there were ghost stories, too, but Abbot Furuta did not engage in earnest in them. He did not see the merit in those stories aside from the scare they gave children and well, some adults, too.

"The circumstances surrounding the coming of a particular artifact to the temple made up a widely told story indeed," he admitted, raising their interest a notch. Though, up until now a story told strictly among the abbots of temples within the temple organization. After all, the story was about an artifact that had come from the family of Prince Shotoku. It had actually come from his descendents many years after his death, which is why this story stood out in Abbot Furuta's mind. It was strange, he thought, that when they brought the artifact and several others to Horyuji, all the family said, it is reported, was that it is important that these things stay with the temple. He for his part was glad to carry out the family's wishes. Like others before him, Abbot Furuta made arrangements for these wishes to be known to whoever would become the next abbot. That set of familial artifacts was under lock and key in a place reserved only for access to and by the abbots of Horyuji. The reason why the abbot considered how the item came to the temple as strange was that while the family knew that the item was to stay with the temple, even the family themselves did not know why. All they could say was that this was the Prince's wish. The monks had figured that this was because so much time had passed since the Prince had passed away. Now the abbots of Horyuji were the ones honoring his memory by carrying out his wishes that had been passed on to them from the family. The family by their own report had received the instructions verbally from the Prince generations before, and they had been passed along to them. This was in addition to what was included, rather vaguely, in his written will, a copy of which they had brought with them. Arguments among family, they said were what caused it to take so long for them to get the artifacts to Horyuji. It had taken more than one hundred years.

"You mean you have the Prince's will!" Bernd exclaimed thankful that they were out of earshot of anyone in the temple grounds other than the three of them in the vault. All the abbot did was to nod his head and smile.

There was no specific description of the significance of any of Prince Shotoku's items given to the temple, only a vague will and that was only in part, the part to be given to Horyuji. In fact, it may have been that the family did not clearly know themselves what the significance was of the items the Prince was leaving to them. It was possible, too, that for some of the items anyway, the family thought their significance would be obvious to the monks and abbots. At any rate it was not clear to the monks at the time of the arrival of the items nor is it now in the present. The monks were stewards of the items through the years, and then they packed the items carefully and stored them down in this room untouched since 1941. You will recall that was the year the United States entered into World War II.

Yuri and Bernd were amazed to find that originally the items had been given to the temple in 792 AD, only two years before the imperial capital of Japan had been moved from Nara to Kyoto.

And now, as unexpected to them as it would have been to the abbot just hours earlier, Yuri and Bernd were standing before a small box on which only the letters P.S. were written. The abbot was perhaps the only one alive who knew what that meant. Bernd couldn't help himself and let out a gasp of admiration for the artifacts before them. It was amazing to be in their presence even without opening the packages and seeing them. Yuri practiced deep breathing or *kokyuu hou* as she attempted to relax herself. Something in her asked her to be calm. She felt like something important was about to be revealed, and this was the same feeling she had that night she surprised Bernd by exclaiming that they must come here again, the night she grabbed his arm on the veranda. She knew that now it was important to keep her best attention to every detail. This opportunity might be brief, and almost certainly would never come again.

The abbot reached forward and drawing the box toward him pulled it into the open from the storage area and placed it on a low table motioning to them to sit beside him. He opened the stained, lacquered, wooden box, and inside was a smaller box about five inches long and three inches wide that he carefully removed and set on the table beside the large box marked with the letters P. S. The inside boxes were marked with the Japanese kanji characters for Prince Shotoku. The P.S. came during the additional box being added during World War II. It was also a result of the push to learn foreign languages, especially English, which began in the Meiji period and continues today. It was also a good way to keep novice monks, who may have wandered down here, from suspecting that there were items from Prince Shotoku himself down here. It would prevent not only snooping, but also potential temptation to view or perhaps even steal something belonging to the former Prince.

After Abbot Furuta opened the smaller box while leaving the other items in the larger wooden box, the three of them could see inside. There was some yellowing wax coated paper covering a very, very old *furushiki* or woven wrapping cloth. Inside was yet another layer of *washi* or Japanese rice paper, clearly older than any extant paper either Yuri or Bernd had ever seen at least at this close proximity. Having removed the waxed paper and *furoshiki* with great caution, the abbot carefully placed his fingers under the edges of the final paper covering and slid his hands underneath the Japanese rice paper very, very slowly. They watched in anticipation while he took the prize in his fingers, raised it up ever so slightly and then asked Bernd to move away the box. Bernd happily obliged sliding the box down and angling it away from Abbot Furuta's steady hands. Then, the abbot angled the artifact down and the paper slid off of it. The abbot looked more confident now. The relief that showed on the abbot's face gave them the impression that the abbot realized the item was not as frail as he had originally thought it might be. He slowly rotated the artifact, and it shone dimly in the candle light. All three were transfixed on the item. While looking at it in utter amazement Yuri exclaimed, "It's a star!"

Bernd exclaimed, "Made out of bronze!"

"True to the time period I might add," stated the abbot, though he looked puzzled, wondering why they seemed so excited upon seeing a bronze star left by Prince Shotoku so many, many years ago. "Do you know something about this star?" the abbot asked, his curiosity piqued once again. He couldn't get over how much these two made him feel excited about everything. He wondered, *Could it be their youth*? Questioning them about what they might have known about the star now made them tense. Yuri was feeling worried and wondering what to do next when ….

"Well, we have been sitting on our veranda and drinking tea under the stars ever since we got married," Bernd added quickly. Yuri breathed more easily relieved by his quick thinking.

"Stars have kind of become our good luck symbol as a couple," she added, somewhat embarrassed. She was a little ashamed to tell the abbot that they had gotten over being angry with each other under starry skies many times even though they had not been married for very long. As for Bernd's exclamation about the star being bronze he answered with renewed questions about how old the temple was, its construction etc …. He explained that this would help him be able to confirm the time period based on the bronze material used. This gave Abbot Furuta the impression that it was all part of his research.

Fortunately, the abbot believed them and was even amused so there was no awkward moment in which they felt a need to try and not tell the abbot about the Secret Society. If Abbot Furuta knew about this business he would have to tell them before they revealed anything to him, they thought. They realized that they had taken being sworn to secrecy to heart and were getting accustomed to keeping this secret, and that things felt somehow safer that way. It was always a little unnerving, still, to realize so many things and yet not always have a clear reason as to why. They often felt as though they were doing things on faith, which they now thought of as a close kin to fate. At any rate all three breathed more easily now.

Next, they looked at other things such as the diary written by the Prince and other items sent by his family including a post card. It was fascinating. Seeing their appreciation, the abbot told the young couple that it might be possible for them to come back from time to time when possible to view the artifacts without disturbances from others. He made them swear not to tell people about this as he did not want the temple to have people coming just to view these items. He had only let them in because they had actually meditated with a meditation teacher, and seemed overall in earnest to learn about the temple's history. These facts were things that he appreciated greatly and took very seriously.

There was no shortage of people coming to the temples of Japan just to see artifacts, and so, too, there was no large gathering of students in earnest to learn meditation, he thought to himself. He had noted many times how people often treat temples as tourist destinations rather than truly places of worship and learning as they had once been. Voyeur tourism as he called it did not interest him. Nor would a barrage of media sit well with him, he firmly noted. The couple understood and promised immediately to keep things secret. This included Bernd's research, the abbot confirmed. Bernd set him at ease by agreeing immediately. Abbot Furuta had chosen two trustworthy people, but had no idea just how good they were at keeping a secret. Their Society connections would serve them well in this regard, they thought smiling at each other.

When they were about to leave they realized that it was late. It was even later than they imagined anyone would be allowed to be in the temple vicinity. Indeed, it was now a beautifully moonlit night, the stars shining. It could not have been more perfect. While strolling by the pagoda they took it all in. The moon was visible behind it, and the stars shined above. They were amazed at the natural beauty of the scene. Then Bernd remembered from one of the mural paintings that there had been a fire long ago and that the pagoda had been on fire. This brought what he hoped would be his final question of the night to mind. He cautiously asked the following.

"I know that it sounds kind of strange, but have there ever been more layers on the pagoda? I mean, there was fire here, right?" He felt a little embarrassed since Yuri had already told him that pagodas have five levels at many temples in Japan. Still he wanted to ask the abbot about this after seeing the pagoda again and this time in the moonlight. The historian in him also wanted to see the pagoda just as monks and Samurai must have in earlier historical periods such as the Tokugawa Period called *Edo* in Japanese.

The abbot looked at Bernd thoughtfully and said, "You know, there were never more than five tiers to the pagoda as far as I know, and the pagoda was restored to its original shape after it was burnt. It seems that it was burned, though not burned completely to the ground by a stray flaming arrow. It was lucky that the arrow only damaged the top part of the pagoda." He reflected for a moment and then said, "You know, there was also something small, like a statue of Buddha that fell during that fire. Unfortunately, no one knows or remembers what it was. This event happened during the *Sengoku Jidai,* or Warring States Period," he explained sighing seemingly at the great loss of life of that time, Bernd imagined. Another thing was clear. The tone of voice Abbot Furuta used told them that he was finished discussing things with them for that night. Yuri realized what he meant right away, and Bernd understood, too, when she nudged him in the ribs with her elbow.

Again, Confucian ethics was at work. Yuri realized without having to be told that the abbot wished to return home, and for them it was time to leave without further delay. She even considered that he may be late for dinner as it was now almost eight o'clock. Bernd was beginning to really understand this, too. It did not escape his attention that the urging them to leave was in no way meant to be unkind. After all, the abbot had invited them, and repeated the invitation. They were to come back at another time. Bernd thought to himself a thought that later surprised him. He thought that he *would like to return here to meditate.* He did of course wish for continued health in mind and body both benefits of meditation, but there was something else in this, too, ...

The abbot, having an intuition about the couple, thought to himself, *I would like to teach these two to harness awareness of body, speech, and mind as my teachers have shown me.* Amidst so much resistance to the understanding of reality, he thought, it would be a true joy to teach these two who seemed so much in earnest. He reflected on how hard it was even for students with interest to attain higher states of awareness.

Bernd took the opportunity as they were taking their leave to ask, "May we come back and look at the Prince's diary tomorrow? I'm doing some research at the university, and that would be of great help. I realize that I cannot take the diary with me and that it belongs here." Again Yuri was impressed by his quick thinking. They both were wondering the same thing. *Could it have been the Prince's star that was knocked off of the pagoda in the fire?* Certainly both of them wanted to see if there was any hint of that ...in the diary.

"You may come back and look at the diary. I hope it is of some help to you. It is a waste to have it here, like a prize, with no one looking at it. On the other hand, you will have to make up some story about how you found the information. I don't want this place crawling with people who are not interested in the sincere study of meditation. Though, it would be nice if some young people, in addition to you two, came here interested in meditation, I might add." And with that he showed them the door, watched them leave in polite Japanese style, and then returned home for dinner, a little later than usual, but inspired more than he would have thought by this chance meeting with a sincere, youthful couple.

The Following Day

Upon return to the inn they ate dinner, had a bath and relaxed until bedtime. They woke refreshed the next day. They arrived at the temple after having a *morning set* at a local coffee shop. This consisted of an egg, toasted bread with butter and jam and coffee. Of course, now that they had returned to the temple their excitement grew with each step they made toward the vault, and yet they had to contain their excitement. They needed to avoid having the abbot ask them more detailed questions as to why they were interested in things about the temple, stars, and Prince Shotoku. In fact they were hoping not to let on that they knew anything special about this "something wonderful" that they had learned about in the ancestral book at Yuri's parents' home. Being questioned was particularly dangerous, they thought, as it may lead to questions they could not answer about the Secret Society. Neither did they wish to get into a position of offending Abbot Furuta who they both respected very much. Just for good measure, and for a little fun, as they walked up to the main entrance of the room through which they could access the vault, they held hands, kept their fingers crossed, and this caused them to giggle.

The previous evening's visit to the temple firmed up their resolve that stars, particularly the metal one that they had seen must have something to do with finding the last point. Still, what that was remained a mystery. They hoped to find some clue in the diary. And having retrieved it from the vault and sitting beside a low table in a side room they began to explore it.

Prince Shotoku, having been a learned man, had a hand in many things, including documents that helped with the formation of the government at the time. He also wrote of helping to incorporate Confucian principles and Buddhism from China and Korea into Japanese life. At least you could see how passionate he was about those things from the entry for July first which they now viewed awestruck.

At last they came to the chapter where it was written that the Prince had helped to found the temple at Horyuji. It was with joy, he wrote, that he had been involved intimately in all of the crowning glory of Horyuji including a *well adorned* pagoda. At this point Bernd paused and thought to himself how he must confer with Yuri later regarding what could have been meant by a "well adorned" pagoda. Later when they discussed the diary they noted that though the Prince made a point of noting it, just how the pagoda had been "adorned" was entirely unclear from the diary. The Prince had left it up to the reader's imagination just where or how it had been adorned, and with what for that matter. For some reason this is how he chose to end the diary. There may be yet another diary, but of this one they were clearly at the end.

Yuri and Bernd were crushed. Since they could find no mention of the star in the Prince's diary, they gave up for the time being and had tea and met with Abbot Furuta. He told them the following anecdote after telling them that Prince Shotoku's life was much earlier than the Warring States Period in Japan. He told them about the fire at the pagoda and about how the lead disciple or lead *deshi* of the abbot at the time nearly lost his life. He recalled details that he'd forgotten the previous evening. It is said that a very large piece of wood fell when the pagoda started on fire, and it nearly hit the disciple, but did miss him. Other accounts had it that the piece of wood "hit" the disciple. Yuri and Bernd realized that this apparently had become quite a story at the time. Of course like all good stories it had gotten embellished to the point where everything except the moon had almost hit the poor disciple, the abbot admitted smiling.

The disciple had been taking the meditation practice too seriously, the stage in which one has a tendency to try too hard, forcing the meditation. He had been out trying to meditate by the pagoda in the midst of a battle raging nearby. Abbot Furuta, upon reading about the disciple had chuckled. He knew that it was not necessary to force anything. *Mu* or emptiness was something that arose naturally out of an allowing of the being to unfold. And this, Abbot Furuta realized, was unique for each individual and was certainly *not* something that could be forced.

The young couple went back to the diary one more time. Continuing to look through it was dissatisfying. "I would give anything," Yuri said out loud, "to find out what was in the Prince's mind on the day he wrote the section of his diary talking about a *well adorned pagoda*." They both wanted to see what he saw in his mind's eye as he wrote, and they also knew that this was only wishful thinking. Unfortunately, one thing had been made clear by the day's search. The star had not been what had fallen when the stray arrow had hit the temple. According to the abbot's story, it had been a chunk of wood and likely had been on fire.

"I don't know what to say," Bernd added obviously astonished at the abrupt ending of the diary. "Maybe the Prince has left us some other clue somewhere," he continued.

"It doesn't seem like it," Yuri said sighing in disbelief, thinking what a shame since they had done so well up until this point. She also considered that if star points had been easy to find, they all would have been discovered centuries ago.

They resigned themselves to further searching and placed the book down on the table in the upstairs side room in which the abbot had first taken them into his confidence. This had been the agreed upon place to leave this treasure. There was nothing that could be done, and nothing else to do for now.

They made plans to continue looking through the items donated by Prince Shotoku's family after lunch. They had already spent several hours looking through the diary. Since they were now taking a break from the search, they realized that they were really hungry. They got up to stretch and go get something to eat when a breeze came in the window. It was just what they needed, a refreshing blast of cool air. This gave them a nice feeling as they were leaving the room to have lunch.

After looking through the items that afternoon, they returned to Tokyo on the bullet train or *shinkansen*. Their feeling was complicated. They had had a great weekend, though it had been both exciting and a bit of a letdown, too.

Once Again in Tokyo

Nonetheless, the next day when they got up, they both felt as though they couldn't wait to be in contact with the Secret Society. They were so excited to tell them about their experiences at Horyuji that they could hardly finish their breakfast of toast, baked beans and sausage that Yuri had learned to make while at Oxford. And then they came back to reality.

They realized that telling the Secret Society wouldn't be easy. They had to wait in virtual silence for the Society to contact them! On this point the Society had been very specific. They weren't even to talk among themselves of the Society. Indeed, they had to continually develop a code to converse at all about the Society. Since Bernd was from Germany the choice was made to call the Secret Society the SS linking the letters not to the Secret Society, but to the storm troopers under Nazi Germany. This was the strategy they used at times in which they felt it necessary to discuss something related even remotely to the Secret Society. They developed various code words to talk of their adventures and exploration.

With renewed effort, they found ways to talk about the Society while at the same time maintaining secrecy about what had been revealed over the last year or so. They took pains to discuss the matter without referring to anything directly or providing too many details. Even so, they realized that they would simply have to wait it out. This of course was frustrating because they so much so wanted to tell the Society of their discoveries at Horyuji that they felt as though they were about to burst.

Their wanting to be in contact with the Secret Society was practical, too. They hoped that the society could give them some clues as to where to search next, since their voyage to Horyuji ended without them being any closer to finding the star point. They realized yet again, that there were too many temples and shrines in Japan to search through each of them …at least not in one life time. They wanted some sort of help as to where to go with their exploration next. They went to sleep late that night wondering what the best way was to approach the journey to the fifth star point.

Though they were anxious, there was nothing that could be done about it. Yuri said "*shikataga nai*," which was Japanese for the recognition that nothing could be done about it. At any rate, they had something to do in the mean-time.

It was clear to both of them that if they were to become proficient at meditating they had a lot of practice to do. So they threw themselves whole-heartedly into the practice. They visited Bentenji in the spring holiday as promised and thereafter planned to go there as often as their work schedules would allow.

They made it the first few weekends in May, but then were not sure when they next would be able to go there. As they were beginners and had real interest, they already had many questions about meditating especially regarding why one would meditate. They wondered about the ultimate benefits of meditation. In fact Yuri once asked the abbot about awakening. In short, like so many who have practiced meditation before them, they wondered what they could get out of it. Abbot Kimura only chuckled and said, "It is not what you gain, but what you ultimately give up," something that left them both confused and now really wondering what it all was about. For his part Abbot Kimura asked them not to worry so much about results and to focus on the practice. There was no arguing with that, the young couple thought. They both had a lot to learn about the practice. This was for sure. This was enough, they understood, to keep them busy *for a while*.

Nonetheless when they were getting ready to leave the temple one day, Yuri just had to ask the following. "Well, sir, if you awaken, what happens then?" she quizzed Abbot Kimura. His reply without any further explanation was simply, "teach."

Though Yuri progressed quickly, the abbot at Bentenji urged her to not think much of it. "You are after all benefiting from the work of all beings, and not only yourself," he continually reminded her. At times he let her know that she may well have been benefiting from work done in a previous life, though he did not make a very big deal out of this, emphasizing that she not make a big deal of it either. Both of them were now coming to an understanding that there was enough to work through in this life time, that even if there was such a thing as past or future lives, that was just fancy wondering. The real work was the current, very real, mundane life and living it well in the present moment as it presented itself day by day.

Yuri had often wondered whether there really was a "previous life." After all, the Japanese even have a name for it, *zensei*. Yuri couldn't help wondering if it was true that her accomplishments were somehow tied to the work done previously by another being in another lifetime. She also wondered just how much of her progress was the result of efforts in this lifetime. Either way, as is often true in teacher-student relations in Asia, when she asked the abbot about her progress he gave no definite answers. Indeed, he would not even confirm whether or not he himself was an awakened being. He just didn't make a big deal out of it either way. This caused Bernd to trust him even more. The abbot simply stated, in response to many of their questions, that they would understand things by themselves if they continued practicing. Smiling he pointed out that this would happen naturally and could not be forced. Yuri, who had so many questions, had no other way of knowing the answers to the many questions that ran around in her head so it seemed that she would have to for now continue meditating … in order to find the answers. The more she understood, the more she began to think that Abbot Kimura was a right clever teacher.

However, most of the time she didn't seem to mind this waiting and meditating, and she told the monk so. The monk laughed to himself thinking that this must be since she was so young, and that this was part of her ego complex, too. He realized that while one would ultimately go at one's own pace, it was also true that a sense of urgency was useful. He did recognize, too, that there were times when Yuri really did not mind waiting, a wonderful gift indeed. The universe is so rich, they both thought.

A Picnic in the Park

While thoughts about the many events that had unfolded since they were married were constantly on their minds, the days somehow passed, and Yuri and Bernd had to completely stop talking about things related to the search not wanting to be secretive every waking hour of the day. This was for a very practical reason; they found being continually on guard to be exhausting. Neither did they wish to reveal anything that would compromise the Secret Society.

Just before pledging to never mention the Society until they met with its members again, Bernd smiled to himself, as he allowed for his last mention of the Society, though in a roundabout way, to Yuri. He noted that the name itself was extremely clever. Since in almost any age there had been "secret societies" having this society's name be simply the "Secret Society" could easily be misleading even if it were overheard. Anyone that heard someone talking about a *Secret Society* would naturally wonder what kind of Secret Society it was. As such the name itself gave nothing away. It was simple and brilliant like other things they knew about the way the Society did things. This simplicity came, they later found out, from the vast and lengthy experience of the Society.

During May, while many were enjoying one of the most pleasant seasons in Japan, and dreading the coming of the rainy season sometime in mid-June, Bernd asked Yuri to meet him for a picnic lunch. This was one of the few chances they had to get together while they were working. Bernd knew that Yuri would be dropping in on editors who worked at an office near Sophia University and that this was among the best of chances for them to get together. Yuri accepted the invitation thinking that as good an opportunity as this should not be missed. They made plans to meet with their boxed lunches, called *bento*s at a small park within the grounds of the university.

"Hey Yuri, over here," Bernd called letting her know that he had claimed a spot below a beautiful tree right beside a beautiful bed of spring flowers bursting with violets, bright yellows, pinks and whites. Yuri hurried over to where he was and gracefully sat down on the foldable roll-up reed mat that he had laid out for them. Of course she was careful to take off her shoes before placing her feet on the mat as he had before her. At first when he came to Japan he thought, *how unnecessary*, but now he thought that this made keeping the mat clean easier. Likewise, it was true that this saved it from being damaged and was certainly worth the small effort it took to remove one's shoes.

"Any trouble getting here?" he asked.

"No, not really," She replied. She continued by way of explaining that "The trains were quite empty considering the location and that it's lunchtime." She was obviously relieved to have had an easy trip. "Living in Tokyo is quite convenient, but I do miss the quiet side of living on the island," she added, while opening the bentos. It could have taken her up to ten more minutes if things had not gone well, a significant chunk of her time off for lunch. On the small island you could bike anywhere it seemed in ten minutes.

"I can imagine you do miss life on the island," Bernd said, smiling as he ate some of the deep-fried breaded chicken that they had made that morning before leaving for work. This was called *kara age* and was one of his favorite Japanese dishes. They made their own lunches because they were adamant about trying to not eat out a lot. The food they made was so much healthier than anything they could get when eating out. This was one thing they both felt strongly about. He was off now to eating, and they both knew his smile meant there was no turning back his chopsticks cutting the spring air. Yuri joined him, and they sat enjoying their lunches on a warm and sunny spring day, content in the quiet space shared between them. Her chopsticks or *o-hashi* were made out of cherry wood. They were a gift from her mother when she left home to go overseas the first time years ago. She only took this pair out for special occasions such as a picnic with her husband.

Yuri brought out some tea just as Bernd was finishing the side dish of boiled spinach topped with soy sauce and sesame seeds called *o-hitashi*. He held up his cup with two hands appreciating her kindness in getting the tea ready for them both. She was happy that he had remembered to bring his cup, because she hated to use throw away cups dreading the waste. The earthy, slightly bitter and almost sweet green tea was a great finish to lunch. They both were enjoying tea when they were interrupted suddenly. Just before Bernd could get out the pastries he purchased for desert on the way to the picnic spot it happened.

A man walking by them dropped a stack of papers that he was carrying. The couple got up to help him arrange and pick up the many papers before they could blow away in the light, spring breeze.

"Hi, Bernd and Yuri, long time no see," came the cheerful voice of the delegate from India. He looked the part of a visiting professor, even being a bit stereotypically clumsy, Yuri thought.

"Oh my god, it's …" she belted out excited to see him.

"Contain yourself, please," he quickly added cutting her off. "I know we haven't seen each other for awhile, I am excited, too," he said. And then by way of a cover for her loud outburst he said only slightly above normal speaking level, "When are you coming to India to study again?" He asked hoping that this would cover her gaffe.

Bernd and Yuri were beaming and let the delegate take the lead from that point forward. He set the time and place of their next meeting pretending that the *grand hall* was a place where plans were being made for students going to India this summer for a seminar on Hinduism and that they would be welcomed to join in on the meeting if they still had an interest in Indian culture.

He then quieted his voice, and told them concisely "Go to the grand hall tonight. Arrive an hour after sunset." They were to enter through the side door that could be accessed next to the window they had come in. He also told them when they looked puzzled to trust him, that he had to go, and that someone would be there to help them get in.

At Long Last the Couple Visits the Grand Hall Again

That night promptly an hour after sunset they showed up on the side of the building they had entered before. Though both of them were puzzled thinking there was no door, at least none that could be seen with normal eyes. So there they were on time now waiting not only a little confused, but also a little impatiently. The moon was not visible yet, only the first planets and stars shone in the western sky. It was not yet completely dark nor was it any longer light out. Being as such gave them a kind of in between feeling.

They noticed these subtleties so much more nowadays. Not only were they more in tune to the changes in the night time sky, but because of their meditation practice they now took greater care in noticing what was going on with their bodies and feelings. That is why Yuri now could tell by the tingling of her spine that she was energized and ready for this night. Bernd, too, noticed how he was tired from the work he'd done that day. Both of them consciously slowed down and renewed their focus for the events that no doubt would unfold yet tonight. Both knew that most likely the night was still young.

Neither was concerned for long, however, as the fire escape alongside of the window rotated to lay flat along the building and became a ladder to the second story. Again, they were surprised by how simple and yet effective the workings of the Secret Society were. The fire escape as it had been, looked entirely out of use, and did again once it was turned back and allowed to hang off-kilter the way it had been hanging before it was rotated by some unseen person or machine. This happened after they climbed up as noiselessly as they could to the second floor "apartment." They had entered the building through a window that was nearly as big as a door. They could not help but notice how quickly the fire escape was returned to its original position as soon as they were inside. The timing was very precise. No time was wasted.

Once inside what they saw was some kind of lab obviously belonging to the members of the Secret Society. It was clear, too, that anyone who walked by the window directly below could be seen from inside on the monitors that hung on the wall to the right of the window they had just entered.

In answer to the amazed looks on both Bernd and Yuri's faces, the reply came. "Yes, that's right we can see any activity outside the window below us, and all around the building." It was the voice of the delegate from Greece.

"You mean you have always been able to see us coming and going?" spoke up Yuri, a bit incredulously.

"No, we installed the observation mirrors after we found out that you two were coming in this way." The Society had brilliantly installed cameras that fed wireless video of the goings on around the building. The cameras were in mirrors erected to help traffic move safely along narrow roadways. The delegate from Greece went on, "We can't allow anyone to get that close again," she admitted matter-of-factly. "At least not get so close without our knowing about it," the delegate said with a shudder and a sigh of relief at the new observation system that was now in place.

"Nor without being invited," the Indian delegate, who had met them earlier that day, added with a smile as he entered the room.

It was the policy of the Society to learn from its mistakes as there inevitably would be mistakes, and it was also policy to not make a big deal out of it. These two policies solved what had been seemingly endless arguments that wasted sometimes decades while members blamed each other for things gone wrong, maps that were overlooked, people who went missing ....

"There is simply blind luck sometimes, too, you know, that keeps our activities secret." The Greek delegate added. "It could be the workings of an unseen universe," she mused. And then, she left the room obviously off for some previously arranged errand the most likely being to tell of their arrival.

A moment later the delegate from Tibet came in and let them know that the delegate from Greece had informed the group of Yuri and Bernd's arrival, and as such all were now waiting for them. It was his duty to see that they safely and quietly made it down to the chambers three stories below. The Indian gladly assisted, not by taking over, but by being of service in any way that he could. He, too, made sure that the couple was sure to get to where they needed to go as smoothly as possible.

Bernd was almost about to ask what had been meant by three stories below, when Yuri guessed what he was thinking. She recalled and now pointed out to Bernd that the delegate from Egypt had disappeared into the archway, when they had been one story below the ground level. As she was saying this, Bernd, too, remembered that he had disappeared by making a curving decent. His feet disappearing first and then finally his maroon hood, too. Three floors down made sense now that they were on the second floor.

Next, they found themselves two levels below ground with people talking at their normal volume, hushed tones being unnecessary. They were in a considerably smaller group of people than when they were with the entire assembly on the previous occasion with whom they had eaten together. It was a smaller room this time. The Egyptian delegate was the next one to speak to them. He began with a word of caution for the two.

"Of course we in Egypt thought that the talk of stars, evident in almost every message found was a reference to sky. To Egyptians, the sky which is home to not only the stars, but also the moon or the sun immediately gave rise to thoughts of Osiris, the god of resurrection, the sun and the moon. This threw members of our society off for centuries." The last part of the Egyptian's statement was said with an emphasis on the word "centuries." "Many also thought that Ra, the god of the cyclical sun was what we should be looking for. It was a confusing time for the Society in Egypt. Arguments continued even after finding several star points around the world with no mention or hint of the moon or sun.

At first, of course, the Society was located only in Egypt. That was because that was where the first star point was found in what we consider to be the *modern period* of this quest. The modern period began once the quest was picked up again so to speak. The *early period* had ended after the first groups had gone out and gotten lost so to speak. The modern period began about one thousand years ago now. Another point wasn't found for five hundred or more years, a long time to wait, for any society, don't you think?"

"Oh, I see," cried Yuri in her energetic though rather abrupt way. She wasn't able to contain herself any longer. She continued blurting out, "We think we know what the symbol or *star* point might have been in Japan, though we cannot confirm where it was or for sure if what we found is the star point indicator yet."

"What do you mean where it was?" the Egyptian shot back a little confused and in disbelief. "It was on the island, right?"

"Well, we think we have found it or some clues about it that will help in our search. And if these clues have anything to do with the actual star point it is no wonder that it hadn't been found until now." Yuri and Bernd looked at each other when she had said, with emphasis, the word star. She went on.

"It had been hidden for many hundreds of years even with the clues to its significance still in place. Of course I mean the island where I was born" she said finishing this all rather quickly in her excitement. She was positively beaming at their potential discovery and the chance to finally tell the Society about it.

"You just heard me talk of Osiris and Ra, right?" the Egyptian replied.

"Yes, of course," stated Bernd flatly, his sense of caution rising at the Egyptian's words. Bernd's tone was cautious, but an attempt to urge others to listen, too. They had been waiting to divulge their discovery for what felt to the couple like a very, very long time. It felt more like years than the months that it had actually been. This did not go unnoticed by Society members present including the Egyptian.

"Well, don't get me wrong. Any news is good news, of course, but we've been wrong so many times before that we must be absolutely sure before we take further action," he said dramatically."I mean we must explore the finding in detail to confirm as much as possible before spreading the news of another "star point." The last time we sent out a false alarm, there were hurt feelings that perhaps did not go away, it would seem until those people, how do you say it in English, *passed on?*"

"We understand," said Yuri, the excitement slowly leaving her face, her eyes as watchful as ever.

"Do you think there is any way to be sure of what you found?" The Tibetan asked as compassionately as he could, clearly having noticed their stunned caution.

"Well, we would like to try," Bernd spoke up. "We are also hoping that you all can help point us in the direction as to where to look next. Especially we'll need your assistance if what we found turns up to be nothing other than an interesting artifact. Yuri smiled inside as she noticed that Bernd unwittingly used the phrase *You all* that could have come from the South in the United States. Of course she knew that it would be stated *Ya'll* in the US. She smiled to herself now, too, as she thought that it might be said in the United Kingdom as "You lot." She blushed a little realizing that it is a bit casual and as such might be considered disrespectful for the members of this community. She was relieved by the continued calm in the room as the members present listened carefully to Bernd. Bernd went on.

"We originally thought we found the point and where it had been knocked down from. Now we realize from talking to the abbot of Horyuji about Prince Shotoku's diary that it was only a piece of wood that had fallen. I mean something had fallen from a burning pagoda at Horyuji, a temple in Nara Prefecture, Japan. On top of that the event actually happened much later than when the Prince lived. The fire had occurred during the Warring States Period. The abbot told us of a piece of wood or perhaps a Buddhist image that may have fallen. If that is the truth, it means that it was not a star point that had fallen at all. We thought from the clue on Yuri's island that the star point had something to do with the pagoda at Horyuji. It was our feeling about this as much as anything that led us to search there.

"Horyuji is a good place to look," the Egyptian continued noting that its buildings were among the oldest existing structures in Japan. He was well studied in the history of Japan as were other members of the society who had been assigned to Japan and therefore present this night. Indeed, being the foremost scholar on Japan among the members of the Secret Society was the reason why the Egyptian was leading the meetings in Japan. A close second to his knowledge of the archipelago was the Tibetan delegate. In other areas it would be someone else leading who was an expert and knowledgeable of that place.

The Secret Society collaborated and shared responsibilities among its members according to ability and need. Upon finding this out, Yuri was very pleased as this made perfect sense to her. She was not one to be bound by tradition that may have relied heavily on the age of a delegate, for example, if they were following Japanese cultural sensitivities. For her, if talent or ability existed, it should be utilized she thought. She noticed how this had changed ever so slightly since she began meditating. She now thought, too, one should do what is necessary, but not in a way that tramples on another's traditions. Her friend's father who was married to tradition now came to mind. He relied on tradition as something that helped him to make sense out of the world in which he lived. It did not seem right to upset his understanding by pointing out inconsistencies in his way of doing things. This would serve no other point than to simply upset him. This did not seem anything like the compassion of which she was now learning about from her meditation teachers and through her own experiences. People could be encouraged to stretch their minds further, but trampling over their understandings was not all right, she now thought. Her thoughts returned to Horyuji. Mostly to herself, but stating it out loud nonetheless, Yuri admitted that there was no conclusive evidence of a star point at Horyuji. Indeed, the only thing confirmed was that the piece of wood fell off of the pagoda. This of course meant that they still had no idea where in if even at Horyuji a star point was hidden. She mentioned the couple's wish for assistance in thinking about the next place to search beyond their exploration at Horyuji.

"You may want to try any other old structures like Horyuji, or any places linked to exchange along the Silk Road," the Egyptian added. He let them know that finding a place with connections to the Silk Road such as Yakushiji temple may point them in the right direction simply because the connection would be very old. Indeed, he pointed out that Yakushiji was connected to Buddhism coming to Japan in the early days in the sixth century. Buddhism, he noted …" had come to Japan along…"

"The Silk Road," Bernd finished his statement for him.

"Thank you. That is very helpful to know. It seems that we are looking in the right direction," Yuri replied ever hopeful.

"We brought you here tonight not expecting that you had found the point, but in order to let you know that we are still with you. We felt that you might begin to feel disconnected from us. In fact, after much debate and many discussions we have also decided to make you an offer," he stated with great gravity, and then he paused. He loved drama as much as he enjoyed meeting new people. Tonight would be some of both he hoped as he believed he would get to know the young couple better this evening.

He smiled and went on. "We've found you two to be unusually reliable and very capable of keeping the knowledge of the Society to yourselves. This is truly remarkable. Usually the level of integrity shown by you both is found in, how shall I say it now? It is found in, well, older people." He looked at them now, patiently and considerately wondering what they were thinking, and giving them time to think. Then, wanting to be finished with the drama, he went on, and at last he asked, "Would you like to be initiated into the Secret Society?" the question that had been on the minds of everyone present and a few absent members, too.

"Of course!" This time Bernd was the first to speak. He had read about so many societies such as the Knights Templar that he was excited at the proposition. He was also honored to be asked to join not thinking that they had even been considered for induction into the Society. After all, they had met the members of the society not so long ago. He would have thought that they would have to earn membership somehow by doing something daring, risky or special. He thought that there would be some sort of requirement for membership. He did not realize that their honesty, sincerity and trust did just that, prove their suitability.

When the members of the Society discussed offering them membership in the Society, the couple was considered more than qualified for membership. They possessed the one crucial quality that all members possessed even if in varying degrees, *trustworthiness*. And in the case of this young couple clearly it was tempered with integrity.

"We believe that you have made every effort to keep our society secret. We think this is true because of what you have not done. Unlike others we have met over the centuries, you have not forced us to abandon a long-term meeting place such as this building by continually coming to see if we are here or not. This has happened repeatedly in any number of places. You have not talked about us with your neighbors, either, we feel since they have not come around looking into the windows, calling at the door, wandering outside …. Please consider our proposal together quietly for a few moments.

"That won't be necessary. We are with you," Yuri stated convincingly and with conviction. No one had even had time to move to bring them tea, the usual protocol for giving potential members time to consider agreeing to such a big commitment. It seemed Yuri was proving her unique capacity as the one who had asked about the symbols on the floor of a hospital in Alexandria, Egypt. Normally delegates would have left the room, though guarded the door, while the prospects conversed in private either amongst themselves or with a member of the group with whom they felt comfortable discussing the matter. This was especially true if there was only one potential new member who needed someone to discuss their feelings with or had questions. Nonetheless, it was a personal choice, and it was made crystal clear to potential members that they could join, but were also free to refuse membership as well. Refusal would require moving their meeting place in Japan to another building, but that was a common story now for the past few centuries anyway. In this case they were lucky. They had been able to keep the number of places they met with the young couple to only the building in which was housed the grand hall.

This method was protocol to be sure but not always easily done. A potential member might take quite some time to get to know before being offered membership. And during that time they may have been to more than one meeting place of the Secret Society. At any rate this young couple seemingly needed no time to discuss the matter.

"Fine," continued the delegate from Egypt, pleased that this was so straightforward. "Will you be able to come back in July? That will give us time to contact important members of our society who are not here now," he said seriously. The couple did not know that this, too, was a sort of test, a check on their seriousness, commitment and suitability for membership.

"We can come back in July," the couple said in unison, however they also shared the thought that they wished it could happen even yet that very evening.

"In the meantime please keep looking for clues," urged the Tibetan. Confirm in any way you can the findings you have come across so far.

"And we will contact you from time to time to find out what you've uncovered," said the delegate from India. We still have faith in you. Perhaps it is our past mistakes more than anything that gives us cause for caution now," he went on to say encouragingly. "That is why we once again, are not going into great detail at this time," he explained in a tone that conveyed respect for the couple and their recent achievements.

"Yuri, we must go and give it our best effort at another temple. It is important to know if the place we have found is anything special or not, something truly "wonderful." We can only do this by checking out other temples that may be of significance regarding the star points. By the way, if we are wrong then there are only about 20,000 more temples to explore in Japan," Bernd said jokingly. "And countless shrines, too," he added now laughing out loud.

With this she and the Society members assembled there smiled, and Yuri realized again how glad she was to be married to him. Her hand brushed his, though did not make a heavy and obvious contact. Her feminine, Japanese side showed in this subtle, yet sensitive gesture that was missed by nearly all present except for some of the Society members standing near enough to feel the positive energy between the couple.

After some general discussion about what to bring to the initiation in July, which would, of course, include a small party to get reacquainted, the couple left to return home. They realized that the Secret Society liked to socialize and that celebrating being together was indeed a major focus of the Society.

It all ended, it seemed, as soon as it began, Bernd thought. Yuri, too, felt that it had all gone so fast after such a long wait to be reconnected with the Secret Society.

It was funny she thought, that life was so unpredictable. She was, as in the past, still fascinated by it all, but now found that she was increasingly accepting of the fleeting nature of life. You could not get any of it back, she thought, and as she was thinking this, something reverberated through her being. She had no clear, logical meaning of what it was, but it left her sort of vaguely feeling, "Why would you need to get any of it back?" and then she felt a little chill run down her spine, and her body quivered lightly.

She considered, while they were taking a long, meandering walk back to their apartment, that Bernd had a good sense of people. At least that is what she told him later that night when they were home and snug in their futons. She came to this conclusion because of the quickness of his response to join the Society that night. "A good sense about people …for a scientist," she said while smiling at him. They had some tender moments together and slept well renewing their strength and intention for the ongoing search for the star point in Japan.

The next day, Saturday was spent relaxing, drinking tea on the veranda and staying at home without anything special to do. This was a much needed day of rest. It seemed they almost never just "stayed home." When discussing this over lunch that day, they noted how this seemed a hazard of living in the twenty-first century.

And then that evening, as Yuri was about to fall asleep, she could not have known that she was thinking the exact same thing as Bernd, but she was. Both were thinking that even if the Prince's star had anything to do with the "star point" in Japan, it was going to be a challenge to confirm this. Both also realized that if this was the final star point they would then have to figure out the connection between all of the star points and further, where they came from, the origin. What *was* the point of origin, she wondered?

So first, before searching for the origin, there was other work to be done. They would have to confirm their findings either useful or not at Horyuji. They would do this in part by searching in and comparing any connections to something that resembles a star point at other ancient temples. This would allow them to determine where the star point might be or to find a clue as to where the star point had been or maybe still is! They would have to rule out Horyuji as being anything special in their search or rule out other temples as the logical repository of the star point in Japan or both. It really seemed as though it would be a daunting task. It could potentially take many, many years.

The next day they awoke refreshed and ready to renew the search. They were glad that neither of them had to work on Saturdays or Sundays.

"Bernd, have you read about other old temples in Japan?" Yuri asked.

"Don't be so sure it is at a temple," Bernd cautioned.

"Now come on, help me with this," she implored.

"Well I don't know how old it is, but isn't Shitennouji one of the temples in the 33 temple pilgrimage route of Kansai?" he asked. "It has traditionally been a meeting place of people coming from Wakayama and Nara into Osaka, too," he added as he was considering their options.

"And that brings to mind the 88 temple walking pilgrimage of Shikoku, you know," Yuri said, almost exasperated at the thought of going to them all and having to figure out how to explore them, confirm star points or even decide where to begin.

"Well, you know," Bernd began, "I really want to go to the flea market at Shitennouji. It would be a good excuse to go. It's held on the twenty-first of the month rain or shine, right?

"I don't know about rain or shine, but it is a big flea market, and it is regular, too," Yuri conceded. She hadn't been there, but had heard a lot about it from a friend who lived near the temple. The market was a bit cosmopolitan, too. There even used to be an Australian man who sold Buddhist wares there, but he stopped selling there years ago now, her friend in Osaka said. She missed his use of *Osaka-ben*, the regional dialect. He was not only good at speaking Japanese he was light-hearted about many things, too.

"What about Yakushiji? Yuri reminded them both of what the members of the Secret Society had said.

"Well, we can go there, too, but I happened to remember reading of Shitennouji first," Bernd replied realizing that it didn't really matter which one they began with since they could go to either. "Anyway there were so many temples," he now considered out loud …. In the end, since it really didn't matter, they settled on going to Shitennouji at least first.

For some reason Bernd began to get lost in thought. He considered that one of the hard parts about learning Japanese was that words or characters more often than not have two or more readings. So the reading Shitennouji was more complicated than at first it might seem. Since the character for "ji" was the same as "tera" or temple, how was one to be sure which reading to use he mused? Another example was the Temple of the Pure Water or Kiyomizu temple in Kyoto that was called in Japanese Kiyomizudera not Kiyomizuji. And in addition to the two readings he now recognized a third. "dera" for "tera." It made for interesting learning, though it also sometimes made his head spin. He went out onto the porch for some fresh air. Yuri followed.

They were both interested now, and so they made plans to go to Shitennouji the next weekend even if it meant traveling all the way to Osaka from Tokyo and coming back the same day a trip called *higaeri* in Japanese. They would have to decide whether or not to stay overnight in a hotel.

Yuri sat down to write a post card to that same friend, who was living in Osaka near Shitennouji. They had met when they were in Oxford. Yuri hoped that she and Bernd could stay at her friend's place, though that was not an easy thing to propose. Going with Japanese custom, staying over at someone's home was not common at all, and if it were to happen, it had to be offered, not asked for. The one thing in their favor was that Yuri's friend had lived abroad. She may or may not be stuck in this regard on Japanese custom. It was decided that even if they needed to stay in a hotel, they would go. Finally, it was planned that Yakushiji would be the next place they went to explore after going to Shitennouji. At least that was their plan for that day.

The Next Weekend in Osaka

Bernd wasted no time. It was Saturday night, and Osaka was where they found themselves, and that meant just one thing to him *okonomiyaki* a specialty food in Osaka. He wasn't sure if the deep-fried breaded pork called *tonkatsu* or *okonimiyaki* was his favorite Japanese food, for he loved them both. Okonomiyaki is often described as a Japanese pancake, but Bernd thought it was better to describe it as a cabbage filled pancake. To him it was more along the lines of potato pancakes he had eaten when his family visited the United States. He made okonomiyaki at home, and he even considered himself a bit of an okonomiyaki artist or technician. For him this meant someone who can flip okonomiyaki without having it fall to pieces no matter what size the thick pancake-like food took. He liked his with thinly sliced pork and cheese. He really liked smothering it in the special "okonomiyaki" sauce and putting on the green sea weed flakes. He did not, however, like the *katsuo* fish shavings called *katsuobushi* that others rave about. When put on top of okonomiyaki they waved in the heat as it rises off the cake, and this he felt was downright *creepy*. He thought maybe someday he might be able to stomach them, but for now he thought, *No thanks*. On the other hand, he was proud of himself for enjoying *nattou*, a dish made from fermented beans. He got used to this food because he had heard of how healthy it was. Now he loved to eat it mixed with mustard and over rice in the way it is often served.

Fortunately, Yuri's friend and her husband offered to put them up for the weekend of which Sunday was the twenty-first day of the month. After spending Saturday night with their friends in Osaka, the next day Yuri, Bernd and the couple, Tomiko and Hiroshi went to the flea market. They were having coffee after a morning of shopping at the various stalls, when Yuri had an idea.

"Hey Bernd, why don't we go to the pagoda and see if it is open or not?" she suggested.

"Sure, why not," he replied sarcastically thinking that there would be no way for them to get into the Pagoda assuming that it would be closed to the public.

"I heard that you can go up any of the tiers in this pagoda," Tomiko noted, putting the couple at ease before there was a chance of having to "have tea on the veranda" as they called their cooling down time after a fight.

"I'm not so sure," Hiroshi warned. "What if it's closed because of the flea market?" He looked worried wanting their guests to have a good time.

"Well, let's try and see, and if it isn't open it's no big deal," Yuri jumped in. She wanted to give it a try before Hiroshi could lead the discussion some other way so he wouldn't lose face by showing the visitors a "bad time." Hiroshi, too, was relieved. Bernd, caught only part of the meaning of this banter and considered how complicated social relations can be in Japan.

So it was decided that after the coffee shop they would return to the temple grounds and give entering the pagoda a try. Soon they found themselves climbing the pagoda having been rushed in so that others would not follow in behind them. It wasn't that it was closed on the days of the flea market so much as the monks acting as caretakers did not want everyone up there wandering around with so many important items stored there. On flea market days the crowd was noticeably more *diverse* than on other days the monks noted. It was obvious that the monks were making an effort to not say that *bad* or *dangerous* people come to the temple on market days. What they said instead was "*Iro iro na hito ga kuru*" that in Japanese meant literally *various people come* to the flea market. Bernd understood what they meant. Their focus, however, was the pagoda and its contents, so they all moved along the stairs further into the pagoda without further conversation.

Had they not been with Bernd, the professor from Germany, they likely would not have gotten in. The monks wanted to protect the memorials and items placed on shelves commemorating, for example, those who donated money to the temple. There were also items commemorating the anniversary dates of those who had passed away and had held prominent positions at the temple among other things. The monks did not want insincere people wandering in the pagoda without some sort of reverence for the items displayed within. A scholar, they deemed, would ostensibly do no harm.

On the third floor they saw plaques and statues of members of Shitennouji who had been important monks, contributors to the temple etc .... It was a kind of museum of anyone who had given anything whether it was service or money to the temple. The list of memorials included former monks and abbots of the temple.

Bernd and Yuri looked at each other wondering if the other was thinking the same thing. *Did the inside of the pagoda at Horyuji have any clues for them?* After all, wasn't the Prince the main benefactor to the construction of Horyuji?

They made parting greetings and thanked Hiroshi and Tomiko for their hospitality and prepared for the train ride to Tokyo. They'd welcome the couple anytime they chose to come to Tokyo.

When they were able to talk on their own, while waiting for the train back to Tokyo on the tracks in the JR Osaka Station in Umeda, they discussed the possibility of finally confirming once and for all whether or not Horyuji held any significance for their search. They would have to somehow get into the pagoda. That might not be as easy as the one at Shitennouji, but they would have to see. For the time being, exploring Yakushiji would have to wait. Horyuji seemed more pressing. Yuri became as determined as ever once again. Bernd wondered from which side of her family came such determination. Either way he thought it made her even more attractive as a partner. She was a combination of determination and positive attitude. This made her incredibly interesting, he mused.

Getting Back to Horyuji after a Brief Time Away

In early July after working for several weeks and completing the dictionary project that Yuri had been working on, they finally had a slower period at work. This gave them the opportunity to get away for a few days to go to Horyuji. Being finished with the project was helpful in that they would be able to leave around noon on Friday as opposed to in the early hours of Saturday giving them almost a whole extra day to explore. Yuri was able to arrange nearly a week away from work. Bernd of course had the summer off as he worked at a university. July was a little busy as the term would formally end in mid-July, but he could fill in grades in the middle of the month as well as at the beginning so there was no hurry to finish right away. He knew the trip was coming, so he had already begun this work.

"What a relief, to have almost a week off. My boss was really glad that I was taking my vacation in part now and later in July instead of during the o-bon ancestral festival," Yuri stated relieved that the Horyuji trip would finally happen. She also noted how so many people in Japan took time off of work around August fifteenth the date of the o-bon Festival. At that time the highways and byways become crowded with the sudden onslaught of people, cars and trains. Therefore she, too, was glad that they were traveling in early July and not mid-August. The only drawback would be that she would not be able to go to the island at that time and be with her family, dance the traditional *bon odori* or *o-bon* dance and hear the drumming of the *taiko* or Japanese drum that accompanied the dancers helping them to keep the beat and rhythm of the dance.

At *o-bon* time people go back to their *furusato* or hometown in which they were raised to get together with family. Family members out of respect for their ancestors welcome back the souls of deceased ancestors and honor their family lineage.

Yuri was not only relieved that she was able to get time off from work, but also feeling like she was finally able to breathe again, having finished the dictionary project. She had been under a lot of stress and was now feeling tired from it. She had practiced deep breathing a lot and became even more interested in meditation, hoping that it would help her not feel so stressed out while working on these projects.

She noticed now more than ever, that work life was quite different from student life. There were many expectations that were not around while she excelled at her studies. Bernd told her that she was making a big deal out of this, since it was so obvious to him that she continued to excel at what she was doing. All she could do was to sigh.

"I'm glad that you told them you would be taking more of your vacation later this month," Bernd said smiling. "I wouldn't want to go to initiation without you," he said pushing her lightly with his shoulder. She responded by putting her arms around him and giving him a warm hug. They smiled at each other enjoying the closeness. And then a jolt went through Yuri suddenly.

"Quiet Bernd, you know we are not allowed to talk about it," she said, hoping to make him look around. She knew, however, that he had taken the necessary precautions, and no one was in earshot. She, too, had looked around to survey the scene as she put her arms around him. Indeed, he had made sure that no one was around let alone nearby. She was relieved, too, because this look around for her proved that no one was watching them hug. And while she was not a conformist, she was aware that it might make others uncomfortable to see them embrace in public. This is because in Japan public affection, while not being scorned, was not common either. She smiled, too, because though he had taken the necessary precaution, Bernd, not being able to help himself did look around to make sure again. Yuri smiled at his sense of caution. They enjoyed teasing each other.

"Let's get moving, the train will depart, soon," she urged. They quickened their pace and hurried along the train platform to ride the *shinkansen* or bullet train. Having only several days, they took express trains each leg of their trip. While this was pretty expensive, it did get them to Horyuji in one day. They now called the abbot hoping that he would not be against them coming to the temple right away, even though it was kind of late for visitors at this time in the early evening whether it was Horyuji or any other temple.

"Well, what brings you two back so soon?" the abbot said into the phone. And then, having enjoyed their company so much on previous visits he continued purposefully not allowing them to answer, "By all means come at once. You must be tired after traveling all day. Let's talk more after you arrive. What time will you be arriving?"

"You are very kind," responded Bernd. And Yuri breathed a sigh of relief. Their time was limited, so getting in tonight was very helpful. Bernd was hoping to set the time at only a few minutes from then since the couple was already near the temple.

They realized that they could not spend a lot of time there. They thought that if nothing came of their search tonight, they would have time to begin circling the 33 temple route of the Kansai region perhaps as early as tomorrow. "We are on the promenade along the street that runs right up to the temple the one lined with tourist shops and restaurants. If it is not inconvenient, may we meet you at the front gate in a couple of minutes?"

Bernd asked this hoping they could meet right away and that the pagoda would be in full view from the gate as even now the evening was gaining on the day. On this trip finally, Bernd would be able to ask the distinction between the Japanese words *nyourai* and *bosatsu*. The Japanese words ran through his mind as he was now on the phone with the abbot. That is if he did not forget to ask the many questions on his mind in his excitement created by actually being back at Horyuji again. He really began to like Horyuji. It started to feel like his temple home in Japan. And he thought to himself, *interesting*. Until recently he wouldn't have thought that this was possible having been raised in a German Lutheran family.

"I will see you there presently," the abbot graciously replied. Fortunately, he had finished his rounds of the temple and was sure that there were no stragglers hanging about. The grounds were empty aside from the normal staff, monks in training .... It was his night to make the rounds. He did not leave it up to only his students. He taught responsibility by being responsible. He was a master of organization, persistence and consistency.

The couple arrived to find the abbot waiting for them at the appointed place. Though the abbot had suggested on the phone that they were back soon, Bernd began the conversation with "It has been a while, hasn't it?" in perfect Japanese that was both polite and incorporated the proper use of honorifics. The abbot was visibly impressed, though considerate enough to spare Bernd any comments about how good his Japanese was. Having met many foreigners who were good at Japanese, the abbot realized that when they knew what they were saying, as Bernd clearly did, there was no need to comment on the proficiency. The benefit was in being able to speak a foreign language, and any comments about it were unnecessary and could possibly be taken as patronizing. Bernd appreciated this wisdom.

"Do come in, you two. What a joy to see you again. Are you still practicing meditation?" he inquired directly, taking them a little off guard.

"She more than I," Bernd admitted, while recovering from the direct question, adding his sense of humor to the reply. "Though, I enjoy it, too," he continued quickly not wanting to sound lazy.

"If you continue, it will not all be enjoyable," the abbot retorted. He smiled after looking at their once again surprised faces. "Nothing to worry about," he added in earnest. "It's all good."

"Thank you for meeting us at the gate," Yuri said, bringing them all back to the business at hand. "I was hoping that we could see the beautiful pagoda in the moonlight." Bernd was amazed that they had been thinking almost exactly the same thing. On second thought he was getting more used to it now.

The abbot brought them to a spot where the moon hung above the pagoda and where the pagoda itself was reflected in a puddle left from the rain that had fallen in fits and sprinkles earlier that day. "From here, this is my favorite night view especially after it rains as you can see," he said. "It is really too bad that we cannot trust people more and allow the temple to be open to the public at night. It has never been open to the public at night. From the beginning, when this temple was young it was guarded, and then in the warring states period in Japan even the monks were forced to take sides almost everywhere," he lamented.

"I have read just a little about the warring states period in Japan," Bernd joined in. "It really sounds like it was a harsh time to live in Japan," he finished seriously, though admittedly unsure. Secretly he hoped that the abbot would inform them further about this period of history in Japan. But that is not what happened.

By way of reply all the abbot said was, "It was a hard time." They noticed the stern, contemplative look on his face. Neither of the couple pursued the topic further.

Again, Yuri chimed in hoping to change the subject. "Abbot Furuta, we were wondering something, I mean remember about your research?" she said turning to Bernd.

"Yes, I was at Shitennouji and had the good fortune to be shown the memorials in the pagoda there. I'm chronicling the founding of the temples on the 33 and 88 temple pilgrimage sites of the Kii and Shikoku areas of Japan. Therefore, being allowed into the pagoda at Shitennouji was very helpful. It gave me some insight into the age of the temple and certain developments since the beginning of the temple. I wonder if you have anything of significance in the pagoda here, too?" he asked boldly. "I mean is that a common practice in Japan?" he asked, embarrassed about being so bold.

"Well, I haven't been in there for a long time myself. My apprentices do much of the cleaning now," the abbot said matter-of-factly while scratching his chin thoughtfully. "I do make the rounds to ensure that they are cleaning it, however, like I said, I haven't been in there in a while." He finished thinking that he would have to clean in there for himself again sometime soon. "There are a few things of interest in the pagoda, but I think you should experience them for yourselves, not have me try and tell you about them," he said. Though he was being more practical than anything, he came across as mysterious to the couple.

He went on, "There's no reason we can't go in there now. Though, we will have to take along a light of course, won't we?" As he mentioned this he was smiling at the two young people who for some reason made him either feel young or remember his youth. He wasn't sure which feeling it was nor why they made him feel this way, but it was such a good feeling that he didn't care. He felt an easy unity with them in a way he did not with other young people around their age. He felt as though he was happy to help them in any way he could. He felt that they were in earnest, just as he had the first time that he met them. And that was what he continued to appreciate, especially in such young people.

He led now as they all walked along the stone path to the pagoda. Either side of the path was lined with pebbles that had been carefully raked and were so daily. Bernd noticed that the pebbles were now askew with the footsteps of the many visitors of the day. The temple had trees planted here and there that were elegantly pruned as well. They stopped briefly as they neared the entrance to the pagoda, something that gave them an opportunity to take it all in again.

From where they stood, Yuri noticed that Bernd's shadow was perfectly aligned with the shadow cast by the pagoda. The shadows were parallel to each other. She made a snapshot of this in her mind's eye. As they began moving again, the abbot smiled as he saw the two young people instinctively hold hands as they neared the building. He held the door open for them, and they entered.

"Wow, what is that?" exclaimed Bernd in amazement.

"That is an artifact from along the silk road. When Prince Shotoku went back to China to learn about Confucian principles in greater detail he also learned much about how Buddhism had traveled to China along the Silk Road. He brought this back with him. It's a scroll from somewhere along the Silk Road between present day Xian and Dunhuang. On it is written the Lotus Sutra," he divulged, his voice now animated. He explained that the Lotus Sutra was an ancient and significant Buddhist teaching.

"Three floors up there was an artifact from the Prince, but that was burnt in the fire the story goes. It, too, was something that came to us from him and was originally from somewhere along the Silk Road, I am told. No one knows what it was. It was one of many items lost in the fire. What damage a stray arrow can cause, eh? It is a shame that we have no record of what the item was."

"Is there anything for us to see in here," Yuri asked. "I mean anything that would help Bernd understand more about the founding of the temple?" she said, wanting to seem as though they were on a scholarly mission.

"Well, let's take a look. As for the usefulness of anything here that is really up to Bernd, isn't it?" he smiled again.

"Can we go up these stairs?" Bernd asked. And with a nod from the abbot, they turned to go up the stairs.

All of a sudden someone was at the door calling for the abbot. He had an appointment or something came up regarding dinner, and this was a disciple informing him of some kind of urgent matter.

Therefore, the abbot gave his leave making it clear to the two that they could look, but not touch the items in the pagoda. He had said this half seriously and half tongue in cheek, as he was not really concerned now trusting them both completely. He gave them the light he was carrying, and then he was off. There was one condition to their search, however. The couple had to promise to check in with him before they left for the night. Yuri thought that this was only what could be considered a normal expectation in Japan, but also wondered why the abbot had made and extra effort to be sure of this before leaving them. He must have been interested in some way regarding their *research*.

"I can't believe it. Perhaps what we are looking for was right up there on the third floor, and now it is gone. We have no way of knowing what was up there nor its significance," Bernd complained. Both of them were, however, wondering the same thing. Was it the star or not? They also both had the same concern. Would there be any way of knowing that the bronze star had been up there or not.

"Don't be so sure of anything yet, Bernd. Remember the warning by the Secret Society," Yuri shot back right away speaking slowly to add extra caution to her tone of voice. All of this of course was done in code.

"I'm sure you're right to be cautious," Bernd said with resignation. "But we have to go see either way."

"What are we waiting for," Yuri replied, and they began to climb the stairs. In usual fashion she had now left him behind and began the ascent only to have him hurrying along to catch up. Bernd imagined several ninja stealthily sneaking up into the pagoda to view the countryside from the small spaces to look out of that were in place of windows. The thought of ninja at night made him shutter. They were so famous for stealth that they could be there with them now, and neither would know it. He recalled the make up of a ninja house he had seen and how there were purposefully false walls and moving trap doors and the like built into it.

Then it came to him. He still wanted to make sure of what they could by going to the third floor, but if nothing else came of their trip, he desperately wanted to find out if the original blueprints for the pagoda and the temple still existed. Then, while this intriguing thought ran through his mind Yuri shrieked having arrived on the third floor before him. He hurried to the landing and saw now, too, what she saw …. He found his way following the trail of light coming from the flashlight she held out for him to see his way up the stairs ….

What caused Yuri to shriek was that on the third floor there was a small hole in the wall. She noticed that when the moon was full, as it was this night, the hole allowed the moon light to shine on a precise spot in the wall opposite the hole. The spot did not have any particular shape to it, though it was a point of light that now looked as though it were included in …a mural on the wall!

From China the story of the farmer and the weaver princess came. The spot on the wall was lighting up an area by one of the stars in the farmer and weaver princess mural. It was the star, Altair that represents the farmer in the legend, a cowherd. He is called *hikoboshi* in Japanese. A different star, Vega represented the weaving princess or *orihime* in Japanese.

"It is only a coincidence," Bernd immediately said, hoping to head off any wonderings by Yuri. He had made it to the top of the stairs and was looking at the same spot that Yuri was looking at. He knew much about Japan, but did not know the details or the history of the *Tanabata* Festival in Japan. He did not even know that it was originally of Chinese origin as Yuri explained to him next. He thought of it simply as a fun thing to do every July, attach your wishes to a bamboo branch and hope that they come true on the seventh day of the seventh month annually. The tree branch used for the Tanabata Festival is a leaflet from a flexible shoot. It is called *sasa* in Japanese and is what pandas eat. Bernd thought that it looked somewhat like a willow branch.

"I wonder if it means anything," Yuri got out having formed the words in her head even before Bernd spoke his mind.

"I don't think that we can be sure of anything at this point. We must confirm everything." Neither of them having more to say about the moon beam, next Yuri and Bernd discussed the origins of the Tanabata Festival briefly.

"How could the star point have anything to do with this tradition from China?" Bernd posed.

"Well, for one thing, no one would think it odd if this is how it looked." Yuri went on. "And well"… stopping in mid thought.

"What is it?" Bernd asked.

"Well, it's kind of far-fetched, but it could be representative of how all the star points are related. You're familiar with the story of the farmer and the weaving princess, right?

"No, not really," Bernd conceded a little frustrated. Usually he was the one who knew these things, but this time he didn't.

"Well, the story goes that the couple fell in love but can only meet once a year during the Tanabata festival when the heavens are just right. That means when the Milky Way is thick enough for them to cross and get to each other. Well, couldn't this be what was meant for we humans, too, existing in places that are star points?" she wondered out loud. We can get connected with each other when the *stars are just right* so to speak."

"Maybe, but it's hard to know now." Bernd said."Let's not jump to any conclusions. Like you said, let's be careful," he cautioned, remembering what the Egyptian man had said. Again, he looked around not wanting to be obvious when discussing something from the Secret Society even though they were using code. Visions of ninja went through his mind again. "Anyway, I think that we have to get going before we make the abbot any more curious than necessary," he pointed out. He noted out loud that they couldn't be expected to get too much done in the dark three stories up in a pagoda at night. Since

Yuri agreed, rather than responding, she headed for the stairs almost immediately. Then in the process of turning away from the wall mural and crossing the room to go down the stairs she was hit right in the eyes by the same beam of light, moonlight coming in from outside. It was seven o'clock.

"Wow, that's bright," she exclaimed. She thought for a moment that she might need help going down, but found that she wasn't as shocked by the light as she first thought she had been. Bernd teasingly offered his arm to her now, but she laughed light-heartedly and went on ahead of him. Bernd took one last look around and realized that now the scientist was awakened in him.

He thought that the light coming in the hole did do "something wonderful," by lighting up the mural. Certainly when it hit the mural it caused the room to brighten, too. It might signify seasons in the year as the ancients had established. For example, it is thought that some ancient Aztec pyramids mark the winter and summer solstices. At any rate for tonight, they were out of time.

He began to look around and then realized that Yuri had gone on ahead. Since he was holding the light that they had brought up with them, he hurried over to the stairs to catch up so Yuri would be able to go down safely. As he approached the top step, he found something on the wall opposite the farmer and princess star mural but couldn't make it out. It was some kind of image, a kind of painting. He shined the light on it and found that it was a map of Buddhism coming to Japan along the Silk Road. Buddhism arrived in China via the Silk Road, and then after coming to Korea, continued on to Japan. Yuri had gotten fairly far ahead down the stairs. He would have to hurry in order for the light in his keeping to be of any help, so he went down as quickly as he could while being safe. Once he caught up with Yuri, he thought, they could talk more, and so he rushed down the stairs, only to find that they would have to talk together alone much later.

At the bottom of the stairs was a young monk who had been sent by the abbot to be of assistance to the two people who were not used to wandering the pagoda after dark. Even he was not accustomed to walking in the pagoda after dark, the monk thought to himself. Also he was a bit miffed having never been trusted with that honorable job, cleaning the pagoda after the day's visitors had left. This was important since it meant that one would be by him or herself with the artifacts. The young monk knew that there were interesting treasures around the temple and would like to have been trusted to go to all places within the temple grounds. The abbot had recognized this tendency in the young monk immediately and thought that sending him this night would be appropriate training for his meditation practice.

The monks were expected to practice maintaining awareness and an even temper. The abbot had laughed with his eyes, but said nothing to the novice monk, who missed these nuances. Thus the abbot had sent this monk on purpose to retrieve the young couple. It was an opportunity to deal with the frustration of not being allowed to do something while others were allowed to do it.

At any rate now the monk led them back along the stone path surrounded by pebbles that reflected the light of the full moon. Soon they arrived at the place where the abbot was waiting for them. There was no time for the young couple to talk right then, and so the map could not be mentioned until they were in the secrecy of their hotel, and even then it was not a good idea to talk freely about it, Bernd thought. Clearly the conversation would have to wait until sometime later.

Bernd realized as he mulled over his thoughts on his own, that his thinking about the map being of significance beyond being a representation of the route, along which Buddhism came to Japan, was pretty far-fetched. What he didn't know, and this laid heavily on his mind, was whether it was coincidence or not that the hole to let light into the room was in the center of the map. *Maybe it was meant to mark "something wonderful,"* he was thinking ...when they came to the place in which the abbot was sitting. Thus, Bernd gave up trying to figure it out for now.

They made their agreed upon and obligatory parting greetings with the abbot and planned to have tea together the next day, before taking their leave of Horyuji. They, too, thought the abbot brought out something positive in them. Yuri, for example, spent four hours meditating that night, and she had planned to sit for only about twenty minutes. She was amazed once again that she had "forgotten herself" while meditating. Bernd admired her stamina, but chose to sleep. He was planning on getting up early the next day to do some Tai Chi. They not only ate healthy foods, but knew that they needed to move their bodies, too. They felt blessed to be able to do both. Yuri and her yoga and Bernd and his Tai Chi had become quite in depth activities for both since beginning meditation practice with regularity. Each noticed that with regular practice it was not only easier, but deeper.

The meditation improved the other activities, and the other activities supported the meditation practice.

Tea with the abbot would provide a chance for Bernd to ask some questions about the construction of the temple and of course the rebuilding of the pagoda. This would have been during the warring states period that he was painfully aware was a period of Japanese history that he knew little about. So if for no other reason than this the conversation would be interesting he thought.

Tea the Next Day

When they met with the abbot for tea, they found that he really could not give them detailed answers to their questions about the temple or the pagoda. True, he told them that the map had been drawn and recreated several times. However, no one knew why or from where the details came. Nonetheless it had been drawn according to the reigning abbot's instructions each time impeccably. And the instructions had been handed down without fail since the original pagoda was constructed where the current one now stood. The origin of the instructions were lost they were told. At this both Yuri and Bernd gave each other a knowing look meaning, doesn't that remind you of something else, but quickly averted their eyes, or they would have burst out laughing. Unfortunately, no abbot for the last 300 years knew why the map was to be drawn as it was in the way it was in the exact place that it was, though each passed on the instructions intact to each successive abbot religiously. Also, no one remembered why there was a hole in the map, but they followed tradition, as the instructions were clear, that a hole was necessary to let in light by day along that wall. And by night, too, Yuri and Bernd thought.

Bernd also considered once again, whether this meant they were barking up the wrong tree and needed to check out the pagoda again during the day. He was wondering where the sun light would fall as it came into the room at noon, for example. Mostly, though, the couple thought that they were at a dead end. How could such clear instructions have not been passed down with any way of confirming if this was a star point or not? It seemed unlikely. It seemed the item left by the Prince may have been lost for good in the fire.

Since the couple was in Nara Prefecture, they visited the famous *Todaiji* or *Todai* temple, in Nara City. That temple was such an important temple during the Nara period 710-794 CE that Bernd thought it would be really useful to go there. The city of Nara was built as one of the first modern capitals of Japan. Indeed, Nara had been built, modeled on the ancient capital of Chang An, that is now known as Xian in China.

It was a nice day for the couple to enjoy each other's company. They took a long walk along *Sanjo dori*, a pedestrian-only street on the weekends. They even walked along part of Mount Wakakusa that borders Nara Park on the eastern side. Nara Park itself was a large green area of the city, and the walk along Mount Wakakusa was especially enjoyable. It was quiet and gave them time to relax, not having to think about Bernd's research or the quest they were on, if only for the while they were on the pebbled and shaded paths.

While walking along, Yuri and Bernd prayed in earnest whenever they came before Buddhist statues along the way, especially the *Jizou*. *Jizou* are the usually small statues, though sometimes large, draped in red bibs or coverings and sometimes adorned with head covers. They are set out along the side of a road for the benefit of travelers. A certain kind created for the benefit of the souls of still born, aborted children or those who died in childbirth are called *Mizuko Jizou*. They are especially notable along pedestrian routes and were striking on the mountain walk Yuri and Bernd were taking. Indeed, some of the Buddhist statues along this walk were really quite old. All in all it was an enjoyable day for them mostly because it was uneventful.

The highlight for Bernd was drinking *macha*, the tea ceremony style green tea, at a roadside stall that was set up to sell sweets, tea and light meals. He had grown to enjoy its bitter taste very much. The experience of bitter taste was a pleasant contrast to the sweets normally served with and before the tea. They spent another day like this going to several temples in Kyoto including the famous *Kiyomizudera* or Temple of the Pure Water and another temple that has an umbrella stuck up in the rafters. Unfortunately, they felt no sense of awe as they felt when standing in Horyuji viewing the pagoda at night. They were at a loss as to how to proceed looking for clues to the star point. And then, being that the week had passed, it was back to Tokyo and back to work. This suited them fine, however, since they had had enough dead ends for a while.

Back to Tokyo

They couldn't wait to be in their apartment again in Tokyo. It was almost painful riding the train for half a day and not being able to discuss what was foremost on their minds. They had long since given up talking in code about their quest and the Secret Society almost entirely. Unless it was something really drastic or thought to be important by one of the two, it was too exhausting trying to get the point across without actually saying it. They only did this when it was of great urgency, which according to both of them, wasn't very often.

At any rate they were now back in their apartment, and there truly was much to talk about.

"It can't be coincidence," Yuri began, "that the star was returned by the family to remain with the temple. It is too bad that they left no instructions as to where it should be kept at the temple," Yuri protested. "Or whether or not it had come from the temple or was being brought to the temple for the first time," she added with a hint of caution in her voice. Even if Bernd thought that it was only a coincidence, she thought that Horyuji and the star *just had to have something to do with the star points*.

"Like you warned, we can't be sure that the star has anything to do with what was on the third floor of the pagoda. In fact, we cannot be sure at all what artifact had been placed on the third floor so long ago," Bernd was adamant.

"Maybe not, but we can ask the Secret Society what they think, and maybe they can help us decide what clues are worthwhile to follow and which ones are not." Yuri wasn't giving up.

"Well, I am almost to the point of raising my voice to the level that our neighbors can hear, so I have to go out on the *engawa*," Bernd said leaving the room. Yuri knew that all that was left for her to do was to make tea. She thought to herself, *shikata ga nai*, it can't be helped and began to calm down. She smiled now that she had time to think; what was almost an argument was over for now.

The water for the tea was boiling, so she put it into the pot and let it steep for about a minute. Then, she poured it out filling the cups to be about eighty to eighty-five percent full the way that her mother had taught her. This was so that the tea, out of consideration for whomever the tea was being served, wouldn't take a long time to cool enough to drink. She also thought this was a good way to avoid burning one's hand on the edges of a really hot cup. This was one thing she liked about tradition. While doing things the traditional way can sometimes seem stifling, traditions often were based on things that made sense. Recently, she thought that following tradition was as good a way to do things as any, but being flexible enough to consider the importance and usefulness of a tradition was important, too.

Bernd had been waiting for her to come out and gave her a hug after she set the tea cups down. This was welcomed by Yuri since he had done a good job of pretending to still be mad about the disagreement though he really wasn't angry. After making up, Bernd told her right away, that her idea was a good one. They would ask the Secret Society about their findings the first chance they got …. He of course kept his voice really low and used code words that they had previously chosen in order to avoid naming the Secret Society out loud in public.

Later That July

When the university mail carrier brought in a special package for the department head of Bernd's department at the university, he had to apologize because there was no one there by the name of Tanaka as it stated on the package. As he passed Bernd's desk while leaving, he dropped the package on the floor. Bernd smiled when he realized that the reason he tripped on his robe was that he was wearing a monk's robe from Tibet.

All that was said was, "same time, same place." Bernd knew what to do since he remembered the previous instructions from the Indian delegate. This meant that *tonight one hour after sunset* he and Yuri would once again be on some kind of adventure. Just what that would be of course could not have been disclosed in that brief encounter not only because there was not enough time, but because of the great need to keep their association secret. Bernd had a feeling that since it was July tonight would be the night of their initiation, the night he and Yuri were waiting for with great anticipation.

Indeed, they had both prepared bags and were ready to go in an instant since the middle of June. He nodded and went about his tasks at the university, but had to use great effort to stay there as long as normal. He knew however, that to leave early while it may not arouse suspicion, would be an unnecessary risk, so when four o'clock came around he said his usual, "*shitsurei shimasu.*" This meant something like "pardon me I'm going now," and then he went directly home.

No sooner was he out of the door, than he was using a brilliant piece of technology to his advantage. He called Yuri on his cell phone and told her in German that he loved her. That was their planned phrase that, when said in German out of nowhere, meant something was up. He knew better than to risk going into any detail and so restrained himself until meeting Yuri face-to-face. When they met he excitedly made the statement that the long awaited "final preparations" would be necessary for that very night.

Yuri and Bernd dressed in loose clothing, though nothing too casual. They looked nice, but wore nothing that was too restrictive such as jeans might be. This was according to the instructions they had received the last time they were with the members of the Secret Society just before parting. They also took off all jewelry, had showered and avoided wearing anything that had a scent like after shave. Just to be sure, Yuri didn't tie back her hair in any way. This was fine with her as she preferred it wild, only wearing it back at work to keep it out of her eyes. Bernd didn't spike his hair as he sometimes did, just in case it would matter. Everything was set.

Having come in the second floor "apartment," they were there precisely an hour after sunset, very nervous, and filled with anticipation. They were ushered down one level to the grand hall, the room with the seals, only moments after the fire escape was returned to its normal position on the side of the building. The moon had just risen, and the light began to shine in the windows illuminating the grand hall, and Yuri noticed once again, the wording written in Japanese nearby to where she was standing. It was somehow comforting. She had not realized just how intensely uptight she felt about not knowing what would happen at initiation. Bernd for his part began successive attempts, some successful and others not, to breathe deeply and in a relaxed manner.

The initiation, it seemed, would begin right away after they arrived giving them no time at all for small talk. This they found out later was out of compassion. The Society had found that giving those who were to be initiated time, even to greet longtime friends, just added to their anticipation and for the vast majority anxiety, too, about the initiation.

Therefore, just after arriving they were asked to sit in the middle of the room. Then, members of the Secret Society they had not met came up from below and mixed in with people they already knew surrounding the couple.

As Yuri's face almost began to show more fear than interest the delegate from India came next to her and standing between her and Bernd so that they both could hear said, "We haven't lost anyone yet," and promptly faded back into the assembly surrounding the couple. This, too, was another agreed upon tactic of the Society. If one noticed *any* member, in this case soon to be members, of the Society in any kind of trouble the first to notice must immediately help to the best of their ability. And further, this was something that was not to be made a big deal of in the way demonstrated by the delegate from India who faded back into the assembly that surrounded the couple. In fact, almost immediately Yuri and Bernd were not even sure where the delegate went upon returning to the group. Immediate help without concern for personal recognition was what Yuri remembered upon thinking of this later that night. She felt that it would be of great use in many contexts over one's lifetime and in one's daily life.

It was the first of many lessons that night. Most of the lessons had to do with openness or rather how to be open to new experiences and ideas.

That was the purpose of the initial experience, not knowing what was coming next. These lessons were to help one to *not take one self too seriously* and to *think of others even before one thought of one self.* The lessons also had much to do with what it means to be in or have agreements, how to achieve non-competition with each other and above all *making things work*, especially through cooperation. These principles looked different in how they were utilized by each culture occupying any of the various star points, and many examples were given as to the differences of each. And sometimes "help" would be greeted by joy in the person giving help and with such appreciation that only later was it understood by the couple to have been an offering of help at all.

Nonetheless, these principles were why the Society had lasted intact so long. On this point all were certain. In short, the principles were: (1) inclusion, (2) immediate action, and (3) collaborative agreement especially with members of the group. There were many other obvious lessons, too, such as acting responsibly and with integrity along with cooperating for the common good ….

On this night Yuri and Bernd were initiated into what it meant to be truly cooperative. Their initiation was a chance for members of the Secret Society to serve them, their newest members. And no one had to be told what to do. They all acted independently trusting each other. The spirit of the initiation Bernd surmised was found in that any doubling up of efforts to serve the new members were seen as funny and chuckled about. Also, he noted that no one made a big deal out of these *mistakes.*

That the room was dark was never a problem. It all went as though it had been carefully choreographed, though it could not have been. It was truly something special, Bernd thought. Cooperative cooperation, Yuri named it later when they were home.

The ultimate lesson was that through real, unaffected, sincere service, one achieved membership in the group without limitation, permanently. Wow, what a feeling and guarantee! They were both so impressed, that it was one of the few times ever that Yuri was speechless. Bernd, normally relying on logic, cried at the simplicity and beauty of the mood and the entire evening. They were profoundly aware that they had just made friends with all of these people …for life.

Back at home it was all Bernd could do to contain his excitement …. "That was the most amazing thing I have ever been a part of. They were truly inviting," Bernd said, after they had settled down on the living room floor both having finished their evening baths. Bathing in the evening was of course customary in Japan. Yuri noted as she was listening to him that it was early morning the next day.

"It was nice of them to agree to meet us again to help with our questions," Yuri said hoping to continue the conversation, but also somewhat interested in going to bed sooner rather than later.

"Yes, they are a grand lot, aren't they?" Bernd replied, again using British styled English he picked up while watching TV as a youth in Germany. "It was tomorrow we are to go, right?" he finished.

"Yeah *same time, same place* as always," Yuri chuckled.

Then Bernd spoke the words she was longing to hear, "Why don't we go to bed and talk more tomorrow." And she was up and putting out the futons as he finished his statement.

"That ready for bed, huh?" he asked.

"U-huh," she replied weakly as he began to help smooth the futons and straighten the sheets on the bottom futon called the *shiki buton*. She began to take out the light weight, summer *kakebuton* or cover futon.

As they lay in their futons just before falling to sleep she thought that though she was tired, it was an *ii tsukare*, a good tiredness. Then, she drifted off to sleep.

Bernd did not sleep right away, but considered once again what it may have been on the third floor of the pagoda at Horyuji that was now missing. Then, he wondered whether or not that thing had any relation to the hole in the wall and what the difference in effect would be when the sun shone bright instead of the moon. This wondering would never be answered it seemed now since the "something wonderful" hadn't been there for the longest time, perhaps since the Sengoku period or warring states period of Japanese history. *What a loss* he thought to himself as he fell off to sleep.

The Next Day

In response to the couple telling about the item missing on the third floor of the pagoda and the possibility of the hole in the wall being somehow related to this missing item, the meeting room was all a buzz. Nonetheless they still were not sure. At least, the long lost artifact was something that would perhaps reveal something to them about the farmer and the princess mural, the young couple wondered and hoped. Part of the conversation centered on the star Altair, or the cow herd star that was illuminated by the moonlight on the night Yuri and Bernd were in the Pagoda. The buzz of the Secret Society members grew ever more intense for a few minutes. Bernd paused to catch his breath and was ready to begin again when the Egyptian added more words of wisdom to the conversation.

"I'm sorry Yuri and Bernd that we cannot be of more help, but you will have to learn to trust yourselves," the Egyptian delegate continued having already talked with the couple for several minutes.

"All we can say, we have said already. You need to trust how you were feeling that night. If you cannot remember what you felt, then you will have to go again. Your gut feeling is all you really have when two or more possibilities open like that. The universe points us the way it does, and then we have to do something with what we get. Again, I'm sorry that we cannot be of more help than that." He also added the standard Secret Society caution of making sure before being sure, not wanting them to get burned. This was in part because as a young man in Egypt at the largest pyramid he had felt betrayed by his feelings. He had been so sure that it was of significance that he was crushed when he found out that it wasn't. The map he had found was an economic map of trade in ancient Egypt and had nothing to do with their quest.

"Well, that is helpful. I continue to feel as though there is some connection, or why would we even have stumbled upon the place," Yuri continued in the same optimistic way as before.

Bernd wanted to restate that we "just don't know," but held his tongue. He thought it would be better now to use this gathering to help analyze what they think they found or what they felt there that night. "I felt as though the map on the wall showing the route of Buddhism from India to Japan through China and Korea was significant."

"It could have been a Silk Road map," the delegate from India spoke up. "It's a common way to explain the arrival of Buddhism, of course."

"I read something about the Silk Road," Bernd began speaking again.

"I wonder now, too, could it have been what someone in that time thought was the "whole world?" he asked to all who were assembled there. He was at the same time asking the group and muttering to himself wanting some kind of clarification.

This caused them all to stop. As they looked around, they noticed that everyone there was from some place that was in some way connected to the ancient Silk Road route though some of them from places that had been along those trade routes even before it had been called the Silk Road. Then, after the pause, the place was really all a buzz all over again. It was fortunate that they had taken the precaution of meeting on the lowest level of the ornate building where noise could not leak up to the outdoors even if it did bounce off of the intricately carved archways. No one in Tokyo realized what the members of the Society were thinking or discussing. No one in Tokyo knew or was aware that a Society that had learned nothing new about their search in over two hundred years had tonight possibly come upon a clue to the fifth star point. Nor did anyone in Tokyo guess that this was something that may have brought them one step closer to finding the origin of their search. And the origin was, many of them now considered, along the ancient Silk Road at a destination from which one of them had come.

When Yuri heard this idea she was excited, but also a little concerned. Whether the origin was in Egypt, China, ancient Maya, India, Japan, Russia, Tibet, Greece, or perhaps even ancient Rome how would one know? Wasn't Rome, that had no delegate here, an end point or perhaps a beginning point along that ancient route? Didn't Rome trade manufactured goods for Chinese silks giving the Silk Road its name? And anyway where or how would one begin to look for the origin? These major questions remained.

Something else also occurred to her while she laid in her futon later that night, once again having so many thoughts going through her mind that she could not sift them all easily. After she had given up sifting and was practicing relaxation breathing she had one thought come clearly to the fore in her mind, "Why, if stars have five-points were they looking now in Japan? It could be that Japan was among the farthest points from the origin, and so it was among the last reached. One had to consider all possibilities. Wasn't that what the members of the Society said so themselves? Wasn't the sixth point, the yet to be chiseled seal, supposed to be the center, the origin? How is Japan related to the sixth point? There is something unseen, something more to what is happening, she thought. What if Japan was the origin? And then, unable to hold back a sudden rush of tiredness, she fell asleep. When she awoke the next day she could not remember what that last thought was she had had before falling asleep. What she did remember was that she had considered it something significant!

Further Exploration Needed

The couple both came to the gloomy conclusion that they would have to begin the search again. They may go back to Horyuji, but realized that aside from their feeling when at Horyuji, they should not think that it would be so easy to find the star point. They were more cautious than ever to think that the first place they had explored would be the star point that has been sought after for many hundreds of years. They realized that their excitement while at Horyuji could simply have been the excitement of being on the search. Yuri felt saddened, but was appreciative of the Egyptian's warning that gave her some comfort. She had really thought that Horyuji was it, the place they were looking for in Japan, but realized that caution was wise. Certainly the Secret Society had been wrong in the past sometimes *for centuries.*

A quick internet search had shown them that the Silk Road connection was certainly not unique to Horyuji. Places like Yakushiji also had prominent displays of artifacts, connections and indeed wall murals and maps of the Silk Road as part of their heritage. Nara, too, had a Silk Road Goodwill Guide program at the Nara Tourist Information Center that promoted the exploration of Nara and its connection to the ancient Silk Road. As for the hole in the wall, that would provide plenty of light during the day for looking at the wall mural the couple imagined. It was likely to be just that simple. It was also small enough that the protection of the overhanging roof parts of the pagoda would stop almost any rain from coming in short of a typhoon. Since they were inland enough to avoid the most drastic of ocean related rain and wind storms this would not be much of a concern. All these things taken together meant that the search would have to continue. The many possibilities left them far from certain about anything regarding the fifth star point! The key question now was where was it that this "something wonderful" is in Japan?

Therefore, by way of comparison and in hopes of proving that the fifth point really was in Japan, they decided to explore two possible places of really ancient Japanese history. They would go to the most important Shinto shrine, the one that enshrines the Sun Goddess,

Amaterasu at Ise. Also they would explore the most unique temple that they knew of, Teruji. After searching the internet regarding things international, they decided that if neither of these turned up any clues they would also go to Zenkouji, a temple with long-term international connections. Zenkouji was located right in the center of the largest island of Japan, Honshu. Maybe that would help them find something special or at least something significantly related to their search.

"Interesting coincidence" was all Bernd could say when he discovered this fact and that being stated only halfheartedly rather than in his usually joyful manner. He, too, was a little down not being able to be sure of their find at Horyuji. They had put their hopes in that place perhaps a bit prematurely.

Though Bernd protested that they should spend their time going to simply the oldest sites in Japan, Yuri was insistent. She had had many dreams about the ancient connections of Teruji and recalled her experiences with the abbot at Teruji while in the midst of meditating many times. After all, though not her main teacher, he had been her first teacher in the sense of a student-teacher relationship, something considered important in the East. If for nothing else it would be an opportunity for her to thank him for his teaching. It did not escape Bernd's attention that it would be, too, an opportunity for Yuri to partake in her favorite pastime, bathing in a hot spa or *onsen*. And so it was decided, they would first go to Teruji.

There was no time to lose both of them realized. They proceeded to the Japanese Inn and the *onsen* the very next weekend, with Yuri learning Lithuanian for a new dictionary project while riding the train. Bernd for his part was correcting history papers about Kaiser Wilhelm the Second. He had given his favorite lecture based in part on the chapter about the Willy- Nicky correspondence in the book <u>Nicholas and Alexandra</u>. He thought people studying about Europe should understand just how interconnected the ruling families were. Willy and Nicky were related. One was the King of Prussian Germany and the other Nicholas the Second, "Tsar of all the Russias," and they were cousins.

They made it to the *ryokan* or Japanese Inn by mid-afternoon, and after checking in went directly to greet the abbot having arranged a visit prior to leaving Tokyo.

"Welcome. How nice it is when old friends come from afar to visit," he stated making a statement almost word for word out of the Confucian Analects. Yuri and Bernd bowed graciously recognizing the great compliment at being called friends and both of them appreciating the historical note and context. "Come in," he continued allowing them into the residence, at which both of them felt honored. "*o-jama shimasu*," Bernd got out at the same time as Yuri, and they entered after using this polite greeting given before entering homes in Japan.

Once inside they sat on *zabuton* seating cushions and waited while the abbot made tea for them. They wanted to help, but the abbot insisted that they act like guests. They both waited patiently and discussed the questions they would ask of the abbot.

"Well, what brings you two back to me?" the abbot inquired.

"We would like to do two things. First, I am here to thank you for teaching me as you did when I was here before," Yuri began. With this she gave him a gift that she tried to give him upon entering, but that he had motioned could wait until later. She had thought this odd since gifts were traditionally given right away upon meeting the person the gift is to be given to. He for his part wished to demonstrate non-attachment to the gift by waiting till after they were sitting to receive the present. He had already guessed that she had come out of respect, and he wanted the emphasis to be on the three of them relaxing and sharing this time together. Indeed, this couple had such a warm glow about them, and he could truly see this, that he felt he would share anything he had with them. After a few moments of getting acquainted, Bernd spoke up with what had been most pressing on his mind, their second reason for coming to see the abbot.

"Pardon me abbot, but we hoped to ask you about the history of this temple situated in perhaps the most eastern part of northern Japan." Bernd had stated this matter-of-factly yet the abbot sat up straight and asked in return.

"Why do you inquire about a temple in the north eastern part of Japan?"

"Well, you see, I am conducting research about the spread of Buddhism in Japan," Bernd responded. "I would like to know which temples were built first and which later as Buddhism spread throughout the islands." This explanation satisfied the abbot and led to an afternoon of discussing Buddhism at the temple, the connection between Shinto and Buddhism in Japan as well as the spread of Buddhism to the north eastern part of Japan.

The abbot was happy to tell them about his temple that was truly very old. It was among the oldest. However, when he showed Bernd and Yuri the old, fading murals that were stored in the basement dwellings where monks used to carry out ascetic practices they came up with nothing that linked this place to the stars, the moon or other star points at least as far as they could tell. For now, they would not rule the temple out, but thought that the name Teruji, or shining temple referred to awakening, as a kind of shining enlightenment that was possible for all humans rather than a hint at it being a star point. In fact they grew a little concerned because they were finding more and more that there were many temples connected with the Silk Road in one form or another all-around Japan. Indeed, direct connections with the Silk Road were found at five of the twenty five temples they viewed on line of the 88 temple pilgrimage in Shikoku. This included Temple number 87, the one affiliated with the birth place of Kobodaishi, the founder of the Shingon Sect or school of esoteric Buddhism in Japan.

At *Koyasan* or Mount Koya in Wakayama they came up empty in terms of finding clues they thought might represent the place as a star point. They considered Mount Koya since it was founded as a monastery by Kobodaishi.

Because they felt as strong a connection to the Silk Road as ever, they also checked for clues at *Hiezan* or Mount Hie in Kyoto Prefecture. Like Kobodaishi, the founder at Mount Hie had gone to China on a pilgrimage to learn more about Buddhism.

Of the temples that the couple thought held promising interest, Bernd had to do much of the leg work as he was off from university all of August and into September. Yuri caught up with him via encrypted emails filled with vague terms and coded messages. These emails were mostly signaling additional temples or places to reconsider as well as places that definitely seemed to have no connection to their search. Sometimes the messages were anything but clear since they could not include details. Several times they were talking about two completely different things since the details were so vague. Even so both of them preferred this to giving away any information that would jeopardize their search or the Secret Society. They both realized that text messages and phone messages could be all over the internet and were a particular risk. Caution was in high demand.

Yuri also got away on the weekends as often as the Lithuanian dictionary project would allow; she met Bernd at temples within a short distance of Tokyo. One exception to staying in the Tokyo area was going to the Shinto Shrine at Ise. Being Japanese, she not only found the idea of going there stimulating and interesting, she held the temple of the Sun Goddess in high regard.

A Fruitful Trip to Ise

Not long after they went to Teruji, they planned a trip to Ise. Causing a little frustration for Yuri, the trip would have to wait. Bernd insisted on exploring various sites that he felt "absolutely sure" had a connection to the Silk Road, the star points or both. One such place was Yakushiji that he recalled from an earlier visit had artifacts on display that had been brought to Japan from places along the Silk Road.

It was true, too, that Yuri could not take off more time easily since she had already used her vacation time before and during their initiation into the Secret Society. She had to plan carefully and was able to go to Ise as part of a trip to the Kansai area cities of Osaka, Kyoto and Nagoya in which she was part of the welcoming committee for foreign officials from Lithuania and other places abroad. She had had to gain the cooperation of a colleague as well to make it all work. Her colleague would fill Yuri in on the international dictionary convention workshops held in Nagoya that Yuri missed while riding the train along the coast of the Kii Peninsula to the shrine at Ise. They would also cover for her if there was need to meet international representatives from the Lithuanian dictionary company with which they had contracted the work to write a Japanese-Lithuanian dictionary. At any rate and finally after Bernd had gone to the places he felt he must, the time came to get Yuri with the cooperation of her coworkers to the internationally known *Ise Jingu* or Ise Shrine.

Upon arrival at the main shrine at Ise, they noticed that it had been several years since the rebuilding of the main shrine building. Bernd had learned that it is rebuilt every twenty years. This was an effort to keep it new, renewed, and fresh that was in line with the Shinto value of purity or *kiyomeru*. It was also, he noted, in line with the Shinto belief regarding renewal or purification, a main theme in Shinto. Yuri was impressed once again with his knowledge of things Japanese. He truly was a *benkyouka*, or someone who likes to learn and studies a lot.

Yuri and Bernd followed common Shinto etiquette by washing their hands and rinsing out their mouths before entering the grounds proper. Troughs with clean water and ladles are provided at every shrine and many if not most temples in Japan. At their best they are filled with fresh running mountain water. That is because running mountain water is considered fresh as opposed to standing water that can become stagnant. Many carry and use a handkerchief to dry their hands, however, more often than not, a towel is hung near the clean water area.

Next, they went up to the shrine and prepared to address the god or *kami* of the shrine. First, they gave an offering of money and rang a bell with a rope that was connected to the bell and suspended in the air in front of them. Then they bowed twice, clapped their hands twice, and bowed yet once more. This brief ceremonial way of addressing the god was packed with meaning. For example, the first two bows can be an offering of respect to the kami or god of the shrine. Then the two claps are a call to the kami that makes a connection between the patron and the kami. And the final bow is a manner of bringing closure to the exchange.

Yuri chuckled because she had been trying to explain this way of addressing the gods at a shrine to non-Japanese when at Cambridge. At that time, as now, what made her chuckle was the fact that two of her Japanese acquaintances there each gave their own and distinctly different version of how to do it. When she told Bernd about this later, he, too, laughed. The couple, however, thought of Shinto as very impressive because no matter how one did this bowing, ringing and clapping, it was all considered correct. Clearly the point was to be respectful of the kami that usually were connected to something real, on earth and of nature such as a large rock, a waterfall or a tree.

The couple immediately noticed the connectedness motif at the shrine, the *shimenawa* or connecting rope. The *shimenawa* intertwined around or between various plants, other natural items, and decorations symbolizes how things are connected, hence the use of rope. They were hopeful that they were onto something seeing the signs of connectedness, the motif of purity, and appreciation of nature common in many ancient traditions.

Then Yuri had a horrible feeling. She recognized something that made her stop everything for a moment including breathing. Then, when she felt she could move again, Yuri gave a sigh commenting that "There are probably more shrines than temples in Japan." Bernd stopped in his tracks and was about to concur when something came to him.

"You know Yuri, you are right. We will have to go to all of the shrines in Japan to find the connection to the star points."

Yuri gave a gasp and grew increasingly disheartened by the thought of traveling everywhere in Japan to each and every shrine. *Hadn't exploring temples been a big enough project?* she thought disheartened by this new realization. Though she loved traveling, *going to all of the shrines in Japan* was not possible in one lifetime she was sure. She began to feel dizzy when Bernd took her by the arm and gently turned her to look at him. She had not realized that his statement was meant to tease her. He was beaming.

"What are you so happy about?" she asked a little taken aback. "We'll never finish even if we grow to be ninety-nine years old," she snapped. He continued smiling and replied.

"Yuri, we do not have to look at any more shrines for at least two reasons," he went on confidently. "First of all, Shinto is Japanese; it has little to do at least in its creation, with the rest of the world. Secondly, the *shimenawa* or rope connects us to the kami or Shinto gods, not each other as we understand the revelations of the star point seals to mean." She wanted to be sure she understood his coded message.

"But by implication it means to each other," Yuri countered.

"Yes of course, but it is only meant symbolically and for one's personal connection to the kami, right? Certainly we will keep our eyes and ears open including any ideas about shrines and Shinto, but I do not think we need to focus on Shinto Shrines. Shinto beliefs, however, do relate to Buddhist beliefs at least in their universal appeal. So let's enjoy the rest of the day, and then get you back to that conference in Nagoya," he stated triumphantly. She became quiet and relaxed a little. All that was left to do now was to go have some coffee. Of course they would leave after praying to the kami being thankful and relieved.

The Search for Proof

Though she did not dream about the place, Yuri continued to have nagging thoughts of another place. As often as they tried to broaden their search to include any possibilities her thoughts and feelings still came back to rest with Horyuji. She even began to wonder if she had been there in a previous life, if that were possible.

"Not that again," Bernd complained when she brought it up as the beginning of September brought some days of relief from the sweltering hot and humid days of August. September remained warm enough, Yuri noted, "to go out into the evening at Horyuji." She wouldn't give up. Something inside of her wouldn't let her. She only wished she knew what that was and why. She wished that she could be more specific about how to confirm her feeling, but when she thought about it nothing certain came to mind.

Bernd wasn't giving up either. He told her that sure he would go to Horyuji again as long as it was next year after he had searched other places he thought were likely to be connected to their search. And for him this meant someplace new. Then, there was a twist of fate as so often happens with the universe.

Something wonderful happened. At least that is what Yuri thought. They received a letter from the abbot on the island of her birth. It was an invitation from the abbot at Bentenji. He asked them to come to a meditation sit. Apparently he was taking the teacher-student relationship that had begun between them seriously. Though it was an invitation, it was clear that it was not a request, and that both of them were expected to attend. This year, they were meeting for the thirtieth anniversary of his becoming a monk at another site, a site that was connected to his lineage in a special way. The site was Horyuji because the abbot there had graduated from the same monastery as the abbot at Bentenji. Yuri could not believe their good fortune. Bernd nearly dropped the invitation when he read that it was to be held at Horyuji. He really was astounded. Yuri had contacted him earlier that day to tell him that they had been invited to a meditation sit by the abbot of Bentenji, but did not tell him where that would be. She wanted to see the look on his face herself. She felt that it was worth the wait. What a twist of fate.

"Well, if we are going back there, it is good that we are going during the day like was noted in the information from the family of Prince Shotoku," Bernd commented. He had resigned himself, albeit begrudgingly, to another trip to the temple. "And I am glad we are going there for meditation. I wouldn't want to be wasting our time chasing the same old thing again," he added a bit perturbed that they were going back before going to other temples that he felt were more likely to be connected to their search.

Nonetheless, several weekends later, though Bernd found himself wanting to explore other areas around Japan and perhaps the world, he found himself heading toward Horyuji on the bullet train from Tokyo with Yuri. It had not been easy for her to get off of work, but having a formal invitation from the temple, really helped. With the emphasis on respect of elders in Japan, were she to be working at a Japanese company this would have been almost a free ticket for her. Since she worked for a foreign company, it took more convincing. It was only because of the earnest input of her Japanese coworkers that Yuri was able to get off for two days. She would have Friday off one week, and then the following Monday as well. This would allow them to travel on the day before and the day after the event if needed.

Unlike usual, Yuri was nervous. She was sure that the abbot would be happy to see them, but was worried about how to make a good impression on two abbots at the same time without seeming to take sides. She was acutely aware of the importance of status in Japan. What she did not know was that the awakening experienced by at least one of the monks excluded him from any concern over status whatsoever.

She really did not have much time to worry as the first thing Abbot Furuta, of Horyuji said to them was, "Come in. We are just getting ready to have a meditation sit. Join us."

Later that day while in the men's shared dormitory, Bernd was rubbing his legs when he muttered, "*It's mid-day. I wonder what the third level room with the hole in the wall at the pagoda would look like during the day.*" Since it was a regular meditation break, he asked permission to go to the Pagoda. His request was granted, and he was let into the pagoda. He had agreed to do his walking meditation by the Pagoda and to get back to serious meditation quickly. This was because taking too much time for his research would be time away from the meditation practice. The concern was that it would allow his mind to wander far away from the meditation, and this concern the abbot from Bentenji had emphasized *twice*.

The only reason the monks had agreed to the unusual request at all was that they could sense how new Bernd was to meditation. And they did not want to turn him off regarding the practice especially since it was evident that he was willing to continue after the trip to the pagoda. In addition, however *new* he might be one of the experienced monks noticed his earnest approach and potentially good karma. The monk pointed out the difficulty of leaving meditation for personal work and coming back to meditation as Bernd was about to do. Normally, this would not have been allowed, but the abbot could see how much this meant to Bernd and had to weigh the benefit of forcing Bernd to stay with the meditation against his being so preoccupied that he could not concentrate. The abbot went along with the request to help Bernd to get this out of his system. It proved to be the correct choice since Bernd was able to practice meditating very well after going to the Pagoda. Indeed, for whatever reason he became quite relaxed, which proved to be very effective that weekend.

That he did not bring up what happened while he was there was not a surprise to Yuri since they were trying to keep things secret. Though even with this being the case she wanted to know what he had found out. Bernd for his part was enjoying not saying anything which was easy for a very simple reason. This was a silent practice retreat at which student interaction was discouraged if not forbidden. Meditating people were not to talk to each other. They could talk only if it was absolutely necessary such as if there were an emergency or something of grave importance to tell another. Bernd used this to his advantage purposefully keeping Yuri in the dark. Thus, nothing else significant regarding the search happened on Saturday.

By Sunday afternoon when the practice was finished, Yuri was about ready to climb the walls wondering what Bernd had discovered. She was almost embarrassed by her lack of mindfulness, but nonetheless anxious to know. Bernd, on the other hand, had found that he got deep into the meditation and was really practicing sincerely by the end. He no longer was hiding anything from anyone. He simply was practicing moment to moment awareness, something he found relaxing, but admittedly incredibly hard to do well especially with any level of consistency. He had renewed his interest in meditation, but not because he felt that he was good at it. It was mostly because he could see that it could be effective as a learning tool, *and* that he had a lot to learn. He felt encouraged to go for it.

Yuri was surprised that she could not put things out of her mind and concentrate, having done so very easily at other times. For her the two days had been very tumultuous, anything but smooth. She saw with a renewed sense that there was still much to learn. Finally, they had a chance to talk.

They both felt as though they had learned a lot. They had received teaching from the abbot of Bentenji, Abbot Kimura throughout the two days. It was clear that since he had invited them and had been their first teacher of any significance that there would be no competition between him and Abbot Furuta. Abbot Kimura became firmly their lead guru or meditation master trainer. He would point out the blind spots in their meditation practice and point them in the right direction. Also, when they had questions about what they were learning, he would be there for them. This was something that the young couple utilized throughout the weekend with a renewed interest in the practice. They also gained a greater understanding of the benefit and importance of working with a qualified guru or teacher.

Bernd had read much about this. Not just anyone would do. The teacher had to be right for the student, and the student had the responsibility to observe the teacher to make sure that the teacher was compassionate and not only teaching to massage his or her own ego. They both felt that the Abbot Kimura of Bentenji could provide this kind of selfless, compassionate assistance for them. It was true, too, that he was no pushover. Yuri appreciated this very much. She would need his clear direction to get over her own chaotic thoughts about her practice, gain a greater degree of mindfulness, and to orient toward a practice that would lead to an understanding that could perhaps help many others, too.

With his assistance she began to understand the Bodhisattva vow. One takes the vow and then continually renews the aspiration to "awaken speedily for the benefit of all beings" as other Bodhisattvas or beings working toward awakening did before them. The couple was now clearly students of the abbot of Bentenji. Yuri chuckled, since the deity at Bentenji was the god of fortune. She thought it was really good fortune indeed, that they found such a suitable teacher and leader in the Abbot Kimura. She thought that if this was the warring states period that it might not have been as easy to become the students of one abbot over another. Then she smiled again to herself.

Finally the meditation and discussions with the abbots was finished. Now that they had some time to themselves they discussed their weekend and their practice.

"How did it go for you?" Yuri asked.

Bernd responded, "Pretty well, I think," though he was unsure of how to describe liking meditating, but not feeling particularly good at it.

"It was really hard for me to concentrate," Yuri admitted, letting Bernd know by her tone that this fact surprised her. Bernd was interested in listening, but the scholar in him came out once more. He felt that now that they were at Horyuji, there was no time to lose.

"Yuri, we have little more time here. I couldn't find anything out on Friday when I went into the Pagoda. I used a mirror to reflect the sun light, but all it did was focus on one spot on the wall. Perhaps that is the origin, but it was near no town in particular even along the many towns painted on that map of the Silk Road. The light gave me no indication whether I was pointing it at the right spot or not. Perhaps we should try it at varying angles," he said feeling dejected at what seemed to him lack of success.

"I give up," he continued. "Let's see if the abbot will let me look over the diary and items brought by the family sincerely as part of my research on temples built around Japan. After that we can move on to other things and places. I have a few more ideas of places we should look." And with that startling revelation, he finished almost as soon as he began which stunned Yuri into silence.

Yuri could not believe it. She had been so sure that there was something more to this place than meets the eye. She was confused about her feelings. She considered that perhaps her attraction to Horyuji had been for meditation and was unrelated to the search for the fifth star point. She mulled over her thoughts while Bernd went to the abbot to request in earnest a final preview of the artifacts bequeathed to the temple by the family of Prince Shotoku.

Bernd found the abbot sitting in *seiza* with his legs folded over front to back and his feet completely under him. Bernd was pleased that he could sit this way for about 30 minutes, but thought that for foreigners, who were not used to sitting on the floor let alone like this it was only normal to find it quite painful. He could sit that way only because he had experience with it. He had sat that way while learning aikido, a martial art for several years. The abbot was preparing to pour himself tea and offered a cup to Bernd.

"So, I thought you were packing up your things. What is it?" Abbot Furuta said.

"We wish to … well, I would really appreciate it if I could kill two birds with one stone and have a look at the artifacts left behind by the Prince's family while I am here. I have no idea when I'll be able to come back," he said looking at the bamboo pattern on the curtains that hung behind the abbot. The abbot sat there in his traditional black kimono that was a long wrap around garment common attire among Japanese monks. He was considering Bernd's fairly bold request.

Eventually, after a conversation that considered points learned during the several days of meditation, he got permission from Abbot Furuta to view the items given to the temple by the Prince's family. Of course there was the customary direction to be discreet and to keep this activity hidden from all others present. Yuri came by just then and joined them. She had finished packing all of her belongings. Bernd had packed his earlier so they were now ready to proceed, but did so with caution. Indeed, it became necessary, with so many people in attendance at the retreat, for them to view the items in a deeper, even more removed side room than before making sure to be by themselves.

Once in the room floored with *tatami* mats and beautifully painted *fusuma*, they sat by a table prepared to carefully extract the artifacts from their boxes and wrappers once more. Bernd noticed the crane on the *fusuma*, a closet door made out of thick paper and remembered that cranes are considered auspicious in Japan, symbols used at times of celebration. Bernd took an interest in the diary and Yuri in the bronze star once more. With lipstick she traced it on the mirror that she had taken out of her purse. She was careful not to touch the sides of the star with lipstick so it took careful concentration and some time. The star only just fit within the size of that mirror. The mirror wasn't very big being one that folded in half on a hinge to fit into her handbag. Yuri wanted a copy of the star as a memento what the Japanese often call a memorial or *kinen*. For her it was just that, a nice keepsake, a very nice keepsake. She planned to trace it onto paper when she got home not having permission to use materials in the room.

Bernd put the diary on the table and got up to get them some tea. Yuri had promised to keep his place for him and reached for the diary as the breeze blew in the window on that cooling late September evening. The pages in the diary blew over and the back cover was exposed. It caught Yuri's eye, but not for the same reason as the ancestral book at her home had done so. This book had no tear in the cover. What it did have was some small markings along the rolled over edge of the cloth covering or so she thought. She investigated further.

"Bernd, Come here," she exclaimed and then lowered her voice immediately. There's something written here at the back." He returned right away, having completely forgotten about the tea.

"What do you see?" he asked. In a few moments both of them were becoming increasingly excited.

The special temple vegetarian meal, *shoujin ryouri* that consisted of various items made of tofu and sesame among other vegetarian items, was about to be served. This caused both of them to think *how do we get out of sitting in with the whole group for the meal unnoticed*? Surely they would be missed. After all it was the final event of the weekend retreat and certainly everyone would want to meet the German.

Their minds raced, going over ways to get out of attending the meal which would seem especially odd since they had been fully participating in all events since Friday. Yuri knew that she would have to do something, she was getting very excited. She thought now that she would bring up being sick. Of course they would have to take the abbot of Horyuji, Abbot Furuta into their confidence. Without out his cooperation there would be no nocturnal exploration. That was for sure.

It worked. The abbot was a little perturbed that Bernd wanted to explore the pagoda again at night, but thought well, it can't be helped. Bernd had convinced the abbot that he needed to finish up his research this year as his grant money was running low. The abbot realized that they needed to go back to Tokyo the following day, so he agreed to allow them to explore the Pagoda yet again at night though he thought it was a little unusual. He planned to tell anyone who asked that Yuri was sick and that Bernd was tending to her needs.

What They Found

Along the hem on the back cover somewhat obscured by the cloth cover, you could just make out that there was something written along the edge of the book where the seam formed by the joining of the cloth covers. After getting a better look at the writing, Yuri thought that this writing was familiar to her. Could it be, she wondered? Was it in the same hand as the one in her family's ancestral book? She believed that it was or she would not have done what she did.

She peeled away the cloth cover and even as she did so prepared to glue it back on as soon as they were done. It was a stroke of good luck that resulted in the glue being available in that room. *For this* she would get over her shyness and use the materials in the room she thought. It did seem that important.

They were in a side room at the temple, but not just any side room. When the temple was open for visitors, this room was used for filling in the *shuuin cho* or temple memorial collection books. People brought the books along for collecting memorial stamps as they went from temple to temple along routes established long ago. Therefore, many stationery items needed for brush writing calligraphy and other writing materials, including glue, could be found in this room. The cost for having the temple memorial information written in one's book was about three hundred yen or roughly three US dollars.

When this was paid, one could have the official stamp of the temple and the date one visited inscribed in the temple book in beautifully handwritten calligraphy. This allowed one to support the temple and have a record of where and when they visited such and such a spot. It was perhaps most useful when traveling along the 33 temple route of the Kansai region of Japan or the 88 temple route of Shikoku Island.

The glue had been left out next to the trough used to grind the India ink with water for brush writing calligraphy. These were found all over Japan, though nowadays one could buy already mixed ink and water that comes in a bottle. This is very convenient, though eliminates the sense of making the ink that can be boring or fun depending upon one's attitude.

Above and beyond her memory of how she thought that the characters were formed, what convinced her that this lettering at the back of the diary was written by the same person as the one who wrote in her family ancestral book was what it said:

"'Something wonderful' happens when the sky is connected to the Silk Road with the help of the moon and a star."

In a matter of only a few moments they found themselves unable to concentrate, and trying to be present in the moment and having failed at both desperately trying to at least breathe normally while rushing as fast as polite walking would allow them to get to the Pagoda. Yuri was numb with excitement and while she had had trouble meditating, she now seemed almost to float not being able to feel herself at all. She did notice that it was a good feeling. She was fully concentrating on the events at hand, easily.

Bernd could hardly keep his thoughts straight, but considered now that the hint "during the day" included in Prince Shotoku's diary proper was meant to throw off would be stealers of the information. After all, on the mural was painted not only the stars and the Milky Way, but also …a moon.

Finally they arrived at the Pagoda, and this time Bernd was the first to the stairs. His competitive side was coming out from the many years of football, the game the Americans call soccer, in his youth. Yuri of course was right behind him, the benefit of regular yoga practice. They hurried up the wooden stairs enjoying the creaking of the wood under their feet in their excitement. In her heightened state of attention brought on by the excitement Yuri noticed *everything* it seemed. She noticed not only the creaking of the stairs on the way up, but also the shadows outside the pagoda and the feel of the wood grain on those same creaking steps, the slight breeze as she entered the pagoda and more.

One thing had not happened …and that was taking the bronze star along with them. In haste they left without it, but each of them for different reasons. Yuri had realized how preposterous it would have been to ask to take a piece of the Prince's possessions out of the protected area within the temple halls. That would have been breaking too many cultural taboos-tantamount to stealing it-and far too great of a favor to ask of the abbot so she did not. Being taken up by the moment, too, she flew into action before giving it much thought. As for Bernd, in his excitement, he just didn't think of it taking no time to pause because of the seeming significance of their discovery. All he thought about was procuring a flash light to take along.

Now that they were standing in front of the mural, they wondered what to do. The first step was easy. It had been a while, and Bernd had seen the map while Yuri had not so he waved her over to where it was on the wall. Yuri stepped across the point where the moon light was coming in and once again was temporarily blinded. Bernd, beside himself, chuckled about this though as Yuri got over the temporary blindness she got an idea. She took the light from Bernd and shined it on various places around the map on the wall, places from which their acquaintances and friends came.

"Bernd, this map is of the Silk Road, right?" she asked, saying each successive word slower than the last.

"Yes it is. Why do you ask like that?" His interest was piqued.

She continued using coded expressions as a precaution to hide the true meaning of what she was saying. To Bernd, who knew the code it sounded something like this, "Well, I was just thinking of the members of the Secret Society being from places around the Silk Road route.

"Yes ..." Bernd said waiting impatiently for her to continue.

"And I got an idea as to a way to see if there is any truth to where the points are from."

"Go on," he implored, though losing patience in his growing anticipation of what she would say next.

"Well, here goes," she said walking across the room to where the moonlight hit the wall mural of the weaving princess and the farmer. Next, she raised her hand up to the wall. Bernd couldn't figure out what she was doing since he was a distance away and since she had turned out the light making the room almost completely dark except for ....

And then what she was doing became easily clear. The room at least in the direction Bernd was standing became brighter. Bernd could tell immediately what was going on because the moon light coming into the room through the hole in the wall had struck what she held in her hand and was now being reflected onto the wall map of the Silk Road.

"'Something wonderful' happens when the sky is connected to the Silk Road with the help of the moon and a star." In this case it was not the bronze star, what was almost certainly what had been intended by the words in the diary, but what Yuri now held in her hand. It was the folding mirror Yuri had traced the star onto which she had pulled out of her hand bag. The moon light was so brightly reflecting off of her mirror that it filled the entire wall.

Certainly, when this plan had been originally devised the people then had not planned on the clarity of modern mirrors, but a shiny, bronze implement. Now that it was night time, the light from the mirror seemed so bright that unlike the light from the sun during the day, it resulted in the whole wall being lit up.

Right away the scientist in Bernd began to worry about the randomness and wide range of the light coming off of the mirror. This concerned Bernd at first and then he saw what Yuri had really intended. It seems that she had guessed correctly as to how the reflection would work. The lines of the lipstick that had been traced around the mirror fell across the map at various points that now captivated the interest of this young couple.

At first they noticed that the lines were not on the map proper. Yuri solved that problem quickly by walking one step toward the map making the outline drawn with lipstick shrink to the general size of the outline of the map. The lines touched Novgorod in Russia, Places in India, Egypt and what was certainly the direction off toward the ancient Maya. The reflection was so well planned that the hole in the wall from which the light was coming in was right in the middle of the star outline from the mirror that was now reflecting that light. The reason that the star was not perfectly symmetrical was becoming clear. The star had one arm on each side longer than the others, and the arms were not of the expected angles to match each other evenly. They had thought this being off-kilter was the result of the level of the workmanship at the time, but they now determined that it had been made that way on purpose. It was brilliant.

The couple was discussing these things when Bernd pointed out that the star reflection was a bit off the mark.

"What do you mean?" Yuri asked.

"Well, the lines match almost all of the countries very well it seems, but overextend the mark in Japan ending somewhere out into the Pacific Ocean. What's more they do not make it to place of the ancient Maya, ending in the Atlantic Ocean. The way the lines do line up could all be coincidence," he mused. Then he went on, "And I am afraid that this could mean we have no idea if Japan or the ancient Maya were part of the quest or not."

For a moment this had each of them thinking in the same way. They were silent for a while, concerned. Yuri now pondered whether they would have to find the origin simply *to verify having verified* the fifth star point. Again the search made her head spin. Bernd for his part was lost in his thoughts his mind wondering what would be the next logical step.

After a weekend of sitting in meditation, his mind was as sharp as ever. He considered several possibilities for their next step in only a few seconds. What he considered was their approach. Would they try to figure more of this out for and by themselves, or were they to go to the Secret Society for advice? Yuri for her part was starting to feel a little down. They were both about to give up when an idea came to her. She, too, had developed a plan in an instant so to speak.

She wasn't sure just how to tell him this, and she was growing more excited by the moment. "Bernd, don't worry," Yuri said encouragingly, but he could not imagine why not thinking that she was only trying to make him feel better. "Try this," she continued. "What if you measure how far the line goes beyond Japan? And tell me what you get."

"About three feet," he answered playing along like a good sport.

"Okay," she went on. "And how far short is it of the ancient Mayan ruins?"

"About three feet short of that, too," he responded.

With that she was now sure of her idea. She gave him a moment for it to sink in, and then she smiled the biggest smile she thought she could. Though it was impossible to see her expression clearly in the darkness on the third floor of the pagoda she didn't care. Bernd's interest was piqued. He leaned toward her as if to go in her direction when she went on, "Bernd, I traced the star backwards," she said, and though he could not see her smiling, he felt her happiness across the room. "It is not perfect probably since the information of the point in ancient Maya may not have been clear to whoever brought the star point to Japan in the first place. It may be an estimation of the routes taken," she said out loud wondering what he thought about it. She did not want to be too sure of herself, remembering the admonitions of the Secret Society.

He said nothing at first wanting to be sure, but eventually he agreed. Then he spoke out. "Obviously all five-points were not reunited so to speak at least not with each other. This evidence on the wall here means, of course, that the return to the origin *did happen. It gave an idea of the original routes as shown by this star.* It must have been true, too, that the original routes have never been verified since this star point had been lost even as it had been founded so to speak," he went on describing his thoughts.

"We do not even know if there are only five star points," Yuri said half to herself and half out loud in contemplation, showing that she understood his point.

"But the routes understood upon return to the origin must have been five since the Japanese or whoever lived in Japan when the journey came here used a star to symbolize the five directions left from the point of origin," Bernd added. He continued, "Yuri?"

"Yes, Bernd."

"Why do you think there is a hole in the middle of the star? I mean the hole in the wall on which the star is reflecting moon light?"

"Yeah, go on," Now Yuri was impatient with interest.

"Well, it makes you wonder if there is any significance to there being a hole there, doesn't it? The hole in the center is perfect. If it was any other way the star points would not make sense and would be off by many, many miles," Bernd continued expressing his thoughts out loud. Yuri could see that when the hole is situated in the middle of the reflection of the star, it made the other five-points line up. As for Japan and the ancient Maya, neither was well understood at the earliest times in which the Silk Road was being used. It made sense that those points were not as accurately displayed by the shape of the star as other points along the Silk Road. Yuri now recalled thinking that the Silk Road must have been what was considered to be the "known" world at the time.

"Obviously you're describing the reason for the hole being there. The hole is in the middle so that the star points line up, and it's that simple, I think," Yuri added thoughtfully. "And it is certainly necessary to have the hole at all in order to create 'something wonderful,'" she was saying when they were interrupted.

Since it was getting late, the abbot's lead disciple came to the pagoda to collect them. They had used up their grace period there and now were told and agreed that they had to join the others, even if that meant that they had to pretend to be feeling better. Yuri for her part would have liked to have tried the temple's *shojin ryouri* or vegetarian temple food and felt sore that she missed this opportunity. Nonetheless, the discovery allowed them both to almost float down the stairs of the pagoda so much was their joy.

Again With the Secret Society

Having become members of the Secret Society, Bernd and Yuri could call a meeting which they now planned to do due to the especially urgent nature of their findings. Meetings could be called, but would only be considered acceptable if there was a legitimate reason for having the meeting. If one had the luck of connecting with Society members nearby, that was one thing, but to call a meeting that would draw people internationally, there was need for careful consideration and planning. This was why only important meetings could be called when meant for large numbers of members or for members coming from far away. As for calling meetings there were several logistical hurdles that needed to be cleared.

Because of the secrecy surrounding communication, a meeting called immediately took anywhere from three to four days to set up, and at earliest a week to make happen, but usually longer.

The couple chose a thoroughfare of Tokyo called Roppongi to call the meeting. This was in upscale area where many young and foreign people gathered from around the Tokyo area. Bernd and Yuri went to Shibuya, a nearby train station and stood near the statue of a famous dog, Hachiko, a favorite meeting place of all kinds of people. They started slowly as the prescribed method went and progressed gradually from what seemed to be innocent back scratching to scratching their heads. It all depended upon whether or not anyone noticed them. Next, if there were potential Society members around who were reciprocating by first scratching their corresponding body parts in the prescribed way and then copying the person who initiated the elaborate ceremony they would move on in the direction from head to foot. The plan, like so many of the Secret Society's efforts was simple. It also was smart since the place to begin was the abdomen, usually scratching one's back and then going to the head. What prevented it being an overly simple process was that it was not only a top down or bottom up approach. This helped to keep it *secret*. First up and then down. To make it more secure, the action would be repeated only so many times and then one would need to leave if there were no Secret Society members around.

After about three weeks, those who could assemble were in Japan. An extra week above and beyond the normal two was given to allow for the greatest number of participants as possible. This was grueling for Yuri and Bernd and an almost unbearably long time, but wait they had to. They had no choice. In this matter the Secret Society would not be flexible. The extra week was given out of compassion for so many who normally might not attend, but would now come as the code red, the highest alert possible was used. This was the most important level of meeting, chosen because the person helping to call the meeting internationally thought it was that important. It was clear that more members than usual would attend this meeting even if it meant being outside their own countries.

Finally the awaited day arrived. Now Yuri and Bernd could give and get information at the first meeting of this size in 250 years. Upon getting everyone together there was a brief time of getting acquainted, reacquainted, and then the meeting was called to order. After introductions, the couple made their brief, but significant announcement about the walls on the third floor of the pagoda at Horyuji.

Almost as soon as they finished their explanation of their finding, the couple heard rather loud gasps coming from around the room. Then as more and more people heard the translation, and it began to sink in, it created such a stir that the meeting came to a halt.

All of a sudden the young couple found themselves along with the delegates present having refreshments chosen from amongst the world's finest coffees, teas and other drinks including hot cocoa from Europe. And alongside of them as natural as could be was the Egyptian delegate who, only about one year before seemed to them the most dangerous person they might ever meet. He had been the one who insisted that out of compassion the meeting would have to be held one week later than originally Bernd and Yuri had hoped.

The Egyptian explained that the announcement caused such a commotion, that after it was made, break out groups were being set up to discuss further action. Before adjourning, they were to come back together and set the stage for the next leg of this journey. The collective gasp was certainly a result of the immediate recognition that they had come farther than perhaps any of them expected that they would, in this lifetime.

The couple, now in their breakaway group, realized with the help of the Egyptian delegate that not only in Japan but on the pyramids, too, there were many pictures related to trade routes of the Silk Road. They discussed once again how the Silk Road routes eventually extended from China to Rome including other places, too. Chinese silks were traded for manufactured goods from Europe, especially from the Romans.

The Chinese, Han Dynasty (206 BCE-220 CE) controlled China around the same time as the Roman Empire was at its zenith. Japan through connections with China was connected to the Silk Road though this was related to the spread of Confucian ethics and Buddhism to Japan somewhat later than the time in which the Roman Empire flourished. It was noted that during the Nara period of Japan the Chinese capital of *Chang an* which is modern Xian was copied when building Nara City. It was also during this time in the Tang Dynasty in China that Buddhism began to flourish in China. These were just some of the things that small group discussed.

The connections went a step further now they considered. They all now realized that the pictures on the pyramids, heretofore not linked to the Silk Road were there because this trade included Egypt, too. What had been missing in the interpretation of the pictures had been a clue such as the hole in the wall at Horyuji that would have told of the connections beyond the immediate area. "You see, Yuri and Bernd," the Egyptian delegate went on, "No matter how good you are at reading hieroglyphics the symbols and maps seem to represent, as many interpret nowadays, an economic map. So many people up until now have thought that these were only maps of ancient trade routes! Certainly some of the maps were not only trade routes, but also related to this search along the Silk Road route for purposes of establishing connections among peoples of the world. Some of the maps must have been created by those original travelers so many centuries ago. All we need to do of course is to establish why, and find out what the purpose of those journeys was so to speak.

I myself had failed to see the pictures and maps in this new light until the discovery at Horyuji that you only told me about in detail the last several days. The interconnectedness of these routes is startlingly simple. Perhaps nothing has been lost by the original clans so much as it is a matter of not being able to interpret what was left behind." After speaking and using his arms to gesture broadly in his excitement he drew for them on the table with his fingers the pyramids and some simple hieroglyphics. Then after speaking he sat down. He sat smiling and thinking to himself, "Wait till I get back to the pyramids. I will explore them again anew."

"You know, this means only one thing," Yuri said seriously.

"Yes?" the Egyptian replied trusting his feeling that he should listen carefully to this one no matter how young she might be.

"Now that we have all five star points, all that we have to do is figure out how they are connected and, in turn, what indeed was or is the origin." She finished this statement while smiling an uneasy smile that let on how she realized that this would not be an easy task.

"Indeed, travel out of Japan to any or all of the star points might be necessary, time consuming and an expensive endeavor. It might be necessary to go to the star points to help sum up what was similar about each point or what was held in common among the points," she considered out loud. "Obviously, this was something that the members wanted to find out to understand the location of the origin," she finished. She was stating the obvious fact that the thing or things held in common to the star points all around the world would have to be discovered to get back to the place of origin.

As a result, Yuri felt exasperated. She had thought they were almost finished, but now realized that what remained could take years. She now fully remembered her thought as she was about to sleep that night which seemed like many years ago, that Japan was only one of five-points. *There is something more going on here than meets the eye* was what had come to her mind as she was about to sleep.

For her this meant that they could not be sure whether the five star points they found were all of the points that existed. Further, they were not even sure what to include or if they should include a sixth seal, though it was already on the floor of the grand hall. This brought out the question in her mind, *Should there be more seals on the floor of the grand hall?"*

As she unrolled a map of the ancient Silk Road, she realized that the center region between the intersecting lines of the star points covered much ground indeed. The dimensions of the hole, when considered were no help either. In fact the size of it left her dumbfounded. There was no single mark on a city, just a rather large hole in the middle of the map. Yuri realized that the hole had been specifically made to be that size according to instructions passed down from abbot to abbot. Now, when drawn to scale on a map it covered quite a large area. Yuri did not know whether or not it was meant to mark only one spot, an ancient city or town or whether the size had to do with how much light was to be let in. If it were the latter case it would in no way be emphasizing how big or not the hole was to be on the map. At any rate it covered more area than would allow them to easily pinpoint any one ancient or modern site in that region.

In addition, she discussed the details with the Egyptian now and a few other members of that smaller group that night. They wondered if all of the connections made may have been symbolic. The origin could have been anywhere among the star points. Everything seemed connected along the ancient trade routes. She was amazed and a little overwhelmed by two things. The first was that there was so much yet to explore, as they had seemingly only just begun to look for the long lost information regarding the origin of the quest. The second was the realization that humans have been connected for so long. In spite of the fact that there has been continual war or conflict somewhere along the route, the connections were truly ancient and this connectedness was truly amazing. Yuri now shuddered as she thought of the Taliban setting off dynamite to destroy Buddhist images in the caves in Bamiyan, Afghanistan. She was happy that the Society members were now making connections anew and still. This gave her some positive energy now and a little hope, too.

The Secret Society adjourned their meeting with one goal clearly set. The members would coordinate and cooperate in exploring the existing star points. They would look for similarities or anything that would in some way connect the points. Then when something was uncovered, the group would reassemble at a geographic location nearest the seemingly most significant find to discuss the subsequent actions to be taken.

Yuri was ecstatic because she and Bernd, with their knowledge of history and Egyptian hieroglyphics were chosen to explore places along the route from Egypt through Greece to Tibet. Of course there would be others searching at the same time not only at other star points, but also along the route Yuri and Bernd were taking. There was more than enough work to go around. Each group would in some way be in contact with the group at large if something of significance was to be found. For this they were thankful of cellular technology and the internet albeit in coded form.

The Search for the Origin

The couple thought long and hard about how to help find the connection to the place of origin of the star points. They wondered if the best way wasn't to go to some of the places that they know were visited by the early explorers and were recognized by the members of the Secret Society. For example, there was Columbus and his explorations in the West Indies or rather information gathered by a member of the Secret Society who had gone along with him to the New World in 1492 and after. The information gathered eventually led to the understanding that there was a star point at the ancient Mayan site. Bernd thought that perhaps in places of early exploration, they could find clues as to how the points were established, maintained and kept hidden. Bernd wondered, too, if there was any merit in one group trying to find clues at all of the five star points in order to find the sixth, the origin. To him that just made sense. One group would be able to sift through the information without the disjointed coordination of four other groups. Either way it would become a great task.

And so next Bernd said out loud, "Going to the five star points by one person, I mean, we'd …volunteer, might reveal clues as to how they are related to each other. And I wonder," continuing out loud, he said "if there is a logical order in which to visit the star points." His scientific mind kicked in to be the most active part of him right then.

The couple would of course begin with their assigned route from Egypt to Tibet. It was clear that while they were new to the Society they were held in high regard. It was also evident that they should not take matters entirely into their own hands. The Society, it was clear, had built the Society on a foundation of cooperation. Going it alone would be looked upon as not only uncooperative, but also somewhat selfish. Yuri and Bernd came to this understanding remembering the Bodhisattva Vow they learned about from the Tibetan delegate and also from the abbot at the temple on the island of Yuri's birth, Bentenji. The vow was: *May I awaken speedily for the sake of all beings.* One Tibetan Lama, they were told by the Tibetan delegate called this the greater compassion. Ordinary compassion was compassion toward oneself or another, while greater compassion had the aspect of being on behalf of *all beings*.

At the mention of this last idea, Yuri's attitude changed and she grew excited. She knew it would be a task that might take years, but she also knew that she loved traveling and learning about the world. Again her optimism and intelligent determination impressed the members of the Secret Society who were still with the couple as others were leaving to begin their search. All groups were aware of how many centuries had already passed since their Society's search began and also that there was no time to lose as there may be much work ahead.

"Bernd, that's a great idea," she concurred. "If we find out indeed *how* each of the places is related to the others, then perhaps we will find some kind of hint that will link us with the place of origin." They knew that the Egyptian star point had been found first therefore they were going in order, kind of, already. Though this was true it was another example of fate. They had been told to go to Egypt first not having chosen it as their first stop. Yuri and Bernd quite happily agreed with fate this time. As soon as they could they would begin the search.

Of course Yuri planned to take a leave of absence from her job and hoped that she could keep it somehow. She knew that this was unlikely, and so prepared her heart for the potentiality or *kokoro no jumbi wo shita* of resigning her position. Then once again fate adjusted her circumstances dramatically. When the company heard where the couple was going, the undeveloped dictionary market in the Middle East and the competitive markets of Tibet that might include work in China, it decided to allow her to use the time out of Japan to make contacts with other companies. She would be able to build business ties as she went around the world. She would have to take a pay cut until the position proved a money maker for the company, but it was a dream come true for Yuri. She was stunned when she heard of the good stroke of fortune. She would have to cross her fingers however, to believe that she would have a job upon return to Japan. She did just that, she crossed her fingers and asked this of the universe. She knew already by her many experiences abroad and in Japan that positive creativity was necessary for things to happen. She was creating many things in her mind that night as she went to sleep snuggled in her thick, yet soft, cotton futon.

After hearing reports from those traveling from Japan to Russia or China to India by way of Tibet or to Egypt from Japan, they became convinced that all of the star points were related by the following things: Each place had a star point designated in a special site and was located along or related to the Silk Road, the ancient trade route of ideas and goods. It was clear, too, that each place with a star point now had members in the Secret Society either living in or being from those places. Though this struck them as obvious and of little importance it was all that they had thus far.

What was encouraging, interesting, and a little daunting was that they still had their route to attend to. Therefore, since they were only beginning with their search, they were open to other ideas as they would come in from others or be discovered by other groups while they made their way along their own paths of exploration. The young couple wanted to find something that connected the star points in some new way whether it was factual or geographical in nature.

For one thing, they wondered just what brought people to the places that became star points and not others? It was clear that the routes chosen were the easiest to travel having been established, it seemed, for trade. What they wondered about was in what way the travelers from the origin had chosen their routes, among the many possibilities, and why. If they could solve that problem perhaps they could find some common connection among the star points. Additionally geographic explanations might be had. For example, was it possible that star points were established along water systems as were the earliest of civilizations? They would be checking these things as they went as well.

Having given their report from their exploration of the Egyptian pyramids, Yuri and Bernd were traveling from Greece to Tibet with the need to report on their findings in Greece as of yet. What they had found in Egypt were clear indications that the hieroglyphics noted the trade routes along the Silk Road. They believed now since talking to the Egyptian delegate, Avaad, that some of these pictographs also told the story of travel around the ancient world to make connections at the star points. Still they found nothing more in clear detail that was conclusive about this.

As for Greece, try as they might there was no connection to their search that they could find at the Parthenon in Athens or anywhere else they looked. Therefore, they continued their search. The route Bernd and Yuri were on traversed the intersection of lines that if drawn on a map would connect one star point with another. One such line ran from Russia to India, for example, and another, now they knew, from Japan to Egypt, the one they were traveling along. These two lines intersected with another line at Tibet. The line running from Russia to Egypt intersected with several other lines in the region that today has come to be called Greece.

Once they arrived in Tibet, Yuri and Bernd planned to compare two ancient traditions. They were the Buddhist initiation with those of the ancient Greek *initiation* as well as the idea of "logos" or the universal aspect of life in ancient Greece. They would also compare these with the Tibetan idea of the interconnectedness of life, Tantra that is also explained at least in part in the Buddhist philosophy of dependent arising. This was the idea that all things do not exist independently in and of themselves. Phenomena, including humans are all related and come about or arise in relationship to each other. In short everything is connected. Certainly they had a lot to learn about these concepts and philosophies. They hoped that these deeply spiritual searches would help them to discover some connection that would reveal the origin some way somehow.

Yuri kept thinking that the best way to gather this information and understand the origin seemed to be by understanding what all of the places along their route had in common. They wouldn't rule out anything until they were certain it did not pertain to the search.

Before they went any further, they noted that Orthodoxy in the form that the East Orthodox Church had taken in Russia was also a religious-spiritual tradition. They would not ignore Islamic influences while on their journey either. Ancient Egyptian rites regarding gods such as Ra had a special place in Yuri's heart after studying about Egyptian hieroglyphics and lore for so long. Even so they did not seem to reveal any direct connection to the origin, at least not for now.

Finding some connecting thread would be the clincher. Yuri laughed as she thought about this, being aware that Buddhist philosophy as taught by Abbot Kimura of Bentenji told them that the idea of dependent origination was often described as a woven tapestry that contained many, many threads each connected in their own way and each a separate yet integral part of the weaving.

They were a little tired, but couldn't stop now. Something as important as this could not wait several more centuries! They also realized how idealistic they sounded. It likely would take several more decades to figure out the point of origin. They hoped that they could find something to logically connect the star points together especially at the points that intersect. It seemed so simple, but was not, the original intention of the trekking being lost. It was lost having not been written in a way they could interpret such as on the maps at Horyuji or anywhere else now it seemed.

Archaeological Dig

Bumping along the road in a jeep the couple was passing through a region that had been part of ancient Babylon on their way to Tibet. They were looking forward to their search in Tibet and could hardly wait to get there when they came across an archaeological site.

Along with traveling to Tibet they also had a secondary goal in mind. They were tracing the route of Alexander the Great, at least in part, hoping that it would reveal something, some way of making sense out of the routes that had been laid down so long ago.

This had been Yuri's idea. They were desperate to find something that would connect all of the points and confirm that their Silk Road theory was leading them on the right course. Since Alexander had journeyed so thoroughly throughout and conquered the ancient world, it made sense, they thought, to see what connections were made by his journey. He had after all conquered an area that was more extensive than any others up until his time.

They were headed toward what was formerly Persia when they happened upon the archaeological site. It was surrounded by sand, a few pack camels, and several canvas tents with a mountain in the distance though not very far away.

The archaeological dig they came across was far from a town of any size. Bernd for his love of history and artifacts could not pass up archaeologically related sites without at least having a look. He just loved artifacts. He had known Yuri long enough to realize that even if they were in a hurry, as they now were, she would not object. She shared his passion for viewing real objects of history. She did after all grow excited just thinking about Egyptian artifacts that would describe the hieroglyphics surrounding them. The finds of bones buried in the pyramids gave invaluable information about the types of people who build the pyramids. In fact recent archaeological finds have altered previous theories from the idea that slaves built the pyramids for the Pharaohs, to the idea that skilled artisans were heavily involved. This made sense to Bernd, the logician. It would take engineers to create that level of architectural greatness.

Yuri, too, had wanted to stop at first when she learned of the site because she wanted to find out if this site was one of the places that Alexander the Great had been. Surely Alexander could have helped to connect places since he was considered to be the one who conquered the entire "known world" in his time. Bernd knew that this theory made sense and wanted to help her check it out. He originally only thought of the place as a nice area to learn something about the ancients and archaeology while on their way. He thought so since it was clear that the dig was being carried out in a very, very old site.

The search for the star points really connected them to so much that it was sometimes overwhelming. He welcomed the side adventure since he wanted something to take his mind off of the search if only for awhile. While exhausting, the search also made them feel even more excited about being together. Yuri for her part was thrilled by new learning aside from the hard work of retracing the route of Alexander the Great from Greece through the Middle East to India.

At this point, realizing that they were in need of new clues pointing them to the origin, they were willing to try almost anything. Nonetheless, both of them realized that they needed to do something other than look for star points for awhile, so they went to the site to check out Yuri's Alexander theory and to satisfy Bernd's wish to explore artifacts. They were unsuccessful at first, however, as they could not gain access without prior approval.

Then Bernd thought of an idea that helped him while at Oxford; he discussed his connections. Eventually the two were granted access to the site because of friends Bernd had at the Sophia University archaeology department. It only took several exchanges of email, a few days, extending much politeness, and then they were in. While they were waiting for emails to be returned they enjoyed, a long needed rest.

While they were waiting for emails to be sent back and forth, they took the opportunity to enjoy one of their passions, coffee. In the village a family business peddled among other things such as silver chalices, ceramic dishes, spices, vegetables and coffee as well. Over coffee they discussed their journey up till then, and smiled at each other. They remembered their wedding day and the cousins from the United States mistaking Bernd's family for English speaking Americans and how they all laughed. Their love for each other had grown with this journey. Being pretty good at using the code that they had developed to talk secretly about anything related to the Secret Society made this discussion much easier than the previous year. At long last the document granting them permission to enter the site arrived.

"Many thousands of years ago," Bernd began, after entering the site and looking around a little, when he stopped abruptly. His face went funny and he sort of scrunched up his eyebrows like he did when he was considering something that he just couldn't believe. In fact, Yuri thought that this was just how he looked when they came across the star from Prince Shotoku's relatives. And then he began again almost as suddenly as when he had stopped. "This kind of temple was very common place," Bernd stated recognizing the simple construction that made this kind of temple easy to build with the geographic resources available.

His part-time hobby of studying ancient structures now came alive. It was only by chance that this one, he noticed, having been built of wood and rocks still looked a little like a temple, and not only a simple, ancient house as it seemed at first. Bernd had stopped when he noticed that one rock was prominently displayed with a star inscribed on it. Not making a big deal out of this at the time was on purpose so that if the star image was of any significance others present at the dig would not notice. He was getting very used to Society business.

Noting that they were traveling through what was ancient Babylon, he recognized that the symbol on the rock of this ancient dig was part of an extremely old temple. It had captivated Yuri, too, for some reason, but she could not place just why.

Later, back at the hotel, after confirming that they were alone, though still using the coded wording, they began to consider the star they had seen that day. What they had noticed, they eventually realized was that this star was different from the star they found at Horyuji. This star was symmetrical while the one at Horyji was not. Yuri wondered why she was so amazed by the symbol. It was not only different from the star at Horyuji, but Bernd noted now, too, that it was also not a six-pointed star as he thought that he might find in Babylon from so long ago. The eight-pointed star might also have been used in the ancient dwelling he mused out loud. Though he now told these things to Yuri, he wondered why this star stood out so dramatically for him as well.

Almost as soon as he looked upon the star, he had a recollection of being back at Oxford. The feeling was, however, faint at the time. He now remembered that feeling, having no other people around to distract him.

Though he tried, Bernd couldn't remember where he might have seen that symbol before, so he dismissed this feeling and began in earnest to explore the archaeological dig the next day when they returned.

It was fascinating. This temple or house, as the locals seemed to think was very, very, old indeed. It was built into the side of a hill. In fact much of the structure was intact because it was made of rock and a dugout part of the rocky hill. Some of the wooden parts had petrified, making them seem almost permanent, but most had deteriorated over time and were gone. So it now was kind of a dugout house in the rock with its face no longer attached.

There may have been other symbols or artwork prominently displayed, but those were now gone forever. The reason the rock with the star, a temple item or perhaps a piece of art in a farm house still existed at all was that it was in a section of the hillside part of the dwelling. They had no way of knowing if this star was the lone adornment to the temple, dwelling or not. At any rate it was time for them to get back to searching the star points. That job had not gone away while they were on this brief, side trip.

When in Rome

When in Rome, do what the Romans do is an interesting saying, Yuri thought, used not only in the West but in Japan as well. *Goh ni ireba, goh ni shitagae.* In Japanese it means something like "When in *Goh*, obey the cultural rules of *Goh*." The saying now was taking on much importance for the young couple. Neither of them had been to Tibet, though Bernd had read about it now and again. Both were aware that Tibetan Buddhism or Tantra also called Tantrayana was popular in the West. Yuri this time was the one who knew that Tantra is also called Vajrayana or the Vajra vehicle that translates roughly to the Diamond Vehicle. Since neither was familiar with the traditions of Tibet they would have to pay careful attention to the Tibetan traditions in hopes of not offending anyone or stepping on anyone's toes. They would do their best to do what the Romans do, well, in Tibetan style. They of course would start with something they heard a lot about in Tibet, the head temple in the region around where the star point had been fixed.

The maroon and golden colored robes of the Tibetans were striking. That the monks chanted at certain times of the day or during initiations was fascinating for the young couple. Since they had expressed interest in Tibetan culture, they were allowed into a monastery though it was clear by the expression on the abbot's face that they could only be there if they were serious about studying and meditating. He seemed to espouse the Buddhist idea that wasting the teacher's time was inappropriate. Seemingly with this warning he wasn't letting them get into the position to waste anyone's time. Giving a warning of what was expected of them was of course consistent with being compassionate. Clearly they would need to meditate.

First, they were ushered into a couple of changing rooms and given their own robes to wear. They were told that monks of many traditions owned only a few things. For example, monks of various traditions only had their robes, that were their sole responsibility to take care of. Monks might also have a begging bowl that was a bowl or basket to receive gifts of food, money or medicine. In some places in Southeast Asia such as Laos, Bernd had witnessed monks coming out to make the morning rounds to collect food, money or other items donated by people who regularly got up fairly early in the morning to prepare. When Bernd was in Laos, he noticed that the monks made their morning rounds at 6:00 AM. Monks did not possess much else of significance, frugality being one of the lessons to be learned in the monastic way of life.

In Laos he had observed people giving monks sticky rice, a kind of rice that is highly sticky in the sense of sticking to itself and also noticeably chewy. It was served almost everywhere Bernd went when he made that trip as a young college student wanting to explore the world. What was striking about this practice was that the giver was the one to receive merit in this interaction. The monks prayed for the benefit of those who gave them offerings, that most often were food. He remembered, too, being ill from very different sanitary conditions than what he was used to.

The Tibetan meditation practice was steeped in tradition. It was extremely interesting for both of them. Yuri had picked up a little Chinese while visiting China as a little girl with her father. Mostly she remembered the vast expanse of the Great Wall of China. Looking across the mountains made her feel special and almost outside of herself in the beauty of that great accomplishment.

She knew that the characters may or may not have the same meaning and only occasionally share the same readings between Chinese and Japanese. For example, the character that means *hot water* and signifies public bath houses in Japan means and signifies *soup restaurants* in China. She was hoping that she could find similarities in the Tibetan language now, too. Bernd had heard how different spoken Tibetan was from written Tibetan. He had heard that it was almost like knowing two different languages. For both of them the language would be an obstacle, but they were interested in all they were now encountering, so they felt confident that they were up to the challenges that may arise from a lack of knowledge.

Yuri had always been interested in other cultures and found that when she went places, being truly interested in the world around her was a large part of what helped her to get along. Each day presented itself as though it was new! What an adventure life was, she thought.

Yuri chuckled when she heard how different spoken and written Tibetan can be. "You mean like having a separate vocabulary for honorifics?" she joked. Of course Bernd knew that she was referring to the honorifics in Japanese. This made Japanese, too, a little like knowing two separate languages that of regular and that of polite word usage. At least that's what Bernd and many foreigners thought and Yuri knew this. Yuri satisfied her curiosity for the time being with trying to learn the spoken language of Tibet at least in part. One thing at a time she thought. The spoken language was complicated enough, she thought let alone what it would take to learn the written language.

The monks in charge of showing the two visitors around took them into their care and began to teach them about Buddhist initiations. They began with perhaps the most famous deity of the Buddhist pantheon in Tibet, Chenreizig.

They taught the young couple the Chenreizig mantra "Om, Ma, Ni, Pad Me Hung." Yuri sat still for a moment and said the mantra quietly to get a feeling for the sounds. Then all of a sudden she realized that this was precisely what the Secret Society Tibetan delegate had said that one night with the group. She also was taken aback at how it seemed that it was a long time ago. She remembered that he had been saying it in a way that made her feel that he was saying, "Oh my god!" or "Lord have mercy," as an American might.

"What does it mean?" she asked.

"It has more of a teaching with it than we can go into detail here, but there are various colors used with each syllable and …well, you need to have the initiation by a qualified teacher if you are to find out in detail," he said as diplomatically as he could. What I can tell you is that the deity, Chenreizig is the deity of compassion," the monk said in finishing.

"Oh you mean like Avalokiteshvara," Bernd spoke up now.

"Yes," the monks said in unison with one of them finishing by saying, "That's right, one in the same."

"And Kannon in Japan," Yuri added.

"True, these all are names for this deity, including Guan Yin in China," one of the monks went on. "Do you see any differences between the Tibetan deity and those in other countries?" he asked hoping to spur them on to use their brains and be mindful, though not as an attempt to be seen as smarter than them.

"Well for one thing it is translated as the god of mercy in English in Japan. That is not really the same as compassion, is it?" Yuri brought out one difference.

"And the Tibetan version as well as Avalokiteshvara are male versions while the others are female emanations," Bernd continued the conversation.

"Yes, those are the major differences we think, too, however, I was only wondering if you knew. It is really not important to emphasize what the differences are. Probably we can all agree that in Buddhism both compassion and loving kindness are key teachings."

"Yes, they are a common theme among the teachings we have received from Abbot Kimura, wouldn't you say, Bernd?"

"Absolutely! That's most certainly the case. But don't you think that it is also obvious that Christianity teaches that loving one's neighbor and being compassionate to those less fortunate are important traits?"

"Yes, these are common themes," the monk agreed adding. "In Islam one of the five pillars or main beliefs is to give alms to the poor, I've read." And with that he turned to the door. Being the one chosen to take them around he prepared to show them more about the temple grounds.

"Today let's take some time to walk around and view the various deities pictured in *thankas* or deity paintings, within the buildings around the temple grounds. I think it will be educational for you to see that there are many, each with a different feeling to it. You see we have many emanations in our teaching, but not any gods in the way that Christians have *a god.* These are representations used for specialized teaching purposes. They are not to be worshipped as separate gods so to speak. At least not separate from you and me," he finished leaving the young couple a little puzzled after this last statement.

While walking around the temple, Yuri and Bernd noticed how their interest was aroused anew. It truly was fascinating. Many of the buildings had been there a very long time. They could not help but notice, too, the rich culture represented by the many artifacts that provided reminders of the Buddhist teachings and were displayed prominently in the buildings within the temple grounds. There were curved knives, and one of them looked as though it were five hundred or more years old though Yuri was not sure why she thought so. In fact, later she found out that it was five hundred years old.

Each thanka had a different color scheme. The monk in charge of showing the couple around said that while he could not explain the details of the thankas to someone who had not received specific teaching about them from a qualified teacher, he could tell them that the different colors were of significance. The specialized teaching about a thanka is called either initiation in English or *Wong Kur* in

Tibetan they were told. The teachings when written down were called *sadhanas*. At any rate it was now time to "relax and have some tea," the monk said with a calm that did not seem as though it could be disturbed.

The monk invited them to have tea at a small hall in the temple grounds that was set aside for getting refreshed after meditation sessions whether long or short. All people needed to allow themselves to be refreshed from time to time, he said matter-of-factly. Bernd thought that it would be good in general for westerners to relax and take time to be calm more often. Most westerners he knew, and many Japanese, too, did nothing but hurry around and try to get things done. Whew! It made his head spin now thinking about the fast pace of the country of his birth and the one in which he now resided. While sitting and having yak tea, a milky, buttery tea, the couple was asked if they wanted to attend the Chenreizig initiation that was scheduled for the coming Sunday.

"Yes," came the simple answer from both of them spoken together in one voice. Delight showed on the monk's face, and with that it was decided. They would attend the initiation. They were told to be ready at 6:00 AM on the following Sunday.

"A bit like going to church," Bernd quipped with a smile. Yuri poked him with her elbow smiling in return.

The following Sunday, Yuri and Bernd were ready before 6:00 AM recognizing that it was important to be ready when the event would begin. And who knew if this might be sooner than the proposed time. *It is important to not keep anyone waiting*, they thought trying to be considerate. Besides, both were incredibly excited. Indeed, attending initiation was so interesting that neither of them could sleep very much the night prior to the initiation. Yuri had been up for hours and had a feeling in her stomach now that she could not explain having never felt that way before. This truly was something she felt that she should be doing. And she had no clear reason as to why she felt this way. She just did. Next was a welcomed surprise.

Waiting for them, with the intent of explaining the proceedings to them was the Secret Society member of the Tibetan delegation. He now revealed that his name when rendered into English was Karma. He apologized for not being with them sooner. He explained that he had been on a three month retreat in order to get into the meditation on a deeper level than one can achieve with, for example, a week of meditation.

Now that they were going to experience initiation for themselves, the two of them decided that they would later have to find a chance to engage the Greek delegate in the differences between this initiation and the ancient Greek *initiation*. Their experience today they realized would be invaluable in that discussion.

As instructed by Karma, first they underwent various simple, symbolic purification and cleansing routines. Then they waited for the teacher in a large hall with the Chenreizig Thanka prominently displayed at the front. They were not the first ones to go into the hall. There were many other initiation or *Wong Kur* recipients. They were among a crowd of mostly males who ranged from boys in their youth and teens to men quite advanced in age.

The room was set before they arrived. There were mats to sit on and cloths prepared on which one could lay any implements or accompaniments one brought along. Traditionally the person who requested the initiation would give a real or symbolic item of food, clothing, shelter and medicine to the qualified guru or lead teacher who would perform the initiation. Some places Yuri heard later use white silken scarves to symbolize the giving of clothing. The idea of not receiving something for nothing along with the feelings of sacredness, respect, reverence and seriousness in the room was so prevalent you could almost feel it.

There was a series of chants, some rice and other offerings of light, incense, and still other offerings. The ceremony was so rich and involved that they could not remember it all this being their first time participating in a Buddhist initiation. During the ceremony Bernd remembered reading of "initiation" in ancient Greece. He recalled that it was secretive and set apart from those who were uninvited.

There was so much going on that Bernd thought of this only for a fleeting moment, and then the ceremony was over seemingly as soon as it began.

"Yuri, what did you think?" Bernd asked.

"It was beautiful with the colors and style," she said.

"I would like to have a chance to learn more about the practice," Bernd said out loud, intending this thought to have been private.

"Well, you can," said the monk who had taken them around the other day. He walked up as the couple was settling down to relax after the initiation. First he explained to them what had been said in Tibetan regarding the practice part to be carried out after the event.

"After receiving an initiation or empowerment as they are sometimes called, the teacher gives a *sadhana* or the text of the teaching to each student. This is done with one condition, if the student promises to undertake the practice seriously. No frivolousness is allowed here. You do the practice or you don't, though to be sure you have a choice. Many monks have already taken the bodhisattva vow to awaken speedily for the sake of all beings. While the practice is truly up to the individual, for the monks, the expectation is that they would follow through on the practice."

Bernd became incredibly interested in what the *practice* entailed so he spoke up. "How does one carry out the practice with the *sadhana*?" he inquired of their new friend. "I mean, what does one have to do if one is serious about undertaking the practice?" he finished trying to sound interested and respectful at the same time.

"Well, you have to repeat the mantra, given during the initiation 100,000 times. It is really that simple."

"If you call that simple," Yuri smiled. She did think that 100,000 recitations was a lot, however, chose to continue finding out about the practice. "How long does it take? It seems like it would be a long time before one finished," she was trying to choose her words carefully now so as to find out what she was wondering, but avoid being disrespectful.

"It takes a different amount of time for each student," the monk told them. "Like anything, it depends on how much effort the student puts forward. Some finish rather quickly, and others take a very, very long time to complete each practice. We can talk more about this later," he said changing the subject and the tone of the conversation. "For now, follow me," he said, and he led them into a side room that reminded them of the room at Horyuji in which souvenir temple cards are written for people to take home as a memento of their trip on the given day of the visit. Both wondered, though neither knew, whether or not it was a custom in Tibet to write out cards in calligraphy that represented the temple's name, the date of the visit etc ….

Next, the abbot of the temple came out and for some reason asked all the attending monks except for the Tibetan delegate to leave them alone to talk. The abbot had realized that this would set the couple at ease. Karma, knowing English fluently from his time in India, would make an excellent translator, the abbot thought, especially since he had indicated that they were already acquainted. He waited patiently while the monks who normally would walk out with heads bowed, walked out of the hall to find something to do such as begin reciting their mantras that go along with *sadhana* practice. Yuri noticed that many of the monks having realized how unusual this was stole a look at their guru and the couple before departing.

When the last monks had left the room, the abbot paused for a moment taking in the mood of the young couple, which created a little tension. Then gradually he began to move slowly and to speak to them a greeting with translations being done by Karma, the Tibetan delegate. He asked of their trip here and admired their interest in other cultures and traditions.

Then surprising all present, he drew from under his robes an old book wrapped in very, very old cloth. He explained that it had teachings from many, many generations before. The teachings, he said were universal in nature. They were not included simply because they were Buddhist in nature. He wanted to share something with them because he had seen the glimmer in the young couple's eyes. This was the same glimmer of light that had been noticed by Abbot Kimura of Bentenji and the old monk in Teruji. Their sincerity and the brightness in their eyes were the reasons he had called this private gathering.

He now began to teach them about Guru Rinpoche, a teaching that is from very long ago when Buddhism came to Tibet from India. Guru Rinpoche, it is said, had hidden teachings in Tibet that were to be found at a later time. Indeed, Guru Rinpoche was instrumental in bringing Mahayana and esoteric Buddhist teachings to Tibet. This fact piqued the curiosity of the two. Since one of them was amazed by history and the other by cultures of the world, with this one story the abbot at that temple in Tibet secured the couple's interest in Vajrayama Buddhism from that day onward. Vajrayana was the form in which the development of Buddhism had taken root in Tibet. They would one day find the diamond in the diamond vehicle it was now hoped by all in that room.

They were told of secret teachings and many interesting things in the book. Some of the teachings in the book had been gathered together from around Tibet the abbot said. Based on lessons from this book, Yuri and Bernd were given a lesson firsthand about the guru-disciple relationship and the great importance in which this relationship is held in Tibet. They learned how the teacher takes it as a great responsibility to have a student in this relationship. The student for his or her part was honored to have a guru to point him or her in the right direction. Here, too, frivolous action was discouraged. The student for his part was bound to the teacher in a learning environment that would go on till the liberation of the student and perhaps for long afterward. In both of them this brought to the fore their lessons and deepened their understanding of their relationship with Abbot Kimura of Bentenji.

The young couple spent the afternoon feeling blessed to be able to learn from and ask questions of the abbot. They felt blessed to know Karma. Their questions were those of deep, Buddhist philosophy. Also they were about this old and magnificent wooden, golden and maroon draped, colorful temple outside of which hung colorful green, red, white, and yellow prayer cloths.

After dinner Yuri and Bernd were discussing the teachings in their room that was a small, wooden, sparsely furnished compartment that seemed to emphasize mainly its functionality. It was truly somewhere in which one only slept or meditated to be sure. They had been discussing the differences between Mahayana Buddhism and Vajrayana when Yuri became so tired that she started feeling drowsy and went to her bedding to sleep. As she was falling off to sleep she realized something important. Immediately she sat up in bed. Bernd, who had been meditating was shocked into attention by how quickly she bolted upright.

"What is it?" he said.

"Bernd!" was her only response.

"Yes?" he wondered.

"I think I know what connects all the star points. We have to call a meeting right away," she said now growing so excited that it would take her several hours to remember being sleepy and to fall asleep later that night.

Like it or not, he was finished with mediation for the night. All of his senses were abuzz and while he was cautious, he wanted to hear what Yuri had to say about connecting the star points. The lessons of the Secret Society, had truly taken hold in him. Especially noteworthy was that of caution.

What Yuri Remembered

Yuri noticed now in her mind's eye that the binding of the book, while being unique, had a symbol on it which she was somehow familiar. It had a star. Though, this was not any old star. It was enclosed in a circle. Remembering this was what had caused Yuri to sit up suddenly as she was dosing off to sleep. It had not registered in her conscious brain earlier that day, but was released into her consciousness from her subconscious just before sleep was to overtake her.

It was a star just like the one on the ancestral book at Yuri's parent's house except for one thing. It was red while the one in the ancestral book was indigo blue. The symbol of a star surrounded in a circle was small and on the inside of the paper that was part of the binding of the book. It seemed to her at the time to simply be part of the design. The symbol was mixed in with other symbols as part of a pattern. It had hardly registered in her consciousness when she was looking at either the ancestral book or today the Tibetan text. Today had given this a context. It was riveting to her now, but it didn't seem to be of any importance to her at the time she was looking at the ancestral book.

The search had changed so much since then. With the many symbols on that patterned cover—moons, flowers, and the like she could not imagine that any of them would have a special significance. Why would they? The pattern was a normal, Japanese patterning. Even now she considered how simple it would be to draw the symbol, a five-pointed star within a circle, and drew one for herself on the ground. For a moment she thought that it might just be a coincidence that two of the same symbols were found in these two places.

This may have nothing to do with the origin, she considered, and her blood went cold.

Still Bernd thought that it was worth looking into. To him, finding a star here in Tibet, like the one Yuri saw in her ancestral book seemed to be significant. However, in order to prove its significance they would have to travel to the other star points and explore in detail places or things in which the symbol might be used. It was not enough to know that there was one on her ancestral book cover and one on an old text in Tibet.

After a long discussion, Yuri was in agreement. Were this to be the way in which the star points were related or connected, they would have to find evidence of the star within a circle at the other sights, too. They were not sure yet whether or not the two they knew about especially being of different colors were of any importance. Nonetheless they had to prove that it wasn't just a coincidence that this symbol was found in the patterns on the binding of two books. It was true that the two places in which the symbols were found were believed by the Secret Society to be star points. It was also true that these were only two of the five places.

So the next day they were out rubbing their backs in a nonchalant manner hoping to attract the attention of any other Secret Society members and hoping, too, that they didn't look silly. After making contact over a couple of days with several members in a drawn out ritual making absolutely sure they were Society members, the meeting was called in Egypt in two weeks.

Due to the urgency of recent events people were largely ready for a meeting at any time, so two weeks was enough time for most to attend. In fact, the Society did not want to waste any time at all. This truly was an engaging time for the Society. It was perhaps the most auspicious time since the inception of the Society. It was also understood that if there was a significant problem, the meeting would be held farther into the future if that became necessary. And they would hold subsequent meetings to be sure. All hoped that delays would be unnecessary. This ritual had been used so carefully that it had taken two full days of people showing up and showing up again before anyone had the nerve to confirm that they were Society members. This was at first troubling, but in the end reassuring for the couple.

This meeting, to be held in Egypt was so important that no key member of the Society could be overlooked. Though it was not the closest meeting spot to Tibet, Egypt had been chosen since it was the beginning part of this leg of their search. It was also the most convenient place to meet for most members of the Secret Society.

Some of the Society members, Yuri and Bernd were told really could not afford to get away from their jobs long enough to attend on such short notice. In this case they would have to lose their jobs by either quitting or being fired. It then became clear to both Yuri and

Bernd, that this finding was considered of such significance that quitting one's job or being fired for leaving it was completely in line with the policies set forth by and were common throughout the Secret Society. Since they had at least two weeks until the meeting began, Bernd decided to take a side trip to London. There was something he wanted to check out …at Oxford.

To Oxford

After leaving Tibet, Bernd and Yuri flew to London and took the train to Oxford. Bernd had research to do now and was more than ever excited about and interested in the search and their findings. This was because it could all be applied to his work.

First he would explore the document that had come to mind recently at the archaeological site. Where had he seen it before? He just couldn't remember. He went back to his familiar college of history to hopefully find some clue that would shed light on just what these things all meant from the search and the ancient document.

Bernd was in the library for about an hour when suddenly he remembered somethings about the ancient document that he came across during his time in Oxford. The document was taken from Jerusalem during one of the "Holy" Crusades. It had been left behind it seemed by Babylonians after they overtook Jerusalem in the sixth century BCE. After overtaking Jerusalem, they were then in turn pushed out of Jerusalem by Persian forces. He couldn't remember the content of the document, though he now knew in his heart that he had to look it up. *What were the Babylonians up to in Jerusalem?* he wondered.

It was unclear to either of the young couple why this text from Jerusalem would be important, but they decided that they would come back to find it after their routine of morning coffee.

While at a coffee shop near the university Yuri asked the following, "Bernd, can you tell me about the Babylonians in Jerusalem?"

Bernd pulled on his collar with both hands so as to straighten it inside his blue wool sweater and went directly into his historian mode rubbing the straight tops of his wire rimmed glasses. "Well, the most important thing for our search, I think, is that they are famous for observing the sky. They were in Jerusalem in the sixth century BCE. Today we are learning about their observations of the sky through clay tablets written in the Babylonian style of cuneiform." He paused to sip espresso from the demitasse or small cup in front of him. Then he continued.

"Babylonian cuneiform, like that of ancient Sumer, was made by pushing wedges into a wet clay block to leave impressions. Babylonian writing in this way helped to clarify and designate the months and seasons.

The Babylonians created clay tablets that documented their observations of the stars and the night time sky. The knowledge gained through these observations was used with mathematically based predictions to help them to understand, months and the passage of time.

Indeed an understanding of and breakdown of the circle into 360 degrees, 60 minutes and 60 seconds, at least in part, comes from the ancient Babylonians. They developed the sixty minute hour based on the passage of the sun across the sky during the day and especially observations of the movement and placement of the heavens at night. And of course as I said, they are famous for watching the stars at night. They were great astronomers," he said, finally pausing to catch his breath. He was so excited by it all.

"I wonder if they were like me," Yuri went on. "Ever since I was a little girl, I have liked looking at the stars and I don't even know why. I just do," she said while contemplating sitting in the bamboo forest looking at the stars at night.

"Anyway, we've finished our coffees. Shall we get back to the library?" she asked

"That sounds great," Bernd agreed eager to return to explore the ancient document coursing through his memory in faint glimpses of imagination and reality. He wanted to confirm his thoughts since he recognized that our long-term memories are only about forty percent accurate.

While Bernd was able to convince the librarian that he really did work for Sophia University in Japan and that he would like to see the ancient document from the Crusades this was not enough to make the librarian get the document for Bernd. It took a phone call from Bernd's former professor, Tom McRobbie in order to get permission to view the ancient document.

Mr. McRobbie had retired, but since he thought so much of Bernd and had been in a senior position at Oxford for so long, the couple finally received the go ahead. Now all they could do was to wait for it to be located.

It took several hours for the document to be located and brought to the special research room prepared for items just like this one. The light was subdued and safe for ancient documents in order to not damage the parchment and paper on which the documents were made.

The wait was well worth it because now the two of them were looking at an ancient document found in Jerusalem that had been brought back to England during the Crusades. They had agreed of course to look but not touch. It was mystical. The document talked of a star encircled. It also talked of the occupation of Jerusalem by the Babylonians.

"Wait, that's it!" Bernd almost shouted, which got the attention of the lead librarian who came over and told the couple to hold it down. Bernd went on, "the star talked about in this document, like the others found in Tibet and in your ancestral book is encircled. Seemingly the star symbol was drawn by Babylonians in Jerusalem, but there was no explanation of its significance, nor proof of them drawing it."

These things they would have to confirm somewhere else since the document while it mentioned the symbol, suddenly finished talking about the star symbol abruptly. The document only mentioned the symbol in passing it seemed talking about it being on a wall in a building in Jerusalem. It lacked any other details about it including where in Jerusalem it had been seen. As such the document could not be considered conclusive.

The document continued with an explanation of the Babylonian rule in Jerusalem and their having been pushed out of Jerusalem by Persian forces. That had been long before the Crusades began.

The star symbol, mysteriously, was not recreated on that sheet. It was not drawn, only written about briefly in the document. Why this was the couple could not be sure and likely would never know. They were not, however, surprised that it came across as secretive.

Bernd remembered their time at the temple in southern Iraq now. He realized that what had caused him to stop in mid-sentence while there was the distant memory of the very symbol that he now realized that he had learned of in this document as a student. While at the archaeological dig he was not able to remember that the description of the symbol was an encircled star.

He now stopped, again being totally speechless. He now knew what had been of significance to him that day. There was some kind of connection to the symbol on that temple and the site the Crusaders had been to in Jerusalem. Or so they both now thought. And Jerusalem and the Babylonian temple both lay generally along the route between the Egyptian point and the point in Tibet.

The symbol had never been found to exist anywhere in Jerusalem. And it struck the young couple as odd that no one had made the connection between the recent archaeological site and any connections around the ancient world, at least not yet. This could be since the site had only been discovered a few months earlier. They also realized how hard it was to find connections so far back. This was evident in how long it took the Secret Society to make connections of old.

Yuri remembered now something important. From the few words of the local dialect Yuri had learned, she realized that the local people thought that this building was not a temple, but a house. They were still wondering about the strange looking stone in the middle of one of the walls. Or at least that's what she thought they meant. She remembered thinking that she would want to make connections for her company in that village! To Yuri, of course, the language they spoke was very interesting.

Now in the library in Oxford, Bernd began to explain once more. "Yuri, this symbol was found or at least written about during the Crusades, but later historians believed it to be a symbol written about by Crusaders. It had not been proven to belong to any one group *in Jerusalem*. There was no way of knowing whether or not the reference to the Babylonians was related to the star symbol or simply a relating of the history of the dynamic city." He excitedly and instinctively stopped and took in the view of the document more fully. He began explaining his thoughts again.

"Of course, many thought that being something written about by people who had been to Jerusalem it represented how they wanted to relate the star with five-points instead of as the six-pointed Star of David that most people think of today as predominant in that land." Bernd went on to explain that it was thought to be a misprint, a symbol changed by historical bias.

Yuri mirrored his excitement, but was cautious, still not wanting to jump to any conclusions in their search, remembering the warning of the Secret Society. "This could be important, Bernd, but it seems like a long shot," Yuri said carefully, though almost as if talking to herself rather than to Bernd. "What if the Babylonians were using the five-pointed star and not the six-pointed Star of David when they went into Jerusalem? What happened? Did Jerusalem and the Jewish people begin using the six-pointed star after the Babylonian invasion?" she asked. "This connection to Jerusalem seems important."

"That's just it Yuri," Bernd blurted out once more while grabbing her arm, then looking to see that the lead librarian was not coming over to scold them again. The temple in southern Iraq was probably built before the sacking of Jerusalem. And almost for certain it was built by the time of the tradition of breaking an hour into sixty minutes. That tradition was developed prior to the sacking of Jerusalem by the Babylonians. This connects them to Jerusalem in the time before and at least by this account during the Crusades. Jerusalem, too, might have been a crossing point as people went from Babylon to Egypt, for example, on their journey from the origin. It might also point to the spreading of the star points beyond Jerusalem, perhaps to Egypt or the ancient Maya?"

He began to pace, "What makes this significant is that all of this was long before the Crusades! The symbol likely was not written about by Crusaders to change the six-pointed Star of David in Jerusalem. It was completely independent of that time having come to Jerusalem earlier."

"The symbol may have gotten to other points, too," Yuri suggested. We *must* go check each star point now. Or at least that's what I want to suggest at the Society meeting in about a week." This confirmed their prior conviction. "We must find out if there is any connection between this symbol found in Jerusalem and the star points when we meet in Egypt. Let's confer with them about this," Yuri noted seriously. Yuri and Bernd had developed a few coded phrases that meant let's contact the Secret Society and discuss this with them. They used these phrases now.

They arrived in Egypt later that week only spending a few days in London. They had gone out to eat and toured some places in London such as Tower Bridge, but did not dawdle there knowing the importance of being on time and the significance of the meeting they had helped to call.

Their brief stint in London did give Bernd a chance to partake in one of his favorite pastimes. He really enjoyed going out for a beer. Bernd liked the beer in the United Kingdom; however, he told Yuri that the best beer in Europe was of course made in Germany. Yuri only smiled at him because she thought that good beer was good beer and that it did not matter from where it came. And she believed that good beer was made in many places.

She proposed a toast to, "A safe and speedy journey to Egypt, for the sake of all beings." This last part came out quite naturally for her, but made them both stop suddenly and think about it. She was repeating part of the Bodhisattva vow they had learned in Tibet and they were both surprised. The original vow went something like: "May I awaken speedily for the sake of all beings." They chuckled at her use of it in a toast.

She was really starting to think about what was good for all humans and not just themselves. Though it was a new feeling, this filled her with joy and she smiled to herself. Bernd thought that it was a little strange coming out so suddenly, but also considered that it was very appropriate based on the things they had been doing the past few years. Clearly they were on a journey that mattered to more than just themselves. A few days later this utterance had been mostly forgotten, and they touched down in Cairo, Egypt.

They dropped their things at the hotel and then went to explore the pyramids. Yuri was incredibly excited for two reasons. She knew many more hieroglyphics than the last time she was there, and she was looking forward to playing again in yet another land that had become one of her "other" homes. This was incredibly exciting coming on the heels of having gone to the United Kingdom. When she told this to Bernd he realized that he felt that way about Japan, too.

The first thing they did was to go to the pyramids in Giza near Cairo. This side trip worked out for them as it required only getting the local bus. Fortunately, Yuri could read enough modern Egyptian to find the correct buses to get there and back. They had just enough time to fit this trip in, but they wanted to go as soon as possible to search for any clues they could find related to their search. This trip also provided opportunities for learning about ancient Egypt. The guide led them around and explained many parts of the temples and their many halls to them. Many of them, Yuri admitted she had previously learned about, but had forgotten since being away. Bernd was taking it all in. He was learning everything and enjoying himself very much since it was all new to him. That made it wonderfully exciting and challenging, too. And he liked a challenge.

Everywhere they went of course they continued to look for the symbol of a star within a circle. Seemingly it was nowhere to be found. This made them a little nervous since they had called this meeting and called it in Egypt, but had no way of knowing whether or not Egypt was a true star point or only a stop along the way to the ancient Mayans. Now they both realized that they would have to go there, too. They planned to go at some time to all of the known star points and if necessary all of the places considered possible star points over the years by the Society. For now, they hoped that if another point could be found, that would be enough to settle on the encircled star as the connecting symbol that would lead them in the right direction to the point of origin. Since Egyptian civilization was among the oldest in the world, the young couple could not even be sure that it was not the center, the origin itself.

As they were wandering in a market their second day in Egypt, they came across the Society member from Greece who they had met when they first came across the Secret Society. She invited them to have lunch along the way and took the opportunity to tell them what she knew about the Rosetta Stone.

"When Alexander came from Greece, he brought the Greek language to Egypt," the delegate explained while they ate. As a result, when the Rosetta Stone was found in the 1800s, the Greek language on it helped scholars to decipher the hieroglyphics that were also on that hardened piece of earth. While hearing about this Yuri, who had heard about the Rosetta Stone first while studying hieroglyphics in university, remembered the hospital and the seal under which were the catacombs in Alexandria. She thought of them and wanted to go back there with Bernd since he was now feeling well. She remembered how Bernd not feeling well cut their honeymoon trip short the first time they came here together. She wanted him to experience for himself the wonderful underground passages that she learned about. They would go there together this time.

After the Greek delegate confirmed what was true about what Bernd had read about *initiation* in ancient Greece, they took their leave of her and went back to their hotel for a rest. They would have to discuss the comparison of initiation in ancient Greece with the Tibetan Buddhist initiation another time. They did not have time that day, and they were in Egypt for important business that would take precedent over this extraneous interest of theirs.

After discussing the catacombs, it was set. They would leave for Alexandria the next day. Bernd's stomach turned remembering his stay in the hospital there, but he was happy to have another chance to go there and to be well. And being able to experience it with Yuri made it all the more inviting.

In Alexandria it took them a while to find the underground passageways they had been in briefly before he became ill, but once there, enjoyed walking around the torch lit passages. True some of them were lit with electric lights made to look like torches, but nonetheless this made it all the more fun to explore.

It was said that Alexander left his mark on all the places he went. And here, too, they found he had some handiwork of importance. First he let it be known that he was the chosen one, the sun god. The inscription they read was taken from a prominently displayed tablet made while Alexander was in Egypt. For Alexander being the sun god was of the utmost importance. His trip to Egypt and a visit to an Egyptian oracle or fortune teller confirmed this point. Alexander had this information posted around the catacombs in various ways. In addition, they found that he left the marks of ancient Greece in certain areas. Bernd told Yuri of the lost library of Alexandria that had been found. It confirmed the great extent of learning in the ancient world. It helped tie the present understanding of mathematics and science to the past. Alexander did something, too, that became of great interest to the couple ....

While walking around the catacombs and enjoying their time together Bernd was thanking heaven, the gods and the universe for his good health now on this trip to the catacombs. They walked hand in hand through the catacombs that were dark, musty, damp and truly old. They both remembered the seal on the floor above in the hospital. Yuri wondered out loud how odd it was that the seal was not below, down where they were. Bernd thought about this, but could not figure out why it was not down in this old section of the city, but upstairs.

Later that night they realized that the Secret Society constructed the seal in view of a window so that moon light could come in, the seal would be visible under the midnight sky but not so below. That was the case when Yuri had inquired about it. It had been after midnight. She noticed it while taking a walk to stretch after sitting by Bernd's bed all day.

The seal was different from the others in Japan, they thought now, too. It was a symbol of the society's meeting place in Egypt, but not the representative seal of Egypt as a star point as was the one in Tokyo. Yuri understood now, too, the puzzled looks on the nurses' faces. Not all of them and perhaps many of them could not see the symbol as it was visible only in the moonlight and by people of the *right orientation*.

Bernd began to talk of Alexander's victories from ancient Greece, the region of Macedonia, to Persia, Egypt all the way to India when Yuri said suddenly, "Stop, Bernd."

"Why? What is the matter? Do you want me to repeat something?" he asked.

Yuri did not answer right away. She was thinking now very carefully about something she noticed. Yuri had been fixing her hair while using a make-up mirror she had purchased while on the trip since she had left the other one in safe keeping back in Japan. In the reflection she now noticed something that caught her interest and was beginning to feel as though it would be interesting for Bernd, too. "Well, we've already been by this area before while walking and recounting our anniversary cruise around the Mediterranean Sea, haven't we?" was her response finally. He agreed with a nod of the head.

"And, why is that of any matter? I was hoping that we could go above and find the seal on the floor of the hospital again," Bernd tried to make sense out of the situation for them both.

"And get some coffee no doubt," she inquired teasingly.

"Well, yes." he admitted amazed at how quickly she figured out his intention, finishing with "Why did you want me to stop?"

Yuri continued with, "See that curved line and two-points?"

"Yes, of course, it is marking the doorway across from where we are standing," Bernd answered her.

"Well, that mark is the mirror image of one we walked past about fifteen minutes ago clear across on the other side of the catacomb.

"Really?" Bernd said, amazed by her attention to detail.

"I think so. Let's make sure," she said, while walking up to the lines that Bernd had thought of as decoration up until this time. The symbol was a dark gray color such as slate that made a contrast against the whitish gray rock used to make the walls of the catacomb. Other places, too, had bluish hues and golden colors as well.

The couple measured the lines and documented the measurements and size of the symbol in the notebook that Bernd always had with him for new items of research. Then they retraced their steps to the previous spot Yuri was thinking of on the other side of the catacombs. The place they were going to was about a quarter of a mile away. Finally after having to make sure on the compass three times that they were walking in the right direction they came to another doorway that led into another region of the catacombs. It was due west of the first door that sat on the eastern side of the catacombs.

As Yuri had expected, the symbol was there in reverse on the opposite side of the door from the previous half symbol. They were sure to measure the distance from the floor to the symbol as well as the size and dimensions of the symbol itself. It was exactly the mirror of the other. Even how far off of the floor it was matched the previous one.

The two were very interested in that Alexander had had the symbol cut in half exactly and used to mark two different doorways. It was something he was known for, making changes to suit himself. Alexander separated the encircled star symbol it now seemed and put it on either side of the door at the points exactly east and west from each other on the compass. It could not be a coincidence. He had planned to conquer the whole world. That was what he then set out to do and achieved. He conquered all-of-the known world up until that time, and the journey stretched across Eurasia east and west.

What Alexander could not have known was that this change made by separating the wall with a symbol and posting it by separated doors had gone unnoticed up until now. It had been enough to throw off the Secret Society ever since they took up the quest to look for the star points hundreds and hundreds of years ago. Since the doors were so far apart, the Society simply had not put two and two together so to speak. And Yuri thought that it was ironic that this location was positioned in almost the very place that became the meeting place of the Society from its very beginning!

She and Bernd had been briefed by the Egyptian delegate of the whereabouts of the underground meeting place when they found that all of them would be in Egypt at the same time. The Egyptian had chuckled when he remembered the stir caused by Yuri's asking the meaning of the symbol on the floor of the hospital above where they now stood. The nurse had become something of a hero now since informing the society of Yuri's inquisitiveness.

With that, the couple realized that there were only three things they could do: first, take careful notes to bring to the important Society meeting in Cairo, second, go upstairs to view the seal in the hospital, and third, to have some coffee.

Secret Society Meeting in Egypt

It had been two and one half weeks after the discovery of the symbol while in Tibet. The relatively old age of the artifact and the symbolism of the image were lost on neither the couple nor the members of the Secret Society whom the couple had contacted immediately. Though they were now able to contact the Society in the time-honored secret way there were some important things that slowed down having a meeting.

Though they tried to make contact immediately it was still true that immediately meant more than a few days to make contact with the Society. Even with the required knowledge to call a meeting, meetings could not be set up *immediately*. A certain protocol needed to be followed. Since this was the digital age, photos could be taken along on jump drives, CDs and various other storage devices that facilitated clear understanding of the significant findings along the routes now being traveled by Society members around the world. This sped up understanding, but did little for speeding up setting meetings, making contact with others …. Secrecy was paramount.

Now they would finally meet all the expert members of the Secret Society. Yuri and Bernd were realistic in their hopes. They realized that if the Secret Society thought the symbol that they found truly was not part of their search, then, they would have to find another way that the star points were connected.

Bernd decided that he would have the star symbol considered again separately as a deeper connection to the Crusades in his ongoing research for Sophia University. Yuri, however, felt it deep within her being and was sure that the encircled star symbol was significant in some way to their current search. Hopefully it would point them to the origin someday. She remained hopeful and now more anxious than ever to meet with the members of the Society.

The meeting was called while they were in Tibet, and now they were in Egypt. This presented them with the problem of once again making contact with other members of the Secret Society, this time locally. The instructions were to do just that, contact Society members once you arrive. The location of the meeting other than saying simply "Cairo" was not divulged so as to not put their meeting place in jeopardy of being found out. Since the couple had never been to a meeting in Cairo, they now were at a loss as to how to find the location.

Their only way forward was connecting with other members of the Society. When they were with the Greek delegate the other day this had not even crossed their minds. They wished now that they had set a time and a place to meet her regarding the meeting that was to happen this very day!

When connecting with members in Cairo, the young couple now needed to employ techniques that had been shown to them at their initiation all over again. There were a separate set of techniques available for contacting members in addition to those employed to "call a meeting." This was so that a member who caught only part of the symbolism would not run off and call a meeting when it wasn't necessary.

They would make signs once more with their hands that could only be recognized by members of the Secret Society. There were several sets of actions to take place to signify whether or not the other really was a member of the Society or simple scratching one's back so to speak.

To start with one began by drawing one's hand up one's back as one does when calling a meeting. Then, differently, one runs three fingers slightly parted that could be run through the hair on one's head. One would give the first part of the sign, and if members of the Society were present they would give the next part of the sign. The second set was to have the person who observed those actions correspond by doing the same action in reverse. When done well, Yuri thought it looked just like one began spontaneously to scratch one's back or run fingers through one's hair. So if one person ran their fingers through their hair, for example, the next person ran them through their hair in reverse. In the case of the back scratching technique the proposed Society member would reply by running their hand down their back in reverse fashion of person who initiated the action.

There were various two part stages to use as one proceeded in finding out if other members were present in a given area. As each sign was matched correctly one would proceed, making absolute sure that the other person making the signs was doing so on purpose, as proof that they were a Society member. If there was any indication that others were making symbols by coincidence that coincided with the Society member's actions, then the game was off, and one simply walked away. Confirming this was not always easy to determine since members were purposefully making the signs as if they were not doing anything on purpose! It was as though they were running their fingers through their hair, scratching their backs or something otherwise that was a normal human action such as itching ones left ear. If there were no members present it only looked like one was being overly elaborate in scratching his or her back or head, and so no harm was done aside from the possible confusion that might occur in an innocent bystander.

Because it seemed too simple to be effective, Yuri and Bernd soon realized how brilliant it was. This style had worked over the centuries to unite members of the Society in far places, and it still worked to this day! They were amazed, and they were glad that it was simple and so effective. Obviously, one thing that made it effective was that members would be actively seeking out other members on occasions such as this.

Many members knew how interesting the recent months had been and wanted to and were prepared to attend. Out of consideration, all members realized that it was important not to leave any interested members out of the coming meeting. That is why it took more than two weeks to confirm the meeting in Egypt and to ensure that all interested were able to attend even with the increased level of interest shown recently. Without the internet, this would have been impossible in this short a period of time. The young couple was told that one month was the quickest that a meeting would have been called in the nineteenth century. Technology and communication in the nineteenth century were slower, but the techniques used to this day had been the same.

Just as they were about to give up, they noticed someone rubbing his back in the reverse order of them. When he turned around smiling they became hopeful that it was a Society member. It wasn't until he winked at them that they recognized Pankaj, the delegate from India. Their joy upon seeing someone with whom they felt an important connection was immediate.

The meeting was assembled in Cairo for its ease of access by plane, boat, camel, or otherwise. The meeting was to be held in the basement of a very old museum that the Indian delegate was presently walking them toward along an old thoroughfare of Cairo filled with shops, people selling their wares in long shirts, wearing lose, flowing, cover cloths and in the midst of the smell of spices, animals and humanity. They passed down some side streets totally amazing Yuri and Bernd. Yuri really enjoyed the sights and sounds as well as the smells of these side adventures when she could take them in the countries she was visiting. This was true even if the smells sometimes made her feel a little queasy. Bernd noticed that the smells were always the strongest recollection for him. Yuri was impressed mostly by the visual aspect of the journey.

Though the building itself wasn't old enough for this to be true, it seemed, that the Society had been using the museum since the original star point was found in Egypt many hundreds of years ago. It was perfect. There was an altar built into the front of the room in which they now stood. What made it perfect for them was this item since they enjoyed having an altar that gave their meetings a sacred tone. The advantage here was that the altar was not built by them. It was part of the museum.

The altar was used to mark the rise of early civilization and especially regarding the Sumerians and their form of writing, cuneiform. Cuneiform was made by using wedge shaped instruments to make impressions in clay tablets that when dried held a story, a ledger for a business and its transactions or some other form of communication deemed important so long ago. The Society did, however, embellish the altar. Since they began using the seals to record the star points both discovered and being looked for, there were smaller replicas of the seals engraved in the walls behind the altar. They were disguised as Sumerian symbols that had been translated into other languages. The two blank symbols were works in progress albeit for two hundred plus years! The claim was lack of funding, agreements, appropriate wording, etc ….

The stewards of the seals had already agreed about the fifth one, found in Japan recently. As for the seal regarding the origin, as of yet, all bets were off.

It had long been a Society tradition that the person most instrumental in finding a star point, such as Yuri, would help with the translation into that language. That is why each seal had been translated slightly differently. It had been so long since some of them had been written, that it made people wonder, too, if the modern understanding of the meanings was accurate or not.

The way in which the person who helped find or establish that there was a star point was significant in how the seal would be written.

What that person decided would be best to describe the feeling behind the search, and the significance of the star point for all concerned is what would be put into the wording. The Society couldn't be sure whether or not any hints at the place of origin were included in the seals as the trek was unique in each corner of the world.

In the case of the fifth star point, Bernd of course, could help with the feeling behind the search. Yuri, being Japanese, would choose the wording for the Japanese star point seal. She of course was free to consult with others about the language to use, but would be instrumental in choosing those words. It was an honor and an important task, nothing to be taken lightly.

On the same wall they looked at the blank seal created ahead of time in preparation for signifying the place of origin once it was found. Having a blank seal representing the point of origin, at one and the same time created a sense of optimism and awe. There was optimism in the looking forward to finding the point of origin and also awe at it being a mystery after so many years. Many have proposed where the place of origin would be, but none has been able to define it, definitely, ever.

The meeting was commenced in this room named by the society *The Sumerian Room*. This they believed was easier to say than the room housing "Artifacts of the Beginnings of Civilization in the Ancient World."

After commencing the meeting, Yuri and Bernd were introduced to the assembly made up of so many Society members that they had not yet met. Briefly they talked about the encircled star symbol and how they had found it in the ancestral book on the island of Yuri's birth. They then told the assembly their two greatest discoveries that the symbol was found in Tibet and of the brand new one found in the catacombs of Alexandria. At this last mention of the symbol in Alexandria, there was a collective gasp in the hall. There was so much bottled up interest and excitement in the room that the Greek delegate acting as host, called a break. During the break the following took place.

Again, the finest refreshments from around the world were present. There was *masala* chai or spiced black tea from India, yaks milk tea from Tibet, the finest in green tea from Japan and green oolong teas from China and many, many more varieties of refreshments. The Americans had made chocolate chip cookies, but the Greeks stuck with their baklava. In addition to sweets there were vegetable options and pure, real fruits that proved to Yuri that the world had not gone completely mad. She loved eating what nature provided in the way it had provided it. She found that with real food, too, she could make very tasty dishes. It amazed her and now Bernd, too, since meeting her that processed food was so common around the world. The Americans had noted this feeling in more than just Yuri, so they took special care to make the cookies from scratch using only naturally occurring ingredients. Society members truly strove to get along. Everything, without reservation was shared. As a result there was ample food and drink for everyone.

During the break, Yuri and Bernd had a chance to catch up with some people who were rapidly becoming like old friends to them. The Egyptian delegate now in his homeland and looking ever the more fine for it, the Tibetan, who apologized for not being able meet with them longer while they were in Tibet and the Greek delegate who avoided the baklava and had salad instead. Yuri chuckled and invited her to go to yoga with them the next day. She accepted immediately. It was among her favorite forms of exercise.

Of course all present wanted to approach the couple at the break, but realizing that that would make them uncomfortable, that did not happen. There was an elegant decorum among those present, and it was not shattered by the amazing things they had heard. After the break, Yuri and Bernd were asked to talk of what they had found. The description of Yuri and Bernd's travels was kept to a minimum explaining briefly how they found the temple in a house in southern Iraq and then went on to talk in detail of Tibet where they were blown away by the discovery of a symbol that they had seen in three separate places, the encircled star.

Yuri and Bernd asked for the assistance of the Society members present in interpreting the significance of the encircled star symbol. Though she had wondered about its possible connections to the place of origin, Yuri had a note of caution in her voice, having learned from the Egyptian delegate to be careful not to assume anything. They were not convinced that the three symbols they found were anything other than a coincidence.

She did not talk of the Alexander symbol in detail, but asked cautiously whether anyone would be willing to be members of a committee to explore a symbol that she and Bernd had come across in Egypt. It was as though the whole room moved when she finished speaking. Virtually all volunteered. Obviously, the Alexander symbol would be explored right away even that day.

Yuri then went on to talk of what she believed or guessed was the significance behind the doings of those early people using stars as symbols along their search route, those who went away from the point of origin. The reason, Yuri proposed to the Secret Society, that the star symbol had been chosen was that stars existed in great numbers. She went on to explain that she thought that the original people recognized this and used stars to represent points along the way. Further, she believed that this meant that all people are included in any meaningful plan as all are included under the night time sky. At least that is what she believed it must have seemed to the ancients.

"Surely," she went on "…any ancient astronomers would have been able to figure this out." There was a slight pause while what Yuri and Bernd said was translated to members around the room and posted in English up in front along side the altar that had been decorated with various bright colors to represent a sense of joy as they assembled together as a group. Once again, the assembly was used as an occasion for celebration.

The members of the Secret Society quickly agreed with Yuri's inclusive reading of the star points. It had to be that the symbol of a star represented something that is truly countless. Therefore, members of the Society now considered the number of star points again. It seemed to them that even though there were only five star points verified that this was not meant to limit the possible connections around the world to only five places. But the five places, being established as star points, would come to symbolize a beginning that would later …number as the stars. The five star points had been points established as people left from the origin on a trajectory as toward legs of a star itself. This they had confirmed with Yuri and Bernd's findings at Horyuji. Bernd, now to himself wondered about the finding at Jerusalem and whether or not it was meant to be a star point or even *the origin.*

The members of the Secret Society again were struck by workings of fate and the good luck of being brought together with Yuri. No one had quite said it like that before. So many had been focused on the shape of stars and where the next point would be found. The symbol of the star they now were coming to see was meant to include all, and being under the same sky was only a beginning. The original members, the people from the place of origin, it was guessed, went on a quest to establish and to make connections to five distant parts of the "known" world. Indeed, now that five connections had been made people could continue making connections anywhere and everywhere it would seem. Also, the possibilities were infinite because the symbol of a star now was seen to represent such great numbers. And some considered that since stars represented night this was significant since clearly it was always night somewhere. This had been the emphasis until now, that the use of the star points was to signify that all lived under the same sky one that was the home of the stars.

One Society member noted that the trails from point to point go through what is now Iraq or ancient Babylon a crossroads of the Silk Road. This prompted Bernd to mention that there was an archaeological dig going on there now. The group thought that it was some kind of out post on the trek from the origin. They thought this because it was in the middle of where ancient Babylon would have been, itself an early outpost of civilization.

There was a pause again, though this time it was not so that translations could be made. It was a commonly felt sense around the room. During this pause, Bernd remembered the Secret Society member's question about how the ancient Silk Road began. He now wondered if it even could be true that the beginning of the Silk Road may have been in part caused by the ancient treks themselves and was not only related to trade.

Was it possible that the Secret Society, going about in search of the star points, would have helped make connections along the Silk Road even further? Why did this idea of Babylon now course through the room and his brain? He would not have been surprised, but he did not know that sitting next to him Yuri was thinking the exact same thing. The image of the temple farmhouse now came to the fore in her brain. The image burned deeper as she sat next to her history-loving, scientist husband.

The idea of Babylon resonated with people around the room in a way that it had not before. After the pause, that allowed for the gaining of insight into the farmhouse discovery at Babylon, here are some of the things that were discussed. She was as glad as ever that he took on some extra work in this research project.

In ancient Babylon because of a long tradition of astronomy and rigorous documentation of the movements of the stars, many things were discovered. For example, they built upon previous cultural achievements in that area of early civilization to make the separation of an hour into sixty minutes. They counted with a base of sixty. This of course ultimately led to the development of a day having twenty four hours that is widely used today. Of course along with the idea of keeping track of the passage of time, and hours and a day came watching the sun travel throughout the sky. Along with this was the related exploration and discoveries of the passage of the moon and the *stars* at night.

It was recognized that this exploration took place not only in Babylon, but also in other places such as ancient China. Marking time by the day and the night time sky certainly touched everyone on the planet and included all. Indeed, this exploration of the night time sky was evident in Babylon as elsewhere with the use of vertical poles that showed the passage of time in the year from season to season based on the length of a shadow at certain times, for example, at noon. (1983, Krupp, Echoes of the Ancient Skies, pp. 47)

In Egypt, this was true, too. The Egyptians explored the night time sky giving significance to the stars and the movements of heavenly bodies. Ra, the sun god, for example, that lived during the day only to die at night and be reborn the next day again ever anew is evidence of this tendency. That this was a widespread discovery around the planet is evident in that there was developed an ancient Aztec calendar as well as ancient "pillars" used to mark the equinox or solstice times in ancient Scotland. Also there is evidence of ancient pillars that marked the spot to stand to view the horizon and the moon or sun rising or setting as the seasons changed in any number of ancient traditions in addition to the ancient Mesopotamian calendars ….

It was agreed. That was what the symbol meant! It meant inclusion for all, and the star was symbolic of the millions and now billions of people who lived on the earth on every continent. They soon realized that the reason this had been overlooked for centuries was the simplicity of it. It seemed too obvious. Stars, too, were a brilliant choice they thought. As they were discovering together now, stars could be seen as countless, limitless and yet inclusive especially when encircled as this symbol was! Stars, too, in ancient Babylon represented gods such as Ishtar, or Venus. Stars are seen as significant in the lives of people around the planet.

Though the star of Ishtar was eight-pointed like the eight-pointed wheel in Buddhism, the five-point star was chosen by those early people. Simplicity once again it seemed to the young couple now who overheard Society members discussing these matters. And then, because of technology and some quick thinking earlier by Bernd the following happened.

The Secret Society was able to see this star image from the site in southern Iraq themselves thanks to the resourceful Bernd. If Bernd had not been working at the university this would not have been possible. He received permission to capture pictures of the "house" and promised to bring the images to the university archaeology lab. He did this with the digital camera he had brought with him. He was not, however, planning to give the star image to the folks in the archaeology department. He went a step further, too, and told the people at the sight in southern Iraq that he wasn't sure, but thought that the symbol may have been a symbol of the family itself like a coat of arms though he did not know of any special importance it might hold. He felt bad about this misleading statement, but thought the needs of their search outweighed the detriment of making this statement.

Again there was a pause, though this one became quiet and was a pause that went on for several minutes. Most people present were stunned into silence. They were stunned by a realization that they simply could not believe to be true. Yuri and Bernd did not understand why there was such a long pause. Being so new to the Society they thought that it was a pause at a certain time such as 10:00 PM or something else that had been agreed upon. They considered that it may have been a moment of silent, group meditation or something like that. This is what followed that long pause.

Another idea began to take over the meeting. And then a noise began to be emitted by the crowd. At First it began as a murmuring, and then it became almost a full-fledged ruckus. Yuri and Bernd were beside themselves wondering just what the fuss was about. The Egyptian, the Greek and the Tibetan delegates were now waving them over to a table at the edge of the room. The Indian delegate had just joined them, and those at the table were in heated discussion. When the couple came over the discussion stopped as all eyes turned to them which of course made the young couple uneasy.

After that moment of disquiet, the delegates got over their shock. Yuri and Bernd were told that nothing was the matter and to not be concerned by the awkward silence. Those at this table began to describe slowly and calmly in more detail the significance of the find as members of the Society saw it.

This smaller delegation told the two that the symbol of the encircled star probably predated modern religions and must have been chosen for its obvious connected symbolism that Yuri had pointed out and to which they agreed. With the round sides there is a connection created by a circle that is encircling and including all. Also the symbol represented connections between all points with its intersecting lines as the star was not drawn hollow. In this case the circle around the star had connected them all. The star having five-points was not separable into pairs of points. Each was interdependent with the others to make up the symbol, in this case the star symbol. *And* that they now suspected that the oldest depiction of the symbol found, the one in southern Iraq, that they designated as Babylon was more than likely to be the *center* or *origin*!

The couple was awestruck. They figured that the symbol was pointing them to the origin, but had not believed that Babylon was it. After all it was not exactly in the center of the ancient world. The Egyptian went on to explain that regardless of its actual geographic location, Babylon was at a symbolic crossroads of civilization. Indeed, it was a key part of Mesopotamia, what has been called the cradle of civilization. Babylon was a centrally located site and became a center even if by different names as time went on along the Silk Road. Once again it came to the fore in Bernd's mind that a Secret Society member had talked of the significance of the Society using the Silk Road route. Bernd realized now the truth of what that meant. The use of the Silk Road by the Secret Society and perhaps those at the origin before them likely made a significant contribution to it becoming the well-traveled route that it did.

And, too, the Indian continued, "You see, a star was a symbol of the unity of the night time sky and the day-time sky in the sense of marking the sky and thus giving humans a way to think about and record the passage of time, especially the seasons."

"Hence," the Greek delegate continued, "this is symbolized by the use of constellations to make sense out of the sky by the ancient Greeks."

The Indian continued, "Since the Babylonians had already developed the knowledge of telling time by breaking up the day into twenty four hours, an hour into sixty minutes and used calendars etc …stars would already have been considered important by them. One would use an important and impressive symbol like this don't you think?" he asked all at the table who readily agreed. The couple began to realize just how much the Society had considered the star points over the years. While they had not found the origin, they were obviously already prepared to understand it in a very detailed way.

"The night time sky further symbolized opportunities for quiet reflection at night as opposed to busi-ness during the day." the

Egyptian went on. "This information, that of the night-time reflection by farmers, we found in hieroglyphics on a pyramid, but that no one dared think was related to those from the origin. Truly the idea could have been put on the pyramid at any time in the past, even the recent past."

The Egyptian began to relate the story to them all. "It went something like this. During the day farmers produced crops and tended livestock in earth's earliest civilizations that we now know developed around 8,000 to 10,000 years ago. This, too, was a very important connection as well. All of the star points started with farmers, real people, or those who were connected to the earth in some sincere way.

In Russia, this responsibility was passed along to Peter the Great at one-point, and he was the only exception to this rule. He became the keeper of the star point in Russia for reasons of safety. It was believed that he could keep the star point safe since the "Tsar of all the Russias" was the most powerful person in a dangerous land. It was felt that he, being of such strength of character would be suitable for care of the star point. At least that is what people thought when they realized that he built St. Petersburg starting in 1703 CE. It was after all to be another kind of connection. He did after all call it the "window" to the west.

This honor of watching over the star point in Russia had been given to him, it seems by a farmer. The farmer was from the lineage of the original group that established the star point. It was significant that his ruling predecessors were not given the privilege of guarding the star point nor were his successors. Indeed, that duty was returned to a farmer, someone close to the land to firmly keep it grounded in reality so to speak at least until keeping track of the star point was lost. Even so, it was fortunate that Peter had done his duty by securing it while the modern system of the Tsars took shape.

That Babylon seemed to be the origin was so exciting and stunning that for all present everything but their beating hearts had simply stopped …for several minutes. Yuri and Bernd were ecstatic that they had helped to find this information. Secretly Yuri hoped that it was true, though still remained cautious.

All agreed, too, that this would have to be confirmed at other sites, the very reason for Yuri's continuing caution. An additional delegation to the ancient Mayan capital as well as to what had been Babylon was organized right away. Other delegations would go to Russia and India as well. It was not enough to know that the star point had been moved to the secluded kingdom of Tibet for safety from India. They would confirm whether or not the symbol was to be found in India, too. Of course, Tibet may have had this symbol simply as a crossroads along the path of those leaving from or returning to the origin. Either way it was clear that it was necessary to confirm their discovery. A delegation was sent to each star point to confirm things once and for all. Though unlike in Alexander the Great's time, it would not be to the entire known world; it would be to all of the known star points.

After arrangements were made to send delegations to explore the newly found symbol, the party was planned. True, they would have to make sure as to whether or not the symbol was present at all the known star points but for now, that would have to wait. The celebration would not be delayed.

The Secret Society had realized this early on. Celebration with a capital "C" was among the most important parts of life. If for nothing other than blessing the fact that one was alive for that day, a celebration was seen as appropriate. Indeed, some saw it as necessary if one was not to be considered among those who were missing out on life so to speak.

Though the party would start right away, many understandably were cautious. Still all were willing to celebrate finding, it seemed, the place of origin. Again, the finest foods and drinks from places from which all the delegates came were served now in plentiful amounts to all present. There were fine curries filled with cumin and cinnamon, nan, the Indian styled bread, Russian caviar, *ikura*, the raw salmon roe fish eggs so popular in Japan among many other tasty, healthy and nutritious foods from around the world.

Though he was skeptical, Bernd took this opportunity to try some American beer made at a brewery in Wisconsin. He was pleasantly surprised to find that the beer made in America was not made up only of the watery thin beer he had tried years ago. The beer he had now was full of taste and very delicious. It was said of that Wisconsin family that they had been brewing that brand of beer for something like five generations.

Yuri reminded Bernd of what the abbot at Bentenji had said. There is nothing wrong with beer, but there is something unwholesome about being blatantly drunk. Bernd shot back reminding Yuri of the abbot at a small temple in Hiroshima who got drunk and laughed about this fact.

All Yuri said was, "guru yoga," and Bernd gave in. He knew better than to go against the recommendations of a teacher who was serious about giving instruction to students. That would bring about really bad karma, he believed. Respect for others, especially the teacher was important in many of the Buddhist traditions he had read about. This was emphasized emphatically by the Tibetans who took Yuri and Bernd under their wing while the young couple was in Tibet. Their guru was at Bentenji. Bernd understood the point and so began to focus on the company around him in a renewed way. The beer had clearly become secondary and people became the main focus. He liked this way of prioritizing very much. It was in great contrast to an over emphasis on the tastiness of beer or food. He liked putting people as the main focus for a very simple reason; it felt good

The Last Treks of Confirmation

In subsequent meetings of the Secret Society, after completion of the treks to confirm that the symbol was truly at all of the star points, this is what was revealed. They found that the original purpose of the group, that they found to be called the Star Gazers Society, was to form societies and groups that would be an example that we humans can all work together and cooperate. It was based in the area of the origin, the temple house in ancient Babylon. In addition, from the beginning, while the members cooperated effortlessly they also did not make a big deal out of this as they did so. This was on purpose. It was meant to represent that working together really should be the norm and not a big deal.

The archaeological dig that Yuri and Bernd had come across seemed to confirm these ideas. This was known eventually by both Yuri and Bernd though not right away. The knowledge came from several contacts that the Society made with and around this temple-dwelling. Because of these contacts at some time later several other things about that place were confirmed.

The Society found out that the temple-dwelling of the original Star Gazers, was the home of a Babylonian farmer. That it was a simple dwelling was that way on purpose they believed. There was a document, a cuneiform tablet, unearthed that had been hidden deep in a hole behind the rock around which the temple-dwelling was built. The tablet stated that there were plans to renovate or move the Star Gazers meetings from that place. On the clay tablet it was made clear that in the end they decided to stay in the temple-dwelling. The main reason for this decision was to foster and maintain the idea of simplicity.

Another point about it was discovered down the line by the Secret Society. This simple farmer's temple-dwelling had an excellent view of a nearby mountain. In fact, the local people bragged about how it provided an unobstructed view for miles around. Apparently viewing the night time sky from there was breathtaking. And these discoveries happened after confirming the remaining star point sites, making it all the more difficult to confirm them.

The symbol had been found to exist, too, in the Mayan area, but only after much research and searching that took over a year. It was found not on the wall of the ancient ruins at which the star point had been confirmed, but found within a very old pyramid shaped structure. It was found included along with part of a ceremonial rite used to mark of all things the passing of time. It was found on the cover of a kind of ancient calendar inscribed in stone. The symbol was included at the beginning of the ceremonial inscriptions written across the bottom of the calendar. As it was in Tibet, it was presented to look as though it was a decoration. Whether this was on purpose or by accident the Society neither knew nor cared. Members of the Secret Society were excited simply to have found it.

Yuri and Bernd were prepared to go out with other members of the Society to confirm star points, but one last thing was running around in their minds unanswered. What was the connection they wondered between an ancestral book and the belongings, a diary, of Prince Shotoku? This was such an amazing coincidence that it certainly made it hard to believe. Certainly if it was planned, then it was brilliant in its unlikelihood. No one would have guessed any connection between Yuri's ancestors and the Prince's. As far as Yuri knew there was none.

The couple decided to go to Horyuji perhaps one last time. Of course since it had been their temple of exciting visits up until now there was no guarantee that this visit would be the last! They met with Abbot Furuta to converse once again about the history of the connection between Bentenji or at least the abbot of Bentenji and the abbots of Horyuji. What they found amazed them now all over again.

The temple arrangements were such that in the past the abbots had shared disciples back and forth. However, since this created such hardships in times when good disciples were hard to find, this practice had ended many years earlier. The disciple "assigned" to Prince Shotoku, Yuri and Bernd astutely guessed was none other than the disciple who had a good relation with Yuri's family many, many lost generations ago. After all, he had been a student at the neighboring temple, Bentenji.

He had been in Horyuji on exchange from Bentenji when the Prince saw an opportunity. It was not clear how much the Prince was involved in the placement of the star point in Japan. Still, that he was a key figure in the founding of Horyuji was enough to make the couple wonder how much he was or was not part of setting the star point there.

This disciple they now realized had written in the Prince's diary while at Horyuji and was employed in the same endeavor on the island of Yuri's birth, too, writing in the family's ancestral book. He had written a post card that had been inserted into the ancestral book, but had been taken out and it seemed, lost. He had left notation within the back cover of the book so that all information would not be lost, they now guessed. Surprisingly, he had been right.

The reason for the selection of the Island of Yuri's birth was simple. Being relatively remote from the four larger islands of Japan and having a connection to the Prince, the star point would hopefully not be lost for all time if those who knew about it passed away. And at the same time, the star point would not be discovered by accident as the clue to its whereabouts was on an island, safe and sound far from Horyuji.

The disciple may or may not have known the significance of his work, however, his handwriting and his loyalty in carefully following instructions allowed the connection to the Prince to go unnoticed for centuries. He played a significant role in connecting the two temples, the two families and the star point in Japan at Horyuji. If it weren't for his loyal participation, finding the star point could have taken much longer, the couple now considered as they were headed back to the train station, hearts feeling assured. It wasn't easy either, they both now thought as they laughed out loud. Keeping a secret such as a star point must have been a lot of work.

They could now move onto other parts of this journey energized once more by their visit and knowledge gained at Horyuji. They had grown to love the temple. And so they prepared to join the Secret Society delegation at the most difficult place to confirm, the encircled star symbol, Russia.

Based on their experiences up until then they were not at all surprised that everything did not go smoothly. In Russia the symbol was confirmed, however, it took two years to find it which led to many people questioning whether or not these symbols really were the connecting factor to the place of origin. This was before the clay tablet was found out behind the rock at the temple-dwelling in what had been Babylon.

The symbol was found in the cloth lining of an Icon, an Orthodox religious painting such as that of a saint or the mother of God. In this case it was on the inside lining on the back side of an Icon of Saint Anthony, *the patron saint of finding lost items* of all things! When Bernd had heard this he laughed out loud. Bernd knew that this was the belief about St. Anthony in the western Catholic Church. The couple figured that this hold over from the western, Catholic tradition made many overlook it in eastern, Orthodox Russia.

    This Icon was particularly hard to get a chance to view, but after Yuri and Bernd joined the other Society members, it became possible. Once again Bernd pretended to be doing a study of Orthodoxy for Sophia University and Yuri claimed that she wanted to look at the image up close for a new dictionary about to be published that included information about world religions. It would be in Russian, Spanish, English, Chinese, French, and Japanese. The church in Novgorod, where the Icon was kept in adoration locked from the public granted permission to view the item. Even so they were only given a few minutes and were made to promise not to use any flash photography. It was easily the most ambitious work on comparative religions yet, the attendant commented as he led them to the Icon.

    Prior to viewing the item it had been agreed that the church would get credit for the image even if a flash were not used. Since a flash was not used, the picture was of lower quality as a result. The picture had in it the symbol. Thankfully it could be seen though it was dim being one layer beneath the outer layer of the thin cloth covering that held the icon to the wooden frame. The outer lining was fastened by nails that looked like staples. Bernd noticed that it was very secure. There wasn't the time or the means to peel back the cloth. Thus what they saw through the photo would have to do as evidence for the Society. Not long after, the archaeological site discoveries were made in Iraq in what had been Babylon.

    The Alexander symbol that had been pointing to two sister pyramids both east and west of where the symbols were found, was confirmed last. The separated Alexander symbol itself had been explored the very day of the meeting in Cairo. What eluded the onlookers until later was the reason why the symbol had been separated to begin with. It was not because Alexander connected from west to east the entire known world up until that time. It was because it designated two places in which the inclusive star circle was found. One was the pyramid where Alexander met the oracle who stated that Alexander was the Sun god. And the second pyramid was in Cairo, of course a pyramid in the Valley of Kings of which Alexander wished to be considered a prominent one. The symbol was drawn in the hieroglyphics of both temples, but though he added significance to them they were not for Alexander. They had predated his arrival in Egypt. That they had been included in the hieroglyphics of the pyramids was because they both were pyramids along the Silk Road routes as established in Egypt as a follow up to arrivals in Antioch from the East.

The Symbol in India had been icing on the cake so to speak. After finding the symbol in Tibet, it was really a measure for peace of mind to look in India. What they found they could not have been sure even existed. Where the Buddha had given his first teaching in Sarnath, the symbol was inscribed on the lower part of a very old relic that remained because it was where he had stood that day. As for the Buddha, he may or may not have known of the whereabouts of the symbol. Bernd and Yuri couldn't imagine that the symbol was known to him at that time. They imagined that he probably did not care, either. Indeed, no one knew why the symbol had been moved to Tibet, there being no record of such a move.

With that, the symbol had been confirmed in relation to all five of the star points. This along with the cuneiform tablet pointed to Babylon being the true center, the point of origin. Members of the Secret Society were beside themselves with joy ... and then it sank in.

The sixth star point seal had to be written now. It could not be written with the help of the ancients; they were no more. It had to be something that expressed the journey from the origin, and the journey as it would be today. It needed to give some idea, too, of the meaning of return to the origin. All thought of it as an important undertaking. Indeed, it would point the way to proceed from here on out.

Experienced members of the society and newer members, some of which had belonged to the Secret Society since only a few years before Yuri and Bernd, would be included equally in this endeavor. Each according to whether or not their ideas were useful or captured a significant part of the journey up until now would play a part. The conditions for choosing which writing and contributions would be used on the sixth seal was based upon the appropriateness of ideas and not based on any kind of seniority system. This was in line with the cooperative and compassionate nature of the Society.

Nonetheless the obvious question arose; what would be appropriate to include? This was now crossing the minds of each and every one of the members present in Egypt that day ....

Attending to the seals...

Here is what they came up with for the sixth seal. It was widely understood now, that the result of their work proved that when all was said and done, nothing was *finished*.

This journey was long from being over. Hence the wording on the seal would honor the feeling of other seals in language that did not suggest only *completion*, but also an *ongoing* journey. And it would also emphasize that the journey was not only not finished, but all together possible, too. The Society member's feelings were not unlike the monks who upon reaching enlightenment under the Buddha's tutelage, found that there was more to do. They would have to help others. The Society members now realized that finding the symbols and the origin were only half of the journey. They discovered that what they had found brought them to an end of a chapter in human history or at least their Society's history. Now it was their turn to complete the work began so many, many years ago.

How would they do this? What did this work entail? Before them, these questions drove away half of the monks who had gained enlightenment under the tutelage of the Buddha. However for them, they thought, it really was quite simple. Again, the simplicity of the journey led to the approach taken, and that the approach taken was simple allowed it to be elusive for so long. They would include information from all the previous seals, especially the most recent one developed by Yuri and Bernd while on the journey to confirm the existing star points. It said: "Ten no shita de kagayaiteiru hoshi no you ni, mina san no kyouryoku ga nagareteiru." This meant: *Under heaven, shining like the stars, flows the collaboration of everyone.* Yuri felt that this wording would honor both Horyuji and the Society ideal of collective collaboration. She also felt that the collaboration between the couple and with the Society was responsible for them finding the fifth star point.

The sixth seal as written said it all they thought: "The world is coming together by making connections numbering as the stars, as witnessed by the stars, with unfolding, creative cooperation revealing possibilities among people" It was stated longer than the other seals, but needed to be longer in order to summarize them all, the members thought. Though there was a spirit of cooperation and several members needed to leave the room so as to not be angry at any other Society members, in the end all agreed to this version for the sixth seal. It was later set in stone or rather sand so to speak.

The following was discovered in the inscription on the cuneiform stone tablet. What had been recognized by the Society from the tablet was that all that was really necessary was to make connections and maintain friendships inspired by the idea that cooperation among humans was possible. It was that simple. Love was what was needed many thousands of years ago, and now today, too, was what was in great need.

Greater friendships and loving relations would come about by people caring about their fellow people enough to look beyond the confines of their lives. The things that bound people to separation on earth were artificial constructs. And by adhering stubbornly to the culture in which one was raised, for example, one could be locked into disagreements for many centuries it had been seen.

Just look at the Arab-Israeli conflict, Bernd thought, as he looked lovingly at Yuri now. He thought he could never dislike her for centuries as odd as it was to think of it that way. Especially, it was important, Yuri was thinking at the same time as Bernd, to consider whether or not one's culture when it was at odds with that of one's neighbor's caused conflict, discord and possibly injury. True, one should learn about one's own culture and try to understand its many teachings, life lessons, and wonders. And at the same time one need not be too invested in one's own cultural traditions so that there was no longer any room for learning from or about others including one's husband!

They, the members of the Secret Society, as a start believed now that they needed to care enough about others to not let their own needs become selfish and self-centered and get in the way of helping others. It was decided that making connections and caring about others would become the priority and primary focus of their activities. Being a society based in compassion meant that they already had a good start on this journey. Realizing that the journey was not over and was only beginning was half of the battle. That there was no time to lose was evident with continual conflict erupting around the globe as was true at the beginning of the twenty-first century in Africa and other places.

Finding the last star point and the origin was appropriately cause for celebration, but also no reason to sit back and rest. As the Latvians say, "One sleeps in the grave." In the same spirit members of the Secret Society did not rest; they began to work in earnest on their new journey.

These things and this approach was why the symbol of the encircled star had been chosen so long ago by the original Star Gazers Society in Babylon. Their dream was now coming true so many years later. What they hoped the search would help beings find was the following: The origin being at the center wasn't only about the beginning being in Babylon, it was also about the idea of not taking oneself too seriously or thinking of one self as too important. That they went out from their *center* to include others on purpose represented this way of thinking.

Since there was complete agreement, the ideas of cooperation and not making a big deal out of things were continued by the Secret Society now as well as the Star Gazers in the ancient past. This included, of course, not thinking of oneself as too important.

Therefore, there had been a plan in place to go back to the center and not think that once you have made it to the far parts of the world and established your star point that it was over. The interconnectedness of the star points when going back to the center was also meant to be a demonstration of the importance of all, and not only the one. Hence there was much importance given to reconnecting at the center. Tibet was a good example of being connected along the way. It had not been the original star point, India had. Tibet was at a historic crossroads of Buddhist civilization and so became a connecting point in the way the ancients had imagined points around the world would become as connections were made.

Most importantly, going back to the center also represented the need to look deeply within one self and finding that what we are looking for is within us at our own origin or core. It was to note that nothing was lacking, but what was necessary was already there inside of each human being.

Further the wonder of being human was to be shared. What is inside of one self is perhaps in need of some polishing, but each of us is complete and whole as we are. What is inside of us is strength, courage to share, and the ability to love. It was not some place in Babylon, Japan or elsewhere that any*thing* is to be found. The ancient Star Gazers Society knew what the Secret Society had been discovering ...that finding peace outside of yourself is at best only finding peace halfway. And also that after learning about peace within, it is important to share that knowledge with others for it to be meaningful.

The star symbol was useful in another way, too. When drawn on paper, or in the sand, it demonstrates connectedness. It represents that around the world there are many points that circle the center and cross each other as is evident by the lines drawn between them making interconnections. All of these ideas come together at the center and show us that being interrelated on this earth means that we need to and can work together. And that each of us is a piece of god, a partner in the universe ...a star point.

This idea was not unique to the Secret Society or the farmer from years ago. After all, the Buddhists call it dependent arising, and the greatest expression of this in a positive sense is the Bodhisattva vow, a vow to *awaken speedily for the sake of all beings*. This, too, can be seen in the Christian idea, *do unto others as you would have them do unto you*. Clearly these ideas were established in any and all of the major religions.

The difference with the Secret Society was that it was purposefully not bound to or created out of any one nation or culture. Nor was it limited in distance or scope by any worldly borders such as that of the United States and Canada, borders in the Middle East, European borders, etc ...lines drawn by people. In short, the Secret Society members were in a position to make connections without reservation or limit, something many organizations aspire to, but many find difficult to achieve. How would the Secret Society members do it? Each day it was becoming increasingly clear that they would do it by making connections ...one person at a time. Their membership would grow and grow.

That is why, after the last "star point" was found and the inclusive star symbol was confirmed at each point, the Secret Society sent its members to the eight-points of the eight directions of the compass in an effort to create connectedness around the world. The societal emblem was redrawn from a five-pointed star to become an all inclusive encircled eight-pointed star that represented the eight directions of the compass. They also considered using the ten directions of the universe as a symbol, but chose the eight-sided star encircled for its ease of understanding being based on the directions of the compass. In this way the symbol became even more inclusive, some felt, than that of the five-pointed star used by the ancients. While some of the Society members did not agree with the change, the overwhelming majority did, and so after discussion and by agreement, it was changed.

The Society continued their work secretly, but their work became work to create the feeling of being included for all beings around the world. The reason for secrecy was not to be secret so much as to not be making a big deal out of their work. This was the longtime philosophical basis of their approach. Really getting to know others, being accepting of them, and most of all sharing with them openly, freely and in an unobstructed manner was what was necessary. Though they were a society built upon compassionate action, this purposefully making connections was a new emphasis to the Secret Society members.

Many were puzzled by this idea of really getting to know another being. How to go about this would be a challenge. It would be a challenge met differently by each member of the Secret Society. Yuri and Bernd had begun some of their study by going to and helping to confirm the use of the inclusive encircled star symbol at each of the five star points in turn, for themselves. And then after that was finished they returned to Japan. After returning, Yuri for her part discovered how she would make connections. This was in summer after returning to Japan.

Tanabata Festival

The first leg of their trip to the places of all the known star points took Yuri and Bernd more than a year to complete. They went around with the delegations appointed by the Society, and also in some cases by themselves, too. They went to confirm all of the star points personally and also to be helpful by exploring places others were unable to get to or would have difficulty getting to explore as in the case of Russia.

The collaboration of the Secret Society members allowed them to find the inclusive star symbol, the encircled star, in all of the known star point locations within several years. After this, Yuri and Bernd took some time off to visit the island of Yuri's birth. On the way to Japan they stopped in Egypt to visit their friend.

They were amazed when the Egyptian delegate showed them personally what the reunited Alexander star, the halves being brought together, looked like in a museum in Cairo. To make this happen had taken the clout of his friend at the most prestigious university in Egypt. He promised to introduce his friend to Bernd someday. The friend was part of a team of archaeologists, in a land of artifacts. Bernd couldn't wait.

With even just hearing of them, Bernd had to count to about a hundred in order to not be envious of them. Yuri pointed out that a German living in Japan was itself by all accounts certainly a wonderful experience. Bernd paused for a moment and then relaxed as he easily agreed. He began counting to one hundred again; only this time he was counting his blessings! He continued counting on the way back to Japan. When he wasn't sleeping, he noticed that he never ran out of things to be thankful for.

Both Yuri and Bernd were happy to be back in Japan and were looking forward to enjoying the summer together. It was early July. It would be an opportunity to see Yuri's family, too, a welcome blessing. Having completed their personal search of the star points, confirming the encircled star symbols for themselves, they looked forward to this sojourn on the island.

Yes, it was a warm July evening. On this night there was a festival on the island of Yuri's birth, and many members of Yuri's family were in attendance.

"Hello Grandmother, how are you tonight?" Yuri asked, seeing her grandmother more clearly and with a level of interest that even she thought was surprising. She was surprised by how she now felt about her grandmother. She had never felt an interest in another this deeply before. Remembering that all members of the Secret Society would begin building an interconnected world one person at a time she began to do so in earnest on that night.

Yuri felt that, starting with her grandmother, she wanted to begin right then to make connections. Also, not having done so consciously before, Yuri was at a loss as to how to go about making such a connection.

"Other than my left knee feeling that it is being torn from my body, I am quite well," responded Grandmother, using the kind of statement everyone had come to know her for. She always seemed to have pain in some part of her body. Only after the words came out as a matter of habit did she notice the intensity with which Yuri was looking at her. Grandmother turned to her and smiled, having had enough experience throughout her many years on this earth, and maybe even some universal wisdom, too, to know that Yuri had grown up a fine woman. Grandmother recognized that Yuri began to see others more clearly than ever before.

Yuri herself was very pleased to be able to truly "see" others and not be only concerned with her own needs. She felt that it was a relief to be not overly concerned with her thoughts. Grandmother noted mostly that Yuri seemed to have achieved this at an unusually young age. Grandmother noted the exception to the way she had thought things were and said finally, "Yuri, I am really doing quite well, you know. Many of my generation died in the greatest most destructive war of all time as you well know. I should count my blessings that I am even still here."

"Yes, I have heard this Grandmother. It makes me sad. I cannot even imagine it, since I was not around then." She had replied with an honesty and seriousness that belied her youth.

"Well, you must try to imagine it, Yuri. We cannot forget the lessons of that time so that they will not be repeated," her grandmother said imploringly.

"That is so true, Grandmother," Yuri said contemplatively and respectfully. She vowed to not let others forget transgressions of human weakness. And then she thought she would take this unique opportunity to find out something else her grandmother knew much about, the traditions of this small island in the middle, edge and side of the world.

"Grandmother?" she said, her voice questioning how much Grandmother would like to share with her.

"Yes," came the calm reply.

"I was wondering if you wouldn't mind telling me about the Tanabata Festival, you know. Not the stories I can find in the books or even what it meant to others generations ago, but what it meant for you as a girl growing up and what it means perhaps even now for you on this island," she asked. She was cautious and hopeful, not wanting to offend her grandmother by asking something too personal, nor wanting to overstep the social boundaries present by their separation in years.

Grandmother leaned forward as she sat on a rock that overlooked the lapping water washing the sand out to sea and said, "Now that is the most gracious invitation I have had in a long time," and paused seeming to think of what she would say next. "Did you know that when I was seven years old, and I found out that the Tanabata Festival was on July seventh, I had been at a loom weaving? You know that it is a festival that concerns a farmer and a weaving princess, right?"

Yuri nodded showing that she knew this point, and smiled, too, remembering the painting on the wall of the pagoda at Horyuji.

"Well, I imagined that I was that princess, and I had only just learned how to weave, you know ...." Grandmother went on and told Yuri stories of her life for quite a while that night and laughed a lot.

Yuri spent the rest of the summer going to the island on the weekends doing everything she could with Grandmother. She enjoyed Grandmother's wit, her stories and learning from her how to prepare and cook many locally developed dishes that she had been too busy studying to find out about before. Luckily Yuri was able to resume her job. She was considered quite an asset now, with all the connections she had made.

And as the summer went on Yuri noticed two things that happened. One was that Grandmother became very active in the household and in the community no longer complaining of pains in her body. Indeed, she cooked more often than not in the home to the enjoyment of the whole family since she was so good at it. The other was that Yuri became enthusiastic about life to an even greater degree than before. This was something that she had not thought possible. She figured it was because being interested in others was more interesting than being interested in primarily her own studies, wants and needs. These weekend visits to the island away from her job in Tokyo were truly a blessing and a pleasure.

She began to meditate on her own almost every day and she made plans to visit the old priest in the ancient temple in northern Japan as well as Abbot Furuta at Horyuji. She made it a habit of seeing Abbot Kimura at Bentenji as often as she could make the journey to the island. She was still excited that there was so much to learn in life and happy about the many opportunities that lie before her to help make connections in her own community and perhaps around the globe.

She noted, too, that her ideas tended to not bunch up all in a stack and seem so that they all wanted to get her attention at the same time. She was never pushed that hard in her thinking mind, finding a calmness that was somewhere in between such thoughts. She was truly happy. And, she found, that this happiness was spontaneous, taking no special effort to achieve.

For all the travel she had done and the many things she had studied one thing stood out now in her mind. It was that most important thing she had learned that she thought of now. It was that *all people count*, especially the small, seemingly insignificant ones who number as the stars, and that none of them are the same.

Epilogue: The beginning

And so one day without warning, after living with an uneasy feeling for some time a man, Jaroul, decided suddenly to go on a journey. He was in awe of nature, completely.

This profound sense of awe he felt about nature made him believe that there was a mystical side to life, and this led to another feeling coming over him. It gnawed at him sometimes for days and then for a while, though very briefly, not at all. After a while it became apparent that there was no way around it; he could not shake the feeling that gnawed at him. He felt a need to take action.

It was because of this feeling that he slowly began to realize that life as it occurred for him day after day seemed in such a strange contrast to the beauty of nature and especially those stars he often viewed from up on top of that mountain.

He began to wonder, question and then eventually deep in his gut to believe that there must be something more to life than just passing time working to live and living to work. Further, all of the self-serving acts that he observed around him made him wonder if there was not something more available to all beings than life as it had been presented to him in his society in ancient Babylon.

When he considered his life, he always came to the same conclusion. He felt that all he was doing was passing away the hours and not getting anywhere only working for a living, and this realization did not sit well with him. Jaroul believed that there was more to life than the solitary existence he was experiencing day in a day out.

Eventually he began to wonder if there were others out there who thought that there must be more to life than just going through the motions day after day by oneself. Jaroul wandered around here and there, first near and then far, and then coming back near to his farm again. Incredibly, he continued to find those of a similar mind to himself wherever he went. He found those who were awestruck by the beauty existing in nature and in people everywhere.

Being anxious and not wanting to wait around, Jaroul continued his journey, primarily around the area along the Mediterranean Sea and made some discoveries ….

What the others felt deep within their souls was that they wanted to cooperate with each other, that it was truly possible to get along with many different kinds of people. Though this understanding, it was clear, had no place in most societies in most regions of the world so many years ago.

Their understanding, however, was not shaken by the chaos that they saw all around. To them the world was truly beautiful if seemingly always in conflict somewhere and in some way.

Not only were there many who felt like him, that there must be something more to this thing that they called "life," but also many felt a genuine need to share their understanding with others.

Eventually, the Star Gazers got together and began to cooperate as best as they could in all they did. They had disagreements, but all in all got along very well. They thought it was such an obvious thing, being happy and sharing that happiness together, that they could not believe their ears when they heard of wars continuously happening around them.

Jaroul realized that it was not enough for them to be happy by themselves in their group. So one day the group got together and made plans to establish groups around the far reaches of the world as far as that may be.

They called themselves the Star Gazers Society. They did not want to lose sight of their original purpose, which was collective cooperation, so they made plans. The power of creativity and their faith in the spirit of cooperation made this happen, made it possible.

No one had remembered how the story began, nor the significance of what took place so very long ago, until the explorations of the Secret Society. What had remained undiscovered for so long were the clues that connected the story of this man in the past with people in the present. Those clues, when found, were the key to how this story began, what was accomplished by this man, and why his actions seemed so important to the world of the ancient past, and are very relevant to the world today!

Their goals to unite the world did come about not only because of careful planning by the Star Gazers, but also because of work by a later Secret Society, some fate, a determined and cooperative couple, …and a little luck.

Pronunciation guide

This is meant to be a simple guide. Students and learners of Japanese can use this guide and the following glossary as a take-off point in learning Japanese pronunciation, vocabulary and culture. Consulting a textbook will give detailed examples of pronunciation. The below cultural points will augment one's understanding of the Japanese language, and the use in the text gives context to many concepts that are often misunderstood.

1.) When two vowels are put together this is to show or make the pronunciation long. Two "o"s side by side are pronounced as a long "o." The combination "ou" is also pronounced as a long "o" sound.

2.) When used as a subject marker "ha" is pronounced "wa." i.e. Otoosan ha Genki? (Otoosan wa genki?). [Consult glossary for meaning.]

3.) The syllables "a," "e," "i," "o" and "u" are pronounced similarly to the syllables in Spanish. Consonants are generally pronounced as in English, though a native speaker, a teacher and or a textbook should be consulted for correct pronunciation and practice.

4.) Many texts include on line support or digital reproductions of the appropriate sounds. Those wanting more details may wish to consult Japanese texts such as the one produced by the *Japan Times* newspaper, Genki: An Integrated Course in Elementary Japanese.

Note: the author does not sponsor any particular textbook and names this one by way of suggestion so that interested people have somewhere to start looking. There are many useful texts available. In addition, the Nihongo Journal is a good source for language and cultural study with digitally produced conversations. I support no one text or magazine, though do support exploration of the many good sources out there such as the "Japan Foundation" on line website.

Glossary

(Honorifics beginning with "o" will usually not be hyphenated in the text as in the term *ocha* thought it can also be written as *o-cha*. Especially in cases where words usually are not separated as in omamori, it will be written together like it is on pp. 68. By way of contrast they are hyphenated below. Some words that are not ever written separately, such as omiyage are written together as below.)

Ao nori: Powdered, dried seaweed flakes often served on okonomiyaki or with yaki soba.

Akagami: Literally a "red paper" that was a compulsory draft notice during the period of the Second World War.

Amida Butsu: The Buddha Amitabha in Japanese. A temple that the author knows of is called Amidaji, a temple for Amida Butsu.

Apaato: Apartment

Benkyouka: Someone who likes to learn and as a result studies a lot. A diligent student; someone who is knowledgeable

Benten: The goddess of fortune (the goddess of music, literature and the arts)

Bento: A boxed lunch prepared in the morning and taken along to work or an outing such as a picnic. The term usually takes the honorific form o-bento.

Bon odori: The o-bon dance held as a community celebration in conjunction with the o-bon festival in which the spirits of the family ancestors return for several days in August each summer. In some places they are sent off again with various small floating boats. This festival mixes native beliefs with Buddhist beliefs.

Bosatsu: Bodhisattva in English. One who is working toward becoming an awakened being. In the Tibetan Karma Kagyu tradition a bodhisattva is one working to awaken on behalf of all beings. This may be true of other traditions as well.

Butsudan: Family Buddhist Altar usually kept in the home of the oldest son of a family if possible, and when the older son either dies or there are no male children, goes to the next oldest child. When the role reverts to women they may even have the requirement of taking on the family name. In the case of them being married, their husband would change his last name to the woman's family name.

Butsudan no ma: The room in which the *butsudan* is kept.

Engawa: A covered walkway that winds around a house along the outside, usually in part rather than surrounding the house entirely.

Enryo: Hesitation, which is an art in Japan. It is considered socially appropriate and good manners to not rush into the accepting of gifts, foods, etc .… This hesitation to put one's needs first is called enryo. Usually after this hesitation, that may be done more than once, during which an item is offered more than once it is perfectly acceptable to receive the item. This has among other purposes the function of having made sure that it would not put the other out to give the item. It is the art of knowing when to pause, and not put one's own ideas or wishes forward at the expense of others. This is socially driven. For example, a teacher or an elder may take the initiative when a student or younger person pauses. This makes the student be or seem less pushy and is considered socially adept.

Furoshiki: A cloth used to wrap for taking along somewhere lunch boxes called bento or other items that need protection or to be kept together while traveling.

Furusato: One's home area; the place one was raised. A home place.

Fusuma: Sliding doors made of thick paper and usually decorated with traditional pictures such as Plum trees *ume* or Cherry trees *sakura* and sometimes with exotic paintings such as tigers.

Genkan: The entry way in a house in Japan.

Geta: Wooden Japanese sandals that hold to the foot by a frontal rope or cloth strap.

Gomen Kudasai: A greeting used to inform of one's arrival at the door. This greeting is used to announce oneself prior to entering a home when there has been no answer at the door. This lets the home owner know that someone is attempting to come in so as to not surprise the residents if anyone is around.

Go ni ireba, go ni shitagae: When in Rome, do what the Romans do. This is an interesting saying used not only in the west but in Japan as well. It means follow the customs of where you are and not only your own customs.

Guru: In Buddhism, this is a meditation master who is also a trainer; someone under which a learner of meditation can study to great benefit. The guru-disciple relationship is prevalent in many societies in Asia. The understudy or disciple does his or her best to learn all which is offered by the teacher or guru. Strict adherence to the wishes of the guru may be necessary and complete trust in a worthy being in both the student and the teacher is sought after and usually possible only after hard work is carried out on both sides. One becomes a guru by having worked hard and experienced the ins and outs of meditation.

Hakachi: A cemetery in which grave stones are lined up family by family.

Hanami: Cherry blossom viewing. Often blossom revelers will get up early in the day to stake a claim at a park with beautiful trees to view. People picnic and celebrate often sitting until late into the night under trees illuminated traditionally by lanterns, but more recently with strings of electrically lit lanterns or lights.

Harumatsu hito: Someone who awaits and looks towards the coming spring especially after the New Year has been rung in.

Hiezan Mount Hie in Kyoto Prefecture. Along with Mount Koya it was founded by one of two monks who had gone to China on pilgrimages to learn more about Buddhism. On Mount Hie there is a temple famous for severe ascetic practice.

Higaeri: Traveling to a place and returning to where one started on the same day. For example, going from Osaka to Tokyo and returning to Osaka on the same day.

Hi no youshin: A small procession of people usually only two or three people, walk through the community, banging pieces of wood together in order to raise awareness of the possibility of fire and thereby prevent fires in that area.

Hondo: Building in which is housed the main altar at a Buddhist Temple

Honshuu: The largest of the four biggest islands in the Japanese archipelago. The other three are Shikoku, Kyuushuu and Hokkaidou.

Horyuji: The temple through which the law flows (my translation). Another term for law is dharma in Buddhist traditions. Horyuji is the oldest standing wooden structure in Japan and perhaps the world. It is considered the first or oldest temple in Japan. It is in Nara Prefecture.

Ii tsukare: A good tiredness or tiredness that is the result of useful or enjoyable effort. For example, hiking or strenuous physical labor such as cutting firewood. Sometimes this is said: ii o-tsukare with the polite marker "o" added.

Imo hori: Potato digging; purplish red on the outside and yellow on the inside are the sweet potatoes in Japan. Some families get together and dig potatoes getting up early in the morning to dig while the sun is not out and it is not yet really hot. Afterwards the diggers and other relatives would gather to knock the dirt off of the potatoes and put them in boxes to bring to market, trade or distribute as gifts to those in one's mutual relationship network.

Irasshaimase: Welcome as in the case of "Welcome, come into my shop." This phrase can be heard all over Japan when people have a place of business and someone comes by or enters their store. It is a greeting used for potential customers.

Iro iro (na) This is an adjective after which the particle "na" follows. It means various, varied, different as in different kinds.

Isseki ni chou: One stone gets two birds. This means the same as the English to kill two birds with one stone.

Jibiiru: Locally brewed beer especially popular at a resort or in a resort town.

Jizou: Buddhist statues often placed along traveler routes. They are set out for the protection of travelers. A kind of Jizou called Mizuko Jizou is set out for the benefit of still born children or those who die in childbirth. They are the usually small statues, though sometimes large, draped in red bibs or coverings and sometimes adorned with head covers.

Kakebuton: The top or covering futon used year round but made especially thick in winter to keep the sleeper warm all night long. Note that the "f" in futon becomes a "b" sound in this word combination.

Kami: A god or gods in the Shinto tradition. Gods are usually the spirit or essence that animates or inhabits so to speak an object in nature such as a large rock, a mountain stream, a tree etc …. Kami are also sometime related to people, especially important dignitaries, though less commonly so. Ropes are symboolic of the connection of the kami and the physical world.

Kan: One's feeling about something. Sometimes this is used in the place of the English word premonition, however, it does not mean premonition out of context. It has to do with how one feels about something.

Kanji: Feeling; sense

Kara age: Deep-fried breaded chicken. It is often breaded with lightly seasoned, salted breading flour.

Katsuobushi: Katsuo fish shavings from dried and cured katuso fish served as an additive to foods such as okonomiyaki, in various soup broths, hot pot meals etc ….

Kimochi: Feeling

Kimono: A traditional Japanese wrap around garment fixed in place with beautifully woven belts.

Kinako: Powdered soy beans often served with mochi or rice cakes.

Kinen: A memorial or keepsake. Especially something that reminds one of a place one has been. The post card sized temple memorials called shuuin are an example of this. Some popular tourist spots in Japan provide stamps that one can stamp into a booklet or shuuinchou and take home. They are called just that, kinen stamps.

Kohaku: A television program aired annually on NHK (Nippon Housou Kyoku), the national television station, on New Year's Eve. It is a competition between the Red and White teams: the red team, all women actresses, singers and performers competes against the white team made up of male singers and performers from around Japan.

Kou in no gotoshi: Time flies like an arrow

Kokoro: Translated as either heart or mind.

Kokoro no jumbi (wo shita): To (do or make) prepare oneself in one's heart/ prepare mentally for a task that is usually seen as unpleasant, though unavoidable at the same time. For example, before one resigns her or his position at work they might prepare their heart to be ready for the change that is coming.

Kokyuu hou: Deep breathing technique

Koseki: Family registry. Usually copies are maintained in the local branch office of the city hall, or in the city hall of big cities. This is a record of who and what relation people are in a family following along the ancestral lineage of a family name. The document upon which the information is recorded is called *koseki touhon* or *koseki shouhon*.

Koyasan: Mount Koya in Wakayama Prefecture that was founded by Kukai whose posthumous and more famous name is Kobodaishi. Kobodaishi is the founder in Japan of Shingonshu or the Shingon Sect of esoteric Buddhism. He was one of two monks who went to China to learn about Buddhism. The other founded a Buddhist tradition on Mount Hie in Kyouto Prefecture.

Kuro mame: A dish made of sweetened black beans cooked with a piece of iron that makes them shiny. It is usually served during the New Year holiday.

Kuushuu: Fire-bombing air raids that destroyed much of Tokyo during World War II

Kyuugamera: An island dialect rendered in standard Japanese as *gomen kudasai*. This term is used to introduce one's presence upon arriving at someone's home. It can also be used as a greeting during the day similar to konnichi ha (konnichi wa) meaning "good day."

Mochi: Rice cakes made from cooked, pounded, especially sticky, glutenous rice.

Momiji: A Japanese maple tree that has petite maple leaves

Morning set: A set menu at a coffee shop offered throughout the morning till around 11:00 AM. It usually consists of an egg, bread with butter and jam and coffee or black/ orange pekoe tea. It is also referred to as "morning or morning service." In this term service is pronounced, *sabisu*.

Mu: A term used in Zen Buddhism that describes a state that at some point one who meditates might attain. It can be described as being in a condition where nothing is to be experienced, meaning that the practitioner would be experiencing no-thing-ness or what Buddhists since the historical Buddha have referred to in many different ways as *shunyata* or "emptiness." It is the Japanese term for emptiness.

Mushi atsui: The condition of being not only hot, but also humid. Hot and humid

Nabemono: Meals made in a nabe or ceramic cooking pot that can be used to cook food over a fire. Often meats and vegetables are put into the broth to be cooked. As a round of food is cooked and eaten another is added till all have taken their fill. In addition to vegetables and meat often udon is added to the broth to complete the meal. Rice is usually eaten on the side.

Nattou: Fermented beans served with a sauce and mustard. There are variation that have shiso, an aromatic plant and ume, Japanese plums, too. Some people add raw egg, too.

Niwa: A yard, a garden in Japan usually of the kind outside a home filled with flowers, shrubs or other plants.

Nyourai: An awakened being

Obi: Wide beautifully woven belts. They hold kimono in place.

O-bon: The ancestral festival in Japan, usually observed around the time of August fifteenth each year. At O-bon time people go back to their furusato or hometown in which they were raised to get together with family. Out of respect for their ancestors, families welcome back the souls of deceased ancestors and honor their family lineage at this time.

Oboradani: "Thank you" in a dialect on one of the Japanese islands of the archipelago. The island is not one of the four largest islands.

O-cha: Tea in Japanese. Usually green tea.

O-haka: Grave site with a grave marker usually for a family and often either at or related to a temple.

O-hashi: Chopsticks. Wari-bashi are chopsticks made out of wood that need to be pulled apart before using. They are slitted, but not fully separated when made. Separating them is called *wari* which is the noun form of *waru*, to separate.

O-hikide mono: A gift given to guests as a thank you for attending a wedding and the reception. It is in line with the idea of giving back having received something.

O-hitashi: A side dish of spinach cooked briefly in boiling water, has had the water squeezed out of it and then cooled. It is topped with soy sauce and ground or whole roasted sesame seeds

O-jama shimasu: Pardon me, may I come in. It is a means of respectfully announcing that one is entering the home one is visiting. It is used as a greeting upon entering especially after being invited in. This is different from another greeting **gomen-kudasai**, which is used as a greeting to announce oneself prior to entering a home when there has been no answer at the door.

Okonomiyaki It is often described as a Japanese pancake. It is a cabbage filled pancake along the lines of potato pancakes. It is often served with thinly sliced pieces of meat such as pork or beef. It can also have shrimp or squid, too. Before it is eaten, it is smothered in a kind of brown sauce and mayonnaise. Mustard can be used, too.

O-mamori: Prayer charms. People buy these and hope that the charms bring them a child, safety while driving or some other worldly wish.

Omiyage: Souvenirs of locally produced goods customarily brought back for those close to oneself such as family and co-workers especially those older than oneself.

Onsen: Hot spring. A natural bath filled with heated water from the earth usually accessible in volcanic areas. These bathing spots are often located in places where one can stay the night such as at a hotel or Japanese inn. While there, one can bathe as many times as one wishes. Traditionally *onsen* were established around natural hot water caused by the volcanic heat within the islands of Japan. Now some *onsen* are made with water that has been heated from some other source such as gas. Sometimes local bathing places in towns called *sento* are not necessarily the result of volcanic heat but are made from water that has been heated in some way.

Oomisoka: New Year's Eve

Osanai: Having the characteristic of being the case since one was quite young. This is said of friends or *osananajimi*, childhood friends.

O-sechi ryouri: Specially prepared food served during the New Year holiday that combines traditional foods, local food traditions and sometime more recent dishes. Beans, and rice cakes as well as root dishes and vegetables are commonly included in the dishes.

Otoosan ha Genki? Is Father all right? Is Father doing well? Are two translations of this term. *Otoosan* means father.

Ozoni: Soup made with miso-salted crushed soy beans. It has daikon radishes, carrots and other vegetables in it. Often mochi is put into the soup until soft, stringy and chewy and then served along with some of the soup. Before being put into the soup, when mochi sits it hardens.

Ryokan: Japanese inn, often established in well-traveled areas especially around hot springs. Often seasonal offerings of local foods are served at ryokan and they have really good food.

Saisen bako: A collection box, usually wooden, at a temple or shrine in which visitors either toss or put coins in as an offering or donation to the temple or shrine.

Sakoku: The closing of Japan to foreigners and by implication foreign influences during the Tokugawa period (1603-1867). The dates are also denoted as 1603-1868 depending on the source.

Sasa: Leafy flexible shoot that is leaf bamboo and looks somewhat like a willow branch.

Sengoku Jidai: Warring States Period

Setsubun: The festival of welcoming into the home good fortune and ousting from the home any evil by throwing beans across the house. The traditional date is February third.

Shichigosan: The Shinto anniversary celebrations of a child becoming the ages of seven, five and three. At these times the family visits a shrine to pray to the kami or tutelary deity of the shrine to ask for help with needs for the child such as praying for a long life, good marriage, healthy child ….

Shikata ga nai: It can't be helped or there's nothing that can be done about it. This term is also used in the case of *cest la vie*, or such is life.

Shikibuton: The bottom futon that is usually stored in a closet along with any cover futons, pillows …and taken out each night and put away each morning. Note that the "f" in futon becomes a "b" sound in this word combination.

Shimenawa: Connecting rope; it symbolizes making a connection with the item in nature, for example, a rock and by implication the kami or gods.

Shingon-Shuu: The Shingon sect of Buddhism in Japan founded by Kobo Daishi and has a base on Mount Koya or Koyasan.

Shinkansen: The high speed rail line in Japan. It is nicknamed the "bullet train." It is fast and on time. It takes about two and a half hours to go between Osaka and Tokyo on the train. There are several levels of trains some faster than others such as the Nozomi, the train that takes two and a half hours to traverse the distance between Osaka and Tokyo. It is the fastest train for that route.

Shinshitsu: Bed room. The room in which the futons are laid out for sleeping.

Shiso: An aromatic plant used as a flavoring in soups and salads or eaten on its own.

Shitsurei shimasu: Pardon me, I'm going now. Used when leaving a place such as the work place.

Shoji: Sliding doors made of wood with many small wooden frames or squares upon which paper is glued.

Shoujin ryouri: A special vegetarian meal made at temples in Japan that consists of various items made of tofu and sesame among other vegetarian foods.

Shotoku Taishi: Prince Shotoku. Taishi means someone of significance or a man of significance, in this case a prince. Kobo Daishi is derived from the same characters. It means the great Kobo. Certainly Kukai, the founder of Shingon-shuu is considered someone of significance as his posthumous name reveals, Kobo Daishi. Monks in Japan may get a posthumous name like this. Daishi means roughly, great person or great dignitary.

Shuugyou: Ascetic practices or practice such as meditation that is employed as training. The result is purification of the body and getting rid of and/ or recognizing conditioned patterns that block one from awakening.

Shuuin: A temple remembrance card. A piece of paper about the size of a post card that has the name of the temple written on it along with a distinctive stamp from the temple and the date of the visit. This can be written and stamped directly in a shuuinchou or temple remembrance book.

Shuuinchou: Book in which memorial post card size cards or paper purchased at temples for around 300 yen or three dollars are pasted to keep a record of one's temple visits. Especially they can be used for pilgrimages such as those made around the eighty-eight temple route of Shikoku, one of the four largest islands of Japan, or the thirty-three temple route of the the Kii Peninsula which is centrally located in Japan.

Susouwake: Sharing of food especially of goods that one has been given. It is usually shared with relatives or others with whom one has important relationships. Even more politely and more usually the term is o-susouwake taking the honorific "o" before the word to make it polite linguistically.

Suzu: Small bells that are enclosed and have a tiny ball bearing inside that makes noise when the bell is shaken side to side.

Taiko: Japanese drum of which there are various types. For example, the oodaiko is the large drum as "oo" comes from the word *ookii* which means large or big.

Tanabata Festival: The Star Festival of Altair, the star of the cowherd and Vega, the star of the weaving princess. The festival is held on the seventh day of the seventh month. The two are banished to the night time sky and can only meet each year in summer on the July seventh, the day they can cross the Milky Way. At this auspicious time people write their wishes on colored paper and affix them to the *sasa* tree branches praying that their wishes will be granted. The festival is thought to have originated in China and been brought to Japan in the feudal period. At first it was only celebrated by the imperial court, but later common citizens as well began to celebrate the Tanabata Festival.

Tatami: Woven reed mats used traditionally in homes and not to be walked on with any type of shoe or footwear other than socks

Tokonoma: An alcove usually set back from one of the main walls of a room in which wall hangings or decorative scrolls are hung.

Tokugawa Period: Also called the Edo Period, 1603-1868 (1867 depending on the calendar). This is the period of the samurai. It is also the period in which Japan was closed off almost entirely from the rest of the world by a policy of self-isolation. (See sakoku above.)

Tonkatsu: Deep-fried breaded pork cutlets usually the size of a pork chop, and often served with sliced cabbage on the side.

Torii: Gate to a Shinto shrine

Uchiwa: Hand-held fan of which there are two types; the kind that has alternating folds allowing it to fold up to the size of a long, rather thick pen or the flat rigid kind that is made traditionally of a bamboo handle that has been cut into veins on one end that holds the paper in place with the help of glue.

Udon: A thick, white, wheat noodle made by kneading flour together with water and salt

Ume: Japanese plums that are red and can be sweet and salty. They are also used to make an alcoholic beverage called *umeshuu* or ume liqueur that is sweet and has a distinct flavor.

Yamato nadeshiko: In Japan following along the lines of Confucian thought, obeying one's parents and being respectful amounted to what was called the Yamato nadeshiko, or essentially obedient Japanese girl filled with "real" Japanese spirit. Yamato is an old name for Japan.

Yaki soba: Fried noodles covered with a sauce and topped with *ao nori* or dried and powdered sea weed and *katusobushi*. This dish usually includes cabbage, sliced carrots and other vegetables.

Zabuton: Floor cushions used for sitting taken out especially when guests arrive, but used for all occasions

Zazen: Japanese sitting style that utilizes the full lotus posture in which both feet are placed upon one's thighs while sitting. It is usually carried out without frills, only a cushion and perhaps some incense.

Zensei: A previous life or life times. A term used to refer to a lifetime before the current existence for those who believe in reincarnation

Zenzai: An o-sechi or New Year's dish made of red beans. It is sweet and served with mochi.

For those interested in finding out more about meditation see:
(www.clearskycenter.org)

CPSIA information can be obtained at www.ICGtesting.com
Printed in the USA
266566BV00001B/2/P